NOVGOROD THE GREAT

NOVGOROD
THE GREAT

Andrew Drummond

Polygon

First published in 2010 by Polygon,
an imprint of Birlinn Ltd
West Newington House · 10 Newington Road
Edinburgh EH9 1QS

www.polygonbooks.co.uk

9 8 7 6 5 4 3 2 1

ISBN 978 1 84697 101 3

British Library Cataloguing-in-Publication Data
A catalogue record for this book is available on
request from the British Library.

Typeset in Fleischman by Dalrymple
Printed in Scotland by
Bell & Bain Ltd
Glasgow

CONTENTS

1

HER FIRST HUSBAND'S PECULIARLY BECOMING NAKEDNESS.

"At last," said Ksenia quite unnecessarily, "the morning."

"And soon," added Horatio, a great hope rising in his breast, "we shall have breakfast."

Ksenia considered him thoughtfully for a moment. "I am, sir," she began rather boldly, "as you know, a woman who has mourned the death of a husband."

"Alas," confirmed Horatio with far too much enthusiasm, anticipating those words which must surely follow.

"A husband," asserted Ksenia, permitting herself to advance from the Particular to the General by virtue of having experienced some of those creatures at very close quarters indeed, "needs his breakfast."

Horatio turned and eyed the front door of the inn which had, a moment before, slammed shut. "But perhaps we must wait a little longer."

"No matter," said Ksenia, so pressed by the light breeze that she leaned slightly into the shelter of Horatio's arm.

"No matter at all," said Horatio, leaning ever so slightly towards the woman, and feeling a tremor. "There are things which are worth waiting for."

"I am, sir," repeated Ksenia, after a pause, "as you know, a woman who has mourned the death of a husband."

"It is a pity," confirmed Horatio, his stomach agitated, and not from hunger.

"There are men," she continued, "who cannot wait for their breakfast, and there are men," she eyed Horatio, "who can be persuaded to wait. My first husband was one who could not wait. My next one should be more tractable."

"Your first husband," answered Horatio, quite incapable of directing the conversation towards the result for which he yearned, "ate, as I recall, horses and wolves for breakfast."

"Infrequently," she assured him.

"My own preference is for strong tea, plenty of bread, and perhaps two eggs." As he served up this menu, Horatio cursed himself for a fool.

"Two eggs, sir?" asked Ksenia, one eyebrow raised. "Is one not enough?"

Horatio wondered whether the moment was slipping away from him, just as rapidly as that log yonder, bobbing and growling in the current of the River Volkhov, slipping away from Novgorod, to St Petersburg and the Gulf of Finland and oblivion.

A commotion within the inn distracted them both for a moment. On turning back to review the river, Horatio paused for one brief instant, and then plunged in recklessly, up to his neck. "What, if I may ask, would a woman look for in a man, should she seek another husband?"

"What she would want," she replied without hesitation, "is one who did not ask so many questions." As she delivered this tart retort, fermented in a long day followed by a longer night, Ksenia immediately cursed herself for a fool. Oh, what is 'Love', she thought, but sweet regret and bitter tears.

Horatio was a man who could readily take a hint. He fell to considering the surrounding buildings, rather than the water. And was enormously relieved to hear, after a solitary cloud had drifted from one tower to another, the following statement of preference:

"If I were to take another husband, he would be one who took his breakfast with me, took his supper with me, and shared my bed at night, every night."

Horatio mentally ticked these items off on the fingers of his left hand and nodded in satisfaction.

"If I were to take another husband, he would be one who would engage in no perilous journeys – no journeys, sir – no perilous service, and no perilous politics."

Horatio completed his left hand, and proceeded eagerly upon his right. The first he could promise; the second he could guarantee; the third lay only in the power of Tsar and the Police, but he must suppose it to be achievable.

"If I were to take another husband, he would be one who took me to my mother's home in Kamtchatka, lived with me there, and brought up our children there."

This final set of demands, taking as its sine qua non a successful journey to the farthest end of the earth, could easily be met: having arrived at the farthest end of the earth, it would be no hardship to stay there and rear as many children as were required. A cottage, a book and a cat would, of course, greatly complement the whole. The matter rested simply on the journey to Kamtchatka – indeed, everything rested on it – for in far Kamtchatka, one would doubtless be beyond the reach of Tsar and the Police, the only other ticklish point so far. A TICKLISH POINT

Horatio pondered the matter of Kamtchatka, the number of versts across Siberia to reach it, and the average degrees of cold (by Réaumur) in Siberia.

At length, Ksenia recalled him to the city of Novgorod the Great. "And will you take your breakfast with me?" she asked. Horatio struggled to determine whether this was – or was not – a firm proposal. Finding that no determination was required, he took her elbow.

The decision to enter the inn at that precise moment was not necessarily the best one. For, as Horatio pushed back the door and ushered his friend before him, his glance fell upon the inn-keeper and his wife, who were both on the floor, entwined in the closest possible discussion of the meaning of the words 'Love' and 'Family'.

"Oh," said Ksenia, unable to avert her gaze. At length, she addressed Horatio, unaccountably reminded of an omission: "Sir, I have not yet told you of the peculiarly becoming nakedness of my first husband."

"Ah," he replied, looking thoughtfully at the ceiling, and attentively avoiding the blissful domestic scene before him,

"BUT I BELIEVE I HAVE HEARD THAT STORY."

2

A PERPETUITY OF SLOTH, IGNORANCE AND BIGOTED SUPERSTITION.

"That story is of no interest," stated Andrew Cochrane-Johnstone unequivocally, before he hawked and spat liberally into the foaming ocean. "You have no stories of interest at all."

His companion, a younger man and one of no great stature, stiffened visibly at this generous critique, but said not a word. John Dundas Cochrane was not a man to contradict his own father, however wrong his own father might be.

"You have stories of no interest at all," repeated the older man. "Now, if you had lived a life such as mine, you would be able to tell stories that any red-blooded man in the world would find fascinating. You could find companionship in any inn or any club or any residence that you entered."

John Cochrane said nothing at all, but gazed up at the stars which heaved and dipped with the motion of the ship. The Frolic, Leeward Islands packet, was not a ship built to a grand scale, and it bounced over the living surface of the Atlantic Ocean at the whim of every contrary current and the least puff of the wind. John Cochrane, saying nothing at all, wished that he had the courage to speak out against his father – whom he loved dearly, of course, as any son should – but feared that to do so would cause between father and son so deep a rupture that it could never be bridged or repaired.

"I will tell you, for example, of my second marriage," continued Cochrane-Johnstone. "After your dear mother died – how old were you, my boy?" he enquired solicitously.

"Four years old, sir," answered his son dully.

"Four years old, aye – leaving you and your dear sister Elizabeth almost orphans," observed the father tenderly. "And what was I to do? A man, in his prime, in a most prominent position, but without a wife: it was a hard thing, sir, a hard thing. I struggled on, as best I could, taking care of you both – did I not?"

"I believe," replied his son, "you were most generous in the allowance which you sent back to us from Dominica."

"Indeed," said the proud father in tones of self-satisfaction. "I sacrificed much to ensure that you were not left impoverished. Some idle tongues go so far as to say that I stepped over the boundaries of proper behaviour to provide for you. Rumours of swindling and embezzlement; and of corruption and wrongful arrest and confiscation. But a man in my position of responsibility had many decisions to make which did not meet with universal acclaim. And of course there was a great deal of jealousy amongst my fellow-officers at my good fortune: appointed Governor of Dominica in 1797, Colonel of the 8th West India Regiment a year later and Brigadier of the Leeward Islands in the year after that. All earned by hard work and native intelligence, sir."

"It was intelligent enough," murmured John Cochrane drily, in a brief display of filial disloyalty, "to marry a lady related nearly to Lord Melville."

"Melville?" exclaimed Cochrane-Johnstone, shocked by this suggestion of nepotism from so nearly-related a source. "Melville was a fool, no more. If he assisted me to my first position, it was no more than I deserved. If he did so in any improper manner, then that was his foolishness and not my fault. Melville, pah!" He spat once more into the froth that carried the ship steadily westwards.

There was a silence of three or four minutes, broken only by the creaking of the masts and the cracking of the ropes and sail. John Cochrane spent those minutes in thinking about the mother he could barely remember; and of the six cold years he had spent as a child growing up in various homes, none of which could be called his own. This had continued until, attaining the age of ten, he was considered old enough to enter the service of the Royal Navy. There, under the eye of sundry uncles and along with countless other young members of the Cochrane clan, he served with enthusiasm and loyalty for seventeen years. His father had featured rarely in any of those years.

"When you joined the Navy, sir," continued Cochrane-Johnstone at length, "I felt that a man in my position had best find a wife. I left it, you see," he added, lest the point be missed, "until you had found your own way in life." He waited for some acknowledgement of the delicacy of his conduct and received none. "Amélie de Clugny," he continued, "the lovely daughter of Baron de Clugny, late lamented Governor of Guadeloupe, and of a departed and loving mother.

THE DELICACY OF
HIS CONDUCTAmélie, left alone at the age of sixteen – another orphan, sir, you see how soft-hearted I am – at first sought refuge with a young Frenchman named Désiré Godet. Wedded together, they lived happily, and she bore a son. Happily, that is, until young Godet died four years later, leaving Amélie a forlorn and abandoned widow."

Cochrane-Johnstone might have been supposed to have shed a tear, for he blew his nose. He did this expertly, with one finger pressed against each nostril in turn, far out over the side of the ship.

"Hearing of her plight, I took myself to Guadeloupe, gave her my protection and – for the reasons I believe you would be interested to hear – married her." He eyed his son in a sidelong glance. His son had made no response and no movement. He continued: "I married her from a goodness of heart, sir, certainly; but I also married her because she had a fine bosom, a pretty face and the whitest, softest thighs a man could ever hope to clap his eyes on."

His son continued to say nothing. He might have been on the far side of the world, in Siberia or Kamtchatka.

"On top of which, she was rich," added Cochrane-Johnstone.

His son gnawed his lip.

"By this marriage, I found you a brother, sir," added the older man, in a tone that suggested he had striven, and failed, all his life to please his son. "Little Auguste, born in the year 1800. He would be five-and-twenty years old now."

"Does Auguste know of me?" asked John Cochrane, turning to face his father, his silence at last broken. A brother – that would have been something – a companion, a friend maybe.

"Know of you? I have no idea," shrugged his father. "I have not seen him for twenty years. It is of no importance now. We were married," he continued, turning his attention to the verifiable facts of the case, "on the twenty-first day of February in the year 1803, a year after the death of the late departed Godet. We were married firstly upon Amélie's island of Guadeloupe and then, one month later, on the French island of Martinique. Once for the wedding-night, and twice for the sake of her wealth. The pleasures of the flesh last a night or a week perhaps, but those of wealth may last a life-time. You should, sir, consider such matters in your own marriages. Of course, Martinique was the island on which the Empress Josephine was born."

John Cochrane cared little to know any of this, but was not so impudent as to say so.

"Napoleon, you know, was the man who annulled my marriage after two short years. This marriage, ordered the Emperor, is not legitimate. It must not continue. On the thirtieth day of May, 1805 – the document said it was the 10 Prairial XIII – our marriage was no more."

Andrew Cochrane-Johnstone shook his head at the ill-usage of a man by his enemies.

"But, of course," he continued, "the joke was that I was not even in the West Indies when the marriage was annulled. I had six months use out of her. Six months only. Tongues wagged, sir. Some said that I had ill-used my new wife; others that I never used her at all." He laughed bitterly. "Oh, I used her all right. I could tell you, sir, in the closest particulars, if I did not think it might offend your sensibilities. But did I ill-use her any more than a man ill-uses a woman?" He waited for his son to meet his eye, for a glimmer of understanding, before he continued. "Napoleon said that the marriage was invalid, as it took place between a Frenchwoman and an Englishman. He was wrong – we are Scotchmen, sir, and don't you ever forget it. Nonetheless, his argument was that – despite all protestations of love, liberty and fraternity – no such marriage should be permitted, and least of all between the Governor of one British island and the daughter of the Governor of one French island. Six months only, for I had in September of that same year to return to London to face a court-martial. Of course, no charges were proven – how could they be? But by the end of that farce, I was no longer the Governor of any island at all, and I was stranded in London – no commission, no prospects, no ship willing to take me to the Leewards, no wife. Maybe," he speculated, "maybe Amélie just got tired of waiting for me. But she did not seem broken-hearted when I left for London. I last saw her as I left Guadeloupe on board the boat I had hired to take me to Montserrat. She stood on the shore with her little son and waved for a while, then turned her back on me."

The old man sighed and looked at his son: "It was a bad affair, sir."

John Cochrane, feeling some faint stirring of filial attachment, observed that, for a marriage to end in such a way was undoubtedly both sad and bad.

His father eyed him with a small degree of pity, and a large degree of scorn. "Not my marriage," he said. "The court-martial." With which words, he tired of talking sense into his son, and strolled back to the grand passenger accommodations of the Frolic. The Leeward Islands Packet Company had furnished its most sea-worthy ship with one large cabin criss-crossed by hammocks, and one small cabin with two bunk-beds, while, for the public room, an airless dark cupboard of triangular shape, with no window to the sea, was deemed sufficient. This room, as a sop to the affectations of land-lubbers, had a plaque carved of wood nailed to the door identifying it as the King George Saloon.

Within the pleasant confines of the King George Saloon, a number of people were assembled, none of who were of any interest to young John Dundas Cochrane. Two ladies claiming to be French were TWO LADIES OF camped upon a broken chaise longue: both of impressive IMPRESSIVE BULK bulk, one young and one who could still remember being young, their professional career had been built around the entertainment of gentlemen. They expected to make a comfortable living in the golden cities of Gran Colombia. Also travelling was Colonel James Hamilton, an entrepreneur of considerable wealth. The Colonel frequently referred to that wealth; it stood in papers which he kept for such purpose in his coat, papers in which Simon Bolivar, Liberator and President of Colombia, Dictator of Peru, Generalissimo of the Armies etc. etc. etc. declared Colonel Hamilton to have the sole steam-navigation rights on the Orinoco River. There was also a young man named John Rundell, partner and son of the well-established firm of Rundell, Bridge and Rundell, which had, from that self-same Dictator etc. etc. etc. of the newly-liberated country to which they were now sailing, been granted the sole rights to the pearl fishery in the Gulf of Panama. "A pearl," declared Mr. Rundell to anyone who asked, "is of itself, but little. A bauble. A mere accident of nature. But on a ring or a necklace, it is transformed by the beauty of its wearer." At these words, he would incline lightly towards Mme. Langue, the less-young of the two French ladies, who spent her days fanning herself languidly and planning the conquest of a fallen Empire. "A pearl upon the chest of a military man," continued Mr. Rundell with enthusiasm, rather unexpectedly changing tack, "is equally splendid; some would even say that it was more so, the delicacy of the one setting off the manliness of the other." When questioned more narrowly, he declared that the noble aim of Messrs. Rundell, Bridge and Rundell was "to raise the young country from a perpetuity of sloth, ignorance, bigoted superstition, and slavery."

There were two other passengers in that cramped cabin: one, calling himself Don Ajue, a Spanish nobleman whose accent was curiously placed somewhere between County Kerry and Seville, shared with Rundell the same lofty motivation for travelling from Bristol to Gran Colombia – as if the downfall of the Empire of Spain and the striving of the oppressed peoples for Liberty was his sole reason for being there in this year of 1825; the accumulation of a fortune, while understandably agreeable, would be nothing more than a happy coincidence. The final passenger, who had claimed for himself and his pipe one corner of the cabin and rarely abandoned either, was a black man named Thomas Smith, a freed slave who did not conceal his aspirations to seek his fortune in the revolutionary states of Spanish America, but rarely spoke to those who, until very recently, he had counted among his masters. They, respecting his reticence and his breeding, barely acknowledged his existence.

THE AGREEABLE ACCUMULATION OF A FORTUNE

After a dreary voyage of over twenty-five days and nights, whose monotony had been relieved only by the increasing instability of their Captain, a man named Massey from Shrewsbury whose apprehensions concerning Ursa Major were frequently voiced, these seven passengers had this night, the sixth of August in the year 1825, come before the port of La Guayra on the coast of Gran Colombia.

For these fellow passengers and their purely financial ambitions, John Cochrane had little time, his mind being fixed upon his own journey: this was a journey which, after completing the small and annoying matter of managing the copper-mine, would take him up into the Andean Mountains and so westwards and southwards until he had conquered each peak and each mile of several thousand, until he stood and gazed upon the Straits of Magellan at the foot of the world. This second great journey, the careful chronicle of which would be published by Mr. Constable or Mr. Murray, would make him the greatest traveller of his age. As for the first great journey, the story of which he had tried to convey to his father with little success, it began as follows.

"In the year 1820," said Commander John Dundas Cochrane of the British Royal Navy, "finding myself not likely to be employed afloat, much less ashore, I determined to undertake a pedestrian journey around the world. Accordingly, I set out from Dieppe, and walked across France as far as Strasbourg, and then I walked across Germany and into Prussia; and from Prussia into Russia, as far as St Petersburg. I reached St Petersburg barely twelve weeks after leaving Dieppe. One thousand and six hundred miles, all told. An average of nearly twenty miles per day. I was, I believe, 'hitting my stride'. From St Petersburg, I took my course southwards as far as Moscow, and then I continued eastwards, down the River Volga and over the Ural Mountains, and into Siberia, across its vast frozen wastes and its fields of plenty, as far as Nizhney Kolymsk, of which, one may concede, few will ever have heard. It lies some six thousand miles east of St Petersburg, in the most north-easterly part of Siberia. This further journey I made on foot, on horseback, on sledge, in canoes, through snows and forests, down vast rivers and over perilous mountains. From Kolymsk, finding that the passage to America could not be achieved by land, I made my way southwards to the desolate region of Kamtchatka, which I explored from end to end; and then I returned, via the borders of China, across the endless lands of Siberia, back to St Petersburg, which I reached once more some three years after leaving it. Sixteen thousand miles all told. This was one of the greatest journeys ever made."

Having, to his own satisfaction, primed and pricked the curiosity of anyone who wished to hear, Commander Cochrane continued: "I have set out the details of this journey in my book entitled

A PEDESTRIAN JOURNEY

Through Russia and Siberian Tartary
to the Frontiers of China,
the Frozen Sea and

KAMTCHATKA.

For those who have not been so fortunate as to acquire my book, though it ran to three editions in as many years and has appeared in several languages, I will now tell the full story without delay or interruption."

3

HE FREQUENTLY MISTOOK A LAXATIVE FOR AN APHRODISIAC.

Eight years later almost to the day, Major George Sinclair was engaged in that activity which old men do best of all, some spending the best years of their life at it: he lay dying. The place where he lay dying was the Russian city of Velikiy Novgorod, once the greatest city of northern Russia, known to all foreigners as Novgorod the Great. His dying was, for the moment at least, uninterrupted by any of those annoyances of modern life – friends, physicians, medicines, priests, prayers. He had contrived to bribe an old woman to come and tend to the few needs of his last days, and to listen to those few words of Russian he had managed to learn. Unhappily, most of those words were more suited to the barrack-room, the gambling-den and the house of low repute, than the sacred bedroom of a dying man or the ears of his respectable nurse. She told him so, using profane language of a different sort. He regretted the caprices of language, but could do no more: in the several months of his residence, he had not learned the Russian for 'apology'.

With these forbidden words alone, Major Sinclair tried to remember what woman had long ago promised with her eyes to share his bed, and thought some more of hot days and stormy nights in the blue seas of Carib. Each neighbouring island had its own Governor, each Governor his own Government and allegiance. One week, an island would be British, the next week French, then Danish, then Swedish and – if a man succumbed to a distraction – the one behind you would suddenly go Dutch. This was no problem, as long as the slaves knew their place.

Six-and-thirty years ago, Major George Sinclair had arrived on the island of Dominica, just as Colonel Andrew Cochrane-Johnstone took up his post. The island lay slightly south of the French stronghold of Guadeloupe, with its smoking volcano, and slightly north of St Vincent, with its volcano that erupted every so often, like an outbreak of the pox. Somewhere away to the west was the land of Gran Colombia, full of proud Spaniards intent on doing each other harm. The French, for their part, oozed treachery: not content with a Revolution in Paris, they wanted a Revolution in the Leeward and Windward islands as well. First they sent out a Revolutionary Commissioner; then they freed the slaves; then they decided that, while Egalité could and Fraternité should be celebrated on certain days of the year, Liberté was best kept for the true white Frenchman.

The British flag, in all of this, flew steady and unchanging. At that time, there was not a whiff of any radicalism to disturb the civilised mood of the British islands – that came later, when all reason was lost. The new Governor of the island of Dominica, mourning decently the recent loss of his wife, and raising a grateful bumper to his patron, Lord Melville, was now at liberty to seduce his women; import his rum; hire his privateers; beat his slaves; sell guns to those that needed them, unless, of course, the customers were slaves – a gentleman had his principles, after all – all as befitted his position and respectability. In the year following his appointment to Dominica, Colonel Cochrane-Johnstone was only too pleased to see Napoleon order the invasion of his own French possession of Guadeloupe. Quell the rebellion of the slaves – put to the sword ten thousand of the rebels – recall the Commissioner to France – re-introduce slavery. Vive Napoleon!

For Major Sinclair, it was not easy to face death with so many happy memories of earlier years still circling in his mind. Here he was, in some forsaken provincial town in Russia, driven from his friends in Paris by a wild burst of hopeless enthusiasm, a lust for fame; now forced by poverty to accept the close attentions of a pugnacious old harridan, forgotten already by the officers in the Citadel, alone. If he had ever imagined his own death, it was not here, in this lifeless spot, surrounded on all sides by a measureless sea of trees, with barely a hill to break the monotony. It was not here, in this town, where every street-corner had its own church to remind you of the sinfulness of the ways of man. It was not here, driven from one place to the next, from the last country to this, by the need to find money, by the unwelcome attentions of creditors, by the obligation to cultivate a new audience for his tales of by-gone glories before all offers of charity dried up once more.

A man should be allowed to choose the place of his dying, if not the time. The Good Lord owed him that, at the very least. Paris, by preference. Being denied Paris, George Sinclair raged for a few days, and then subsided into regret. Here he was, a fine example of the kind of pitiful wretch of whom the chaplains had always preached. They had not been right, they had never been right – but it had to be said that they could not be proven wrong if they came across him in this hour. Major Sinclair's spirit rose into the air above his bed – to where, had the bed been in its prime, the tapestries would have been suspended to block out the sky – and he looked down upon himself. Not for the first time in his long and wasted life, the sight filled his heart with self-pity.

In the evening of the ninth day, by the old Russian calendar – and twenty-first by any other Western Calendar, except that of Greece – of August in the year 1833, Major Sinclair remembered his early days: a boyhood spent in the north of Scotland, a place he had never returned to, once he had escaped. He spoke aloud, if only to hear for one last time a friendly voice, talking in English.

"My father," he said, "never forgave me for not taking a commission in the Navy; it is too expensive in the Army, said my father. But I learned from my uncle William, who had seen some skirmishes in Europe, that an Army man could make more of himself than a Navy man, and have all the women too. On a ship, you have rum, weevils and the rough backsides of slippery midshipmen you cannot love; on land, wine, lice and the smooth—"

He checked himself, fearful of a slap from his croaking nurse. He was surprised to find himself alone. Where were his fellow-officers? "You lazy old witch!" he cried, "Where are all my friends? I told you that they should come!" The old witch slumbered on, oblivious to her dereliction of care. Indeed, the cry of anger was so weak, that only a beetle and a rat heard it, and neither of them could assist in any way. They passed down the passage-way in philosophical companionship, considering briefly the odd manner of the death of men and women, which took so long and meant so little.

"My father," he continued. "That was Mr. John Sinclair, apothecary and penny-pincher of Nairn. He was not a patient man, he learned carelessness, and frequently mistook a laxative for an aphrodisiac – his customers did not know whether they were coming or going."

Major Sinclair surprised himself much with this unexpected play on words, and laughed aloud. Such amusement could yet be found in Nairn. His mirthful outburst had the effect of waking his nurse, which was greatly beneficial. She cursed him with some religious Russian phrases, which meant nothing to him. Only the tone in which the words flew at him gave any indication of their significance. That, and the manner in which she approached his bed with a grey rag, and scrubbed his sweating brow, as if, instead of beads of sweat, it was garnished with mud.

"I was talking of my father," he exclaimed, when she stood back to admire her handiwork. "My father, do you understand?" Yadviga neither understood nor did she care, but she was more than adequately satisfied with her efforts upon his fevered brow.

Major Sinclair shrugged as if he cared no more; and then, with that miraculous facility by which a man and a woman can understand each other without the use of a common language – more commonly seen amongst the young than the old – he gave her to understand that he required warm food and strong drink, and that she was not to lose any of his money, his food or his drink in the river Volkhov. All of these complex instructions, by the simple expedient of pointing at a few coins which lay in a diminishing pile next to his bed, the single gesture containing within it the distillation of fifty conversations of like nature.

After several minutes, during which she arranged her attire and demeanour fittingly for the gaze of the notables of Novgorod – the sun had not yet set, and was unlikely to do so until close upon eight o'clock – the lady finally let herself out of the door of the residence of Major Sinclair, and with a sigh and a shake of the head, undertook a journey which had as its object the inn of

THE APOSTATE VLADIMIR IVANOVICH VORONOV.

4

NEVER WEAR RIGHT AND LEFT SHOES.

"In the year 1820," began Commander John Dundas Cochrane, "I decided to undertake a journey which had as its object the ascertaining of the course and determination of the river Niger."

He paused, wondering whether, in the darkness of the room, his father was asleep or simply uninterested, a deep and unresponsive silence being the mark of both. The inn, known as La Venta, might have been set amidst the circling stars: it was perched high above the port of La Guayra, whose harbour had been reached by the Frolic against all expectations of her captain, who was certain that the ship would founder, as had several others in recent months. When the ship had dropped anchor in the harbour, the passengers were hastily disembarked, and then captain and crew rowed off to a low drinking-establishment some distance down the coast. Colonel Hamilton and Thomas Smith had made their way on a road that led southwards towards the Orinoco River, accompanied, for reasons that no one could determine and which he did not wish to divulge, by young Mr. Rundell, who refused to acknowledge the fact that the pearl fisheries lay to the north and west. The French ladies and Don Ajue had found accommodation in the only house of La Guayra which still was possessed of a roof, the great earthquake of 1812 having caused so much devastation that the inhabitants did not know where to begin to repair it; it seemed that the three had come to an amicable agreement on payment, a contract which left Don Ajue in transports of delight, and much poorer. John Cochrane and his father, finding that they had been out-manoeuvred by the combined European finesse of the wily Irish Spaniard and the two Cockney Frenchwomen, were obliged to hire the only mule still left standing on this side of the mountains, and proceed upwards towards the city of Caraccas. A condition of the hire was that the muleteer should accompany them, a man so exhausted by years of ascending and descending the sheer wall of mountain which overhung La Guayra that he was obliged to ride the mule himself, sitting on top of Colonel Cochrane-Johnstone's bags.

By the time, therefore, that the Cochranes had climbed the many hundred feet of the muddy path that formed the principal highway from the coast to Caraccas, the father was liverish and exhausted, and the son was stroking his elegant moustache in a manner calculated to inspire terror in foreigners and surliness in servants. Alas, the night had swiftly succeeded upon twilight, and the stroking of the moustache had no effect upon the muleteer Fernando or his mule. On their arrival at La Venta, the mule and Fernando enthusiastically commandeered suitable lodgings in the stable, while father and son sat down to a handsome supper, which included several bottles of Canary wine. At the conclusion of this fine feast, they repaired to the only room in the inn, which had neither window nor chimney, but made up for these omissions by a fine view of the stars through the thatch of the roof.

Andrew Cochrane-Johnstone, smoking a cheap cigarillo he had scrounged from Fernando, fell upon his bed with a grunt and said no more. He was in the company of his son, with whom he had spent perhaps a total of seven hundred and thirty days of his life, in the past two-and-thirty years. He was little inclined to add to this accumulated credit by exploiting this latest opportunity: there had been no point then – even less now. He grunted once more and fell silent, leaving his son to determine whether or not he slumbered. The pin-prick of his cigarillo glowed regularly in the darkness.

"In the year 1820," re-commenced Commander John Dundas Cochrane, feeling more at ease with the world, "finding myself not likely to be employed afloat, much less ashore, I decided to undertake a journey into the interior of Africa, which should have as its object the ascertaining of the course and determination of the river Niger. I had, since the conclusion of a general peace, traversed as a pedestrian the countries of France, Spain and Portugal, and now I wished to follow the course adopted by Mungo Park in his first journey. It was my contention that a man alone, relying solely on his own wit and the hospitality of a native people, could discover more about barbarous lands than any number of grand expeditions with half-a-dozen officers, a hundred soldiers and enough baggage to provision the invasion of Spain. The Admiralty, of course, refused this request, although I asked no money of them, simply their permission to go there alone, to accompany the caravans in some servile capacity, to sell myself as a

TO SELL HIMSELF AS A SLAVE slave if that would accomplish the object I had in view.

"On being refused, I determined instead to travel round the globe, as nearly as can be done by land, crossing from Northern Asia to America at Bering's Straits. I intended to do so on foot, for the best of all possible reasons – that my finances allowed of no other. Having procured two years leave of absence, which was doubtless most welcome to the Admiralty, I prepared to traverse the continents of Europe, Asia and America.

"Accordingly, I filled my knapsack with such articles as I considered requisite to enable me to wander the wilds, deserts and forests of three quarters of the globe, and quitted London. A mere forty hours later – the longest and dreariest part of my journey, you may be certain – the packet-boat arrived at Dieppe; and on the following day, my twenty-seventh birthday—"

"I remember it well, my boy," murmured Cochrane-Johnstone, whose thoughts commonly ranged widely over matters of marriage, bastards and heirs. "That would have been the—?"

"—the fourteenth day of February—"

"Indeed," agreed the proud father complacently. He resumed his smoking in silence.

"—my journey began in earnest. Stretching my legs across the north of France, I reached Paris in two days, and remained there to receive signatures for my passports. Paris was dull. Dull, and a regular vortex of dissipation. I resolved immediately to quit it and set out for the Rhine, which I intended to cross at Frankfort. There is little of interest to report, except that I fell in with one of Napoleon's soldiers who imparted much good advice to me on the subject of blistered feet. Firstly, that, on going to bed, I should rub my feet with spirits mixed with soft tallow; and secondly, that I should never wear right and left shoes – that is a bad economy and indeed serves to cramp the feet. Such advice I followed for sixteen thousand miles, and have never once had occasion to complain of it. This military man, I may add, had been captured in the fighting around Vitebsk, and had been marched along with five hundred and thirty of his compatriots to Tobolsk in Siberia, from which a mere twenty-three emerged alive, two years later. Eight months it took them to be marched to Tobolsk – it took me barely three, sir, barely three.

"Just beyond Sarrebrück, I crossed into Germany where the scenery is wild and interesting; many cultivated spots smiled through the immense dark forests. Here and there I found snug little public-houses which reminded me of home. After a walk of a mere forty miles or so, I supped with a band of itinerant Jews on true German fare, to wit: milk-soup, fricasséed veal, pancakes, roast joint, and a sausage; and for our dessert, apples, pears, nuts and good wine. I could not feel else but happy. It was on this short journey through the fairest of countries, that I was able to remark upon the difference between a German and a Frenchman. It is this: address a German, however poor and vulgar his condition, upon any subject, and his answer will prove that he has been at least partially educated. Accost a Frenchman in like manner, and you will have for answer: 'Monsieur, cela je ne puis vous dire', with a shrug of the shoulders."

"The German woman," observed his father sententiously, "is, in my experience, robust, a quality for which one might pay good money and receive a good bargain. But the French woman is beyond price."

John Cochrane at that moment did not care to doubt the paternal words, which seemed imbued with a profound knowledge of human intercourse, of which he himself had learned not much and cared little to hear more. "I continued," he continued, "as far as Frankfort, Hanau, Fulda and Erfurt, then into Prussia. It was in the town of Dueben, the first in Prussia, that I met a reception which could be described as uncivil, if not inhuman. Here, the guards at the frontier were whiskered ruffians. Here, the landlord laughed at me when I asked for supper, and here, when I demanded a bed, he pointed to the floor, where not a wisp of straw lay. For some time, he strutted about, taking immense quantities of snuff and acting the tyrant over all who dared to enter his inn – until, yawning terribly, he made his bed in a large wooden box, furnished with a pillow and some straw, wrapped a blanket round his person and lay down inside. No sooner had he done so than I made it my business to escape from this den of vice – I climbed out through a window and took the road to Wittenberg, where I arrived at eight o'clock in the morning."

Colonel Andrew Cochrane-Johnstone, once the Governor of Dominica and subsequently honourable Member of the Westminster Parliament for the constituency of Grampound, sat up suddenly, squinting across the acrid smoke towards his son, and said in a tone in which were mingled both disapproval and admiration: "You never told me this, my lad. You, climbing out of a window to avoid paying the bill? – an outrage!"

The son protested in vain. The father eyed him and shook his head. Such is the scene when parents are disappointed.

"I came to Berlin after a number of days," said the reprehensible son, "but found it to contain only the most hardened military despots and no smiling faces. I saw no modes of gaining a livelihood, or even of passing the time honestly – billiards, cards and dice succeeded to the spectacle of the parade. I shrugged off this town as easily as I shrugged off Paris. Indeed, all the capitals of Europe have little to recommend them. From Berlin to the ocean was a long, dreary road. The authorities and inn-keepers gave me little in the way of comfort, and in the town of Schlaws arrested me for smoking in the streets."

From the other side of the room came an astonished silence; THE UNNATURAL stupefaction at this assault on the basic Rights of Man. PREJUDICES OF Truly, the tinder-box of civilisation had not opened upon PRUSSIAN OFFICIALS Prussia. As if to emphasise the point, the cigarillo shed a final puff of smoke; and died thereof. The gentleman, still struck dumb by the Unnatural Prejudices of Prussian Officials, lay on his bunk and licked his dry lips, hungering after a fine Mexican cigar, and wondering whether the inn-keeper had a supply to hand.

Unaware of these yearnings, the pedestrian narrator continued: "I made my way to Danzig, through a country infested with bands of robbers. Fortunately, I looked so poor, and my shoes were not worth the trouble of stealing, that I reached the city in safety, pausing merely to examine the fine cathedral and to receive a gift of stout English shoes from the British Consul. There is little of interest to say of the rest of my journey across that flat and largely execrable land. There was rain, mud and snow. There were frozen lakes and frozen seas to cross. Some of the towns were fair to view. But I observed mostly ugly women and long-bearded men.

"At length, having left the town of Riga far behind me, I came upon the St Petersburg wagon. Having stout shoes and a light knapsack, I did not join it. Its pace was so slow that I overtook it. In any case, I found it more convenient, and considerably warmer, to push on. Within a day I had crossed the frontier into Russia and was quite soon in the comfortable city of St Petersburg. There, I had the good fortune to attract the attention of the Emperor himself, who was most solicitous, and begged to know, through the British Consul-General, whether I had need of any money, promising me that I should be supplied from the Imperial Treasury as necessary.

"But I had little need of money, since my object was to make the crossing of Russia and Siberia without spending so much as a guinea. My only need, ably supplied by the ministers of the Emperor, was for passports and letters of introduction."

There was a lengthy pause. Cochrane-Johnstone broke off from a fretful calculation of the likely bill to be thrust at them by the inn-keeper when this night was through, and reflected that he had never come across such largesse as that exhibited by the Russian Emperor. Would that the Spaniards, or the French, had been so open-handed, then perhaps today he would not be obliged to travel seeking a financial opportunity, in the company of a son who could not and would not be shaken off.

"Ah, father!" exclaimed Cochrane after a minute or two, "I forgot to tell you of an amusing incident."

"Did it involve a woman?" yawned the old gentleman, seeing in such a possibility at least some small salvation for his son's soul.

"Not at all. In the town of Narva," explained Cochrane, "I encountered a man who was travelling to St Petersburg by coach. In his good company, I travelled the remaining miles in style, he having two grand

coaches under his command. He travelled in the first coach and I in
the second. I had a specific charge from him to use no ceremony in
abusing the coachman, if he should slacken his driving. I soon forgot

ABUSING THE this admonition in a sound sleep, for which I afterwards
COACHMAN received a severe reprimand. My new companion was
much distracted in his attempts to engage the affections of the chambermaid at the inn, and it was not until the final day of our journey
that we found an opportunity to converse. But father," he said, turning towards the dark corner where his elder and better lay, "if I tell
you that this new companion of mine was a black man – as black as
any man upon Dominica – what would you say?"

Cochrane-Johnstone, who had by now lost all interest in the story,
chose to say nothing, save to bestow, in the pitch darkness, a black look
upon his son. He wished only for an end to this interminable story.

Not disheartened, Cochrane continued: "When I showed him the
passport I had, this gentleman observed my name and asked – note
this, father – if I was related to 'Admiral Kakran, who was in de West
Indies at de capture of de Danish Islands in 1807?' Being informed
that I was the admiral's nephew, he then asked: 'Are you de son of
Massa Kakran Jahnstone? ' I confirmed this. 'You are den,' said he,
'dat lilly Massa Jonny I know at de same time.' It turned out that this
black gentleman had been your servant and my uncle Alexander's
servant thirteen years before, when I was still a boy and came to visit
you. Imagine that, if you will! To come so far across Europe and
stumble across an old friend!"

"Astonishing," said his father, sourly.

"Unfortunately, he seemed little inclined to tell me how he had risen
so high in Russian society. It was only when I reached St Petersburg,
and called upon a friend, that I discovered, of course, that he was not
the wealthy dashing merchant as he put himself about, but a humble
servant of Prince Labanov, whose winter coaches he was conducting
to the Prince's winter quarters."

At this revelation, Cochrane-Johnstone at last slipped off the edge
of the precipice of sleep and swung into

AN ABYSS OF DREAMS AND NIGHTMARES.

"That man," said Commander John Dundas Cochrane, after some deliberation, "what was his name? I could not remember then, and I forget it now. He knew my name, but – was it perhaps —?"

5

AT THE SIGHT OF THE INN-KEEPER'S DAUGHTER, HE RECOVERS HIS APPETITE.

Then, as now, his name was Horatio. At a time when the sun was setting over the north European plains stretched far to the west, two carriages rolled up the road from the south. From the town of Krettsy, to be exact, in that day's journey, and from Moscow some two days earlier. The carriages were visibly those of a man of considerable wealth. In the first carriage, a coachman sat upon the seat, wrapped in furs despite the warm day, and having every appearance of a brown bear that had seized the reins, cracking his whip idly at the two horses which, tired though they were, pulled him along at a steady pace. Inside sat a man tall and massive, probably a merchant; occasionally he leaned dangerously from the window to hurl abuse at the coach-man – one might think that there was some desperate business to be transacted before night-fall – but in reality it was simply a diversion, a sport. The carriage which raced barely yards behind had as a coachman a short thin man, almost a boy, dressed in a costume with a faintly military air about it, and topped with an enormous fur hat, which would have suited a figure twice his height and width. Anyone who stopped to stare – and these were but few in the hot summer air around the town of Novgorod the Great – would have seen that there was no person inside this second carriage. Perhaps it was reserved for rich silk and money-chests; English shooting-shoes and heavy cloaks; bottles of Russian and French champagne; drugged secretaries and listless countesses – or, according to taste – braces of pistols; and books, books, books. Or perhaps, as it roared by, it was empty.

As the two coaches passed close to the shores of Lake Ilmen, the passenger was seen to gaze out upon the still waters with some despondency, and then, as the gloom of the evening settled and the mists rose over the water, to sit back again and curse and roar passionately at the coachman; who, fearing – it must be supposed – for his position, re-doubled his efforts with the whip and urged the horses onwards with bear-like growls. The driver of the rear coach, anxious lest he should be left behind, lashed the last ounces of energy from his team, and together the carriages swept up to the dilapidated gates of Novgorod the Great.

From a distance, as any traveller knows, the might of Novgorod is apparent: it lies in the height of the outer battlements, each corner presided over by a tower perhaps a hundred feet high, scowling over the surrounding lands; and in the glorious battle-array of the spires of its churches, each topped with a golden cross which, at this time of day, gleams brightly in the sun. Had a traveller time to name them all, and a book by some authoritative guide to tell of their wonders, she or he would start with the cathedral of St Sophia, highest of them all; and then would proceed to the cathedral of St Nicholas; then the great church of the Yuriev Monastery, and the rival one in the grounds of the Antoniev Monastery; then would be named the church dedicated jointly to St Peter and St Paul; the one of the Annunciation, another one of the Assumption, and yet another in memory of the blessed St Parasceva; and perhaps grandest of them all, the Saviour Church. With such a great catalogue of churches, one for every saint who might be interested in the mercantile activities of the people of Novgorod, and perhaps one for every saint who long ago abandoned the city for the bright lights of St Petersburg, and one for each family of monks, and finally one for each of the rest of the holy days of the Christian calendar, there would barely be time to mention those whose towers do not poke up above the walls of the city: time only to list in turn, and in no order reflective of the relative spirituality or power of the saint in question, the chapel of St Nicholas (a man obviously in great demand); the churches of St Theodore; St John the Almsgiver; Saints Peter and Paul again, these two clearly went around in pairs, perhaps for safety, perhaps just to impress people all the more; of Christ's Nativity; St John; all of the Holy Apostles together; St Demetrius; St Simeon; St Theodore Stratilates; St Blaise; the Myrrh-Bearing Women – so that the ladies do not feel forgotten – and Saints Boris and Gleb. And then there are the chapels – but the traveller, thirsty for knowledge, must stop there, for, really, the chapels are too numerous to name; one only hopes that a building which does not merit a mention here is not dedicated to some Saint or tangle of Saints on whom, one day, our traveller might rely.

"Who can resist the Gods and the great Novgorod?" muttered Horatio obliquely to himself as the carriages rolled closer to the outer walls. Alas, since some poet wrote those self-same words, Novgorod has become quite resistible (the Gods, on the other hand, have not). For the Imperial city of Novgorod has seen many unhappy times. The massacre of some towns-people by Ivan the Terrible in 1570 was only the beginning of a swift decline: for a city that once boasted near to half a million inhabitants, trading with all the peoples of the East and West, South and North, had now, on the ninth and twenty-first day of August 1833, been reduced to a mere ten thousand or so, ten souls for every church, if certain calculations are correct.

A DISGRUNTLED CONGREGATION OF SAINTS
Leaving the Gods and the Great Novgorod behind them, all who were mighty and rich, and all who were aspirants to mightiness and richness, and all who followed those who strove after might and riches, have fled to chum up with Peter the Great in St Petersburg: even Peter's inseparable companion, St Paul, was abandoned in the flight, it seems. The Gods fled, leaving a disgruntled congregation of Saints.

The Gods having fled, so Horatio arrived: at the south gate to the city. Like all gates which might be breached from within or without, this gate was guarded by a janitor. It was not clear whether the grizzled hero with one leg and a stout stick was part of the military establishment, or whether he was just a pensioner acting on praiseworthy initiative. He brandished his stick under the noses of the leading pair of horses, and the carriage stopped. Horatio pulled down the window and leaned out of the carriage.

"Whither are you bound?" demanded the old man.

"For Novgorod," said Horatio, vaguely waving his arm at the battlements towering above them.

"For Novgorod the Great?" asked the guardian unnecessarily.

"For Novgorod the Great," confirmed Horatio. "And we are in a hurry to find our quarters for the night."

The veteran looked at them sceptically, stroking a thin beard, then mentally valued the horses and the second carriage, which now stopped behind them.

"Well," he said at last, "I suppose you must be let past. But can you spare a moment or two to hear the story of an invalid soldier?" He looked up at Horatio through one infected eye, a pitiful whine in his voice.

The traveller was an easy man to sway, his feelings planted, like the grasses of the steppe, close to the surface. Sighing within, he smiled benignly upon the soldier, while the coachmen above and behind growled wildly. "Certainly, sir," he replied, "if you think I might be interested."

"Oh," said the janitor confidently, "all are interested who hear my story. For it is one to bring tears to your eyes, and make THERE WERE NO you step without delay to the gilded chapel of St Andrew, LADIES ABOARD to offer up prayers for the salvation of men. The ladies, especially, like to weep," he added, peering hopefully into the carriage. There were no ladies aboard.

"Well now," says he, leaning comfortably on his stick, "it was in the year 1828, barely five years ago, you would not believe it to look at me, I was a young man then." Indeed, there was no reason at all to believe it, for the man looked to be at least sixty years of age, one foot in the grave, the right leg having preceded it. "The Great Russian Imperial Army was in the south, pushing back the heathen Turk from our fields and woods and mountains. We had been there over a year, leaving our loved ones in the north, fighting for Emperor and Faith." He crossed himself, at the utterance of the two holy words. "Well, then – sir, would you mind," said he, clambering up on the step of the carriage and forcing open the door, "if I sat with you inside, for the evening chill gets into my bones and I find it hard to stand so long?" Without waiting for an answer, the soldier displayed some of the skills of assault and attack which had brought great glory to the armies of Imperial Russia in times gone by, and was instantly seated opposite Horatio, upon velvet cushions, gazing in unstinting admiration at the pastoral motifs painted within. Through a window up at the front, the first coachman bent his ear to the proceedings. "There we were, sir," he continued in more relaxed manner, "two thousand of us against five thousand of the heathen Turk, at a place known as the Gates of Iron, above a great river. The Danube, it was called. Have you heard of it?" Horatio admitted that he had indeed heard of it. "I knew it, sir," exclaimed the soldier, "from the very first moment, I saw that you were a learnèd gentleman, who had travelled far. Perhaps you have seen the Gates of Iron?" Horatio denied this. "Also known as the Iron Gorge?" Horatio denied it twice. A superstitious man, not wishing the question to be denied thrice, the soldier moved on.

"So there we were, one thousand of us, and maybe nine or ten thousand of the Turk. Have you seen the Turk, sir?" Horatio denied this experience, just once. "Also known as the Ottomans?" Horatio denied it a second time. "Arrayed in battle, sir, what a splendid sight! The Imperial Russian Army, defender of the Faith and of all Christian civilisation— " here he waved at the city of Novgorod, now so abandoned, behind him, "—against the scourge of all Europe. The worst enemy in all the world."

"Except for Napoleon," interrupted the second coachman, who, by this time, was standing on the step of the carriage, listening in.

The veteran looked askance at this interruption. "Napoleon, sir? He was no trouble at all. A scourge, certainly, but never a threat: a horse-fly, not a wolf. No, sir, my money is on the Turk." He continued. "So, the Lieutenant had a plan. That would be Lieutenant Simeonov, sir. You have heard of him?" Horatio denied once. "Now Captain Simeonov. Surely?" Horatio denied it once more. "That is disappointing, sir. The Lieutenant's plan was this: in the night, we would cross the river and take up a position just before the enemy's camp, and then we would attack them by surprise. Ah, a grand plan it was."

Horatio knew little of military strategy, but conceded that such a plan seemed to be rational, if scarcely grand.

"So, when the moon was new, and the night was black, and under the cover of the thick mist which rises above the river every night in these parts, we took boats across the fast-flowing river, all one thousand of us. Have you seen the Danube, sir?" he asked. Horatio denied it. "Also known as the Donau?" Horatio denied it twice. "Sir, it is a mighty river. Wider and stronger than even the Volkhov here. Well, we crossed in safety. Silence was the thing, you see: absolute silence. Not a word was spoken, not a command was necessary. We were good soldiers, then. Not like now..." He rolled his eyes in the direction of the inner city, despairing of the lily-livered military of the present day, whose representatives were doubtless gambling, drinking and arguing noisily in the mess even now, while all around in the evening shades the enemies of Russia were gathering.

"One drink of brandy to warm us up, then we rowed across in the mist. Would you have any brandy about you?" he asked hopefully. Horatio denied it. "Or perhaps some vodka?" Horatio denied that also. The old soldier looked offended, cursed the inadequacy of travellers; but continued.

"Well, the sun came up, but the mist did not clear. We could barely see our hands in front of our faces. We had to sit tight where we had landed. All that day, all that night, and into a second day. Still the mist did not lift, became thicker, so that we could not see the end of our nose before our eyes. A third day also, and still we could not attack. And then, on the fourth day, one of the guards left behind on the north bank arrived, cut to ribbons, missing two arms and a leg, but nevertheless he had rowed across, using his own severed limbs as oars.

Before he died, he told us that the Turk, cunning fellow that he is, had had exactly the same plan as ourselves, and had taken boat to our side of the river. We must, sir, have passed them on the river that very first night. Well, the man promptly died of his wounds, and the Sergeant made up his mind: we had to go back and deal with the Enemy upon the Soil of the Fatherland. Some men would be left behind in enemy territory to maintain our bridgehead."

Horatio objected: "But there was no bridge?"

The old soldier sighed at the ignorance of civilians, but made no great play of it. "It is a military expression, sir, which we old soldiers understand. A bridgehead – it is a secure place within enemy territory, from which an attack may be launched."

"Ah," said Horatio, musing on the imprecision of military language.

"I was among those left behind – myself, and a small detachment with two great cannon. All the others took to the boat and rowed off – silently, mind – back across the river. We never saw them again."

"Dear me," said Horatio, concerned. "Did they drown? Were they also cut to ribbons?"

The old man wiped a welling tear from his good eye. "Ah, sir, we never found out for sure. All we know is that there was a great deal of shouting in the mist. The cries in Russian, and the cries, as we knew, in the Turkish language. The prayers to God Almighty, and the prayers to Allah. My guess is that the Turk had again the same idea as us, and were coming back to deal with us; and the two armies met in the middle of the river. Five hundred against twenty thousand. But, by St Peter and St Paul, our Russian heroes did not die in vain!"

Horatio looked questioningly at him.

"No, sir," said the veteran proudly. "For, if none of our men came back, neither did a single one of the Turk. A triumph! After an hour or two, the shouting and cries and sounds of battle died away, and we were left alone in the mist, listening to the beating of our own hearts. Then, sir, on the following day, the sound of a single gun. I'd swear it was the kind of cannon that the Turk uses. First the explosion as a mortar landed in our small encampment, from out of the mist; then the sound of the gun as it fired. But the skill of the Russian gunner is far greater, and we immediately fired back. All that day, we fired backwards and forwards. One by one, my companions died, hit by debris, shells, heads torn off, limbs flying, innards spilled. Myself, I lost this here leg." He proudly displayed his stump to the three members of his audience. "It was a terrible fight, but at last the gun of the Turk fell silent, and then the mist cleared."

THE SOUND OF
A SINGLE GUN

"And what did you see?" asked Horatio anxiously, imagining a river running blood, landscapes of carnage, a gorge of gore.

The old soldier looked awfully at them each in turn. "Sirs," said he in an unsteady voice, "there was nothing to be seen." Both the armies had vanished into death, and not a single body was left behind, apart from those pieces around me. Being the last man left alive, I took a boat that still remained undamaged, and rowed back to the Homeland, Mother Russia. When I got there, all I found was another small detachment of Russian gunners, also blown into tiny pieces. Never a Turk did we find."

"Never a single Turk?" asked Horatio, startled.

The solder denied it.

"Not one Turk out of ten thousand?"

The soldier denied it twice.

The two coachmen whistled in admiration.

"And not a single Russian apart from yourself?" asked Horatio further.

The soldier confirmed the sad facts.

"Aye, sir," said he. "I made my way back to the army of General Rayevsky, which was encamped further to the east, and made my report. Lieutenant Simeonov had already returned there earlier, the better to plan our next attack. But the General himself, sir, congratulated me on my efforts and accepted my report, and had me sent back home with a good word or two, which got me this post here. It seems that, single-handedly, I had repelled the heathen Turk from the very threshold of our glorious Russia."

The two coachmen applauded, and heaped words of congratulation, not to mention pouches of tobacco, upon the man. Horatio found it necessary to hand over some money, for the pitiful tale of military incompetence he had just heard. His mission accomplished, the veteran leaped nimbly from the carriage and waved them through the southern gate of Novgorod the Great, then turned his gaze hopefully to the road from the south, seeking out further charity.

By the time the travellers entered the city, the sun had set and there was little light to guide them. As befits a city that has been abandoned to past glories, there were few lights in the windows, fewer people at large; and, out of courtesy, those who were at large made themselves very small indeed at the approaching sound of two great rumbling coaches. Within the city walls, the travellers negotiated the wide boulevards and other winding streets without further interruption, it being supper-time for all sentries, and, though the two carriages might contain a whole army of marauding hordes from north, south, east, or any other direction from which a marauding horde might reasonably be expected, supper-time was not the time to be stopping them. On the east side of the river, among the streets of merchants' houses and overgrown pleasure-gardens and the small churches of a host of commercial saints, they stopped at last outside a grand and darkened mansion.

A stable-boy emerged, half-asleep, and guided the two coaches into the yard. Horatio dismounted, nodded once to the two coachmen, and left them to their immediate purpose of stabling the horses and dusting down the carriages. For his part, the weary traveller retraced his steps towards the river. Rich merchant that he was, he found it more convenient to establish himself by night in the inns that lined the main highways of Russia and Europe, from Paris to Berlin, from Berlin to St Petersburg, from St Petersburg to Moscow, from Moscow to Kiev: in the inns, there were greater opportunities to pick up gossip and passing trade. In the inns, also, Horatio found that there was usually a young chambermaid or serving-girl with a twinkling eye, who could be persuaded to have a kiss snatched from her, or to repay a small present with a certain set to her skirt. Girls in inns were impressionable, and there was no need to speak the language of the region. Of course, as a successful merchant, Horatio spoke Dutch, German, French and English with an impeccably thick accent; but these words were the words of trade, and his dealings with the girls in the inns could scarcely be described as trade.

But he was turning weary. This travelling no longer suited him. He wanted a home, a bed, a wife, a small orchard, a seat behind a sunny window, a cat; he wanted nothing more than to get up in the morning and open the shutters and look out upon a small garden that he need not leave until the day he died. He wanted a book of poetry: everyone wanted that, he was told, though he had never read any. 'Pushkin,' they said, puzzlingly: 'you will, of course, like Pushkin, being the African that you are.' Poetry he must unravel. He had lost all appetite for travel, for the endless dusty road that never led anywhere except a foreign land, to a town that was not his.

Complaining inwardly thus, he came to an inn by the river, and stood outside, judging whether it was worthy of his custom. As he stood there, a girl emerged from the front-door, shook out a cloth, caught a glimpse of the weary traveller, smiled, turned back indoors. With a sigh of admiration, he observed the swaying hips of the inn-keeper's daughter, removed his gloves, and followed the smile through the welcoming doorway. "For today," he said to himself in justification, "I HAVE RECOVERED MY APPETITE."

6

HE VACATES HIS MARRIAGE-BED FOR THE HONOURED GUEST.

"Do you have a good appetite?" the inn-keeper asked solicitously.

Both of his new guests nodded politely. The inn-keeper expressed his satisfaction at their politeness, settled himself into a chair beside the stove and began his welcoming speech.

"This city of Novgorod has seen many unhappy times. Let me recount to you the massacre of its towns-people carried out by Ivan Grozny in the year 1570—"

"That would be," interrupted Horatio knowledgeably, for the enlightenment of the lady and other persons innocent of Muscovite history, "Ivan the Terrible."

The lady took this news calmly. "Ah, the period of the Oprichnina," she returned. Then she raised her eyebrows at Horatio and cocked her head slightly. The gentleman blushed to be so sweetly enlightened.

The landlord roared his approval at her observation and, to give proper expression to his appreciation, reached sideways to slap the passing maid-servant upon her behind. Displeased with this treatment of the staff, Horatio frowned; the unfortunate girl reddened like the beetroot and ran off to the kitchen.

"Ivan Grozny," continued our historian, "Ivan Vassilievich, Ivan the Fourth, grandson of Ivan the Great, Ivan, as our friend says, the Terrible. In the year fifteen hundred and seventy, he was—"

—interrupted by his wife, who emerged from the kitchen, as a wolf emerges from its den upon a winter night, seized her husband by the throat, snatched him up from his throne and dragged him off, meanwhile screaming in his ear that he had best leave his hands off the maid if he wished to be able to piss ever again in the cold morning light. The husband was heard to list his excuses as the devoted pair tumbled back into the kitchen.

It had not always been thus.

Once, twenty-five years ago, the inn-keeper and the inn-keeper's wife were newly-wed, and could scarcely be prised apart, even for the very necessary purpose of keeping their guests in food and drink. A traveller would sit for hours at the table, wondering why his supper did not arrive; on entering the kitchen in a quest for enlightenment, he would fall over the entwined bodies of the happy couple, or strike the door upon the back of an intimate animal embrace, and find himself as an unwelcome maggot in the banquet of love. Alas – that was twenty-five years ago. A daughter and two sons had arrived since then, and a wild succession of young girls keen to be chambermaids or maid-servants – the younger son had run off with one, another had run off with the elder son, others had run off with customers, the vast majority had simply run off. In one long winter, 1822, five new girls had come and the same five had left. As his wife grew larger and her figure began to wander, so the eyes of the inn-keeper did likewise and he found the distractions too great to bear; as his wife felt the whole burden of managing the inn slip upon her rounded shoulders, so, at the same time and at approximately the same rate, did her husband feel his enthusiasm slipping away from him.

In these latter days, the inn-keeper felt excluded from the management of his inn. Therefore, to maintain his position as master of the house, he decided to treat all of his guests in a most unequal manner. If a guest arrived who did not suit him – perhaps the guest was from Austria, or from France, or looked as if he might have unorthodox views, or expressed some opinion on the state of Russian literature (it did not matter which opinion, for in the inn-keeper's judgement, no literary opinion could ever be justified, there was far too much literature in Russia in these dangerous times) – then the host made every effort to encourage the guest to leave as soon as possible. Sometimes this involved the careful disposition in the public room of all manner of rubbish from the cellar: old barrels leaking sour dregs, rat-gnawed horse-cloths, rusted implements left there in the seventeenth century by a passing invader – so much filthy clutter, in short, that there would be no place for the weary traveller to sit. At other times, the inn-keeper would arrange his features in a very good approximation of the creation of Victor Frankenstein, as one insulted and cultivated guest pointed out, having a knowledge of modern European literature which a little surpassed that of the inn-keeper (and for which advantage he paid with a cold and sleepless night tied up in the yard, examined by hens): his uncommonly ugly features, set between a bristling black beard and a wild mane of unkempt greying hair, would be contorted into all manner of shapes, while the owner thereof lurched around the room, spilling water upon his guests and trampling on their feet; instead of speaking, he would grunt like a boar; his clothes would be torn and rags would trail into any cold and sour soup that might be set upon the table. In most cases, the guest would take the hint and leave, the inn-keeper would feel a small gratification that his house was once more his, and his wife would scream at him for half the night. In other cases, the guest was obliged to stay put and suffer a thousand punishments which Ivan Grozny himself would have greatly admired.

On the other hand, if a guest arrived to whom the inn-keeper took a fancy, there was scarcely enough that he could do for him or – less frequently – her. The very best crockery and cutlery would be pulled out from the cupboard, the kitchen-girl would be stirred into an hysterical condition, and the landlord himself would serve all the very best dishes, in person, and then sit down and once more begin – but never complete – the story of the massacre of the inhabitants of Novgorod by Ivan the Terrible in the year— yes, even the blankets on the bed of the honoured guest would be shaken out and cleaned before nightfall, in order to ensure that the bugs were at least spruce and lively. On one famous occasion, the landlord was moved by such enthusiasm for a gentleman traveller from the Caucasus, bringing the glad news of the fate of the Decembrists, that he vacated his place in the marriage-bed; both wife and traveller were so mortified by this unexpected hospitality that neither slept a wink all night, each fearing those advances that the other might make.

THE BUGS WERE SPRUCE AND LIVELY

On the arrival of Horatio, the inn-keeper was struck by such a strong emotion of generosity and well-being, that he ordered from his house the only other guest, a surprised traveller, a man with large ears from Krakow who was obliged, without notice, to exchange his place by the stove for the cool airs of the falling night. For convenience, the traveller was ejected from the inn by the back-door – a small social embarrassment might have resulted otherwise. A sumptuous meal was arranged, beds were aired, a huge conflagration set up in the stove, to the great danger of the inn and all the remaining wooden houses of Novgorod the Great. Had there been a pig to slaughter, that pig would have died on the spot. Nothing could be too great a trouble for the new arrival. Noticing that Horatio had, on first entrance, set his eye appreciatively upon his daughter, the inn-keeper ensured she was sent in and out of the room, swaying her hips and with a knowing smile upon her lips, at every possible excuse. What was it that melted that heart underneath the inn-keeper's gruff exterior?

One reason might have been Horatio's appearance, which was unusual for that part of the world, at that time of the year, at that time of the century. Horatio was built large, which indicated either nobility – of which the inn-keeper was greatly in favour – or an insatiable appetite – to which the inn-keeper was less well-disposed; but principally, Horatio was built black. Black all over, as far as the inn-keeper could tell, as he spied out the new arrival through a crack in the kitchen-door. The inn-keeper, for all his other faults, cultivated the unusual amongst his clientele; and here was a man, so unusual not just in size, and not just in the whiteness of his teeth, which he showed frequently in the first few minutes to the inn-keeper's daughter, but most especially in his similarity to the Devil. The landlord – his name, painted above the front-door, was Vladimir Voronov – felt that the view through the crack was by no means enough, and emerged to greet his guest; was immediately impressed by the glowing colour and texture of his skin; was even more impressed by the firmness of his hand-shake; was finally overwhelmed by the gravelly nature of his voice.

At that very moment of greeting, a second traveller stepped in through the door and paused briefly, looking around. In the instant of that pause could be heard the scuttling of a mouse across the floor; the dropping of a large lump of fat into a red-hot pot by Mrs. Voronova; the sudden closing of the back door, followed by the sudden closing of the front door; a sound like a musket; and the arresting of young Miss Voronova in her passage across Horatio's area of easy observation. In the following instant, a memory stirred within Mr. Voronov at the sight of a woman he had first seen some years previously – but he could not place his finger on the who or the when or the how or the why; and Horatio felt an imperative urge to abandon his dissolute ways, at the sight of this woman, for the reason only of the sweetness of her smile and the careful movement of her feet.

The lady was distracted from the transfigured stares of the occupants of the inn by the pouncing of the cat, a sudden curse emitted by Mrs. Voronova, the slamming of the door behind her, the explosion of a piece of wood in the over-heated stove, and the stamping of Miss Voronova's foot; and by any other of several dozen small disturbances which served to startle a tired and nervous traveller.

"Do you," she said at last, turning to the inn-keeper, and avoiding, for the moment at least, the gaze of Horatio, "have a room for the night?"

There could have been no man more willing in all of Novgorod the Great, in all of northern Russia – apart perhaps from one – than Mr. Voronov. "You shall have," said he, rubbing his hands eagerly upon a cloth, "the very best of rooms. Girl! Girl!" he shouted, until the maidenly incumbent of the lowest position in all of Orthodox Christendom arrived from the kitchen, "See that our best room is aired and the bed warmed for our guest!" Seeing the confusion in the girl's face, and guessing that she was about to ask which of many luxurious chambers might be considered the 'best', he chased her out of the room again with a slap to her rear, and turned back to the lady traveller, to pursue with her the matter of food and drink. But by the time he had turned back, the lady's glance had ceased its wandering, and fixed itself upon the face of Horatio; fixed itself and thereby discovered that deep within her heart there was a gulf; and the man who could fill that gulf, even if only for this minute and this hour, had been observed; in such a small space of time do the hearts and loyalties of men and women change. It takes but a single glance, even half a glance, and all other rational consideration becomes pointless.

This sudden change behind his back did not, contrary to anyone's expectations, turn Mr. Voronov from genial host to tyrannical beast;

THE LOWEST POSITION IN ALL OF ORTHODOX CHRISTENDOM

rather, he felt an invisible halo burst out from and surround the two guests, like a blossoming golden fire, and he observed in their eyes a most pleasing hope for the future of all mankind. The priests would call it a miracle; Mr. Voronov remembered it dimly as tender and unreserved compassion. Seeing his daughter make a sudden sally into the room, on no business that she could possibly have there, he hauled her back and pointed her at the kitchen: "Go and help your mother prepare a meal," he ordered, "instead of flaunting yourself like a courtesan before these good people." The girl hissed and wriggled, then retired as commanded.

The stove was blazing fit to crack and hot-spiced ale was produced. Had the pair been his old parents, or a rich and childless aunt and uncle in the final days of life, the inn-keeper could not have been more attentive. Both Horatio and the lady took off their cloaks and hats, and brushed the dust and mud from their boots, and they settled down, one on each side of the stove, with a table between them that threatened to ignite from the licking flames and make the supper their last one. Once, years ago, Horatio had seen a dinner-table burst into flames and consume all the dishes thereon, before the guests had had a chance to do the same. It had been an entertaining sight, all the more so since the flames were only doused by the intervention of a half-dressed medical officer and sixteen bottles of sparkling wine, a matter for which the unfortunate officer was later cashiered; but this was not an event he wished to see repeated, on this night, in this place, in this company.

The lady introduced herself: "My name is Ksenia Ivanovna," she said quietly.

Horatio introduced himself as a gentleman should. He bowed. She courtesied.

Horatio asked Ksenia Ivanovna if she had travelled far.

"Yesterday, from St Petersburg," she confessed, her eyes fixed upon his.

"You have a carriage?" he enquired politely, his eyes fixed upon hers.

"I came with the diligence," she answered, looking down.

"The diligence is rapid, is it not?" he observed, looking up.

"Not as much as before, sir: it has lost a wheel," she replied, looking away.

"Ah," he murmured, looking back, "That is unfortunate."

A short silence followed, fed by the roar of the stove.

"You have a carriage, sir?" she asked, timidly.

"I have two carriages at my disposal," he answered, obliquely.

"You are travelling southwards?" she breathed, her eyes upon him.

"I am travelling northwards," he regretted, his eyes upon her.

There was a lengthy moment while these significant facts were digested. She examined his great hands as they lay, one atop the other, on the table, and admired them as if they were powerful bears asleep.

"A long and tiring journey," said he at length, gazing with admiration upon her tiny hands that rested quietly on her lap. "I know the road intimately. And are you bound for Moscow, perhaps?"

"I am, and much farther," she confirmed. "For Moscow and then a great distance beyond." Again, their eyes met, and locked, and there was a long silence, in which each saw a choice being made. The silence was eternal, interrupted by two hiccoughs only.

Eternal, or at least as long and as wide and as high as it took the landlord to enter the room bearing a steaming pot of stew.

Mr. Voronov had a simple view of Life After Death: when we are faced with oblivion, the long white tunnel stretching before us would simply lead us to a pot of stew, or a plate of beans, or a dish of potatoes dusted with grated cheese, or a thick soup, or a baked fish. The Dead, if not the living, should eat. Could any fault be found with that, he wondered? Would any priest deny us this, he argued? And for those who deny an Afterlife, a Last Supper is always advised. One last good meal, then an eternity of digestion: or, for the literary-minded, of indigestion.

THE DEAD, IF
NOT THE LIVING,
SHOULD EAT

After the two hiccoughs, Mr. Voronov placed the stew upon the table, thereby tugging on the ties that bound one simple soul to the other. "Do you have a good appetite?" the inn-keeper asked. Both guests gazed benevolently up at him, and he down at them. Large lumps of black bread were placed within easy reach, and the meal began.

The inn-keeper now settled himself in a chair beside the stove. "In the year fifteen hundred and seventy, Ivan the Terrible was—"

But, since Mr. Voronov got no further in this romantic exposition, for reasons already noted, and since he then left the room unexpectedly, the travellers were left alone in the corona of their own making. As they ate, now one, now the other would remark upon the dangers and the ills of the journey, or the beautiful scenes they had observed as they proceeded across Russia. Their conversation took in the simplest delights, and the most spiritual ones. They talked of spring water and also of souls.

As they talked thus, Horatio found himself admiring every visible nook and cranny of Ksenia: the gentle curve of her chin, the curl of hair which floated above her left ear, the dark down on her cheek, even – it should be noted, as he grappled without ulterior motive under the table after a lost piece of bread, which the mouse already had its eyes on – even her impressively strong ankle; but more than that, he found balm and comfort in the sound of her voice, and he suffered Galvanic excitement from her silences. He had lost all sense of the passing of time. He was overwhelmed by a passion that he knew that a man may only experience once or twice in his life, however long he lives: he let the passion take over every last breath in his body; and passed her the bread when she had not even asked for it.

"Sir," said the young woman, at last throwing caution to the four easterly winds which blew across all Russia and in under the loose-fitting door. "I must tell you that my first husband once travelled this road."

"Your first husband?" asked Horatio cautiously, suddenly interrupted in his distraction; he looked around cautiously for any second, third or fourth husband.

"I am alone," she assured him.

"QUITE ALONE."

Horatio nodded and fell once more to an agreeable contemplation of the lady's black eyebrows.

"And what I wish to tell you is the story of his peculiarly becoming nakedness."

7

A COUPLE OF RESTLESS HOURS ON A BED OF MOSS.

"I am reminded," said John Cochrane, "of the time when I was stripped naked by ruffians, and tied to a tree."

Lying at rest, somewhere in the darkness, by day or by night, in the land of Gran Colombia, John Cochrane could not put his finger on what had reminded him precisely of that one moment in his pedestrian journey which had led to much after-dinner jollity. Perhaps it was the fact that, to calm the shivering and shaking of his body, he had put on all three of his shirts; the shivering would soon pass – a day of some sixty miles of walking lay ahead, and physical exercise under the sun had until now always driven out such aches and cramps.

"It was," he continued, so as not to lose the thread of his argument among the strange clouds which drifted through his head, "the day after the night on which the Emperor's retreat at Tsarskoe Selo burned down."

"Fire," said an irritable voice from out of the darkness, "is the most dangerous element of all. Captain Massey of the Frolic frequently reminded me of that. He forbade me my pipe. It was, he said, not safe on a ship. The man was a fool. Not safe on a ship!"

"And not, indeed, in a summer palace," agreed Cochrane. "Having left behind me the glories of St Petersburg, on the night of the 24th of May, the moon being near full – ah! you do not know, perhaps, that Mr. John Barrow of the Royal Society in London thought he had me caught in a lie on this point, accusing me of having invented a full moon. He was ignorant, of course, of the finer points of the Russian Calendar: it runs twelve days behind the calendar of Great Britain. He lost the debate; the man is a fool," asserted the great traveller, searching to retrieve his thread. "So, on the night of a near full moon, I set out from St Petersburg. For a traveller with few possessions, the roads at night are no more dangerous than the roads by day. Robbers are of diurnal habit. And," he added, "it is frequently cooler at night.

"As I proceeded in the company of some simple carters from Germany, there suddenly arose to the south-east a tremendous blaze. Immense masses of fire, and sparks, exploded and separated like rockets. As we advanced, we came to the beautiful town of Tsarskoe Selo, and found that the Emperor's favourite palace was ablaze, a palace – I had been assured – that was one of the most exquisite buildings in Europe. When we came closer to the scene of devastation, we found thousands of people employed in the attempt to extinguish the flames, and the Emperor himself directing the operation. There was nothing I could do to help, so I retired to the gardens, where I passed a couple of restless hours on a bed of moss, amid herbs and flowers, their sweet scents mingling with the acrid fumes of smoke. I was awoken by the crashing of the dome of the church, which, in its falling, set fire to two other parts of the palace, until then considered safe. It seemed to me that the entire palace was lost to the flames.

"I breakfasted therefore with Prince Theodore, and amused myself with his small children, then set out southwards through the day to the town of Tosna, which I reached at seven in the evening—"

"One moment, sir," interrupted Colonel Cochrane-Johnstone from the darkness, the red glow of his pipe the only indication that his spirit still lived. "You did nothing more to assist in this dreadful calamity?"

"Nothing, sir: all was already lost. What more could a man, even an energetic one such as I, do to assist? I had slept, sir, and had breakfasted. What else does a man need? When I walk, sir," replied the pedestrian, "I walk. I therefore left the blazing ruins of Tsarskoe Selo and set off by daylight. And I encountered no robbers. Robbers? Fire? A true traveller must not be diverted by matters such as the destruction of a summer palace. Perhaps I can read you a few words from my Journal?" Without waiting for permission, he struggled with his three shirts, then pulled out a small bound volume, and by the light of a stub of candle which illumined barely the ends of his finger-tips, read as follows: "Go and wander with the illiterate and almost brutal savage! – go, and be the companion of the ferocious beast! – go, and contemplate the human

GO AND WANDER WITH THE ILLITERATE AND ALMOST BRUTAL SAVAGE!

being in every element and climate, whether civilized or savage. Make due allowance for the rusticity of their manners. Avoid all political and military topics, and remember that the proper study of mankind is man." He snapped the book shut once more and attempted to tuck it into his coat pocket. He failed, for his fingers seemed to have lost all power of philosophy. The book dropped to the ground.

Colonel Cochrane-Johnstone applauded slowly in the ensuing profound silence: "Did I teach you that, my lad?" he enquired.

"I must believe that you did, sir," stated the son loyally.

"No, I did not," said the father, confirmed in his belief that his son was simple; he proceeded to suck upon his pipe rather too noisily for his son's liking.

"On the following day, I encountered robbers," went on Cochrane. "They stripped me of all my clothes. I was sitting smoking a cigar at the side of the road, when suddenly I was seized from behind by two ruffians. One of them, holding an iron bar in his hand, dragged me by the collar into the forest that bordered the road, while the other pushed me with a bayoneted musket. I gave no resistance. A boy was stationed at the road-side to keep a look-out."

"A wise precaution," said Cochrane-Johnstone, ambiguously.

"We got some fifty yards into thickest part of the forest, and I was ordered to undress. I stripped off my trousers and jacket, my shirt and shoes, and they proceeded to tie me to a tree. I surmised that they were about to shoot me. Fortunately, they did not. Instead, they proceeded to rummage through my belongings and appropriated such items of little value as I possessed – my spectacles, compass, sextant, some roubles; then they obliged me to share with them my own black bread and a glass of rum, and to swear that I would not inform against them, and then they made off with all my clothes and my stout shoes, leaving me tied to the tree. A few hours later, a boy – perhaps the same one who had stood look-out – heard my cries for help, and released me. Having been left with two waistcoats only, I rigged myself a dress that would not look out of place amongst Scotchmen, and trotted on down the road with an empty knapsack and a merry heart. After a few miles, I came upon soldiers employed in making a new road. With some difficulty – language, clothes, documents – I gained an audience with their commanding officer, who showed me great kindness: he provided me with food and offered me new clothes. I accepted the former, but declined the latter."

"You chose to remain in undress?" asked his father in naked bewilderment.

"I found, sir, that my dress was peculiarly becoming."

"You are, I suppose," said the father, "an idiot."

There was a long pause, as father and son separately considered matters. It is troubling for any father to see, reflected in his own son, the falling-off of higher values and moral principles. It is troubling also for a son to realise that his own father has neither understanding, nor sympathy, for his free-and-easy manners. Troubled, the pipe glowed and the candle guttered.

Cochrane sighed and continued his narrative. "Through the kindness of the officer, I left for the next town on his carriage. But I soon discovered that riding in a carriage was too cold, so I dismounted at an early opportunity and walked, bare-foot as I was, to Novgorod. Novgorod the Great.

"There is a proverb, 'Who can resist the Gods and the great Novgorod?' It is an easy task, for the city is much fallen into ruin and neglect. Many handsome edifices are now in ruins, lamentable proofs of its former grandeur and present decay. All that there was of interest to me was, through the kindness of a Russian merchant there, the happy consideration of a complete refit of clothes, which I could not refuse. Thus re-supplied, I walked on from Novgorod, to the towns of Yedrova, Vishney-Volotchok and Torjock. There were many interesting and handsome objects to be seen – the canals, the monasteries, the low hills and the foliage of the woods."

Cochrane halted and lowered his voice, so that none might hear. "But none so handsome and interesting, I believe, as the widowed sister of the unfortunate Captain Golovnin, who was so inhumanly exposed in a cage at Japan until rescued by the estimable Captain Rikord of Kamtchatka. Ah, Mrs. Golovnin, barely past her teens, so kind and so lovely a woman! At Torjock, which I reached amid rain and thunder,

Mrs. Golovnin got all my secrets out of me – all but one – and in return, sent me some tea, and washed my linen. Had she—" Here, John Dundas Cochrane paused for a moment. It was with some surprise that he felt a great regret, a vast and hungry longing arising out of his own words. He peered into the darkness now surrounding him. He lay alone under the stars, confronted by the accusatory finger of his memories, much as a man must stand before the Judgement Chair.

"She offered me the contents of her purse. Had she offered me her hand and heart, I should certainly have replied in the affirmative. Why did I not?"

To that question, there was no single answer. "Because I had to walk to America. Because I am not a man to stop long in one place. Because she was too good and too kind. Because I was too good and too kind. Because I was a fool. Because I was no fool. Because I cannot settle down like other men."

He shook his head from side to side, slowly, as befits a man who must ponder on unusual matters. "Mrs. Golovnin," he apostrophised her as her sweet face, slightly faded by the months that had past, appeared in the darkness above, "what if you had had my final secret and become Mrs. Cochrane?" Mrs. Golovnin, despite the trouble in Cochrane's soul, offered no reply.

One minute passed, one hour, two minutes, two hours. Outside, there were the mysterious rustlings and footsteps of an unfamiliar town at night. The breeze stirred a dead branch that scraped back and forth across the beetle-eaten shutter. Time passed, as did regret.

"But I had barely walked two thousand miles," said John Dundas Cochrane genially, rousing his spirits from sad and romantic thoughts. The shivering had eased a little, and he cast off his spare clothing, surprised to find just how much the sweat was now pouring from every pore in his body. He pushed off his blanket and felt the coolness invade his body. "After quitting the interesting town of Tver, I walked for thirty-two hours without a break through rain, to reach Moscow: a distance of ninety-six miles, which, I would venture, was one of my greatest pedestrian trips. Napoleon having burned Moscow to the ground in 1812, the town was full of rapidly ascending magnificent buildings, and gaieties. I quickly left it behind. The most important sight in this city was a new pair of leather trousers, which I received from a Scotchman named Mr. Rogers, who manages the agricultural part of Count Romanzov's property, he who was once the Chancellor of the Empire. I made my way across vast expanses of well-tended estates and fields, to the town of Nizhney Novgorod."

"Ah," intervened his father hopefully, from out of his silence. "You were already on your return journey, then?"

Cochrane explained patiently. "I had travelled but two thousand and three hundred miles, sir. You must not confuse the town of Nizhney Novgorod – or, Novgorod the Lower – with the town of Velikiy Novgorod – that is, Novgorod the Great. I travelled eastwards, you will understand, not northwards."

Cochrane-Johnstone sighed with impatience and diverted himself with a memory of the bodice of Mme. de Clugny, which, unlike Novgorod, the lower it hung, the greater it seemed, and was very pleasant to linger over, on a dismal night in his dotage. THE LOWER IT The beautiful memory was best remembered with eyes HUNG, THE GREATER IT SEEMED closed, and thus he succumbed to a remorseless slumber.

"I did not linger at Novgorod, it being a rather ill-built town, crowded with all nationalities who had come to a great fair, but instead embarked on the River Volga on a lighter bound for the city of Kazan, taking with me a pair of stout English shooting-shoes, provided through the kindness of my host Baron Bode, in whose garden I had slept, although he had insisted on my occupying a comfortable bed of down. Working my passage on the Volga, and sleeping on the deck wrapped in a sail with three others of the crew, we reached the celebrated city of Kazan after twelve days. Here I was introduced to some of the nobility of Russia, and then I sped eastwards once more, to the city of Perm. I covered the distance in three days, arriving there on the 6th of June: I regret it was not on foot, for I had been offered a lift in the Governor's kibitka, a wagon whose motion much jolted me, even though the roads were of the finest in the world. And from Perm I began my approach to the mighty Ural Mountains, the first object of my travels.

"As I approached the frontiers of Siberia, I began to give way to groundless, though perhaps natural, apprehensions; and indeed as I neared such a supposed scene of cruelty and misery, I became agitated. Hitherto, Providence had protected me, but although I felt thankful for the past, I could not but be concerned for the future, reasonably doubting how, where, and when my pilgrimage would end. At the town of Krasnoufinsk, an ill-built place shrouded in fog, I received a deputation of the inhabitants, who requested I should rest a couple of days, to be present at a dinner given in honour of the first Englishman to have visited the place. I felt the compliment nationally, but thought best to decline it, as perfectly unmerited by the individual; contenting myself only, when shortly thereafter I stood with one foot in Europe and the other in Asia, with strawberries and cream, which the poor people of Kirghizhantsky Krepost presented to me.

"On descending the far side of the Ural Mountains, I visited the town of Ekaterinburg and—" He was forcibly reminded, for the second time in that dark night, of affairs of the heart: quitting Ekaterinburg – of which industrious town, he made a note, he had not yet informed his father; his father would, had he not very obviously fallen asleep, his pipe being cold and his breathing being fitful, perhaps be interested in the copper and gold-mines there – he had passed some time with an enterprising Englishman named Mr. Major, whose three daughters were fine young women of a beauty sufficient to arrest the progress of a Siberian traveller.

"But I had no time to fall in love," he told himself in the manner of a manifesto, thinking again of the widow Mrs. Golovnin, again of the Misses Major, of other young women across the breadth of the Russian Empire, and again of Mrs. Golovnin. She was perhaps – as a young and beautiful widow – as one with whom he had barely had time to converse – his one great regret. "No time at all. Time only to kiss their hands on parting. Three thousand miles I had travelled, I was into Siberia, it was high summer and I had a timetable. A man who will explore the unknown world has no time for road-side dalliance."

John Cochrane spoke these last words in a tone of disbelief. He knew them to be true. He knew the Truth to be unassailable.

He knew the Unassailable to be a monument to regret. He knew Regret to be false.

"But should I not have married her? Perhaps. Should I have married her? Perhaps not." He paused and then he sighed:

"OH, MRS. COCHRANE, MRS. COCHRANE!"

8

SHE FOLLOWS THE DEVIL THROUGH THE CLOSING DOOR.

Ksenia Ivanovna had left behind the last houses of St Petersburg some two days previously, on a day that promised searing heat and baking roads. The diligence was heavy, and lumbered down the roads at a rate, as calculated by her tireless first husband, of no more than five-and-one-half-miles-per-hour. For this reason, the weekly diligence took two full days to travel between St Petersburg and Novgorod, and a further five days to travel from Novgorod to its final destination, the final destination of many whose hopes of riches at the hands and feet of the Tsar had vanished in a puff of Baltic smoke: Moscow. Although the windows had been opened to their fullest extent, the air inside the diligence was hot, oppressive and curiously scented. Something, perhaps, to do with the vast parcel of herring triumphantly cradled by a gentleman from the countryside near Tver. There were but four other passengers on the coach, all inside: the fishy gentleman; an English officer who presented himself as 'Lord Lochrin', drank heavily from a flask and spat frequently from the window; and two priests bound for a monastery in the neighbourhood of Torjock. The Englishman alone thrust his attentions upon Ksenia; she, for her part, wriggled herself between the two priests who, although profoundly shocked by this impudence, said nothing, and glared at the fishy gentleman and the sodden Lord.

All that was dear to Ksenia was in her stomach and in the small bag she placed very carefully upon her lap. She did not look back at St Petersburg until it was far too late to do so, when all that could be seen was the mid-morning sun glinting off the domes and gilded spires, and far above in the sky the watery reflection of the sea to the north. Her face was turned in determined fashion to the south, the road to Moscow. For ten hours on the first day of travel, the coach lurched and trundled through the dust, each jolt more sickening than the last. Every so often, the coachmen would pull up at a wayside inn, or simply a shady spot where the road ran through a forest, and the gentlemen travellers would burst out and either quench their thirst, or relieve their bladders, or both. Ksenia seized upon these brief moments of respite to re-arrange herself; she dreaded the return of her fellow-travellers – a halt at an inn was always followed, for at least an hour, by belches and foul breath, and worse.

Having passed a sleepless night in an appalling inn somewhere beyond Tsarskoe Selo, Ksenia boarded the diligence in the morning, and settled down to another day of intimacy and conversation. Conversation generally centred around the herring, whose stench had not greatly improved overnight; but both the English officer and the gentleman from Tver had a lively interest in dead fish. The priests had little to say on such worldly matters, and preferred to stare out of the windows. Shortly after mid-day, on a particularly rough part of the road, there came, of a sudden, a sharp crack, a shout of panic from the coachman; and the diligence tipped relentlessly to the starboard side, throwing the priests and Ksenia upon the bag of herring. The door at that side flew open with the sudden pressure from within, and all fell out, the herring slithering away into a ditch, seizing this first opportunity to escape. They did not get far.

One of the four enormous wheels had broken. Its spokes pointed this way and that, some shattered, others simply knocked out of the rim. The priests quite reasonably demanded that the wheel be mended, immediately. The guard justifiably pointed out that they would have to go for help first. "You think we should carry a spare wheel, your honours?" he demanded, respectfully. "Do we look like simpletons, or what?" In the meantime, the gentleman from Tver guddled in the ditch, ably assisted by the eager young postillion, while 'Lord Lochrin' strode about, white-faced and cursing Russia in a manner that could not profit diplomatic relations between the two great nations. Ksenia, quietly, approached the guard and asked him how far was it to Novgorod? This person, a man of some fifty years of age with failing sight, replied that it was barely eight versts or so – "a man," he volunteered, "could walk it in two hours."

"A woman," suggested Ksenia modestly, "might do as well?"

The guard snorted and strenuously thought not.

Ksenia held her bag firmly in her hand, and set off southwards. Before leaving, she took the precaution of notifying the coachman that she would meet them in Novgorod. He was less incredulous than his colleague. He also had far better power of vision, and was therefore prepared to acquiesce to anything that such a lady might say.

When a rain-storm burst about her head at the fourth hour of the afternoon, she found shelter with an old woman who lived in a hut in the forest. The rain crashed through the trees and rattled against the roof and poured through cracks; the two women warmed themselves against the tiny stove and sipped at wooden beakers of black tea.

"You are travelling far," observed the old woman, carefully feeling the cloth of her guest's cloak. "Far gone and far to go." This was not a question, so Ksenia said nothing, merely nodded vaguely. In the warmth of the hut, she felt drowsy.

"I was once like you," said the old woman, and lapsed back into such a silence as only the very ancient can maintain. Such a silence usually indicates that they have forgotten who they are, where they are and what they were just talking about. But in this case, that rational conclusion would be mistaken, for she continued, as the water in the hut began to rise. "I was once like you. Many years ago it was, long before that small Frenchman came. I was young – I was a good purchase for the money of any man that came by along the road. Just like you."

SHE WAS A GOOD
PURCHASE

At these words, Ksenia gasped. "I am no loose woman, selling myself beside the road!" she exclaimed. "How could you think that of me?"

The old woman looked at her surprised, as if seeing her for the first time. "No, my dear," she said, "you are quite right, I thought you were someone else." She sighed. "I see so few these days, I see so few."

Her guest was immediately concerned. "When did you last have a visitor?" she asked, beset by an onslaught of tenderness for one who might be herself in fifty years' time.

"Oh," said the old woman vaguely, "I cannot tell. Last year, maybe." She nodded brightly. "Last summer, a priest stopped by. It was raining then, too. I don't know where he went afterwards."

Where did he go? She looked around, half-curious, as if expecting to see the priest still sitting in a corner, stroking his beard and fingering his cross on a chain. "Perhaps he is back there." She nodded to the back of the hut, beyond which the forest stretched endlessly to Siberia. "We talked of old times, Father Pyotr and I. He visited me once when I was young. Such fine hands he had. You would have liked his hands."

"Oh," answered Ksenia, following this train of thought, "I prefer men whose hands have battled with the elements and the hazards of the wilderness. With such hands, a man can do something."

"Ah," sighed both women together, each seeing their own memories.

"Not any more," said the hostess.

"Not for some time," said her guest.

The rain had by then eased off, although great drops and streams of water still cascaded off the trees and on to the ground. A regular stream had arranged itself under the ill-fitting door of the hut, and, after invading each corner of the room in turn, had pooled up against a side wall, prior to making an egress. A small frog appeared and hopped about in the puddle. The drinkers of tea watched it idly.

"Once," said the old woman, "I had a man here who bathed naked in the pond behind the house. He did not stop with me, but he was a fine enough sight to see. That was not long ago."

"But you said you had not seen anyone for a year or more?"

"No, it was not long ago – perhaps ten or twelve years," confirmed the old woman. "It was fine be reminded what a man looked like. They come, you know," she observed, looking wisely at the traveller, "in all sizes."

MEN COME IN ALL SIZES

"Indeed," said Ksenia. "I am little experienced in such matters, having only had two to compare." She compared for a moment, then nodded. "You may be right."

"Oh, I am, I am," said the ageing seductress. "I have made sure of that. Perhaps," she said, enlivened by the cut and thrust of the discussion, "you might like to hear of the time when four generals—"

"I think," interrupted the unwilling disciple, "that I must be on my way now that the rain has stopped. Goodbye, mother." With which kind words, she opened the door to admit a high tide of water from a pond which had silently formed outside, watched in alarm as the rush of water bubbled and hissed around the cracked and broken stove; then she hastened lightly over the forest-floor to the road, which was now alive again with pedestrians and horses. The rain had washed clear the air. The afternoon, though dull, smelled of seeping pine. The remaining versts slipped past without remarkable effort.

At around six o'clock, having had her eyes fixed on the glint of Novgorod's many gilded roofs for over an hour, Ksenia came to the northern gate of the town. Here was a place, she thought, which was holier than many another place upon God's Earth. When still in St Petersburg, she had heard the priests talk of Novgorod as other men talked of heroic passages of arms or of legendary vanishing islands – with a look of wonder in their eyes and a tone of dissimulating insouciance in their voices: from such a look and such a tone, she knew it to be a place of great marvels. Every hundred paces or so, the enthused traveller felt obliged to shut her lovely eyes and say a quick prayer of satisfaction and hope. At every mile-post which she passed in sight of Novgorod the Great, she stopped and drank in the splendid view. At every monastery and church which stood crumbling beside the road – and the closer she came to Novgorod, the more there were, as if every church and chapel in all of Russia was slowly and painfully making its way to a grand assembly of saintliness in the city – at every church, she stopped and knelt, and admired the soaring white walls, the haphazard roof-lines, the weathered wood-work, the hurrying priest or monk. Truly, thought Ksenia, without a trace of naivety, this is a holy place.

Close by the northern gate to Novgorod, as the sun was setting, she came across a wonder of wonders, five grand churches clustered around the walls. Here was the Church of St Simeon, set in the Zverin monastery; here also the Church of the Intercession, since monks have more need of churches than sinners do; St Nicholas the White had his church just down the road, as did Saints Peter and Paul, who never, from Kamtchatka to the western boundaries of civilisation, stepped out alone. There, across the fields to the west, and in the distance, the Church of the Holy Trinity offered a cast-iron hope from within the walls of the Monastery. To the east, a great river slowly burned in the evening light, and, on the far bank, more churches.

Beyond the Church of the inseparable twins, she was accosted by a vigilant sentry. He was but a boy from Nizhney Novgorod, a city not to be confused with Velikiy Novgorod (the Great), the one having a thousand magnificent churches, the other having none to speak of, the one having retired from a millennium of greatness, the other a mere parvenu. The boy from Nizhney Novgorod had been sent here by pure administrative accident, the military clerk concerned having no idea about geography or the vastness of the Russian Empire, and clearly no imagination. As a result of this unfortunate error, the young soldier, far from home, was daily teased and tormented by his comrades, who would wave to every fallen woman who passed and greet them as "Mother!" or "Sister!" on his behalf.

The boy from Nizhney Novgorod was thus understandably of a nervous disposition, and alert to all the possible dangers of the road in and out of the city. On this day in August, at this hour, he had expected the arrival of the diligence, but, to his surprise, it never appeared. When he heard the light footsteps which came up behind him, he turned swiftly and observed the young woman who approached.

On this day in August, at this hour, the young man, far from home, fell instantly in love with the fair traveller.

She gazed kindly at him as he stuttered out a question as to where she was going. "I will spend the night here," she said, "and then I am bound for Moscow."

The soldier swallowed noisily, unable to say a word in return, then wiped his nose in desperation.

She smiled and placed a small hand lightly upon his arm. "Am I permitted to continue my journey, then?" she asked brightly.

In response, the private dropped his eyes and laughed wildly. Ksenia understood this to be an affirmative answer and passed on her way, leaving the disturbed young man to gaze after her, boiling over like a soup-kettle that has been forgotten. He would never enjoy sanity again.

As if in a pleasant dream, the insouciant traveller came upon the streets of Novgorod: before her the wonders hid among the houses. Hurrying on as dusk came over the town, she crossed the river and found herself in the Market District, looking up and down the street for an inn. There was one in the distance, upstream from the bridge, in the gloom which now washed below the twin domes of the Churches of the St John and St George, standing high enough to catch the very last rays of the sinking sun upon their iron crosses. She hastened towards the inn, pleased to have finished another day of travelling without having been killed in an accident, ravished by an English Lord, or set upon by any and every manner of highwayman. And then she stopped suddenly. With a thrill of discovery, she noted that a man in appearance alike to the Devil had removed his gloves and ducked into the shadowy doorway of the inn.

Quite rightly, she halted and considered her position. She looked up and down the deserted street of Novgorod, and saw nothing and THERE WAS NO no one who might welcome her in for the night. There was no OTHER INN other inn in evidence. She consulted the river, the stars, the moon, she prayed to this saint and that saint, two out of many – but clearly the wrong ones, since neither gave solace or good advice. She paused for five, ten, fifteen minutes, not knowing where to turn. At last, she turned with determination, faced the door of the inn. "My God!" she said softly, "am I indeed reduced to this circumstance?" She gripped her bag more tightly, blinked away a tear, and followed in the footsteps of the Devil.

It was not unusual in those troubled times, if a traveller is to believe poets, painters and novelists, for a man or a woman to sell his or her soul to the Devil. It happened all the time. All the indications were that the bargain is at first a sound one, albeit detrimental to the immortal soul. Ksenia had had books read to her by her first husband and her other suitors, in which a Christian soul in the prime of life might unwittingly strike up with Satan, and partake of the fruits and the treasures of this life, only to discover The Mistake too late and find that All Hope was Lost, for All Eternity. Another might sell his shadow and be shunned forever. A third might gain incredible powers at the expense— no, the possibilities were endless. What, she wondered, in that timeless passage as she stepped inside, might be her fate were she to fall in with the Devil and sell her soul to him? Would she be transported through the thickening airs, on the wings of the storm, wherever she wanted, instantly? Would she speak with her dead husband and lie in his arms once more, only to wake up in the cold morning dew, arms entwined around some rotting corpse or worse, with snakes and poisonous frogs in her hair and an abyss in her heart? Would she find favour with the highest Princes of Russia, in their grand palaces, only to find, each time she entered a church, that the candles blew out, the censers poured forth putrid stenches, the ikons wept tears of blood and cried out Horror! at her name?

HORROR !

The Devil, she had been taught, was some Turkish gentleman. But here she was in the presence of a Devil from the Indies, such as abounded in the back parlours and entrance-ways of the most splendid houses of London. It would be no hardship, she mused briefly, to fall in with the Devil; far worse things had happened to her in the few years gone by.

The door slammed behind her, a mouse scuttled, some turmoil took place in the kitchen. Avoiding an aweful and unhinged contemplation of the handsome face of the Devil, Ksenia asked the inn-keeper if he had a room for the night. Arrangements were swiftly made to accommodate her and a pleasing conversation, such as has already been recorded, unfolded above a tasty meat-stew, before the hot stove.

The conversation passed from diligences and carriages to fellow-travellers and charlatans. "You must understand that another man's soul is just darkness," said Horatio by-the-by, peering gloomily into the deep.

"What nonsense!" said she, peering deeply into the gloom. "We must begin by understanding that another man's soul is just clear spring water. Only, it is so clear that we know not whither it flows."

"At least we are agreed, I hope," said Horatio peaceably, "that the soul of another is something of a mystery?"

Ksenia considered the man and this proposition and then hic-coughed. No man had ever before been so ready to make peace with her. 'Love' – what is it? – a curious feeling of panic that seizes the chest, and as quickly threatens to empty the bowels of all reason. Ksenia felt the panic and felt the loss of all reason. She sighed and hiccoughed once more. Horatio brought a cup of water to her lips. She drank. Then she succumbed to that curious feeling. Some other events and debates, with which Ksenia little concerned herself, took place within the room of the inn. But, just as she decided that she must discuss her first husband's nakedness, the door of the inn was flung open and a huge creature of incredible age,

PERHAPS BABA YAGA HERSELF,

stood wheezing upon the threshold.

9

AN OLD GENTLEMAN BLEACHED BY THE SHADOW OF DEATH.

Baba Yaga, revered Goddess of Death and Regeneration. She haunts the darkness and eats people. Usually children. Children are more tender. And more credulous. She lives with two sisters, some say three, but they all share the same name: Baba Yaga. Their common childhood had been a time of confusion. Her home is in the forest, a curious hut that spins on the giant chicken-legs, surrounded by a palisade of human skulls and bones. When she wishes to travel, she rides through the air in a mortar, steering through the air with a giant pestle. Is she old and ugly, is she young and irresistible, does she impart wise advice or punishment? She is both and all, and neither and none; and anyone who listens to her is a fool or a wise man. She vies for the souls of all Russians with Chernobog and Mokosh, with Pyerun and Ved'ma. And her constant companion is – Death.

She plunged through the door from the dark night of Novgorod the Great, demanding Flesh.

Hearing this command, Mr. Voronov fought his way past his incandescent wife, and back into the public room. "Ah," he said, presenting, for the benefit of his glorious guests, an altogether incredible illusion of equanimity, "it is you, Yadviga Petrovna?" He bowed with evident ill-grace to the old woman who had arrived in such a state, and offered her his arm.

"Come," joined in Ksenia, seizing Yadviga's other arm; together they hauled her before the humming stove – it was no easy task – it might have been easier to haul the stove to the woman; "Come into the warm and sit yourself down. You have come far today?" she asked innocently.

The old woman stared at Ksenia blankly. "She says have I come far. I should say she doesn't know anything. Who is she in any case?" she demanded of Mr. Voronov.

"No matter," said the inn-keeper testily. He turned to Ksenia. "Do not be misled by her appearance, young lady: Yadviga has come merely from the other side of the river." He raised his voice. "A long journey, mother, eh, from the Sophia Side to the Market Side, eh?"

The old woman lunged at him with a strong arm. "Is that your insolence, Voronov?" said she. "You think I'm deaf? Why do you say that to a poor old woman like me? In any case, I'm tired." She sat down suddenly in the seat rapidly vacated by Horatio. "I am an old woman of sixty-seven, you mark my words. Sixty-seven. You think I can still manage to walk so far?" The old woman had every appearance of having been hewn from a massive tree, a true indestructible Russian tree – her bulk was simply overwhelming, her arms bulged from their sleeves, her head was the size of two heads, but chopped from one block and wrinkled like an old trunk.

While Ksenia made the old woman comfortable, and Horatio did his best not to get in the way, Voronov stamped off in a pique to the kitchen, where he could be heard briefly, complaining to his wife. She, however, was in no mood for it: the maid, in tears of anger and joy, had given her notice and, two minutes previously, had departed into the night without even a son of the house or a customer in her baggage. Mrs. Voronova therefore sent her husband out into the yard, where a vast pile of logs required chopping with an axe. "And don't you dare come near me until they are all done," she warned, "or I will take that axe and cut off—"

His manhood

thus being threatened, Mr. Voronov had no choice but to submit and soon the night air was alive with the merry sound of chopping and cursing. At the sound of the axe upon wood, Yadviga shortly burst into a series of cries and groans that would rend the heart of any traveller on the road from Moscow to St Petersburg.

"Oh, that noise, that noise!" she wailed, "Is it not the knocking of death upon the door?" Had Mr. Voronov been still in attendance, he might have suspected the old woman of paying far more attention to the poets than was decent in a pious old Russian woman.

"In any case, my dears," she said, recovering rapidly, as Horatio stood before her on her left side and Ksenia stood before her on her right side, each gently warming the old woman's enormous hands in their own, while she, whenever she could escape their grip, sipped on a small mug of mulled wine which had thoughtfully been left unguarded. "In any case, my dears," said she, "all I can say is that the old gentleman is bleached by the Shadow of Death and is not long for this world."

"Oh dear," said Ksenia, full of sympathy. "And is your husband very old?"

"My husband?" asked Yadviga, almost prepared to crack open the slabs of her face with laughter, but deciding providentially not so to do, "My husband who has been dead thirty years or more? Or is it twenty? In any case, he is dead and gone. All I can say is I'm better off without him. Call him a husband? Call him a man? He was no better than a helpless child, whatever did I see in him, whoever told me he could be good for me? The wastrel. The drunkard. God rest his soul, I'm glad he's passed on, you mark my words. In any case, by the blessed St Sophia, it is not my husband who lies dying, it is an old foreign gentleman. Foreign like yourselves, I would say?" peering down at them in a fair depiction of native cunning.

"I am no foreigner," said Horatio, black as night amongst the whitest Russians of all.

"I am no foreigner," said Ksenia, a lone woman traveller of Eastern appearance, unaccompanied on the roads over the vast plains of all the Russias.

Yadviga felt completely vindicated by these evasive replies, and nodded her heavy head. "Well, I can't argue against it," she continued. "I expect you would like to pay a visit to the old gentleman, you being fellow-foreigners and he having no relatives or friends to see him through his last hours, he dying in poverty where once he lived in luxury, he wasting away to the whiteness of his bones upon the black pillow of death, he waiting now for his last meal which I must fetch back to him from Mrs. Voronova here?" Horatio hesitated at the invitation, thinking a far more pleasant evening was to be had in gazing at the curve of the mouth and the two barely crooked teeth which emerged from within when she smiled and the shadow of the cheek-bones and the tiny curl of hair behind the left ear of Ksenia;

Ksenia, however, having lost enough men from her life, but never at close quarters, was eager to depart forthwith. Yadviga begged leave to recover herself before the stove, this spiced ale was doing her a power of good, and so they sat around for an hour, while within Mrs. Voronova cooked up a small supper for the dying man, while without Mr. Voronov, to maintain his rhythm, cut the head off every literary gentleman that had ever taken the road to St Petersburg.

"Here," he hissed, as the axe-blade swung down on the necks of these wooden dilettantes, "Here's for your Pushkin. Here," he grunted, as the axe swung down again, "this is for your Zhukovsky!" Displaying, for one who denied their very right to existence, a remarkable knowledge of the cream of Russian scribblers, he continued with considerable verve to chop the heads off your Batyushkov, your Delvig, your Prince Vyazemsky, and, most importantly, your Baratynsky. Having despatched them to his own satisfaction, he proceeded to range at his feet the headless bodies of Sumarokov, of Kheraskov, of Ozerov, and then dealt admirably swiftly with Fonvizin and Karamzin. By the time his chore was done, the landscape of Russian Literature was denuded, chopped down, laid waste: all neat and tidy. He stood back in admiration and leaned on his axe. Let the Salons of St Petersburg weep, let them rage and fulminate; then let them listen to the true soul of Russian people: let them hear the story of Ivan the Terrible as he came down like a wolf upon the city of Novgorod and—

"Are you idling out there, Vladimir Ivanovich?" demanded his wife, MUST SHE COME who had come to the door to see why the sound of OUT AND USE THAT chopping had ceased. "Is there so much time in the world AXE HERSELF? that you must waste it? Must I come out and use that axe myself? What do you think? Eh?"

The inn-keeper returned to his task. Lamenting another interruption to a story he had never, in twenty-five years of playing the host, managed to tell to the end. One day, he thought, one day, the true and unabridged story, which my father told me, of Ivan the Terrible and his visitation upon the unfortunate towns-people of Novgorod will be—

He was interrupted in his bitter reflections by a threatening voice from the kitchen, reminding him of the several uses of an axe.

What his dear wife said was true – there was not so much time in the world that it could be wasted in reading books and dreaming of matters which do not concern us. In future years, he would satisfactorily deal with Lermontov and Griboyedov and Gogol, not to mention Dostoevsky and Tolstoy, whose weary long works left the Russian People choked in paper. Had he lived into the twentieth century, he would have found ample scope for his thinning of the forests of words, and a host of collaborators across the terrestrial globe to share his vision. He did not – he missed it by a long way: but his great-grandson was a grand axe-man.

At last the work was done without, and within the old gentleman's supper was prepared and a flask of spirits supplied; Yadviga had fully recovered, and the two travellers followed the nurse outside.

"You spoke just now," said her new admirer, as they stepped out into the night air,

"OF YOUR FIRST HUSBAND'S PECULIARLY BECOMING

NAKEDNESS?"

10

THE ENDLESS ROAD AND THE TYRANNY OF THE COACH.

"I did, sir," she sighed, "and it is no agreeable tale, as you, being a man of feeling, will understand."

"But if the recollection upsets you," said the man of feeling, "please—"

"Let me just gather my thoughts," begged the lady.

Conversing in this intimate manner, the two travellers stepped out of the warm air of the inn into a cool Russian night. Up above, a thousand stars and one shone down, some alone, some strung, some bright, others dim, from others only a hint of their light was felt after the pedestrians turned away from them: each one of them – Horatio thought, in poetical mood – an Analogy of Love. Before them, from left to right, the waters of the River Volkhov grumbled past. Across the river, tinged by the light of a half-moon, the vast walls of the kremlin of Novgorod stood, draped curtains of blackness. A short walk ahead of them, a long low bridge crossed the river downstream, passed below the wall and vanished completely into the shadows.

Ksenia Ivanovna shivered and clutched her cloak around her to keep off the cool breezes. In a sympathetic action, her companion pulled his fur hat tighter over his massive head: it was cool – but it was not cold: there can be little excuse for furs – it was summer – alas: the man was a foreigner. In the meantime, he held the lantern lower so that the woman could pick a path between the dried ridges of mud on the street.

"The poor man," she said, by-the-by. "May St Peter and St Paul take pity on him and save his life."

"Save your husband, madam?" enquired her friend cautiously. "But I understood him to be dead?"

"My husband?" asked the young lady, stopping suddenly and turning to her companion in undisguised astonishment. "What are you talking about?"

"Your husband," began Horatio. But got no further.

"My husband, yes, my dear husband is dead: dead and gone, and—" she paused once, "—you have no cause to remind me so sharply of his death." Reminding herself again, she paused twice. "What a cruel and cold-hearted man you are, for all your kindly ways and attentions!" She turned away from him; there was a hint of a catch in her voice. He was mortified. "You men are all the same – you want us only for our favours, and treat us cruelly when most we need kindness!"

Thus characterized, Horatio peered down at her. All he could see was the shawl covering her head, and her shoulders raised slightly. "I am sorry," said he, "if I raised painful memories. I thought we were talking of your husband before, and then—"

"There you are again!" she cried, turning back to him and folding her arms tightly across her chest. "Can you not leave him in peace, asleep in his grave, wherever that might be?"

Horatio, in an ill-advised attempt to retrieve the situation, left the husband in peace. The wild passion which had coursed hotly through his veins barely an hour ago, had suddenly turned into two icy fists squeezing at his innards. It was no comfortable feeling. He doubted whether he would see this woman for much longer.

"So you have, then," asked Ksenia coldly, after a few moments had passed, "no interest in his grave?"

Horatio, in an ill-advised attempt to retrieve the situation, asked after the grave.

Ksenia sighed: "I do not know. It is in a place named Valencia, in South America. That is all I know. I have not seen it. It is, I suspect, in a hot jungle, surrounded by wild beasts."

Horatio did not know whether to remark upon such a burial-ground, so far removed from the colder forests and plains of Russia. As he paused, musing on the mysterious attractions of this plain-looking widow; and the even more mysterious – but imperative – reason for walking with her, when he could be sitting in the inn, with the maid-servant upon his lap, far more lively and with a sweeter face—

the Brute

—he received for his thoughts a sharp tap on the arm. "Are you not listening to me, sir?" Ksenia peered up at him sternly. "Look, the old woman wants us to hurry along, and you stand there humming like a bull caught in the bog. Come along, make haste, or the poor man will have died. If he dies, he will miss our visit!"

The three night-wanderers met at the northern end of the wooden bridge, where an ancient sentry lounged beside a glowing brazier, nodding fitfully in his dreams. Passing him by quietly, so that the nightly retreat before Napoleon should not be interrupted, they set foot upon the planks of the bridge and climbed directly into the long shadow of the walls of the kremlin. Underneath them, the whispering waters flowed from Lake Ilmen to the sea, over a hundred miles to the north. Horatio had seen Lake Ilmen earlier that day, its waters ruffled by the wind, its shores peopled here and there with gloomy brown and black birds, poking without conviction in the mud or taking wing to cross that vast stretch of water. Horatio sighed for the dullness of Russian birds. Horatio sighed for the cold European winds that obliged him to wear a fur hat even in summer. Horatio sighed for the endless road and the tyranny of the coach.

Hearing him sigh thrice, and quite mistaking the reason, Ksenia laid her hand gently on his arm. That simple touch – unassuming, he supposed, but recognising him as a man of feeling – unclenched those two cold fists that sat within him still and set once more the blood running, pumping to his head: Horatio would at that moment have followed her anywhere, without hesitation. She led him therefore blindly into the darkness. He hesitated. She pulled him. He followed.

The boards of the bridge creaked ominously under their feet. But they had creaked for two hundred years and more; the bridge but rarely fell down. In republican days, the bridge had trembled on wooden piers – but now, thanks to the autocratic engineering principles established by the early Romanovs, the piers were of solid stone. Not far out over the river, the pedestrians found the ascent less steep. The old woman panted and grumbled as she stumped along in the lead, clutching to her mighty bosom a bottle of spirits and the package of food purchased at the inn. Not three paces behind her, Ksenia stepped along cheerfully, as if she were out for a market-day errand on a spring morning, rather than paying the last social visit that a dying man would receive. Horatio's heart beat faster at the sound of her footsteps; he padded along in the rear-guard, leaving behind him the lower part of the town, the Market Side with its merchants' halls and churches and inns and dogs and cats and coachmen and inn-keepers who could not keep their hands off the maid-servants and wives of inn-keepers who could not keep their wrath to themselves and not many other people besides, for Novgorod was but a shadow of its greatness in times gone by, so the inn-keeper had said—

"Sir!" exclaimed Ksenia, turning to him in genuine surprise, "You are loitering again! Is there so much time?"

"I was merely reflecting—" answered Horatio.

"Please do not reflect, then, we have a vigil to conduct, not philosophy." With which sensible words, she tugged at his great-coat and jerked him from the spot to which he had stood rooted, lost in the contemplation of the abandoned scene behind him. After a few minutes, they completed their crossing of the bridge and the waters below; and found themselves on the Sophia Side. The old woman hurried forward, but Ksenia hung back, looking to the left and upwards, towards the impending walls of the citadel. She called softly to their guide.

"Can we reach our old gentleman by passing through the fort?" she asked, all innocence.

"Well, I won't say we can't," conceded the old woman, "but why should we? In any case, we're in a hurry."

"And will we be watched over then by soldiers?" she pursued her object, without affectation.

"Well, I can't say we won't," confirmed the old woman, "but why would we? This other way is quicker."

"I would like," said Ksenia, decisively, "to pass through the fort, and be watched over by soldiers, on such a black night as this." So saying, she pulled Horatio along without resistance, and set off up a path which led southwards along the bank, directly under the massive battlements. There was a rumble of exasperation from the old woman, but she lumbered along behind. After a few minutes, they climbed hard up to a huge gate that was now faintly visible in the dark curtain wall. As the party approached, a soldier stepped out of the shadows and peered closely, a lantern held above his head, a musket in his left hand.

"You again, is it?" he welcomed the old woman. "And who are these you have brought with you?"

Pausing at length to regain her breath, the old woman confirmed that it was indeed her again, and why should it not be, by the holy ikon of St Theotokos, and were these kind people not friends of the old Captain – was he not, as everyone well knew, passing on his last journey to Heaven, in a disgraceful condition, with never a word of comfort from his fellow-officers, and was it not permitted for an old woman to tend to her patient with all the tenderness and charity that the priest says is our due upon this miserable earth, were she not so old and frail she would box him about the ears for his pitiless inquisitions – she boxed him anyway, he reeled slightly, and not merely

SHE BOXED HIM
ANYWAY, HE REELED
SLIGHTLY

for the sake of appearances – come along let us leave this man to his ignorant sinfulness, do you see, my girl, these are the kind soldiers you wished to have watch over us.

The soldier, unabashed and ignorant in his sinfulness, turned his attention to Horatio. "Your purpose?" he demanded curtly, as his duties required.

Horatio told all that he knew – there seemed little point in evasion – they were being taken, as the old woman had said, to visit an old military man.

Hearing the same story twice, the sentry relaxed a little: he had received instruction in military intelligence – if two intruders told different stories, they were to be shot out of hand. "And did you serve with the Captain in the army, then?"

Not wishing to seem backward in such tender circumstances, but feeling constrained to a non-committal answer by the impatient tugging of his coat by Ksenia, Horatio gave the impression that, while he had not exactly served with the old gentleman – "Ah, a gentleman he is: I have met him several times!" exclaimed the soldier, slapping his own chest in a fit of pride, as if gentlemanliness could somehow be transferred, like typhus or the pox, by physical proximity – which may, of course, be the case – he thought that it would have been a great honour to have served with him, in some land, in some capacity, at some time, if only he had known him earlier in his life. Having amused himself with the contemplation of this generous sentiment, the sentry lit a pipe and conversed some more.

"You know, during the great days of my service, some twenty years past, we chased the Frenchman Napoleon from our holy soil. Ah, my friend, the tales I could tell you of that, if you have a moment or two, you being an old soldier yourself and by your colour likely having served in many far-off lands?" He looked hopefully at Horatio, suggestively tapping his fingers on a hollow-sounding pewter flask which had appeared as if by a conjuring trick from some pocket in his jacket.

"Well, of course, I'd be pleased to hear your story—" Horatio began, but he failed to finish his sentence and was soon on his way across the moonlit interior of the citadel of Novgorod the Great. HE FAILED TO FINISH HIS SENTENCE There is not much room to feel at ease here, thought Horatio to himself, as he was hurried along. Here a small church; there a large church; over there a building which looked like a gaol, walls, wooden stables, one or two soldiers sauntering with obvious intent under windows, hardly space to swing a censer. The ancient republicans of Novgorod had clearly wished to pack in as many buildings as possible, to cater adequately for body and soul.

At the far side of the fort, a narrow lane led to a small doorway in the western wall, manned by a soldier younger than the first, who, relishing the unusual circumstance of not just one person in transit but three, including a pretty young woman, made the most of the situation. He began by grabbing the old woman round the waist, a romantic gesture so fruitless that he soon abandoned it and gave her a good slap across her mountainous rear portions, an action scarcely courteous and rather unpleasant to witness. Next, he turned his attentions to Ksenia Ivanovna, into whose charming face he peered with all the rigour and discipline owed to ensuring the safety of a military establishment. He straightened the shawl to obtain a better view of the eyes and nose below, and spread out the cloak to admire the neat figure within. Noticing after a short period of objective distraction that Horatio was considerably larger than himself and was fidgeting dangerously from one foot to another; noticing also that Ksenia Ivanovna's spare hand, the one not gripped in the sentry's for his better appreciation of her several charms, was held firmly within Horatio's, he curtailed his close examination and turned in more military manner to the final member of the party.

"Where are you bound?" he demanded to know. Horatio explained, again, as best he could, their purpose on this chilly night.

"Ah, the old Colonel," nodded the soldier. "I hear he's a cantankerous old buggar, is that not right, mother?" The old woman, still fighting for breath and clutching desperately at the bottle of spirits, from which, in a brief flash of inspiration, she drank to assist in her recovery, was in no mood to answer, and obviously, after the intimacy of her examination by the sentry, was in no condition to answer. "Well, he's got the Devil in him, and there's no mistake. Do you know, when he first came here he took all the back-pay off the garrison, every one, in just two nights of gambling?" He shook his head in admiration. "Every last one of us. Aye, and we never won but half of it back in the spring. And then, of course, he got the fever, and not once have we seen him out – how long, matushka? – maybe two months now since we saw him. Aye, he's the Devil's own servant, it's my belief." With which remark upon the household of Satan, the soldier leered once or twice at Ksenia, ignored the bitter curses of the old woman, and turned his attention wholly upon Horatio. "But if you have a moment, I can tell you the most extraordinary story of my father."

Horatio, always an easy prey to story-telling, from his earliest days in – but this is not the time to relate his earliest days, for there is an old man a-dying, and a young woman tugging at Horatio, and an old woman pleasantly surprised for the ten-thousandth time by the restorative power of a bottle of spirits that has been hauled with such great trouble from the inn on the far side of the River Volkhov, and continuing to admire such power as new life flowed back into forgotten parts of the body with which the Good Lord had furnished her, and which – the parts, that is – she had neither seen nor felt for some months – Horatio leaned back against the wall of the doorway and warmed his knees before the brazier which burned at the threshold to the sentry-post.

"My father," said the soldier, "Nikolai Nikolaievich, like myself, his son, was a man of great merriment and great rages. Once, when I was a boy and we were out hunting, we met a large white bear and we stopped our sledge—"

"Ah," said Ksenia, unable to restrain an expression of interest, despite her work in adjusting real and perceived disruptions to her clothing, "you are from the east of the country, then?"

"I am from the east of the country, then," confirmed the soldier, "I grew up in the fortress of Nizhney Kolymsk, next to the White Ocean."

"How extraordinary," exclaimed Ksenia. "My first husband—"

—of whose becoming nakedness and distant grave Horatio was forcefully reminded, but was careful enough to make no mention of – the matter could wait a few minutes – instead, he solicitously adjusted his companion's shawl, allowing the warm light of the flickering fire to shimmer and drown in some black curls which poked from underneath the woollen material.

The soldier observed this procedure with some fascination; however, he was not so easily diverted from his purpose. "As I was saying, my father and I were out hunting. We came across a large white bear. We stopped our sledge. The bear was not pleased to see us. He immediately set upon our dogs, with some ferocity." A LARGE WHITE BEAR

"Oh, how fearful!" shuddered Ksenia. "I have seen a bear being set upon by dogs, but never have I seen dogs set upon by a bear."

"How fearful. Well," conceded Nikolai Nikolaievich Nikolaiev, after due reflection, "I suppose the dogs set upon the bear first, and then the bear set upon the dogs."

"It was like war, then," observed Horatio, quite unnecessarily.

Disconcerted by this observation, which seemed to have no meaning for him, the Corporal stroked his moustache. Eventually, he continued: "The bear, set upon by the dogs, immediately fought back. The dogs got all tangled up together under its feet. The bear managed to bite the throat of one—"

"Oh!" gasped Ksenia.

"—and tear the tail off another—"

"Ah!"

"—and break the neck of a third—"

"Mercy!"

"—threw my father into a bush—"

"The poor man!"

"—and then, jaws dripping with blood, it turned upon me—"

"May St Peter and St Paul preserve us all from bloodshed!" Ksenia put her hand to her mouth in dread anticipation of what should come next. Horatio found himself counting the soldier's visible limbs.

"—whereupon I, as I had been taught by the priest, thanked the Great and Holy Father for His Larder of all beasts and birds and fishes—"

The old woman crossed herself and muttered a prayer to the Great and Holy Father and all His priests and anything that might be left in the larder.

"—rushed upon the bear, and with one—"

At this very moment, an officer of the guard, who had come marching across the parade-ground of the kremlin, demanded to know what all the fuss was about.

"Corporal Nikolaiev!" he barked, "Either shoot these people or let them pass! Is this some tea-room in St Petersburg?"

Nikolai Nikolaievich Nikolaiev professionally considered the two options; and then

HE UNSLUNG HIS MUSKET.

HER SAD ACQUAINTANCE WITH MEN.

"Perhaps," suggested Horatio, at the instant of this presentation of arms nervously recalling their nocturnal commission, "perhaps it would be better if we went on our way. Unless, that is," he added, turning to the officer – it was understandable that he should appear over-eager to adhere to protocol – "we have some other formality to complete?"

The officer, being a man of some historical learning, wondered for a moment if the black man before him was another Abram Petrovich Gannibal, sent by the Tsar to rebuild the fortress of Novgorod. Deciding, after some rational thought, that this would be wholly unorthodox and not national at all, he turned his undivided attention on Ksenia, whose glassy gaze was fixed upon the unslung gun. "This one is dashed pretty, dashed pretty, is she not?" he said, more to himself than to any other, although all could hear. Addressing Horatio with some obvious distaste, he enquired whether the lady was perhaps his wife; and, on receiving a negative and sorrowful answer, instantly insisted on lending his arm to conduct the lady to the far end of the small passage which led out through the south wall of the kremlin. For which minor courtesy she was very glad, finding just enough strength of character to lean decoratively upon the arm and glance gratefully up at the officer, whose name, announced after barely three steps had been taken, was Captain Simeonov, late of the Turkish Wars.

With some interest, Horatio noted the name – it was that of the hero of the Iron Gorge. But there was no time to pause and ask questions. He glanced up and down the short passage. The soldier Nikolaiev stared gloomily at the retreating backs of his superior officer and the young lady, and re-shouldered his weapon. Horatio muttered some words of embarrassed leave-taking and then, in embarrassment, took his leave. The soldier said nothing in reply, thinking no doubt of the end of the story of his father, the dogs, the bear and all others embroiled in that captivating moment of boyhood. He, alas, would not hear the end of it.

At the far end of the passage, a second door was opened, which gave out on to a precipitous path leading down from the kremlin into an area of houses and gardens, a vista washed here and there by the cascading light of the moon. Dimly visible at the foot of the path were the massive battlements that doubtless had kept at bay all manner of horny-helmeted invaders, Ivans, and less terrible domestic malcontents. Captain Simeonov was so kind as to assist Ksenia down the steep steps, leaving both the old woman and Horatio to fend for themselves. The former plunged down the path like a runaway cart in the mountains, or a hag in a mortar, accustomed, no doubt, to passing up and down this road every day of her long life. Horatio shambled down, slipping and sliding, grasping at phantom bushes and snapping off saplings as he went, to the very real peril of the party arm-in-arm below him; but such temporary presentiments of doom came to naught; all four reached the foot of the rock and finally stood on firm ground between citadel and outer walls. At the start of a small foot-bridge which led from the walls, across a dark moat, a soldier stood smartly to attention and saluted. Captain Simeonov ignored him; Horatio, unused to military courtesies, nodded apologetically.

At the far side of this foot-bridge, once again outside all the walls of the kremlin, Captain Simeonov seemed in no hurry to surrender the arm of his lovely companion; no more was she – for it would seem, at least to Horatio who stood restlessly at a respectful but immarital distance, that she had grown attached to the handsome officer, as indeed – had he but known it – she had been attracted to officers the world over. "I regret, ma chère madame," said the Captain casually waving up at the kremlin from which they had just escaped with their lives, "that that soldier is not quite comme il faut. Comme il faut – I expect you have not heard that expression? It is, I believe, French."

"But of course I have, sir," said Ksenia, with more than a little indignation, "I have travelled half of the civilised world and have met more people who are not, as you say, comme il faut, than perhaps there are in the whole of the Imperial Russian Army put together."

Captain Simeonov bowed politely. "How many of such people are there in the Imperial Russian Army, you ask? I think, perhaps, you would be surprised to learn just how many of such people there are in the Imperial Russian Army. Very surprised. I myself was surprised. However, madame, your sad acquaintance with men like that should put you doubly on your guard. On your guard, I say, madame. Doubly. No: triply."

Ksenia, reciprocally bowing her head in acknowledgement, turned slightly towards Horatio. Anxious to take part in this conversation, wherever it might go, for fear of losing the attention of Ksenia, that gentleman blurted out: "And what is this unfortunate man's particular affliction?"

The Captain looked darkly at Horatio; whether for his rude intrusion upon an intimate conversation or for the purpose of setting the scene for the imminent revelation, was not to be determined. "What is his affliction, sir? We know what his affliction is," he announced. "Yes, we do. The man is an imerach. An imerach, sir."

"Ah," said Horatio blankly.

"Dear me," said Ksenia with but dim understanding.

"You may say 'Dear me'," said the Captain with a note of triumph in his voice. Somewhere nearby, a clock in a tower struck nine times. "We know what imerachism is, do we not? You are fortunate to depart from him unhurt. You are acquainted with this disease? No? Well, I will acquaint you with it. First, I will tell you the story about a white bear he encountered in the woods—"

WE KNOW WHAT IMERACHISM IS

"Oh," said Ksenia, cutting him short, "but I believe we have heard that story," forgetting for the moment that she had not yet heard the gory climax, nor yet the unexpected denouement, of the tale of the bear.

Nothing disconcerted, the Captain continued. "Am I surprised that you know that story? I am not. But there is another. I speak of the day when a man came hammering at the door we have just passed through. What did the man want? He demanded entrance. He excited our soldier Nikolaiev. How much was he excited? He was so much excited that he seized a young cadet who was passing and began without further ado to beat him with his fists, to the same rhythm as the man hammered at the door, crying to be let in. Pad-a-bang, pad-a-bang! He only left off when at last the door was opened and the traveller gained admission. Was it amusing? It was highly amusing. Did we laugh? We laughed greatly. Pad-a-bang, pad-a-bang!"

"And the poor young cadet?" asked Ksenia approaching the humorous story from quite the wrong angle. "Did he laugh also, and was he much hurt?"

The Captain expelled breath through pursed lips, indicating an inconsequentiality, and waved away the question as entirely unimportant.

"Nothing that a swift dip in the river could not assuage."

"And did he go into the river of his own accord?" asked Horatio.

"Did he go in the river of his own accord? I cannot say – but he came out of his own accord," said the Captain barely mastering his impatience at these pointless civilian interruptions. "But pay close attention – here is another example of the imerach's curious behaviour. We sent him into the wrestling-ring with a soldier from Chudovo. Where is Chudovo? Chudovo is some distance north of here. What did we observe? We observed that every time his opponent shouted at him, or threatened him, or raised a fist or smote with a leg, our man responded exactly likewise, with a roar or a fist or a leg. Did he win? His energy was without limit, and he won this fight, and every fight that we arranged with the other bold fellows of the company. Is the commander at Chudovo now our sworn enemy? The commander at Chudovo is now our sworn enemy, for the amount he lost in wagers that day." The officer struck his leg in mirth and laughed in a manly way.

"So," said Ksenia earnestly, "the poor soldier is afflicted with a disease which forces him to repeat in action or word exactly what is said or done to him, as if," she concluded, "he were a mirror of the world?"

"Bravo!" shouted Captain Simeonov with unchecked enthusiasm, "For a woman, you are uncommonly clever! Women are not often so, I find. Women are not designed to be clever. Yes, the imerach is an unwilling mirror to the rest of the world. Is this a good thing? No, it is not the best attribute on the parade-ground, from which he has frequently been dragged to the punishment-block. But is he fierce? Place him in front of the fiercest warrior, and he will become the fiercest warrior. Try to terrify him, and he will terrify you in return."

"He has, then, no will of his own, the poor man," murmured Ksenia.

"He has no will of his own, nor has any of this garrison – but only he is the imerach."

"And if," said Horatio, who had been following the description closely, and had been reminded forcefully of the Halls of Mirrors in a hundred palaces the length and breadth of Europe, with which he was intimately acquainted, "And if the regiment were to recruit a second imerach, what would, do you think, Captain, be the consequence?"

Captain Simeonov looked sideways at Horatio, unwilling to adjust his stance square in front of a young woman who might be supposed to be watching in admiration. "A second imerach? What perversion is this, sir, that you imagine for us? The effect would be unimaginable – although..." The Captain began to muse, rolling his eyes upwards to the whirling constellations in a most alarming manner, muttering, "if he did what he did, and then he did what he did, and then he did exactly what he did ...then— "

At last he shook his head regretfully. "You have asked an unreasonable question, sir. I do not commonly answer unreasonable questions. I will commonly flog a man for asking an unreasonable question." He looked Horatio up and down. "But I will answer it. I am obliged to say that, in the event of a second imerach appearing in the garrison at Novgorod, the very discipline of our regiment, of the entire army, on which all military might is built, would crumble. It THE RUSSIAN EMPIRE ITSELF WOULD FALL would crumble, sir." He paused, stroking his considerable moustaches. Then he announced: "The Russian Empire itself would fall."

At this considered response, Horatio was momentarily diverted by the thought of an entire regiment afflicted by imerachism – a marvellous and deadly fighting force, capable of defeating the most furious and vicious marauding invaders, repelling from the very borders each and every assault; but fatally weakened and divided by dissent in the barracks, every command a cause for countermand, every countermand a cause for argument, every argument a cause for a fight, every fight a fight to the death, a regiment so riven by the clash of unstoppable forces that it would be unable to leave the barracks to fight the furious and vicious marauding invaders, the Army would be pushed to the very edge—

"Sir!" cried the officer angrily, "You must be careful that you do not fall in!" At this, Horatio was snatched back from the very edge of the moat by the Captain, who asked: "Do you think that if you fall in, you will come out? No, sir: if you fall in, you will not come out. Many fall in, but few emerge alive! Stay over here, on the other side of this street, where it is safer." The Captain shook his head in disbelief at the actions of the civilian population; it was scarcely safe to let them wander the streets on their own, the army must always be there to help out, or, at the very least, push them back at the point of a sabre.

In the background, the old woman was examining the bottle of spirits she had so carefully brought over from the inn. To the untutored eye, the bottle was now empty; to her own experienced eye, there was always a drop left in it – the trick was in knowing how to soak up that last drip. To which end, she was vigorously shaking the last drops into a small ball of bread clamped over the mouth of the bottle, until the bread was thoroughly soaked; at which satisfactory outcome, she sucked noisily at the bread through the gaps in her teeth. In these days of conspicuous waste, such economy is praiseworthy.

"Do many of your men drown in the moat, Captain Simeonov?" enquired Ksenia, full of concern.

"Of my men? Drown? In the moat? No, I would not have such fools under my command." He eyed Horatio belligerently, inviting him to raise an objection to the neat comparison to a fool. Horatio, however, had turned his attention to the remaining food in the old woman's bundle, and heard nothing to his detriment. Taking advantage of this distraction, the Captain seized an unwary Ksenia around the waist, bent her backwards like a young sapling, and planted a monstrous kiss upon her lips. "Madame, that was most satisfactory," he observed, releasing her once more. "No, indeed, those who drown in the moat are dogs or drunkards or small children who have run away from their parents. Is that not a tragedy? It is a tragedy. It is the responsibility of my men – my men, mark you – to haul out the drowned bodies with ropes and hooks, and lay the poor water-logged bodies upon the bare earth so that their masters or wives or parents may identify them and lament long and loud."

"Oh dear," sobbed Ksenia, but whether her tears were for the kiss that had been forced upon her, or for the sad picture of row upon row of little drowned white bodies and dogs, she could not be certain.

Horatio returned to the discussion, clutching a piece of ill-defined meat that could equally have come from a chicken or a drowned dog. But certainly not from a child. "And do dogs and drunkards drown often?" he asked, greatly interested.

The Captain laughed long and loud. "No," said he, wiping foam from his military lips: "Only once."

It was now that the old woman decided that the time had come to make haste. What if the old man has died waiting for his supper, said she, looking vaguely at the crumbs that now remained of the food. Carefully, she replaced the stopper on the bottle, shaking it one last time to ensure that not a drop remained, then re-tied the small bundle that once contained bread and meat and a roasted turnip. Reluctantly, the Captain handed Ksenia back into the care of Horatio, planting a kiss upon her hand and issuing a final salute from a set of teeth that gleamed like candles at a funeral. At the sight of which gallantry, the old woman cursed, castigating all young men of the army who had lost any sense of reverence for their elders; then turned and led the party away from the moat into the town beyond.

"You spoke," Horatio reminded Ksenia, to while away the passage to their destination, which could scarcely be far now, "of your first husband's peculiarly becoming nakedness?"

Ksenia Ivanovna, who had retrieved Horatio's arm in the absence of any other, sighed.

"SIR, I MUST NOW TELL SOMETHING MORE."

12

HER MOTHER ADVISED HER THAT A
WOMAN NEEDS HAVE SEVERAL HUSBANDS.

Alas, the road to their destination was shorter than either of them could have desired or expected, and before Ksenia could gather all her thoughts on the ticklish matter of her marital relations, the old woman suddenly gripped Horatio's arm in her extraordinarily large hand, which was well-appointed with hard and sharp nails. "Make haste, your honours, we're here now, you mark my words," she croaked, indicating with a gesture of triumph a row of considerable dwellings, the most magnificent on the Sophia Side of the river. Ksenia and Horatio gazed upon these villas and mansions, and wondered which of them could shelter the dying man. Was it that one with the stables? Or that one with the lighted windows?

It was none of them. The old woman marched up to a dark shape which appeared at first to be a pile of timber, but turned out to be a dilapidated lodge set apart at some distance from any other building. Under the flickering moon, it could be seen that the roof was in places open to the sky, which was a comfortable feature in the warm summer evenings, no doubt. A thin spiral of smoke emerged from a chimney, but the windows were as black as a starless night.

"The old gentleman is here? In this place? Ill?" asked Ksenia, in a manner which left Horatio in no doubt as to her disapproval. Wisely and without any hesitation, for he was a man who had seen the rages of many females, he stepped back sufficiently that his shadow no longer fell in front of his chosen companion. The old woman glared at Ksenia, but merely muttered ill-defined obscenities in reply. Laboriously she pushed open the door, which was rotten for most of its height and whose smooth passage across the door-step was hindered by mould, moss and leaves from some long-forgotten autumn. There was a hushing sound, not quite a squeak. Then she stepped into the dark interior, closely followed by Ksenia; Horatio took one last look over his shoulder, up the street and down. There was no one to be seen.

Did the careless sentries of the kremlin preside over an abandoned city? The towns-people of Novgorod the Great might as well have been put to the sword, and their corpses thrown upon the majestic and oblivious waters of the river Volkhov by Ivan the Terrible himself, who, as he had been informed—

"Make haste, sir!" instructed Ksenia, not unkindly, stepping back out of the lodge to take Horatio's hand. "Or must you always stand and dream?"

"I was only wondering—"

His friend sighed once more; she had no regret, she knew that her first sight and impression of the man had been faultless, that the man was as solid as any man she had ever known, that he could and would conceal nothing from her; but he seemed to be filled with dreams – it was not a fault, it was just – she now hauled him indoors. There was a strong smell of melting tallow and of the smoke from an ill-used stove. A short passage-way led onward to the back of the house, and a door stood open to either side of the small party. The old nurse had tip-toed in to the room on the right. Horatio heard a sharp gasp.

"Oh," asked Ksenia, fearfully, "is it too late?" She stepped quickly through that door.

The sharp gasp turned out to be the old woman settling herself in her chair. Nothing worse. Of course it was not too late, she announced a little tetchily, the old gentleman was only sleeping, was he not still alive, but by all the saints that watch over us, it will not be much longer before he receives the mercies of God, you mark my words. Amen, thought Horatio, remembering with a lump in his throat the slow and lingering death of his own mother, reduced to the appearance of a corpse well in advance of departing the wicked world. The darkened room, with its ill-lighting, reminded him sharply of things he did not care to remember so well.

The old nurse, with never a pause for breath, made herself comfort-able beside the poor stove, and wrapped herself in several blankets. There were few other pieces of furniture in the room – just the bed, half-lit by a ray of the moon through the ceiling; a small table creaking under the weight of a jug and a plate; and this chair beside the stove.

Just the bed: but a bed, as shall be revealed, unique in all the world: a bed that had once been a magnificent four-poster, draped with the most luxurious curtains, and covered with silken sheets, on which lay, night after night – a personage whose identity will later surprise the visitors and outrage the nurse; this bed was a three-poster, the fourth having been vanished long ago, and it lay open to the sky.

Horatio, man of action, soul of chivalry, slave by trade, and servant to all who asked, stepped out into the corridor to gather some of the finer comforts of the world. In the other room at the front of the lodge, there was very little to be seen, except for a huge mortar from which an enormous pestle poked, placed under a hole in the roof and filled to overflowing with rain-water. At the back of the house was a small room with a filthy window, as full of shadows and as terrifyingly empty as the deepest sleep of a man of no imagination; and a vast kitchen, residence of a family of rats. The rats stared at the intruder with quizzical amusement before returning to their ungainly leaping. A door led into a small garden at the back of the house, which had a small veranda, furnished, to Horatio's great delight and satisfaction, with two small chairs. One chair had four legs, the other three, but one or other would almost certainly, he thought, hold the delicate frame of Ksenia; he himself would stand, he decided, he would stand all night and all the following day if necessary; and if he felt tired, he simply lie down on the floor and sleep.

In triumph, Horatio bore the two chairs back to the old man's chamber, and with the greatest possible modesty, installed Ksenia in the four-legged chair. The old woman looked at him sourly, but said nothing. As soon as Horatio, now in a more pragmatic mood on the matter of chivalry, even thought of seating himself upon the three-legged chair, it burst asunder beneath him: silently, as suited the place; and irrevocably, as suited the time. Picking himself up from the filthy floor, Horatio carefully collected the many pieces of the chair – which, when he counted, now appeared to have had more legs than was commonly the case – and inserted them one by one into mouth of the stove.

After five minutes, the only sounds being the crackling of the chair in the flames, and the laboured breathing of the dying man, Horatio turned to Ksenia and said: "You were about to tell me—"

The old woman pulled a malevolent face and shushed him. "Young man," said she, keeping to herself the while some doubts on both age and gender, "are you going to seduce this young woman with idle chatter? Have you no consideration? Is there not an old man breathing his last here, and all you can think is the dirty thoughts of men? Well, I can't stop you, that's for certain – but be off with the pair of you and do it outside – have you no respect?"

SEDUCING A YOUNG WOMAN WITH IDLE CHATTER

Ksenia Ivanovna stood up and pulled the embarrassed Horatio towards the door, and they proceeded out through the kitchen, much to the delight of the rats, who had not seen so much of the sad and beautiful affairs of humankind in all their livelong years in their lodge, into the back garden. This hidden paradise, on closer inspection, resembled the forgotten forest of sleeping princesses and excitable princes, at least in the thickness of thorns and creeping bushes. Up above, the sky had cleared sufficiently to show the vast white ribbon of the Milky Way shimmering overhead. Ksenia lifted her charming face and looked pensively into the million stars which hung and twinkled above.

"My husband—" she began.

"I have learned—" said Horatio, beginning at precisely the same moment.

"—used to say – oh!"

"—the names of the stars – ah!"

"Oh!" said Ksenia, for a second time.

The two looked at each other, anxiously.

"Please," Horatio begged, "you were saying?"

Ksenia demurred: "No," said she modestly, "it is your turn to speak. I speak too much sometimes."

"No, no, no," said he, protesting too much, but courteously.

"But I do," said she, grasping at his hand with hers. Gratefully, he enfolded that one offered hand in his, and breathed deeply.

"You said you knew the names of the stars?" she reminded him after several minutes, the stars themselves wheeling expectantly upon an invisible axis in the sky.

Horatio now demonstrated his acquired knowledge. It was adequate, and would certainly have satisfied all those of a slight astronomical and astrological bent: he could see Cassiopeia and Pegasus and the Swan, and that there was Andromeda and there Perseus, over there Medusa and up there the Eagle, while over yonder he could name the Great Bear, the Plough (or Little Bear) and Arcturus. Ksenia, who knew all of these names, and more besides, having been intimate with explorers and sailors, nevertheless murmured with admiration and delight, and shivered with terror when the two bears and their guard were mentioned. How much more fascinated might she have been, had poor Horatio but known of the great story of human arrogance, divine retribution, and over-arching love played out in the several constellations he mentioned. But the story of Cassiopeia, Andromeda, Perseus and Medusa had evaded him thus far, and he was not able advance from the gruesome particular to the sadly general.

HAVING BEEN INTIMATE
WITH EXPLORERS
AND SAILORS

"You know so many things," said the lady kindly when the last stars had been named. "It comes, I suppose, of travelling the Empire in a carriage."

Horatio blushed and denied this. "You know far more than me, I suspect," he said, gazing once more at the depth of her jet-black hair.

"I could name for you," said she hopefully, "the names of all the churches in Novgorod."

"That would be," he considered, "almost as many as the stars in the sky?"

Leaving Horatio to count, and to interpolate silently or otherwise with speculation, she proceeded to name those of which the traveller as yet knew nothing. She named the churches of: the Myrrh-Bearing Women; St Parasceva; the Assumption and the Annunciation; the church of St George; the rival one of St John; one for St Michael himself; yet another for the Old Believers; for Elijah, who might also be known as Pyerun, God of Thunder; just one for Saints Peter and Paul; one for the not-to-be-forgotten Apostle Philip; another for all

Twelve Apostles – did these include perhaps both the good and the bad Judas, wondered Horatio silently, and raised thereby in his mind a number of questions which should not be answered; one, not unnaturally, for Our Saviour; one for Our Lady, and, to be certain, a church of the Nativity of Our Lady; one for the Assembly of Our Lady; and yet another, the distinction perhaps not being clear, of the Nativity of the Holy Virgin; and then she returned to the churches of less likely saints such as Demetrius; Procopius; Clement; Theodore Stratilates; and – perhaps a brother or a son? – Andrew Stratilates; the Saints Boris and Gleb; St John the Divine (but, no, she did not know if the Divine John was one and the same as the Saint John previously mentioned); one church for St Nicolas; another for St Nicholas; a different one for St Nicholas the White; two more for Saints Peter and Paul; one for St John the Alms-giver— THE LESS LIKELY SAINTS

"This John," punctuated Horatio again, "would that be the same—?"

"—I know not, but I cannot stop," said Ksenia, rather breathlessly and continued with—

—the Church of the Intercession; of the Entry into Jerusalem; of the Persuasion of Thomas; and then, allowing no time for doubt, and in a final release of incense, the churches of St Blaise, St Sophia, St Simeon, and two of the Holy Trinity.

"Which makes another six," said Horatio, trying to salvage some flotsam from the on-coming tide of names, whose number was for him now as numberless as the stars in the Milky Way. His accidental wit did not meet with a kind reception.

"Both of my step-fathers," she said, deliberately lifting her hand from Horatio's grip, and using it to pluck some dead leaves from a bramble-bush whose intentions were far from honourable, "greatly admired my knowledge of the saints. My first step-father was a priest, until he died."

Horatio bowed his head in anguish, and cursed himself for a fool. 'Love' – what is it, but the immersion of two separate lives in the barren seas of each other's loneliness. One cold word, one wave higher than usual, and the entire depth of the sea becomes apparent, and the height of the sky and the vast and impossible distance to the invisible horizon. Horatio felt himself going under. Ksenia saw this, and pulled him back to the surface with a forgiving glance.

"Do you know what it is to lose so many fathers?" she asked, not expecting an answer. "Or a husband? It is confusing. It is not tragic, as some seem to think, who have never lost anything. Tragedy is a word used by those who do not suffer. When you lose a father, or a husband, or a child, or an entire family, it is sad, truly, but never tragic: just muddling. You do not know what to believe any more. And when you lose several, one after the other, you just feel that life is – well – unsuitable."

Horatio, having himself experienced loss and tragedy and far worse than those, correctly voiced no contradiction. Ksenia felt obliged to weep some tears: the day had been long, and the evening was longer still. Horatio offered her one of his handkerchiefs, which she proceeded to abuse fearfully. Horatio assisted her in this procedure, by various supportive acts of his arms and hands and once even with a brief touch of his lips against her swollen eyelids, an impulsive action that he dared not repeat, even though Ksenia screamed silently inside for him to do so. After some long moments of yearning, the orphaned widow turned her attention to her dress, which had become unaccountably dishevelled. She employed both the light of the moon and her useful companion to tug brambles from her petticoats and burrs from her hair.

When all was at last put to rights, she said: "My second step-father is in St Petersburg: he is Captain Rikord—"

"Ah," exclaimed Horatio, "the Captain Rikord who is now the respected Governor of the port of Kronstadt?"

"Yes!" exclaimed the lady happily, grasping Horatio's hand in friendship. "Captain Rikord has been a kind father to me, as Mrs. Rikord has been a watchful mother. For four years, they raised me as their daughter in St Peter's and St Paul's – that is," she mentioned in explanatory fashion, keenly aware that few outside of a select circle would have any idea of the vast geography and many municipalities of a distant province of Russia, "the main town on Kamtchatka, the residence of the Governor. Captain Rikord was, as you must know, the Governor there until 1823. I love them dearly, as they love me. And when my first husband appeared, they approved of my marriage, although I was so young. And when, without great delay, I became a widow, they took me back in to their home in St Petersburg. And there," she faltered, visibly looking for the courage to say something; she paused, concentrated her attention on a weed which had wrapped itself around her feet; pulled it off with an air of satisfaction; then began again in a rush: "And there in St Petersburg, I met—"

Just at that moment, the old woman appeared on the veranda to demand whether the old gentleman was not waking up and, if they had nothing better to do than stand and paw each other, should they perhaps show a little respect and come at last to see him? Which they did, Ksenia brushing down her petticoats, Horatio guiding her gently past the deferential rats. As they entered the old gentleman's room, the widow whispered brightly: "My first mother, when I married, advised me that a woman needs have several husbands in her life to truly appreciate the merits of each of them."

Before her confused companion had time to consider all the words of this innocent statement, let alone the rocks of hope and despair which they, individually and together, revealed to a drowning man, a voice from the death-bed interrupted:

"My sweet young thing, your mother was wrong: it is a man who must have as many women as possible, to appreciate the merits of each and every one of them. A woman," he continued, in a voice scarcely weakened by his impending demise, "needs nothing but one experienced husband."

"Sir," said Ksenia Ivanovna, bridling up, "you insult me!"

"I think not," said the man on the bed.

"STEP CLOSER AND PROVE ME WRONG."

13

IN SPITE OF HIS TEETH, HE WAS STILL A FRENCHMAN.

"Sir," protested John Dundas Cochrane from the blanket on which he lay alternately sweating and shivering. It was nothing, a mere chill contracted from the sharp rise from sea-level to the highest peaks of the eastern mountains. When he had accustomed himself to the great elevation above sea-level, and to the thin air, he would feel better: it had happened before. "Sir, you insult me."

"Indeed not," said Andrew Cochrane-Johnstone, un-corking, the better to castigate his errant son, a small bottle of rum. "I can prove you wrong. You speak to me of some Cochrane or other – what was his name?"

"Captain N.D. Cochrane. I cannot tell what the 'N' signifies – Neil, perhaps, or Norman."

"There!" replied the triumphant father, "I rest my case. You ask me to stand astonished here because you met some clerk in Yakutsk who had served on a ship with some cousin of yours. Do you know this cousin's name? No, you do not. But you expect me to know his name. I repeat: the navies of the world are crawling with Cochranes, like weevils in the biscuit or maggots in a round of salt-beef, bastards like yourself or legitimate ones, I care not. Do you know how many brothers I have? Eleven. How many of them are in the Navy? Eleven. How many have produced sons who are in the Navy? Eleven. Small wonder that half the world has met a naval Cochrane. You can add up the numbers yourself, and I will insult you once more, if you like."

"The man in Yakutsk, father," said John, seeing that an argument would be useless, but stubbornly persisting with his story nonetheless, "was no mere clerk: he was the governor of the place, Captain Minitsky of the Russian Navy, and had passed many years in the English service, three of them with my cousin. That is all I said. It is true. I thought perhaps you would be interested to know."

"No," repeated the father, again tiring of his son and this endless journey and this endless impenetrable darkness that seemed to slip in between and around them whenever they conversed. "I have no interest in what you say and even less in the doings of the Cochranes – have I not spent my life trying to get away from them? They are a pack of wastrels and spendthrifts. They have never done anything worthwhile: consider my brother Charles, who was killed at the Battle of Yorktown in 1781 – he had his head carried off by a cannon shot when standing close to Lord Cornwallis. The fool. Whenever I have had dealings with them, I have faced ruin. Your Captain N.D. Cochrane is without doubt as tedious and as worthless as all the rest. Do not parade your Cochranes in front of me, sir!"

There was a silence of several minutes, and then, surprisingly, the old man spoke up again. "Ah, now – my brother John that went to Canada: he did something right – got a son and never married. And there you have it – Captain Nathaniel Day Cochrane – the bastard son of my brother John. That's the man you want."

John Dundas Cochrane felt weak. It was not the chill, it was the hopeless task he had set himself of effecting a reconciliation with his father, a man who had barely featured in his childhood; had never been present when he needed him; and who had spent a life, rumour and scandal had it, embroiled in dubious schemes – but was nonetheless his father. But his attempts were being rebuffed at every opportunity. And it was not that what he had to say was without interest. He said it again, certain that his father was now asleep, and uncertain whether he could remember all of the detail: the important thing was, not to lose the detail.

"I quit the government of Perm at the small town of Kamishlov, a government I felt as little regret at quitting, as I had fear of entering upon my return. It is a place most unfortunately situated – between Europe and Asia, civilisation and semi-barbarism, in short between vice and virtue. But the road was good and I made good time between the stations, albeit with a somewhat awkward indication of ulcers upon my feet. After the city of Tumen, the road grew worse – a land of swamp and marsh, poor roads, worse bridges, miserable inhabitants and wretched habitations. Each small town or village I reached seemed to be named 'Malaya Dervenya', a circumstance I considered rather confusing for the traveller, until I discovered that the words meant 'Little Revenue'. At length, I reached Tobolsk, the capital of Western Siberia, half-drowned and famished, all but naked, and certainly in no condition to accept a kind invitation to dinner by the Governor.

"It is a vital necessity," he continued, "to have a water-proof knapsack, and a Cossack for a guide, should one wish to cross Siberia. Accordingly, I acquired one of each in Tobolsk. The knapsack did me very well for the next two thousand miles, the Cossack did not so well – I was obliged to change one for another every so often. We travelled through the lands of the Tartar, deviating from the great Siberian road to visit some of the smaller villages, and enduring considerable incivility among the population. On several occasions, I was obliged to sleep out of doors and in the rain.

"My Cossack proved perfectly useless in such matters. At a wretched place named Toukalinsk, I had the misfortune to lose all my belongings – passport, letters and papers – all held in a tin-box. In vain did I point out the man who had taken them. I was obliged to move on to Omsk, where, more by good fortune than by any assistance rendered by my Cossack, I was able to send back to Toukalinsk and retrieve the tin-box – which the offending party had thought contained money. One should never, sir, cross Siberia without papers.

HE SHALL NOT DALLY IN OMSK "There is little to say of it, beyond the fact that it is named after the River Om, so I shall not dally in Omsk. I ventured across the lands of the Kirguise and Calmuck peoples, from Omsk, some one hundred and fifty miles, without seeing anything of interest; and I cannot say that the succeeding five hundred miles were any better. The land is devoid of cultivation for a large part, and infested with robbers; my Cossack, being half-drunk for most of the journey, gave me no protection against the robbers, and indeed, on one occasion, I strongly suspected him of being in collusion with them. I dismissed him near Poyanoyarsk, and marched ahead on my own. The country to the east of the Irtish River is quite different. To begin with: melons."

"Melons, sir?" demanded his father, raised briefly from deep in his slumbers. "Who talks of melons? Melons are from Spain."

"In this part of Siberia, sir, I saw melons of a prodigious size. Selling at one kopek each, that is ten for a penny. For five guineas, I might have filled a ship with them. I speak, of course, entirely figuratively. There are few ships in Siberia – a matter of importance I have raised with the Governor-General himself. Trade is carried on but poorly there. Melons and cucumbers. More of cucumbers later. At Ubinsk, a vile, dirty place, I acquired another Cossack; and came at last to a wide and fertile land, with mighty forests on the wild and beautiful mountains, and an endless plain of grass under the skies. At Boukhtarminsk, I procured a guide and made a slight detour to visit the frontier with the Celestial Empire of China—"

"How slight, sir?" Colonel Cochrane-Johnstone wished to know the full extent of the madness of his son.

"A matter of sixty miles or so, sir," replied the son dutifully, not feeling the barb in the question. "But it is a land, surely, of milk and honey that I saw – rich in cattle, corn, melons, cassis, vegetables, wild-fowl, game and fish – all set amid the loftiest mountains. A paradise on earth, with its black soil and rich resources. No part of the world can offer greater or more certain advantages to the agriculturist than the right bank of the Irtish River; neither rent, nor tax, nor war will for ages disturb such a speculator. It was with some regret that I had to quit this place and return to my main route, and, after dinner, by boat and foot, set out taking the road from Boukhtarminsk to Ustkamenogorsk.

BOUKHTARMINSK TO USTKAMENOGORSK

"Sir," stated Cochrane, without much hope, "you may be surprised to learn that the commandant at Ustkamenogorsk was a Frenchman."

There was no reply. The Frenchman could as well have been a Cochrane, for all the interest this unusual fact aroused.

"Indeed," he continued, pulling his blanket closer around his throat with shaking hands, for he felt the cold knives slip between his ribs, "M. Delancourt had been thirty-five years in Siberia, doing anything or nothing. I asked him if he ever intended to return to France, but he answered with a heavy sigh that, since he now had wife, position, and a large family of marriageable daughters in Siberia, it was most unlikely. And yet, in spite of his teeth, he was still a Frenchman: he frequently lamented 'Ma pauvre France!'

"Returning to Ubinsk, where there was decidedly nothing of interest except the good and modest looks of its female inhabitants, I procured a Cossack to attend me to the town of Barnaoule, a short stretch of two hundred and twenty miles. This Cossack was, of course, a mere useless fellow. No, more," Cochrane corrected himself: "He was a saucy and useless fellow. I discharged him before we had reached our goal. It made no difference to my progress. I reached Barnaoule in good time, and was introduced to the Governor-General of Siberia, Mr. Speransky. He took me at first for a religious dissenter, for I had not cut my hair nor shaved in eight months and consequently had a long beard—"

The young gentleman's father snorted. John could not determine whether this was some deliberate insult, or one of those night-noises which innocent sleepers emit.

"—and longer golden locks; I wore, at the same time, a long swaddling grey nankeen coat, and a silken sash round my waist – I was indeed a great buck. I hardly knew myself, sir," said Cochrane, reminiscing easily. "But of more importance than General Speransky's kind attentions, was the fact that he furnished me with the especial authority to make my way to the River Kolyma, to join the Russian expedition then exploring the north-east cape of Asia under the leadership of Baron Wrangel. As you might imagine, I wasted no time in setting out for the Frozen Sea. With a new Cossack, I set out for

HE DID NOT
DALLY IN TOMSK

Tomsk. Within two days, my Cossack got drunk, lost his pipe, his cap and his senses. I left him behind. He soon caught me up, expressed regret, demanded forgiveness, which I most willingly provided; with the result that immediately he got drunk on the strength of it. On reaching Tomsk, I was disappointed to find that Society was far from good. For that reason, I did not dally in Tomsk. And of the land from Tomsk for many hundreds of miles eastwards, there is little more that can be said. It contains forests, musquitoes, unwholesome vapours, few inhabitants – and they of the most worthless kind – many rivers, and the worst roads in the world. It would indeed be a fine thing, sir," observed Cochrane to none who was listening, "if those whose responsibility it is to manage roads were obliged each day to travel on their roads by horse-drawn sledge or cart. Those whose bones had not been knocked out of them entirely would doubtless take a keener interest in their work.

"But I must press on, for we have barely reached Irkutsk, where I met the commander of the Navy, Captain Koutigin, who was kind enough to put me up in the Admiralty House. Irkutsk has little to recommend it. There is a splendid prison, which would have commanded the approbation of the humane and philanthropic Mr. Howard, a military school, a dozen churches, and the person of Mr. Gedenstrom, the famous explorer of the Icy Sea and one of the ablest men in all of Siberia. Also there, should one seek Good Society, sir," – here he directed his voice most specifically towards his father, but met with no response – "is my venerable countryman, Mr. Bentham and his homely Cockney wife. Or, should I say, there is now only the widow Mrs. Bentham, for the gentleman has in the meantime died after forty years in Siberia."

HIS WIDOW GAVE MUCH COMFORT TO LIEUTENANT HOLMAN

John Dundas Cochrane lowered his voice: "His widow, I believe, gave much comfort to Lieutenant Holman, he who named himself, solely for the purpose of self-aggrandisement, The Blind Traveller."

John Cochrane paused, weighing his words carefully. "You should pay no attention to Lieutenant Holman or his Journal," he said at last, a little uncharitably. "The man was blind. What could he see of Siberia? He was overset by the slightest problem. By a great misfortune, Mrs. Bentham's sister-in-law died of an apoplexy just as Holman knocked on the door, and he was mistaken by her servant for a charlatan. Mistaken, I say: but there is sometimes truth in these misapprehensions. In any case, I, John Dundas Cochrane, far out-stripped him in my travels. His Journal should not be permitted to stand. There is some injustice in this, I believe, that people know more of Lieutenant Holman than of Commander John Cochrane. But I shall soon rectify that matter, in this new journey which I have undertaken."

Cochrane threw off his blanket, as the heat boiled without warning through his body. With some difficulty, he poured himself a large mug of water from a jar which had been placed next to him on the floor, and drank it down in gulps that rasped like vitriol against the constriction in his throat. What was this place? Cochrane could not remember. It was beyond the mountains that loomed high above the port of La Guayra; it may have been in Caraccas. Or had they gone beyond Caraccas? No matter, the Andean Mountains were just outside the door.

"I stayed in Irkutsk but a week, furnished myself with a fresh Cossack, and struck out for Yakutsk, at first on foot, and then by canoe on the River Lena, by which means I was able to travel a hundred miles in each day. The people were most hospitable: indeed, I have no doubt that a man may travel through the Russian Empire, as long as his conduct is becoming, without wanting anything – not even horses and money. The winter was rapidly coming upon me. At the town of Vittim, I encountered the first ice-floes floating on the river. Thereafter, whenever we were entangled in the ice, the Toungousian boatmen who accompanied me were obliged to wade in waters at five degrees of cold – they suffered a great deal as a consequence, being quite uncertain which limb to bring back to life first. For a time, we had to abandon the boats and return to our preferred mode of travel. My Cossack was, of course, quite useless, being quite knocked up from cold and want of exercise. However, I was able to return to the canoe during the last four hundred miles, and reached Yakutsk on the 6th of October, with the river freezing over, the snows beginning to fall and the atmosphere very dark.

"I found myself in the hospitable and comfortable residence of his excellency, the Governor of Yakutsk, Captain Minitsky of the Russian navy, who had passed many years in the English service, and three of them with my cousin, Captain N.D. Cochrane. Is that not an astonishing circumstance?"

His father merely muttered, for the fifth time in that long darkness, "The navies of the world are crawling with Cochranes, bastards like yourself or legitimate ones."

"Sir," protested John Dundas Cochrane from the blanket on which he lay sweating and shivering, for the heat of the day and the intolerable warmth of the night had combined with the plummeting temperatures of the freezing wastes of Central Siberia to make him quite weak,

"SIR, YOU INSULT ME."

14

HE SPEAKS OF THE NOCTURNAL SECRETS
OF HIS HAREM.

"Sir," said Ksenia Ivanovna, bridling up, "you insult me!"

"I think not," said the man dying on the bed. "Step closer and prove me wrong."

Ksenia charitably obliged, remembering that the old gentleman was likely never to see another young woman again in the few short hours that remained to him of this world. He raised himself with difficulty on his left arm and peered up at her face. One or two candles shed some light on her, but by far the greater illumination came from the man's eyes. With that light, he could see her well: she was every young woman who had ever had the good fortune to submit to his wild imaginings; she was that woman who was detected standing behind a tree, or lying under a bush; she was that woman who had fled into the shadow and never been found. She had black hair, golden hair, brown hair, she had a squint, she had one eye, she had eyes as deep as pitch, she had white teeth, yellow teeth, no teeth, she snarled, she screamed, she softened her lips, she prayed, she bit and drew blood. They all had had names at one time, but he could not now remember what these were. Even before, the names had not been important, only their limbs and their mouths and their willingness – or, more frequently, unwillingness – to spend a half-hour with him when it seemed that neither strong drink nor the thrill of gambling would douse the fires within. 'Love' – what is it? It is immoderate lust. "But lust is lust," a fellow-officer of poetical persuasion had once said to the Major on the island of Dominica, "it is all-too-human and cannot be denied: moderate or immoderate, paraded shamelessly or hidden shamefully, naked or fully-clothed, an animal imperative turned by the touch of the poet into Love." Beautiful words, thought the Major, as the pair of them stepped a little drunkenly from the officer's mess to seek out the women of the night: "Beautiful words, whatever they mean." He had never forgotten them.

"Ah," said the old man, "I see you all now." He sighed and sighed twice.

Ksenia, imagining in her innocence that the old man had made out her pretty face and, with the strength which this inspired in his last moments, was now reconciling himself to God, smiled upon him. The smile, when he perceived it through the black smoke of his dark soul, revived him at once.

"Give me one more drink and I will tell you all the nocturnal secrets of our harem."

With unbecoming haste, Ksenia pushed a cup to his lips; he drank shallowly and with difficulty as the water dribbled onto his parched tongue; then he fell back on his mattress and prepared to parade his dubious memories.

Horatio meanwhile stood near the stove, wishing he had a chair; a chair to sit on, not simply to throw on the flames to warm up the cool night. Although neither of the women was sitting now, HE WISHED FOR A CHAIR it would scarcely be the move of a gentleman, nor an act of respect for a dying man, to possess himself of either remaining chair. For should the one chair promptly collapse, he would be exposed as one who did not learn his lessons well; and the other was clearly the chair of old Yadviga, who was, as he had already seen that night, not one to dispossess. And he was disturbed, more than reason could explain, by the sight of the old man and the sound of his voice. It felt as if the old man was familiar to him, and that the place and time in which he now found himself was pre-ordained from many years ago. This broken house in Novgorod, this starry night, this placement of people, that mysterious woman over there, myself over here, the old nurse—

"You – fetch some more water," ordered Yadviga, thrusting a jug at him. "Or do you mean to stand around here like a sleigh with no runners?"

He turned away towards the kitchen; the rats ignored his passage out to the back garden where, under the light of the moon and with the practised eye of a man accustomed to observe such things, he had previously seen a pump-handle. He filled the jug to its brim with star-light, and brought it back indoors. In the front room, little had changed. The old man had not yet revealed the secrets of his harem, for which mercy Horatio was pleased; unless, of course, there had only been one secret to tell, and both women already knew what it was?

Yadviga, anxious that the young lady should not hear any more of the old gentleman's outrageous lies, of which she, Yadviga, had heard more than enough these past few weeks, pulled the blankets roughly up under his chin and held them there firmly.

"I suppose," said she, "you wish to tire yourself out, eh?" She turned to her visitors. "I'll have you know, I once nursed a small boy who over-excited himself with his imaginings. Of course, he died."

"Oh no!" exclaimed Ksenia. "How sad!"

"How sad, she says," acknowledged Yadviga, softening her grip upon the old man's throat, so that he began to breathe his last again. "How sad, in truth. Mark my words, it was a week of fever, then up he sits and dies. But not before he had had the time to imagine for himself all manner of dangerous excitements. In any case, did you know that he was a prince?"

Ksenia did not know this interesting fact, but was more than pre-pared to admire it as a pearl among facts. "A young prince? And he died? What a tragedy!" Horatio felt for his handkerchief, so that he might bound into action by her side, and wipe away any emerging tear. But his handkerchief, as he now recalled, was already in her possession. He therefore remained at his station and used his boots to persuade the fire in the stove not to depart this life before the old man did.

"How many years ago was it?" demanded Yadviga, subsiding, as the earth subsides in the thaw, into her seat; the old man continued to lie quietly, and Ksenia settled herself warmly in her own chair, which Horatio had kindly left vacant for her, a fact she acknowledged with a certain look. No one dared answer the question. She continued: "When I was your age—"

"Ah," observed the dying man, thinking he knew the answer, "that was many years ago indeed." His comment was unnecessary.

"—was I not employed by a great family to nurse their small children? In any case, I was not yet married – ah, why had I not realised that such a grim fate still awaited me, unseen, round the corner? All I can say is I was just as pretty as you—"

"Not possible," observed the dying man.

"Surely not?" thought Horatio, startled: this old woman was perhaps the ugliest he had seen in his life, so fascinating in appearance that – had he met with Baba Yaga's ugly sisters – he would surely have made a favourable comparison.

"—and I thought myself the best nurse in all of Russia. After all, the children love me, and I love them. The prince, he says he would trust me with everything that concerned the children. His wife, she says what he says is right. In any case, there were five of them, from one year old to ten years old."

Horatio stopped listening, for there was nothing, he found, so dull as the forgetful ramblings of an old woman on the delights of children. Did she not know that from those innocent caterpillars, such as were small children, there emerged the pestilential black moths of larger children? – and from those, if they lived, and most especially if they were of the noble class, the distant, vapid, ugly-faced, charm-less young men and women, such as populated all the countries of the world? He had once been a child himself, and he had seen the children of his masters grow up and turn, like rotting blooms. Once, only once, indeed, had he found one child who had made something of himself. But what, he wondered, had Ksenia been like as a child? Of course, she would have remained silent and composed, in the face of disappointment and fear.

"Then," continued Yadviga, in her endless reminiscences to which few now listened, any more than anyone would listen intently to the muttering of the stove or the sudden pattering of the rats as they decided on some course of action in the night, "Then Prince Labanov says to me, he says—"

"Labanov?" asked Horatio, proving that he – at least – was paying attention. "Surely not?"

Annoyed at the interruption, Yadviga turned majestically to him and pursed her thick lips. "And why not, in the name of St Euthymius the Great?" she wanted to know.

Horatio shook his head. There were certain things he should not reveal.

"Then what business is it of yours?" said the old woman, scowling at him. "In any case, if you wish to be helpful, give the old man another drink."

Horatio stepped forward with jug and mug, and proudly obliged. As he held the mug to the old man's lips, he mumbled some words of encouragement, the old man mumbled some distracted reply, and there was a passing moment of recognition.

In the manner of the imerachs, both men looked away simultaneously, unable and unwilling to believe. Each passed a hand across his eyes, each felt a tingle of sweat on his brow. The old man recognised, in Horatio's, the kind of face he had never thought once to scrutinise for anything other than obedience or rebellion. Horatio A PASSING MOMENT recognised, in that other face, a man who had never thought OF RECOGNITION twice to witness beating, starvation and humiliation. It was in those eyes: all around, fashions could come and go, a body would decline and decay, limbs might fall off, skin could wrinkle, but the eyes preserved the Soul. Recognition. Or so thought Horatio. He was perhaps quite wrong. But this was not the hour to ask after an identity that should better remain hidden. In the space of a single minute, Horatio found himself twice entwined in the sticky web of his past, from which, were he ever to escape, it would be with the woman he thought he could cherish.

Horatio gazed upon that dying man's face and fretted. In that instant when the pick-axe struck the tin-chest of his buried memories, he began to cast his mind back over his early years as a slave in the West Indies. Born to slaves, raised as a slave, working as a slave, living as a slave, punished as a slave, and with a fair expectation of dying as a slave, it was with some surprise that he was, at the age of twenty-seven, summoned before his master and told that henceforth he was a free man. By then, of course, it was too late for his mother and father who, born as slaves, raised as slaves, died as slaves. To be another man's chattel, to know that another man, white, could at any moment punish him, torture him, put him to death – these were, for a man now free for eighteen years, thoughts that were not to be measured, only felt as splinters in the heart. If it had been right, as many now claimed, to liberate all slaves, surely it had been wrong to have been one; if it had been wrong to have been a slave, why was the black man still a slave in all but the name of the law? Puzzling thoughts such as these, Horatio turned over in his mind as he looked askance at the dying old man.

His very name was the name of a slave. It was not the name he had been born with – for that, as he remembered as something his own to hold on to, given by his mother, was 'John': the name of a slave, perhaps, but not a slave-name; Horatio was shackled to his new name later, when he was twelve and was entrusted with various household duties in the home of his master – "Horatio, we'll call him, like the British admiral". He had thought, later, of changing his name as a free man – but to what? 'John' was probably just another British ne'er-do-well and the names with which his ancestors had been born were lost in the mists of time. He found that, in Liberty, 'Horatio' suited him, for all that he had no pretensions to naval matters or heroism: but the ladies remembered

SKILLED IN MARITAL ARTS AND MARTIAL CRAFTS

him for it, and the Russians greatly admired the name, as belonging to one skilled in marital arts and martial crafts. It was not much to salvage from a life, but—

"You clumsy fool!" exclaimed Yadviga, slapping his arm with the strength of two good peasant women, "Are you trying to drown the poor man?"

Horatio looked down and found that the jug had tilted forward in his hands while he contemplated the red-raw landscape of his younger years, and that he had managed to dribble the contents upon the blankets. The old man said nothing, just looked up at the invisible ceiling with distant eyes. At last, he shifted his gaze to Horatio, who was busy wiping pools of water from the blanket on to the filthy floor, and repeated, with a pleading tone to his voice: "Give me one more drink and I will tell you all the nocturnal secrets of our harem."

The slave, the merchant, John, Horatio, the freed black man, the recaptured black man, felt a humming string snap within him.

"No," said he firmly, his voice at first hushed, "you shall tell us nothing of such things. I know all of your sad stories, and these ladies do not wish to have the dross of your wasted life paraded before them. You," he finished loudly much to his own great surprise, quite convinced that the words of excoriation had come from another mouth, "will tell us nothing of your dissipation. Be silent rather, and make your peace with your own conscience."

After which: after an appreciable interval of profound silence; after the flames had consumed the last ashes of the old stool; after the water had dripped slowly from the blanket to the floor; after an owl had hooted reflectively and the rats scuttled sternly and the echoes had died away; then both the old man and Horatio began shaking with the deep, dark sobs that are dug like sticky clay from an opening grave. Ksenia looked upon each, anguished, then placed an arm around the broad shoulders of the living.

"My dear, kind man," she said softly, "you are filled to the brim with goodness. Let it overflow, let it go. And be assured that no harem in this world holds any secrets for a woman who has experienced marriage and loss."

Horatio shook his head and, through his astonishing grief, replied:

"IF ONLY THAT WERE TRUE."

15

NO BLANKET – A GREAT OVERSIGHT IN A SIBERIAN WINTER.

John Dundas Cochrane shook his head to clear it. Somewhere beyond the enveloping darkness and gloom, there was a shimmering light, which drowned a different world. Could that be the daylight? It was not possible to tell, for he was trapped at the bottom of twin wells of blackness, numbed by the pains in his limbs. He was half-way up a mountain, he thought, or in some quiet spot in the impenetrable forest. He could not remember. But really, it did not seem to matter. He had barely reached Yakutsk, and had two thousand miles to go before he reached Nizhney Kolymsk, where Baron Wrangel eagerly awaited his arrival. He was filled to the brim, and overflowing with happy anticipation and elation, for the main goal and significance of his long, long journey was now within his grasp. The lands of Siberia and the Frozen Sea could no longer hold any secrets from him.

"I remained at Yakutsk some three weeks, making the needful preparations for the journey across the frozen waste. As soon as the River Lena should become passable on the ice, I would leave. I paid particular attention to my dress, for I heard such accounts of the cold that I considered myself exposed to death, without even having the satisfaction of expecting to be buried, since the earth to the north of Yakutsk is perpetually frozen. While I waited, I spent my time in making a study of the commerce in furs, which is considerable; and in moving in Good Society, cracking nuts with the ladies, sucking

CRACKING NUTS sugar-candy and eating biscuits: I found that it was
WITH THE LADIES common practice to return such lumps of candy as had
not been sucked entirely to nothing, to the sugar-bowl, and such crumbs of biscuits as still remained after having been sat on, to the biscuit basket. An interesting instance of economy, I believe.

"I packed my knapsack, furnished myself with some roast beef, a few dried fish, twenty pounds of sugar-candy (you may be sure it had not yet been sucked), a keg of vodka, and a new Cossack, and set off, in seven and twenty degrees of frost – Réaumur, that is – on the last day of October (Old Style) in the year 1820. I may say, of course, that I had no second parka, no knee-preservers – an omission I later much regretted – no blanket or bed, an indifferent pair of gloves, and a cold cap. Captain Minitsky kindly provided me with two horse-drawn sledges, but I found that sitting still upon a sledge was too cold, and preferred to walk alongside.

"After six days, we crossed the Aldan River, and soon became enveloped in a lofty chain of mountains, named the Toukoulan Mountains, and passed a night in the open air. The Yakuti guides who accompanied me were more habituated to the cold temperatures – while I woke every hour and had to run around to restore my circulation, they seized every such opportunity of my absence to move more and more of the fire to their side, with the result that they kept snug while I all but froze to death. On the following night, however, I built a fire in the shape of a horseshoe, and lay down in the centre. I had no trouble after that, you may be sure.

"Can you see the height of the mountains before us, this meagre spur of the Great Andes? Imagine if you will, that the clouds you see here were fields of ice, and the trees that grow up there were fields of snow. Thus, the mountains appeared to me, which barred our passage. It took us six days to cross those mountains, in which time I was constantly on the watch for a bottomless abyss, or a mis-timed slip. And in the succeeding days, it grew colder – we walked for miles in temperatures of thirty degrees below the freezing point measured by M. Réaumur. We were hospitably received by the Yakuti people, who gave us frozen milk and the marrow of freshly-killed deer. Which we sucked raw from the bone and warm from life: I should consider it a great delicacy."

John Cochrane smiled to himself and brought his two hands before his face as if he had the foreleg of a deer there; he sucked longingly and imagined the soothing, warm marrow running down his throat, easing the agonising pain that accompanied his every breath.

"Of course," he continued, "the gluttony of the Yakuti people is proverbial. I have heard tell of one man who was accustomed to consume at home, in the space of a day, the hind quarter of a large ox, twenty pounds of fat, and a proportionate quantity of melted butter for his drink. I myself observed a child, whose age did not exceed five years, swallow down two candles made of tallow; I fed him a third – down it went; my steersman gave him several pounds of sour frozen butter – down it went; a piece of yellow soap followed with great ease. There was nothing that he could not devour.

SEVERAL POUNDS
OF SOUR FROZEN
BUTTER

"During the month of November, we continued our journey, now beating up mountains, now glissading into ice-bound valleys, here chopping across the ridges of ice on a river with hatchets, there digging a path for the horses in the snow; frequently, we had to tie cloths to their feet, and lead them one by one across a frozen stretch of ice. Every day, the tremendous cold bit into my face and my hands. My feet gave me much pain, as the frozen perspiration turned to blisters. The very rocks below were cracked by the cold and yielded up strange substances: such as stone butter, a soft clay that is yellowish in appearance and not bad to the taste. We did not, however, eat it, for the eating thereof may bring unusual consequences."

The pedestrian traveller paused, amused by some memory. He relished these memories, for they were the very events which had driven him forward, ever anxious for the next challenge, the next remarkable suffering, the unusual taste and the bizarre pain, which hauled a man out from a rut of duty and routine and dragged him, if willing, to the pinnacles of adventure and experience. They were experiences which, he honestly wished to believe, more than compensated for the endless loneliness of his existence.

"On the last day of November, I came over a lofty mountain to the town of Zashiversk. Of all the places I have ever seen bearing the name of a city or town, this was the most dreary and desolate. It is the first considerable halting-place after Yakutsk, a half-way station, lying at about nine hundred miles from any civilised place. You may ask me what it contained?"

There was silence. No one asked anything. In the distant shimmering light, the outraged sound of large hawks and falling stone.

"This dismal and desolate town," continued Cochrane, in a tone of impatience, "contained two clergymen, a non-commissioned officer and his second in command; a merchant, a post-master and an old widow, each in their own habitation. I have during my service in the Navy, and during a period when seamen were scarce, seen a merchant ship with sixteen guns and only fifteen men; but never before did I see a town with only seven inhabitants. However, it abounded in food – fish, bear-meat, wolf-meat, fox, reindeer, hares – all manner of meat. The taste of raw fish melting in the mouth, I can assure you, is more delicate even than oysters, or clotted cream or the finest jelly in the world. Oh, and at the village of Sordak, we dined well in the morning, for a wolf and a horse had fought each other to death in the night, on our very door-step. It was an unusual breakfast, but one which contained much sustenance for the journey ahead.

A TOWN WITH ONLY SEVEN INHABITANTS

"As we crossed the flat endless plains, the cold was so intense that I suffered much, especially in the knees, which, although not sensibly cold, had a feeling of deadness and painful fatigue. A passing pedlar explained to me, by signs and words which were easy of comprehension, that I would lose both my legs above the knees if I did not protect the joints from the extreme cold. Accordingly, I bought from him a pair of knee-preservers, made of the skins of reindeer's legs; astonishingly, from that moment I had much less pain and far more heat. I would advise all travellers to furnish themselves with knee-preservers – for when once the knees are frost-bitten, adieu alike to them and life.

"We reached the village of Sredne Kolymsk with little further excitement, and on Christmas Day I left there my Cossack – the first and only one of my Cossacks who were of any value at all, my dear old friend Peter Trechekov. On the second last day of my journey, thirteen dogs and a driver were provided for me. A philanthropic act, no doubt; but, enveloped in a bear-skin and a warm blanket, with a pillow for my head, and enclosed in a sort of tent made of oil-cloth, I have seldom felt so sick and angry, for the want of exercise cruelly afflicted me. I was never so distressed from the cold, and would have died of drowsiness, had it not been for the great kindness of my driver who used all his exertions to rouse me from my lethargic condition.

"And finally, on the very last day of the year, I came upon the town of Nizhney Kolymsk, the head-quarters of Baron Wrangel and his companion Mr. Matiushkin. I had travelled sixty-one days on a most tedious, laborious and dangerous journey; twenty of these nights were passed in the snow without even the comfort of a blanket – a great oversight in a Siberian winter, as was the omission of a second coat or even a second pair of boots. But here, on the shores of the Frozen Sea, I might enjoy health and every comfort I could desire!"

Astonishingly, at this moment, having fought through two thousand miles of the worst landscapes of Siberia, in temperatures so low that many a man in St Petersburg could not credit the truth of the matter, eating food that would turn pale many a man in London, travelling without a word of protest, without resentment for the discomfort – John Dundas Cochrane now laughed; and then cried tears. It was not clear to himself whether they were tears of joy, of frustration, or of sadness; or simply the overflowing of his heart as he remembered

THE JOY OF KNEE-PRESERVERS.

16

NEVER MIND LONDON, HE SAID, HELP ME TO PISS.

As Ksenia dried the tears which had erupted from the eyes of her confused admirer, she was reminded of another day when tears had flowed from a man. At the very thought which thus burst in unannounced, a dew-drop welled up in her left eye, and a jewelled companion in her right eye, much to the consternation of Horatio, who had just enjoyed one hundred heartbeats of undivided care.

"Ah, fool that I am," said he, now regretting his weakness, "I fear I have caused you to weep?"

"No, sir," said she, brushing away those two tears of remembrance with the back of her hand. She smiled upon him. "It was not your doing. It was a memory of my first husband."

Horatio reacted to the familiar words. "That would be he who—" he began.

"Near Yakutsk," she interrupted, against all expectation, "I fell off a horse and remained senseless for twelve long hours."

Horatio exclaimed and laid his hand upon her arm. She did not remark upon it.

The old man muttered from the bed that he had once fallen from a horse, having been senseless for twelve hours from an excess of rum, and that the fall had woken him up.

Yadviga had never fallen from a horse, but remained, for the moment, senseless.

"Horses," remarked Horatio, remaining a man of the very deepest sympathy, "horses can be beasts of great danger. I have made it my business not to go upon a horse. Far safer," he continued, plunging recklessly into the Dangerous Marsh of Opinion, "to travel in a diligence."

Ksenia considered this principle with some earnestness. She could see in it considerable merit – "except when the wheels break" – but: "If you travel from Okhotsk to Yakutsk, and from Yakutsk to Irkutsk, I fear that such a comfort is not always possible. The roads are not made for coaches or diligences. They are not roads at all. They are blocked by snow for half the year, and by mud for the other half. And my husband was in such great haste to return to his own people, that there was no argument could persuade him to walk. We must travel by horse. I did not mind that I had, until then, never seen more than three horses in all my life; my husband urged me; I must mount. My first horse was most tame. I do not like the tamest of things, sir," she added, patting his hand as it rested on her. "I like the wilder things."

Horatio nodded agreeably. With the hand which he had laid quite unconsciously upon her right arm, when first she had fallen from her horse, he was manacled to happiness. The longer his hand rested there, in that soft, warm corner of the night, the more difficult it was to remove it. Such an arm, he knew, was connected, through all the surrounding darkness, to a woman; and the woman maybe to a wife; a wife to a small cottage; and the cottage to a cat, to a sunny window with shutters, to a book of poetry, to Pushkin maybe, and an orchard.

"Sir," said Ksenia, breaking in upon his sun-lit orchard after several minutes, "I must sit now."

Horatio obliged, sighing for the loss. She sat with a sigh of exhaustion; the chair sighed for the lightness of weight, to which it was not accustomed; the stove creaked with a sigh of satisfaction, settling its hot lips around another log; with a sigh of regret for the loss of wild things and the emptiness of spirits, the old woman shook the empty bottle; the dying old man sighed from pain and kept the secrets of the harem to himself; and some water dripped from the old man's bed to the floor. There must have been a passing shower of rain, or of tears.

"Thus, I changed my tame horse for another. The second one did not like me."

"For shame!" murmured Horatio, now confirmed in his antipathy to horses.

"It lost no time in throwing me to the ground, and, had it not been for Providence and two medical men who travelled in our party, I might have died upon the spot. My husband feared the worst, and was sorely troubled as to whether he should continue his journey home, or return my corpse to my father in Kamtchatka. My recovery of my senses relieved him of this worry. Such a dear man he was!"

The old nurse sniffed disbelievingly, but otherwise said nothing. She had seen in her life whole armies of young girls throw themselves blindly in love at heroes and travelling novelties, moths round the flickering flame. And had even one emerged without a broken heart, broken wings, or – in most cases – a broken head?

"It was, indeed, the third time that we had come close to death," continued the young widow cheerfully, "and scarcely had we set off from Kamtchatka! On the first occasion we witnessed a great disturbance of the heavens and the earth as the volcano of Avacha erupted and set fire, it seemed, to all of Kamtchatka. Had we been closer to the shore, we would surely have perished in flames. PERISHED IN FLAMES, And then, driven by gales, we were all but ship-wrecked SMASHED UPON ROCKS upon the Kurile Islands. Only my husband's great skills saved us from being smashed upon the rocks."

Horatio grumbled at her husband's lack of consideration. No man should, he thought angrily, be so careless as to lose his wife three times in a row: first by fire; then by water; then by earth. What next – death by air, an accident in an aerostat? Fortunately, he kept his opinion to himself, for—

"—the fourth time was the worst of them all," she continued with some enthusiasm. "After we had crossed the Ural Mountains and come into the city of Kazan, my husband complained of rheumatism and palpitations of the heart and thought he was like to fall into dissolution. As for myself, I was racked by such aches in my back and my side that I remained three and twenty days in a bed of torment."

"Journeys," said Horatio gloomily, "are full of so many dangers."

"Had it not been for Mrs. Yeremeova, the niece of the Governor of Kazan, we would both have died in some stable."

Yadviga felt obliged to state that a lady of good rank would always find a welcome with the niece of a provincial governor. She spoke from considerable experience.

"A stable, madam?" asked Horatio tentatively.

"A stable, alas. For such were most frequently the accommodations that we were offered as we came into Europe from Siberia."

"But stables," observed Horatio warily—

"—are for horses. Indeed, sir. For horses and for Russians who are born in Kamtchatka, which is not Europe." There was the slightest trace of bitterness in the young woman's voice. After several moments, during which she prodded sadly and distractedly at Horatio's handkerchief, she continued her story.

"The aches came not from walking, or from sailing upon the lakes and rivers, nor from riding from horses—"

"—perhaps from falling from them?" asked Horatio.

"No, indeed not, although since that day I have a pain in my right temple – just here – can you feel the lump?"

She brought Horatio's fingers to that spot, and he caressed it gently, feeling no bump, only providence.

"—but from the roads of Russia, which are suited neither to coaches nor diligences nor sleighs. Why, at Yekaterinburg, the ruts in the road were of four and five feet deep, so that our coach threw us with great violence from one side to another, and we received concussions without number, until at last my husband decided that we must walk the thirty versts that remained, were we to reach our destination alive."

Horatio looked troubled by this poor judgement of the roads of the Great Russian Empire. Had he not, that very day, travelled in great comfort and smoothness upon a Macadamized road, that led almost all the way from Moscow to Novgorod? It was not to be denied that on lesser roads the ruts and bends and holes and depredations of passing floods were not conducive to a slow and calm digestion of dinner, nor for the easy passage of – say – a pregnant woman – at which thought he gazed with some concern upon the young woman by the stove – then banished the thought – then reflected again – and finally decided that the place of a man in the mysterious world of a woman is to keep silent and to observe only. Besides which, he had done with travelling on foot some fifteen years ago, having met a man of uncompromising religion who observed that, If God had wished men to wander the roads on foot, why then had He set carriages and coaches upon the Earth? Pedestrian travel, the religious man had con-

IF GOD HAD WISHED
MEN TO WANDER
THE ROADS ON FOOT,
WHY THEN HAD
HE SET CARRIAGES
AND COACHES UPON
THE EARTH?

tended, led easily to Perdition, while wheeled transport whirled down the road of Salvation. This was an argument that was hard to refute.

The old woman, feeling the aches in her bones that came neither from Perdition, nor Salvation, but simply the lack of movement of any sort, commanded Horatio to the back-yard to fetch more wood for the stove. He obeyed.

Left alone for a few moments, Ksenia fell to serious reflection on the matter of travel, hospitality, and the vast expanses of Russia. Some ten years had passed since she had made that long, tedious and apparently endless journey, interrupted only by dull days and weeks in provincial towns which were quite alien to her. Her husband seemed to abandon her quite frequently. He probably had important things to do, although she never quite knew what these were. Shaking at last the dust and mud of Siberia from her feet, she found herself in a land – still Russia – which had other morals, other concerns, other distractions from those she had grown up with. She was a foreigner in her own country then, and there were not a few people who had reminded her of that, tactless, probably, rather than cruel. And then came Moscow, with its countless streets and busy people and tall towers, all calculated to leave her astonished but not at all enthusiastic; and then the wonderful, miraculous theatre which she had visited with her husband and that blind man, where she had permitted herself to laugh. She shook her head in embarrassment now to think of that moment – she who was now a veteran of the gayest theatres of London and St Petersburg, with their dramas and comedies, their impossibly handsome actors and frankly wanton actresses.

Could she, would she retrace her steps on that journey, if given the chance? Not perhaps in such a rush as before; but – given the right companion – given that word of encouragement which had nothing to do with 'travelling' and everything to do with 'staying' – given the slightest excuse – she felt now that she could do so. At the very thought, a sudden excitement took her. Should she? She got up from her seat, for her legs would not stay still. She turned rapidly out of the room and sought out the traveller who would not travel, the companion who could not stay.

Out in the cold night, all was still. Somewhere a bell tolled four times, then fell silent. The stars wheeled overhead, numberless and hissing. As Horatio stood there, admiring the endless night, he heard the young widow emerge from the lodge and stand beside him. 'Love'? – what is it, but the deepest reciprocal need for companionship, two people wrapped in tranquillity, gazing side by side upon the night sky, not a single word required to pass between them. While they stood, he with a bundle of wood under his left arm, she with her hands around his right arm, the night passed, then the day passed, then the month of August, then the year of 1833, then the century, the stars fizzled and died, the edges of time grew dim, all that was grim did pass away—

THE STARS
FIZZLED
AND DIED

"Here!" came the complaining voice of Yadviga, who had stamped out from the front room to see why her promised fuel had not arrived, "Have you no respect for the dying? Do you want the General to breathe his last in a room as cold as a tomb? That is no way to treat a brave old soldier, you mark my words."

The lovers made haste to return to the only furnished room of the house; Horatio carefully piled the wood upon the glowing embers in the stove; when that had been completed to her satisfaction, Yadviga sat herself directly upon the hot tiles to ensure that the old man would not be troubled by the unusual heat. She nodded – it was a sign of considerable contentment.

"When we were upon the steppes and marshes of Siberia," continued Ksenia, now relinquishing her memories of the roads which were not roads, "we travelled often under the stars. In the space of a hundred and one nights, my husband taught me the names of every star that appears in the sky. He was, of course, a sea-faring man – oh!"

Horatio blushed at his ignorance. Ksenia looked for forgiveness. Ignorance was forgiven, and forgiveness was not ignored.

"Were you," asked Horatio, in order that his stupidity might be obliterated by the pretence of acuity, "not eaten by the wolves, as you travelled by night?" He understood Siberia to be a place of criminals, wolves and intoxicated hordes, not to mention desolation and frozen lakes.

Ksenia laughed as only a young woman can laugh: "Do I seem to be missing any limbs, sir?" she asked, standing up and twirling for his easier examination.

Before he knew what he said, the words were out: "I think I would have to conduct a more thorough examination before I could tell that for sure."

Ah, thought Ksenia Ivanovna approvingly: a man in a rush of blood. Accordingly, she sat down quickly and lowered her eyes. From the bed of the dying man came a lewd laugh, followed by a coughing fit, to which Yadviga felt obliged to attend, grumbling at the two young fools.

"But the cold was a far greater danger to us than were the bears or wolves or flies," said the bold, four-times-saved traveller through Siberia. "My husband used to complain that I withstood the cold far better than he."

What sort of a complaint is that? thought Horatio, that a husband should complain that his wife is not so cold as he? He said nothing, determined that no words should crack the fragile shell of the night.

"Indeed, on our journey I was obliged to allow him under my blanket far more often than a wife is bound to."

Oh, thought Horatio, pleased that he had said nothing: that was the sort of complaint it was.

"My husband grew up in a hot climate; I grew up in a cold climate. That was the cause of our difference."

"I may mention, madam," said her admirer hopefully, "that I too grew up in a hot climate, and feel the cold more commonly than most in Russia." He need not have said anything.

"He frequently told me that, if he had not fetched me from Kamtchatka, then he would assuredly have died, frost-bitten, on the way home."

Yadviga, having dealt with her patient to her own satisfaction, had resumed her post by the stove; a marvel it was that she did not burst into flames herself, like the Burning Bush of the Scriptures, being so basted in fat and flushed dangerously crimson. Hearing these last words of the young widow, she voiced her approval that the woman's late husband seemed a man of uncommon sensibility.

"And yet you came safely across the frozen wastes of Siberia and the dangerous mountains of the Ural, and reached Moscow intact?" observed Horatio, anxious to bring the conversation back to places of which he had at least some knowledge. The endless cold did not suit him: Horatio preferring, summer or winter, to stay indoors by a well-heated stove and a samovar.

"Not merely to Moscow, sir. After eleven months of walking on roads and riding through marsh and sailing upon the rivers, we arrived at St Petersburg on the fourteenth day of June in the year 1823. Ah, almost was it yesterday—"

"Yesterday, she says?" interrupted Yadviga. "You talk of yesterday? Was ten years ago yesterday, you foolish girl? Twenty years, that is maybe yesterday. Is it not twenty years since my own dear husband died, and left me all alone to make a living by caring for the dying? Thirty years, that is maybe yesterday, when my own son died at Austerlitz? Fifty years, yes, that is indeed yesterday, when I was a foolish girl like you, in love with a man who was never any good, and never colder than I? Yesterday? – all I'm going to say is: pah!" After which brief warning, she said: "Pah!", and spat on the stove – at which, the stove spat back. Having delivered her lengthy pronouncement upon the curious funnel of the passing years, she fell silent.

Ten years ago, thought Ksenia, ten years: no, it was not yesterday at all. It was eight long years now since her first husband died. It was hard to believe now in those months travelling across Siberia and Russia; at the time, it had been like some fairy-tale for one so young as herself – or so she had forced herself to believe. What else could it have been? She was married, she had a handsome husband, they were travelling with due haste to the most unlikely cities of the world. And all because she had been the pretty one in among a crowd of a dozen giggling girls. Like the fairy-tale, it had all vanished: she had woken up, the kiss was gone, the prince was gone, the magic was gone – had it gone even before he had died?

At this thought, the new widow surprised herself in weeping. Horatio, horrified and having no handkerchief, hastily ripped a strip of material from the ragged sheets upon the bed, and passed it on for the sake of the floor, already damp from sadness or the rain or jugs of water. She took it from him and filled it with tears.

The dying man in the bed was now awake. "The women," said he with a note of singular satisfaction, "crowd around my bed and mourn for the passing of a libertine. Let them mourn!" To give comfort to the dying was the cause of their visit, so Ksenia cried some more, with vigour. Having cried some more, she dried her eyes, passed the rag back to Horatio and continued her story.

MOURN FOR
THE PASSING OF
A LIBERTINE

"In St Petersburg, my husband was informed that the Tsar himself had been anxious for his safety on the great journey to Kamtchatka, and was now pleased at his safe return."

Yadviga crossed herself fervently at the mention of the Tsar, and revived her national feelings with a cup of bitter black tea.

"The British Ambassador told us that a ship lay at the harbour, waiting for the first fair wind to take passage for London. We engaged a cabin from Captain Smith, and sailed upon his ship, the Peter Proctor, to London. The captain had lately dined with my husband's father, whom I regret never to have met, in Dominica."

"Dominica?" exclaimed both men in the room simultaneously.

"And so," continued Ksenia, neither hearing nor paying attention to the interruptions, "we set sail and left Russia behind us. In no time at all, we had reached the city of London." Ksenia turned inconsequentially to the black window, closed her eyes and whispered in rapture: "Ah, London, London, can any city ever be so great?"

"Never mind London," mumbled the old man,

"HELP ME TO PISS."

17

HE TALKS BLITHELY OF REVOLUTION AS IF IT WERE OF NO CONSEQUENCE.

"It was in London," began Horatio, as the women crowded around the dying man, to assist or hinder him in his attempts to piss for the last time in his life, "It was in London that I heard for the first time of Russia."

No one in the room was listening to him, for the dying man was weak and his efforts to pass water were not of the most determined. Ksenia made cooing noises, Yadviga hissed like a snake; together they brought the old man to a coughing fit; which drove away his urge to piss. Horatio might as well have talked to the rats in the kitchen, who were far more polite. Nonetheless, he ploughed on with a brief history of Europe.

"Three years ago, I was in Paris—"

"In France?" asked Ksenia Ivanovna in a tone of some interest, diverted briefly from the task in hand.

"In France, indeed," Horatio confirmed, "when King Charles attempted to dissolve the Parliament, remove the vote from honest men, and restrict the Press. Ah! the July Days – days of barricades, of fighting in the streets, guns and swords. Five hundred artisans died, all of them young men—"

Ksenia Ivanovna sighed with a heavy distraction.

"—and a hundred and fifty soldiers—"

Ksenia Ivanovna sighed a sigh deeper still.

"—it lasted three days only, and then the King of France fled." Horatio paused to admire the ways of a democratic people. It did not seem such a simple matter in Russia – he had seen what became of the Decembrists. But this was Russia and that was France – a nation which had sucked in Revolution at its mother's breast. "Then the journalists wrote that the barricades should come down, and Louis-Philippe put on the uniform of the National Guard. He became King of the French, and did what he was told."

"All I can say is more men should do so," muttered the old woman unambiguously, struggling with the patient's breeches, inside which was trapped the object of her immediate concern. Having at last unearthed it, she smacked the dying man firmly on the leg, and ordered him to piss, if he would. "In any case, when will you get another chance?" she demanded, giving the old man pause for thought.

When, indeed? he reflected silently. A man takes some things for granted – but he must stop and think: is this the last time I will piss?

"All of Europe was suddenly ablaze with revolution," continued Horatio, lost in his dream of liberalism. "Little Belgium cast off the shackles of the Netherlands. The people of Poland, once more, took up arms against Russia; and, once more, failed to throw off their oppressor. Conspirators flourished in Italy. In Berlin, the students waved flags in the streets. In Brunswick, they dislodged the Duke. In every town I travelled in that year of 1830, there was conspiracy and talk of Revolution. Not since the days of Napoleon had there been so much government and democracy, and –" he shook his head in weariness, "– so little to show for it." IN BRUNSWICK THEY DISLODGED THE DUKE

"Sir," said Ksenia, neglecting for the moment her responsibility in the matter of pissing. She stood up, pressing her hands to the small of her back as she did so – it was a long night following a long day. "Sir, you talk blithely of Revolution as if it were of no consequence."

Horatio started out of his fond reminiscences of smoke and bloodshed and the throwing-over of foreign powers and autocrats. He gazed upon the widow as if from a great height. "No," said he, "I do not consider a Revolution to be of no consequence. It is of the greatest consequence, and, in short, the most beautiful act of humanity. Has not Revolution," he continued, warming to his subject, oblivious to a certain cooling in the manner of his companion, "led to the liberation of the Spirit, not to mention the liberation of Slaves?"

"It has led," came the reply, "to war and the death of many a brave sailor and soldier. It has led to smoking ruins, the raping of women and the slaughter of innocents. It has led to the scything down of handsome young men. It has led at last—"

"At last!" exclaimed the old man, "At last! Aaaaah!" He began to piss, and screamed in agony – he was pissing fire, not water.

"Ah! at last," echoed Yadviga, greatly contented, "has he not managed to piss at last?"

Ksenia abandoned her critique of Revolution, and attended to the patient; who seized the advantageous moment to bury his tears and his sweating brow in her soft bosom; he groaned quietly. Left alone again, Horatio considered the Revolutions of the white man and of the black man, for they were not the same, and convinced himself that Revolution had at least led to the loosening of chains, not the shackling of nations; it had at least led to the flight of the mind through the airs of hope, not to its drowning in the quicksands of despair; it had at least led to shafts of light being beamed upon human affairs; it had led unequivocally to the voicing of unspoken hopes. From every Revolution flowed two rivers, the turbulent River of Progress and the bloody River of Reaction; but the stronger current of the two was always the current of Progress—

THE TURBULENT
RIVER OF PROGRESS
AND THE BLOODY
RIVER OF REACTION

"Sir, you still stand there! Are you forever dreaming of Revolution?" scolded Ksenia Ivanovna. "Fetch, rather, some warm water, that this poor man may lie in comfort for the remaining hours of his life."

Horatio hurriedly renounced all thought of Revolution, and brought warm water from a pot that stood on top of the stove. There followed several minutes of hot and damp activity, from which Horatio, knowing now something of the old man, kept his distance. Yadviga demanded more wood for the stove. Horatio obliged. Ksenia begged him to bring a cloth. Horatio obliged. When the old man was settled once more, moaning in a more comfortable manner, Yadviga commanded that more food and drink be brought from the Inn. Horatio obliged.

Finding himself, from his acts of obligation, out in the cold night, Horatio pulled his coat tighter around him and took his bearings. In his left hand he clutched the bottle which, under threat of a cool reception should he fail, he was commissioned to have re-filled with strong spirits "for the poor Captain"; in his right hand, a cloth in which to wrap some food. Uncertain which way to turn, for he had not paid close attention to directions earlier, being engrossed in the contemplation of a far more beautiful thing than the road before him, he paused and gazed at the wide northern skies of Novgorod. Then he thought more of Revolution and Europe, of Schiller and Goethe, of Hegel and Voltaire, of Rousseau and Radischchev. And then he stamped his feet.

As if waiting for this signal, a short man appeared at his elbow.

"It is indeed a night full of significance," agreed the short man, with no formal introduction. Horatio could not remember having made the suggestion, but was pleased nevertheless. "A night," continued the small gentleman, "in which lovers may meet, lovers may weep, may fall into each others' arms."

"Certainly," replied Horatio, with a heart-felt sigh.

"A night," continued the other, considerably encouraged by this reception from a man of such strong sensibility, "A night in which lovers may part, lovers may weep, may pass from each others' arms."

"Certainly," said Horatio, feeling all too keenly the emptiness of every embrace. Having no handkerchief, he dabbed at his eyes with the cloth for victuals, and placed the empty bottle in his left-hand pocket.

"A night in which—", the shorter gentleman made to continue. But the was this time interrupted by Horatio who, finding that such sad words pinched like too-tight breeches, placed his free hand over the mouth of the other.

TOO-TIGHT BREECHES

"A night," said he rather, "in which to renew one's spirits. Do you know the way to the inn owned by Mr. Voronov?"

The short gentleman nodded vigorously. Horatio uncovered the man's mouth. The man made sure to say nothing, but elegantly bowed and indicated the road to be followed. The two men set off down the street which led back in the direction of the kremlin. After a hundred paces, Horatio's guide could contain himself no longer – words burst forth.

"My name is Nikolai Mikhailovich Karamzin," said he, offering a hand for Horatio to shake.

Surprised, Horatio shook it and introduced himself: "Horatio Alexandrovich."

"You have not, then, heard of my name?" asked Mr. Karamzin, after a pause, and in a disappointed tone.

"I am a visitor to Novgorod the Great," explained Horatio apologetically. "I have not had time to become acquainted with all those who count for something in this beautiful town."

Something placated, Mr. Karamzin forgave the ignorance of travellers, and guided his companion onwards. When they reached the foot and entrance of the kremlin, Horatio made to advance, but Mr. Karamzin guided him to the left. "This is a quicker way across the river," he explained in a whisper. "And, in any case, the soldiers make me nervous."

Horatio was pleased to make the detour, having no desire to force his way past so many unstable sentries again. To meet an Imerach once is to shy from him twice; and likewise the Imerach. Together, the two night-strollers made their way around the northern side of the citadel, their way lit only by a flickering moon. The only sound was the hissing of the wind in the trees, and the padding of their footsteps – which, imperceptibly as they progressed, merged from two sounds into one.

"You seem a man of some sensitivity," said Horatio, prompted of a sudden to unburden his feelings upon another human being. "Have you ever known Love?"

Nikolai Mikhailovich Karamzin, by way of answer, stopped dead in his tracks, brandished his despairing arms at the sky and mouthed some prayer to the unseen God. His supplication lasted more than an instant. Then he turned back to Horatio.

"Not only have I known Love in all its many sad and tragic forms," he explained, "but I have frequently written of it – something you seem not to know."

Horatio was mortified. He launched into a futile apology. It came too late. Mr. Karamzin was offended. They walked together in silence, now out of step with each other. Their footsteps echoed back from the empty mansions they passed, a battalion of the defeated. The wind died down. It was not until they reached the great wooden bridge which spanned the river that Mr. Karamzin consented to speak again.

"What is it that you wish to know of Love?" he asked.

"Oh, it was nothing," said Horatio.

"It was something," countered his companion.

"It has no importance."

"But it matters greatly to you."

"Just a trifle," muttered Horatio.

"There is no trifle in Love – it is all or it is nothing," came the reply.

"Ah!" exclaimed Horatio, "Just as I thought."

"And so?" urged Mr. Karamzin, "And so – what is your question?"

"What is 'Love'?" asked Horatio.

"If you have to ask," came the considered reply, "then you have never known what Love is." With these words, Mr. Karamzin turned on his heel and, without a further word of explanation or courtesy, disappeared into the shadows.

Horatio stood at the bridge, looking into the waters, thinking of Love and Revolution, of Life and Death, until a passing dog that avoided his eye reminded him of his present obligation. He crossed the bridge, passed the slumbering sentry, and walked gloomily until he reached the door of the inn. It was shut and locked. Horatio knocked on the door. There was no answer from within. He knocked louder, and shouted for Mr. Voronov.

A shutter was flung open above him and a voice snarled. "What do you want?"

Horatio stepped out of the shadow and peered up. "I have been sent back for more food and drink," he said.

"What?" exclaimed the inn-keeper, recognising him and changing his tone. "At this hour?" A pause was observed by both parties. Then: "Where is the young lady?"

"She still attends to the dying man," explained Horatio.

"Ah," said Mr. Voronov, in a softer tone. The very thought of such an angel attending to the bed-side of an old soldier greatly softened his heart. "I will come down immediately."

Some minutes elapsed. In this interval, Mr. Voronov had an altercation with the woman who shared his marriage-bed. A door was slammed. Mr. Voronov's night-cap was flung from the window. A feminine voice bawled, "And don't presume to come back here tonight!" The shutter was viciously pulled shut. A splintering of wood ensued. Horatio picked up the night-cap, still warm from its wearer's head; shook out the dust; and stood waiting for his host.

As he did so, someone tapped his arm. It was his recent companion, Mr. Karamzin. "Sir," he whispered with no apology, "I should have said: if you have to ask, you already know what Love is." With that remark, which gave no assistance to a man who truly required it, he slipped away again into the darkness.

The door to the street was unbolted, and Mr. Voronov's face appeared above a candle. Horatio offered him the night-cap and stepped inside. The air within was still hot and thick from the stove, which had been heated beyond endurance earlier in the evening. Horatio fished out the bottle from his pocket, and passed it and the cloth to the inn-keeper, for his attention.

"And how is the young lady bearing up?" asked Mr. Voronov solicitously.

"She bears up most admirably," admitted Horatio.

"And the old general?" asked Mr. Voronov, as an afterthought.

"He will soon be dead," murmured Horatio.

They passed into the kitchen, where the inn-keeper busied himself with replenishing bottle and cloth. A rat sat and stared at them, dumbfounded by the interruption to its nocturnal meal. Mr. Voronov threw his axe at it, missing by several feet. The axe-head buried itself in the wall; by good fortune the blade split the forehead of a famous poet, whose printed portrait had been pinned up and much admired by Mrs. Voronova. The inn-keeper grunted with satisfaction.

THE BLADE SPLIT
THE FOREHEAD OF
A FAMOUS POET

"You found your way back here without difficulty?" he asked.

"I was fortunate enough to meet a man who showed me the way," answered Horatio. "He was most obliging."

"That is unusual in Novgorod," observed Mr. Voronov, carefully adulterating a cask of spirits with water before he decanted some into the bottle.

"I find that everyone I meet in this town is most obliging," said Horatio, wondering whether he ought to remark on the inn-keeper's actions. He decided against it: a man should be free to do as he wishes in his own home.

"Did this man have a name?" asked the inn-keeper, replacing the stopper on the bottle. He turned his attention to several jars of pickles and an accumulation of cucumbers.

"He gave it as Karamzin. Nikolai Karamzin, that was it," announced Horatio, placing the bottle in his pocket. He did this with so much care and thoughtfulness that he did not notice the sharp intake of breath from the inn-keeper. Only when the bottle was safely stowed, and he looked up again, did he see that Mr. Voronov's mouth hung open.

"Karamzin?" asked Voronov nervously. "Nikolai Karamzin?"

"That was it," said Horatio pleasantly. "Karamzin."

Mr. Voronov, such was his distraction, placed in the cloth a cucumber that was almost fresh, having only just begun to wrinkle. "Do you not know, sir," he muttered, looking over his shoulder at the moonlit yard outside, "that Mr. Karamzin has been dead these past seven years?"

"Dead?" queried Horatio. "Surely not? He spoke to me of Love."

"He spoke to many of Love," said Mr. Voronov, "he wrote of Love and the tragic consequences of Love. And broke the hearts of all who read his words. Poor Liza!"

Horatio grew troubled at the thought. His heart was not yet broken, for he still had great hopes of the night. But he was willing to listen to the voice of reason.

"What do you know of a broken heart, Mr. Voronov?" he asked.

In reply, the inn-keeper indicated the cold night-cap. Both men regarded it thoughtfully.

After a moment, the inn-keeper recovered his spirits and his axe. "All writers break hearts and deserve no more than ignominy, disgrace and death. Mr. Karamzin is," he said happily, "dead. But the canker of literature is eating through the healthy body of Imperial Russia, every line from a poet is another dagger in the heart of our Nation, each line of—"

THE INN-KEEPER RECOVERED HIS SPIRITS AND HIS AXE

"Ghosts, now," remarked Horatio, thinking along other lines altogether. "Not two years ago I was travelling in a carriage through the kingdom of Bavaria. Near the small town of Freising, there was a great storm. We stopped to rescue a traveller from the flooded river. Like Mr. Karamzin, the traveller turned out to be a ghost, a man who had drowned one hundred years before in the swollen river and who returned each stormy night to visit the scene of his demise. We should perhaps have realised, when we saw that his eyes had been sucked away by the eels. We left him at the monastery, where he was interred once more, and his story was told to us—"

"—there are three things which our glorious Emperor holds dear: these are Orthodoxy, Autocracy, and Nationality. The Church, the Emperor, the Nation. Not once does the Emperor Nikolai mention Literature, or Poetry, does he, eh? All that is a sickness and treachery at the heart of our—"

"—and being sick at heart from the treachery of his beloved Lisa, he threw himself from the bridge over the Isar into the turbulent waters, and died of his injuries. Such a desperate—"

"—country," concluded Mr. Voronov. The inn-keeper brooded for several minutes more on the treachery of Poets, unburdened himself of six pickled eggs, and tied a firm knot in the cloth. Horatio held out his hand for the package. The inn-keeper denied him it.

"Ah, but this city of Novgorod has seen many desperate times," he began. "Let me tell you of the battle with the Teutonic Knights in 1242—"

"A dying man awaits his final meal," said Horatio firmly. "He cannot be kept long waiting." He possessed himself of the cucumbers and pickled eggs, thanked the inn-keeper for his attentions, and stepped out

ONCE MORE INTO THE NIGHT.

18

THE PASSAGE OF LARGE ARMIES
OF MICE.

"If Boukhtarminsk was the land of plenty for cucumbers and melons, then Nizhney Kolymsk super-abounded with fish," said John Cochrane. "While still at breakfast on my first day there, I received as a New Year's gift, two large fish in frozen state for my personal use, each weighing about two hundred pounds."

"To what use did you put them, my boy?" asked the other innocently.

"I set them aside for the hungry months to come," replied Cochrane unimaginatively. "I received also gifts of new trousers, cap, boots and leather hose, a bear's skin for a bed, and a blanket of hares' skins; and gloves, from the ladies."

"Ah, there were ladies in this God-forsaken place?" asked the other in a tone of mockery. "And Good Society, I would wager?" He laughed aloud.

"Good Society," said Cochrane rather testily, "can be found even in the most desolate and hidden places of the world. Indeed, sir," he went on aggressively, "I have found that Good Society is more readily found where European Society is entirely absent. Baron Wrangel, for example, was kind enough to provide me with a complete suit of the dress of the Tchuktchi."

"The – ?" asked his companion blankly. He thought for a moment that Cochrane had yet again sneezed or coughed. The man had been coughing for the past two days; it was greatly nettling; there was no remedy.

"The Tchuktchi," repeated Cochrane in clear tones, "the people of that part of the world, from their physical appearance probably related to the American native peoples of the north. They survive well enough in the worst conditions of life I have ever encountered. Disease is rampant, I fear, particularly the scurvy, leprosy, apoplexy and venereal."

"Do they perhaps have a cure for such diseases?" asked the other with rather more medical interest than might be expected of a man familiar with Good Society.

"Only for scurvy, for it is a disease which never fails to abate with the arrival of fresh fish in the summer."

"Ah," remarked the other in a disappointed tone, never yet afflicted by that particular disease, nor indeed by leprosy or apoplexy.

"Also imerachism, which is an interesting ailment. I must remember to talk more of it later. In Nizhney Kolymsk," continued Cochrane, warming to his theme, "I passed the months of January and February of the year 1821. We joined in the simple amusements of the natives, and I read the journals of Baron Wrangel. The weather proved exceedingly cold – forty degrees of frost, Réaumur, was not uncommon."

"That, in plain English, would be what?" demanded his disputant, impatient of foreign terms.

"Forty degrees of frost at Réaumur, sir, would be minus fifty-eight degrees of Fahrenheit, or minus fifty of Celsius," was the ready reply.

"Impossible," stated the older man. "No one could survive in that. Nonsense. Fantasies. Get a grip on yourself."

"In such cold, I have seen iron axes split in pieces, sir," countered Cochrane, "and have observed the ill-effects of touching iron, glass or crockery with the naked skin. I have seen log-books of certain honest explorers, who have recorded forty-three and forty-seven degrees of frost of Réaumur."

"Honest explorers who had died, I'll wager," came the reply in a voice shredded by a shiver. "Aye man, you've made it cold in here. I'm freezing to death!"

Cochrane himself shivered a little: was it the night air turning against him again, he wondered? He had not managed to shake this off; it was a small fever. It would pass when once – if once – he was up and about again, and not lying helpless on the filthy blanket.

"Fish," he hissed into the darkness. "Fish, that's all there was. The salmon and the sturgeon, the moksou, the osioter and the nailma. Let me outline how many fish. From the settlement of Nizhney Kolymsk to that of Malone is a distance of eighty miles; the number of inhabitants in the two places may be six hundred. And yet, in one year, these communities consume nearly two million pounds of fish. Allowing one hundred and twenty families to represent the six hundred individuals, it follows – let me see – it follows that each family consumes about fifteen thousand pounds of fish per annum, or forty pounds a day. Of course, there are also many dogs to be fed. But in the seasons when fish are scarce, the inhabitants consume vast quantities of elk, sheep and reindeer. And dogs, if the season was especially poor.

"Baron Wrangel and his party leaving us on the 27th day of February, I attended him ten miles down the river, when, with three cheers, we wished him every success, and returned. From the mouth of the Kolyma, his party proceeded round the north-east cape of Asia, in search of strange lands. I was not permitted to join this party, despite my admirable qualifications, in consequence of my being a foreigner. I was greatly disappointed. I was left behind to read the appalling nonsense written by Captain Burney in his Chronological History of the North-Eastern Discoveries. Finding it so badly informed, I lost no time in addressing a memorial on the matter to the Royal Society in London. But we know, do we not, how the Royal Society received my honest, if unpolished, commentary? Indeed: with slovenliness.

WITH THREE CHEERS, THEY WISHED HIM EVERY SUCCESS

"I would add, for the sake of a complete narrative and history of the exploration of this part of the world, that, while Baron Wrangel strove north and east, a party led by the brave Captain Anjou explored the territory to the north and west, and made many remarkable discoveries which marvellously complemented those of the Baron."

"Baron Wrangel," said a voice from the gloom, "did he find those strange lands to the north?"

"He found no strange lands," replied Cochrane. "He met me on his return, and told me all that he had found in his journey around the headlands of that part of the world. But no strange lands at all."

A lengthy silence enveloped the conversationalists. Outside, the Siberian winds whipped up the snow and carved the Frozen Sea into grotesques and mountains.

"Having been thus thwarted in my aspiration to accompany Baron Wrangel's expedition around the north-east cape of Siberia, I had an urgent desire to treat with the Tchuktchi, to be permitted to travel through their country as far as Bering's Straits and so to cross over to America. I may say that I failed utterly in my attempts to persuade the Tchuktchi to allow me passage; I travelled especially to their annual fair at Ostrovnaya, in the company of Midshipman Matiushkin.

"Furs!" he exclaimed, clutching feverishly at the threadbare blanket which was all that lay between him and eternity. "That's all there was, furs – vast numbers of furs which had been trapped over the previous year – so many, I believe, that there are now great fears for the survival of the beasts which yielded the furs: otters, white and blue fox, red fox, elk, sable, wolves, martins, beavers, bears, sea-dogs. Furs and – oh yes – tobacco in untold amounts – but not one man of significance could I persuade who would permit me to cross their lands. At first, they agreed they would allow me to do so, so long as I paid them fifty bags of tobacco – that is, five thousand pounds in weight – an amount so monstrous I could not hope to muster even a hundredth of that; and then they decided that, as I had neither the Russian nor the Tchukskoi languages, I could be of no use to them. No use at all."

The disappointed pedestrian pondered this second failure gloomily.

"Mice!" he muttered after a while. "That's all there was. Mice may traverse the lands of the Tchuktchi in their thousands and millions. They pass between Asia and America each year in large armies, and need no passport nor any bags of tobacco. But I—"

As his exasperation rose, his throat contracted; he shuddered and his voice faded to nothing. "I might have died there," he whispered to himself, "for all the assistance I received from that empty-countenanced and wild-looking people. In the darkness, unattended, not having attained the object I had in view – I might have died there. And never, ever have experienced the bliss of that marital life which the poet praises. Ah, Mrs. Cochrane,

WHAT IF I HAD NEVER MARRIED YOU?"

19

LIBERTY! – THE CRY OF THE FRENCHMAN AND THE END OF ALL HONOUR.

"He married you, heh?" said the old man, snuffling to himself in his mirth. "Marriage – it is good for one thing alone and that is—"

"Sir," cautioned Ksenia Ivanovna sternly, "if you are a gentleman, as you say you are, you will not finish your sentence."

The invalid paused for three breaths of reason. Then he started again: "Marriage is not for bringing children into the world. Any woman can do that for you. Any woman at all, given half a reason. Or just half a bottle of rum."

"Or just half a man?" observed Yadviga. She intended no malice.

"Or just half a smile," thought Ksenia. She felt something stir within her.

"Or just half a guinea. No, madam," continued the dying man, "marriage is for wealth and position only. Did you," he wondered, casting his red-rimmed, half-closed eyes upon his nurse, "marry for wealth and position? Or was it for – love?" Upon the last word, he managed to drip a greasy sauce of derision, as if preparing it for a feast of cynics.

Ksenia Ivanovna sighed, smelling only the dish, not the sauce. "Yes, it was for love," said she, confident in her knowledge. "His heart was mine, as mine was his. My second father was an important man in Bolcheretsk, but he would count for nothing in Okhotsk, or Yakutsk, or Irkutsk, or Moscow. My third father would count for something in St Petersburg, but certainly for nothing at all in London. But I did not know that then."

The old man looked sharply at her. "And you for him, then? Was your marriage to him not a great advancement for you? Did your fortunes not, with one kiss, increase tenfold, and with a marriage-night, a hundredfold?"

Ksenia Ivanovna stood up rapidly, turned on her heel, and stepped to the stove. After several moments, she turned around. "Sir," said she, her voice shaking, "I was the wife of Commander John Cochrane of the Royal Navy. I married him for what he said and what he had done and what he dreamed of and how he laughed and how he honoured me; not for his name or his rank or his family. In any case," she added, "he had no family, beyond a father whom he had not seen for years and who – he said – had left Great Britain and gone into retirement." Having delivered herself of this defence, she folded her arms and turned to Yadviga.

"All I can say about not being seen for years is, where is that no-good black charlatan?" demanded the latter. "Has he gone off and got drunk with my money, like every man who once stood upright in Russia? The worthless fool – he's fallen in the moat, hasn't he?"

Ksenia gasped in horror. "Oh, the poor man! It cannot be true!" But it seemed most likely.

"All I can say is, if he has," pursued Yadviga, pursing her lips grimly, "it will be the hundredth time I've done without my spirits when most I needed them."

"Commander Cochrane?" murmured the old man, puzzled by something. "Do you know," he said, turning his head towards the red glow of the mouth of the stove, "I served with Cochrane." He struggled for several breaths. "Yes, I had once that honour: Andrew Cochrane-Johnstone."

"Alas," grieved Ksenia Ivanovna, so greatly disturbed that she flatly ignored the Major's reminiscence and ran from the room, to mount guard upon the deserted street outside the lodge from an advantageous position at the mouldering front-door, "if he is drowned, he will never hear what I have to tell him about my husband!"

"It is a family tradition of those Cochranes," said the Major, "to die in poverty and in exile. But at least I will die somewhere other than Paris. Pah! Paris – a city of death, full of old men and corpses and Frenchmen."

"Paris?" exclaimed Ksenia as she passed back through the room, looking this time for a lantern, and stopping as she heard the old man's apostrophe, "Ah – a fine city, sir. Full of young men and the uniforms of the corps franc. Have you been there?"

"I'd sooner die," spat Major Sinclair bitterly, "than return to Paris!"

"You mark my words," mumbled Yadviga, raised briefly from her devotions by the excited tone of the young widow, "you'll get your wish."

"His brother Archibald, he who sprang the family fortune into the air with his alkalis and coal-tars and other phantasies, he died in poverty in Paris. Not two years since. Do you know—?"

But Yadviga had fallen into a doze and knew nothing. And Ksenia was – inexplicably swiftly and once again – outside, eyes and ears directed down the road that led from the kremlin.

"Cochrane-Johnstone," he repeated loudly. He was Velos, master of ceremonies at the Dance of Death. No one, however, listened – the dancers had other things on their minds. Ksenia had stepped to the front-door and was peering out into the darkness, anxiously listening for the sound of a step, the fall of a foot, the fall of a heavy body into water. Yadviga, exhausted with the endless night, mumbled prayers to the stove.

The announcement continued: "Colonel of the glorious 8th West India Regiment, Brigadier of the Leeward Islands, Governor of Dominica, Member of Parliament." He paused for a moment, listening for memories. "And several other titles, too numerous to mention." Ksenia returned for a shawl to pull over her head, the night was cold; then she ran back to the door. "Major Sinclair, he would say to me, Sinclair, I am the twelfth and final son of the eighth Earl of Dundonald and the brother of the ninth Earl of Dung, Coal-tar and Ruin. Gentlemen, this was my comrade-in-arms, my fellow-Briton, my partner-in-folly: may I present to you Colonel the Honourable Andrew James Charon-Johnstone."

THE EARL OF DUNG, COAL-TAR AND RUIN

Levering himself up on his pillow, he tried to find someone nearby who would be interested in his introduction. There being none, he fell back. The pain had spread throughout his body and burned dully in his head. But the burning was a relief. He succumbed to its flames for a while – minutes it might have been, or nights.

"Cochrane-Johnstone said that Archibald was a fool, and Alexander no better - he died in Paris too, last year, just as I left. One brother, another brother – the third brother cannot have long to go. Well, you will not find me dying in Paris, eh?" Yadviga crackled and hissed. The stove passed no judgement.

"That young Thomas Cochrane, too. It's just a matter of time before he dies. In poverty. In Paris. The fool. Got caught, but tried to remain an honourable gentleman. When you're caught, you don't stand and bluff – you clear out! Much good did it do to complain. Sailor-boy for the Spaniards, and the Greeks, too. Paris beckons, young Thomas, Paris beckons!"

Ksenia popped her head round the door on hearing the repeated shout of the name of the Greek hero, startled by the old man's hectoring tone. But all was once more silent, and she quietly resumed her vigil. There was no sign of Horatio. The dear man could not be dead?

She ran out of the garden and into the road. There was no one in sight. She ran on and on and came within a short while, panic in her breast, to the moat at the foot of the kremlin walls. A faint light trickled down from the moon, and the gentlest of breezes ruffled the stagnant water. She peered this way and that, but could find no up-turned face of a drowned man, nor the floating debris of abandoned provisions. There was a dim lantern up in the walls of the fort, but no one moved. On the road which circled the walls, not a soul, not a dog, not a bat. In despair, now she had missed him on the road, now he had been attacked by robbers, now he had found refuge with the monks, she retraced her flight, as swiftly as she could, to the broken lodge and final resting-place of Major George Sinclair. Horatio was not there. Within, all was once again quiet, apart from the heavy breathing of the old woman and the laboured breathing of the old man.

At the disturbance caused by her arrival, the dying man opened his eyes and continued from where he thought he had left off, no time having passed.

"Thirty years of age," he said, "and there we were. He was Governor of the island of Dominica and all its riches, all its slaves and all its rum, all its women and all the islands. There I was, a Major, but in snug and close with the Colonel. It was all there around us for the taking. Not a bad billet, heh? A ticket to wealth, if only you knew how to use it. The Colonel, he knew how to use it. This was his island to rule as he saw fit, in the name of King George. Admiral Alexander, he had the Leeward Islands – Commander-in-Chief, Admiral, whatever he chose to call himself. He left us alone, to windward and to leeward."

The dying man laughed as only a dying man can: without humour. "And then they court-martialled him! Him? The Governor of Dominica, recalled to London and brought to face charges of corruption? What was it they said? – wrongful arrest of citizens, diverting troops into unpaid labour, embezzlement? – everything they could think of. They have the wrong man, I told him. The man they want to try and judge and hang, he is in Paris! He's in Paris!"

Ksenia popped her head round the door, but said nothing. Yadviga mumbled in her sleep, dreaming of a thousand and one nights in Paradise, with murderous Frenchmen hanging from gibbets and vodka hanging from the trees.

"Aye, said I to the Colonel – Napoleon is the man they want. All that was bad and corrupt and evil in the Windwards and the Leewards came from the revolutionary Frenchmen and their reckless cries of Liberty. Liberty! – the cry of the Frenchman and the end of all Honour. But even Napoleon got a bellyful of Liberty when he saw what the black men were up to. Madam," he cried aloud, turning towards the window and toasting with an invisible bumper, in a horizontal position, "Madam, I give you Toussaint Louverture, Victor Hugues and Léger-Félicité Sonthonax! May they burn in everlasting hell-fire!"

TOUSSAINT LOUVERTURE, VICTOR HUGUES AND LÉGER-FÉLICITÉ SONTHONAX

Satisfied for the moment with this happy remembrance of the villains of the Caribbean, the old military man drank off several bottles of rum, then, with a start, recalled where he was.

"Napoleon – what was she to you? Ah! Amélie!" he exclaimed. Ksenia, despairing of ever seeing Horatio again, returned to the dying man's bedside, thinking that no doubt he had called for her. "Amélie, is that you?" With a desperate and clumsy lunge, he tried to raise himself and embrace the young woman. She was too quick for him, and he subsided. "My dear girl," he was at last able to continue, "widowed so young. So beautiful and so fragile."

Ksenia patted the old man's dry hand for his unexpected condolences.

"Her father was doubtless an honourable man, but he died of the fevers."

"Alas," sighed Ksenia, "my first father died when I was young. My second father died soon after I left home. I shall never see his kind face again."

"And her mother, gone in the night."

"Oh no," protested Ksenia, "I am certain that my mother still lives."

"And then she married that young man – what was his name? – ah, her marriage, aged fifteen, or sixteen, it was the talk of all the parlours from Martinique to St Eustatius!"

"May St Eustatius come down among us and distribute among us his many blessings," prayed Yadviga unnecessarily, forgetting that Novgorod was already over-crowded with Saints of every persuasion and skill, and unlikely to welcome one who had never shown his face there in eight hundred years of trade.

"What was his name—?"

"John," replied Ksenia tenderly, a lump growing in her throat. "He died of a fever."

"Godet, yes," remembered Major Sinclair. "Désiré Godet – he died young, also of the fevers. And she the young widow, only twenty years old, helpless, and with a young son to look after."

"Alas," sighed Ksenia Ivanovna, placing her small hands upon her stomach, "there was no child."

"You needed a military man to take care of you."

"Any man," agreed the young widow with some emphasis, "I thought a military man would do. But one who did not wander."

"The world was dangerous, you were an orphan."

"My parents were at the other end of the world: I was like an orphan."

"Madame: I, not the Colonel, would make you my wife."

"Sir," said Ksenia regretfully, "I cannot allow you to do that. But I thank you for your proposal."

"But the Colonel, not I, prevailed: they were married, on the twenty-first day of February. Thirty years ago."

Ksenia sat back, puzzled. It was now clear to her that she was not the grieving young widow under discussion.

"Amélie," said the old man, a look in his eyes suggestive of admiration, "you had the beauty of all of the islands in you, the cool aspect of European nobility when you walked under the trees, and, so I was told, the vigour in bed of a—"

Ksenia threw her hands to her ears, and did not hear more. By this act of propriety, she failed to learn what 'Love' is: it is the exploitation of beauty, whether the beauty be inward or outward, by one whose soul has nothing of nobility.

Unable to sit still any longer, and finding herself the victim of a false identification, Ksenia now eased herself up from the bed and silently hurried once more to the door of the lodge. Believing that Amélie had a second time slipped away from his grasp, the Major fell to a consideration of the Cochranes who persisted in dying in poverty in Paris.

"Archibald: that man was a wastrel. Nothing excited him more than digging for coal and setting fire to his manufactories. All the Cochrane's wealth was sunk in him, and he squandered it all. All he needed to do was go to war like the rest of us, and he could have burned all the gas he wanted. What is war for, if not to make a fortune, I ask you that?"

Despite the importance of the question, no one answered.

"Archibald – Paris, poverty, dead. His brother, Admiral Sir Alexander Forrester Inglis Cochrane, so proud of his exploits in the American War, so proud of his sorties against the French. He said the Americans bred the French, and he was right in that at least. So proud of all his sons and nephews, so disappointed in all his brothers. Disappointed." The Major savoured the word – he repeated it – it contained all the world in its four syllables – a good British word: the French had shrugged it off in two syllables – décu – he had found superficial. "Commander-in-Chief of this, Governor of that: but where did it get him? Paris, poverty, dead. Disappointed in himself, I expect. And now that young Lord Thomas inherits Dundonald's debts, or has paid them off with his Chilean and Brazilian gold. And my Colonel Cochrane-Johnstone – he dreamed of everything, was left with nothing. Paris, poverty, probably dead." Sinclair paused, running out of words.

Yadviga, whose dreams ran more frequently around the matter of food and drink, and rarely around Chilean gold or Greek heroes, woke up suddenly feeling cold. She peered around crossly. Of course it was cold: the door was standing wide open. That idle young woman was nowhere to be seen. Neither was that useless lump who could not carry out a simple errand without getting drowned, or lost, or worse. She heaved herself with a curse from the stove, and shuffled to the front door. She reached it, asked irritably whether the night was not already full of death, did they want another one on their hands? – just in case the young people were standing outside staring like calves at the moon – then pushed the door shut.

Scarcely had the door made contact with the crumbling wood of the frame, than it flew open again and in burst Ksenia Ivanovna, crying, "He's back, he's back!" without even trying to conceal her delight in the presence of mortality. She pushed past Yadviga, hurrying to light another candle, and to pile wood into the stove. As she so busied herself, Horatio entered, not so cold as Ksenia imagined, but in need of a simple warmth that she alone – so he had imagined this past hour – could provide.

The new disturbance roused Major Sinclair from his drowsy reflection. "But the Admiral's son Charles was made of even less enterprising material," he began.

"HE EMBARKED ON THE LIFE OF A TROUBADOUR."

20

HE FOUND THE LIFE OF A TROUBADOUR MOST DESIRABLE.

"I have here," announced Horatio, proudly displaying the fruits of his daring enterprise, "eight pickled eggs, four cucumbers and a large bottle of spirits. I did not drop any of them. Except once, and that was merely a cucumber."

Carefully, and with a smile that fully rewarded his journey into the night and compensated for the dubious companionship of Mr. Karamzin and trade-practices of Mr. Voronov, Ksenia Ivanovna brought relief to Horatio. Having placed his burdens down upon the rickety table, she pulled him to the stove and began to warm his bear-like hands with her own. Disregarding the fact that this tender exercise made no difference to the coldness of his hands, which were in any case barely cold, Horatio considered staying there for the rest of his life. The clock in the citadel struck twelve times, for no reason that anyone could think of – not the dying man, who heard the twelve shots of the cannon upon Guadeloupe – not Yadviga, who had un-corked the bottle to ensure that not a drop had been spilled and had taken twelve sips as substantiation – not Ksenia, who heard her heart pound twelve times with emotion – not Horatio, who was listening rather to the sound of twelve words in his head, stating that he who asked what Love was, must already know what it was. Or was it that he who asked what love was, would never know what it was? Or he who needed to ask another, was better advised to ask himself? Or that—?

"You! – have I not asked you twelve times already," repeated Yadviga in a voice that was cracked with exhaustion and smacked of petulance, "did you bring no bread?"

Horatio indicated with a nod of his head the right-hand pocket of his coat. He dared not release his hands from the chains that held him. A prisoner of Liberty maybe, but he would not be liberated from his prison. Yadviga cursed the folly of the pair, and, with the practised hands of a nurse, dug unceremoniously into the coat pocket, wrestled with whatever she found there, and finally pulled out the few crusts of bread that Mr. Voronov had wrapped in a cabbage-leaf. Uttering words of condemnation upon both scheming and dreaming fools, she turned away to take a full inventory of the night's feast – and prepare a last meal for her patient, perhaps – or at least to ensure that not a drop of spirit escaped.

"When my first husband returned to me in Irkutsk," remembered Ksenia Ivanovna, "he brought me the fur of two silvery seals from Lake Baikhal."

Horatio now regretted that he had only managed to acquire eight pickled eggs. Against the fur of a silvery seal, it seemed but little.

"But more than that, he brought companionship, for Society – the ladies, the military and the merchants of wealth – had all left Irkutsk a week previously to visit the hot baths of Verchney Udinsk, or the fair at Kiakhta. Irkutsk, without Society, is a dull place."

Horatio had heard of places without Society, and could not imagine how dull they were; rather, he thought, how peaceful, full of balm for the soul. He made a mental note of Irkutsk.

"Which month was this that you describe?" he asked tentatively.

"February," she replied. "Dull and very cold."

"And your husband," asked Horatio discreetly, "did he – was he also very cold? Did he have sufficient clothing?"

Ksenia Ivanovna smiled. "When my husband went off on his own explorations, he never complained of the cold. Men's faces might crack and bleed from frost, rivers turn to stone, but my husband was always warm enough. Even when the temperature fell to 30 and 35 degrees below the freezing point of Monsieur Réaumur, he wore naught but his ordinary clothes – shoes, worsted stockings, coat, waistcoat, trousers and hat. Gloves never graced his hands."

"But you mentioned that he once felt the cold worse than yourself," protested Horatio.

"Oh no," said she, remembering with some heat, "he felt the cold only when he was with me."

"Oh," echoed Horatio, remembering with coolness an earlier explanation.

"When one is in Siberia," she noted warmly, "one is frequently cold."

"In February," said Horatio.

"Exactly," agreed Ksenia.

"And your husband—?"

"He left me."

Horatio gazed down upon her in stark horror. "He left you alone, far from your home, in February?" he repeated. What graceless character of man was this, who strode off, almost naked, into the frozen wastes, leaving a pretty young wife behind?

"You must understand, sir," said Ksenia Ivanovna in a tone that signalled to Horatio a slight lowering of the temperature, perhaps by one or two degrees of Réaumur. Horatio understood the thermometry of Mijnher Fahrenheit and Master Celsius to be of greater interest to some Russian philosophers, but as to the conversion of measurements from one of these scales – the zero of both the Swede Celsius and the Frenchman Réaumur being the freezing-point of water, which for the Dutchman stood at 32 – incomprehensible unless one understood that Fahrenheit took the freezing-point of salt-water to be his zero, understandably from a man of Holland, land of pickled herring – while the boiling point of water stood at 100, 80 and 212 degrees respectively – to convert from one another was not something to be undertaken lightly at dead of night in Novgorod. However, 35 degrees of cold in Réaumur did look to be very cold indeed, it was perhaps—

FAHRENHEIT AND PICKLED HERRING

"Are you at all interested, sir, in what I have to say?" demanded Ksenia Ivanovna, seizing the opportunity to release those hands from their imprisonment. Her dark eyes threatened anger. "Or are you content to dream the night away? If you wish me to keep quiet, please do not be afraid to ask."

Horatio felt the thin ice on which he stood crack dangerously. In one instant, he would fall through, and all life would pass away in two or three breaths. "I'm sorry," said he quickly, "I did not mean to seem uninterested. I am interested. I was calculating merely how cold one might be in Siberia."

"And have I not just told you?" enquired the young widow, frostily.

"Yes, but –" Horatio stood miserably, thinking of nothing he could say.

Ksenia repented immediately of her coolness, seeing a man weaken before her eyes. "He left me to travel, as I said, to the borders of China. He was two months gone. On the occasion of my birthday, he was almost dashed to pieces by a horse. But he then returned to me, safe and whole."

Horatio mumbled gloomily at this. Aloud, however, he said: "And no doubt he rested well after his expedition?"

"Oh no," said Ksenia lightly, laughing. "My husband was not one to rest. Scarce was he through the door than he went back out again to arrange a sledge to take us further west."

Horatio, in the same position, would never have left the shelter of home and wife again. Never. He had plans to sit holding the hand of his wife in a small garden or orchard, and listen every day to the humming of the bees and watch them in the blossoms.

"He stayed only two days in Irkutsk, and then we were off to Nizhney Udinsk, where the temperature was 32 degrees below freezing."

Horatio fought manfully against the temptation.

"It was cold and most of the inhabitants of Nizhney Udinsk were drunk."

"All I can say is that is disgusting," said Yadviga in sharp disapproval, shaking her head at the three-quarters empty bottle.

"The mayor, however, was proud to tell us that his father was a cockney shoemaker, and we were well-treated. It was a blessing sometimes to be subjects of the British King."

"Long live King George," muttered the dying man, ears sharp enough for any words that resonated. "And give me a drink."

Yadviga being otherwise occupied, Ksenia hurried forward with a cup of water. Outraged at the taste, the old man pushed her away, screaming "A drink, woman, a drink!" Horatio seized the bottle from the lips of Yadviga – threw the water from the cup and poured some of the spirits in – handed the cup to Ksenia – Ksenia offered it the old man – the old man sighed with satisfaction – Yadviga fought for breath against disbelief and outrage – Ksenia returned the bottle to

Horatio – Horatio re-positioned the bottle at Yadviga's lips – she recovered rapidly.

"God save him!" announced the old man. Ksenia understood this to be a vote of thanks to Horatio, for his charity, and smiled prettily upon him. Horatio wished for none of that man's good wishes, but quenched his anger under the sparkling fountain of the young widow's smile. The bottle now being returned to her, Yadviga crossed herself and invoked the patron saints of good spirits.

"My dear husband thought that I would find Moscow a most delightful place," said Ksenia. "It was of interest. I kept my enthusiasm for better things, however."

Horatio nodded sagely. He, of all people, knew what it was to keep oneself for better things. He had kept himself thus, so far, well.

"Is it not astonishing," said Ksenia, now seated at Horatio's side, keeping two bodies warm, "that in Moscow, when we finally arrived there, we met a fellow-officer of the Royal Navy? This gentleman proposed to walk into Siberia upon the same roads as we had travelled."

Horatio was astonished – not so much by the chance meeting of two British officers in Moscow – more so by the implausibility of two men having lost their senses in exactly the same way. Was it perhaps an effect of the recent wars? Or was it in the discipline of warriors at sea, that they should risk death upon land? Never, he suddenly realised, had he met so many Royal Navy officers, as in Russia. He was not permitted to pursue this thought, for Ksenia was looking closely at him.

"Astonishing, indeed," he exclaimed hurriedly. "Did the Naval gentleman understand the perils which awaited him?"

"Indeed not," said Ksenia sadly, "for the man was blind."

Horatio pondered this unexpected news for several moments.

"Blind?" he asked cautiously.

"Quite blind," sighed Ksenia.

"And yet, being blind, he proposed to travel across Siberia. But what would he hope to see there?"

"Alas, he would see nothing and yet feel everything."

"Like a man in love," thought Horatio to himself.

"Like a woman in her drink," hoped the old man.

"Like a man in the grave," said Yadviga, with every evidence of enthusiasm.

"My husband thought that Lieutenant Holman, being blind, might as well go to Siberia as anywhere else, for he would see just as much. Nevertheless, he tried to persuade the Lieutenant that in Siberia there is so little to be seen even by those who have use of their eyes, that there was little point in a man, having no eyes, travelling there."

In this, and perhaps in this alone, Horatio found himself in full agreement with the young woman's late husband.

"And could the Lieutenant's companions not dissuade him?" asked Horatio, in all innocence.

"Sir, he travelled alone."

Horatio was struck forcibly by the enormity of this revelation. "But the poor man would surely never return from such a journey?"

Ksenia nodded. "Indeed, sir, that was my thought too. Nevertheless," she added, struck by a happy memory, "my husband was kind enough to give Lieutenant Holman some letters of introduction, bequeathed him our carriage and our Cossack, and wished him well."

A HAPPY MEMORY

"Then there is perhaps hope that the Lieutenant will return home safely," said Horatio with a baseless charity which surprised him.

"I believe he did," said Ksenia with some measure of coolness. "He was displeased with my husband. He had experienced some adversity in Siberia, it seems."

Horatio considered this. "Then," he judged, "Mr. Holman would be wise never to venture forth again."

"As," said Ksenia, "I thought my husband would do, once we had settled in London."

At the mere mention of the capital of the Empire, the Colonel groaned and announced that he must once again piss. No one paid any attention – Yadviga had a more pressing concern – Horatio had gone deaf in his right ear, the one nearest the window – Ksenia Ivanovna was walking down Regent Street.

"We took rooms in Kensington, and my husband settled

immediately to the publication of his narrative. It would, he thought, make his name as an explorer, and allow us to raise a family in some comfort. Mr. Murray was kind enough to publish my husband's book in 1823, and I am told that it has been printed many times since then. Even, I am told, by those who have travelled in Europe, has it been translated into German, Dutch and French. My husband would now be a famous man, I believe." There was occasion for a sigh. "Had it not been for the Royal Society, I think he would still be at my side."

"Ah," said Horatio, in a tone of sudden comprehension, "did the Society kill him? I have heard such things of secret societies—"

"No, sir, they did worse than that," exclaimed the young widow, "they ignored him. He had sent the Society a long letter from Kolyma, describing the coastline of north and east Siberia, which Captain Burney had so falsely described—"

"Burney?" asked Horatio puzzled, "I have not met him."

"Burney is not a man I have met either, sir," said Ksenia, "and I do not wish ever to do so, for the Royal Society took Mr. Burney's word over that of my husband – my husband, who had walked there, who had talked to Baron Wrangel himself – over Mr. Burney, who had barely stirred from his ship and talked only to fools!" Horatio admired her flushed face, and gently drew a shaken dark curl to one side of her face to cool her down.

"Thank you, sir," she said quietly as an aside. "The Royal Society chose to ignore my husband's letter. He was obliged to take issue with them in his book. They ignored him again. In a rage, he took ship for Colombia to prospect for gold and copper. It was, he said as he left me the first time, more profitable."

"You were, madam, left alone in London?" asked Horatio in a low voice.

The Colonel moaned quietly.

"In London, yes. Colombia was no place for a lady."

"So I have heard."

"It was no matter: what is 'Love', sir, but the ability to wait forever for the return of the loved one?"

Horatio pondered this universal truth. He found it wanting in some respects. A faithful man, such as himself, would wait forever for a woman of such virtues; but that a woman of such virtues should wait forever for a faithless man such as her first husband – this seemed but a hollow proposition.

"And in Colombia, then, he died?" he asked, steeling himself for the reply, for he knew by now he could only be wrong.

"Not then. He returned, after less than a year. I held him in my arms. And then he set off once more for South America, and on the twelfth day of August he was dead. I waved farewell and never saw him again alive." There followed several passages of grief, timed only by the crackling stove and the heavy breathing of Yadviga.

"John went into Colombia and his cousin Charles came out," the widow said at last.

Horatio's mind reeled. Cousin Charles? Had he missed something? Had he fallen asleep? What was he to say? Wisely, he said nothing at all.

Ksenia explained. "Charles had been in Colombia for two years, and arrived home in the month of May in the year 1824. He closeted himself with my husband in a coffee-house. My husband was excited at the prospect of copper. Or perhaps it was the mountains and the jungle?" She shook her head, to clear it of her husband's dreams. "Within the month, he was off. When he returned six months later, he talked of copper and Simon Bolivar, of flesh-eating fish and of croco-diles, of poisonous frogs and precipitous mountains, of the admirable life of savages and – very frequently – the avarice of inn-keepers."

At that precise moment, the door was pushed open with a great shriek of the rusty hinges.

MR. VORONOV MADE ENTRY.

21

LORD BYRON SWAM THE HELLESPONT, AND JOHN COCHRANE THE OKHOTA.

"I had failed, through the avarice of savages, in my purpose of getting across to the opposite continent. So I determined to proceed to Okhotsk, by the direct route, for I wished to avoid re-tracing my steps through two thousand miles of sameness. And I was amply rewarded for my determination, for the hardest day's work was followed by the happiest evening, and the soundest sleep as I lay down on my snow pillow."

John Dundas Cochrane R.N., trapped below deck on a ship – the Frolic perhaps, as it failed once more to make the perilous harbour of La Guayra – a ship which was holed and slowly disappearing beneath the dark green shifting waters, consoled himself with the memory of his greatest triumph: the astonishing journey that he made from the Frozen Sea of the North to the shores of the Pacific Ocean.

"On the 27th day of March 1821, I left Nizhney Kolymsk, heading south for the port of Okhotsk. I travelled in some style, in a sledge drawn by no fewer than thirteen dogs, which took me 180 miles in three days. Not long afterwards, I changed my sledge for a horse, and I met a wolf. It was large and grey, and my horse nearly threw me at the encounter. A bit horse dreads a wolf – the one I rode had so suffered. But no harm was done. We continued. At Sredne Kolymsk, I met my old friend Peter Trechekov once more, and there awaited a fresh Cossack, who was ordered to attend me through to Okhotsk, which lay some six hundred miles ahead. Of course, the one who was selected was useless: he was love-sick. His sickness nearly proved his own ruin, and mine."

At the thought of love, John Cochrane released the breath that had built up inside him against the watery death at sea. As the bubbles burst out and exploded to the pitiless surface of the waves, he felt the tug of the bottom of the sea and floated easily downwards. He remained silent for a good five minutes thereafter, admiring the shafts of light that penetrated, as in a cool and dark cathedral, to the depths. His silence was like the pearl within a shell, the shell under the sand, the sand under the sea and the sea under an endless heaven. He had, perhaps, felt the sickness of love, but not in the same way as that foolish young Cossack.

With that determination, he breathed deeply once, and hiccoughed.

"In a place named Kasachey," Cochrane continued at last, shaking off these unwelcome thoughts of love and sickness, "I met a Cossack's daughter who was much afflicted with hiccoughs, or dieaval ootra, as the Yakuti termed it – the devil in the belly, le diable au corps, sir. It was a sad case, for she hiccoughed all night, and deprived all, herself included, of sleep. I have seen bad cases of it. The parties afflicted by it are generally most delicate and interesting in their appearance but it is seldom that the individual is cured. In females, it prevails to such an extent as utterly to prevent pregnancy. It is a most melancholy illness, and one of several complaints which much plague the Yakuti.

"It was still winter as we travelled, and many times we found our-selves struggling in deep snow; once, we spent an hour digging our horses from the snow, only for the beasts to run off without us or our baggage, abandoning us in a dreary cold waste. The road was scarcely a good one. And so we struggled on: myself, my milk-sop Cossack and a jovial Yakuti guide, to the next yourte and sent back for our baggage. In that part of Siberia," observed Cochrane, on the matter of roads, "when there is much snow on the road, then there is more labour; and when there is no snow, there is much water; and when there is just a little snow, there is much ice and more danger.

A MILK-SOP COSSACK AND A JOVIAL YAKUTI GUIDE

"We soon entered the mountains, bold and perpendicular. The rivers we frequently had to cross were torrents of freezing water, with ice piled high on either side. The horses had great difficulty in crossing them; my guide was blind from the glare of the sun upon snow; and my Cossack was afflicted with severe diarrhoea, brought on from want of food – until then, we had eaten partridge and other game from traps; but this soon failed us, and my Cossack was unwilling to eat horse-meat.

"By day, the temperature reached eighty degrees of Fahrenheit, which melted the surface of the snow; and by night, the surface froze again; so that we were walking over fields of ice. We camped in the most inhospitable valleys you can ever have seen – without grass, moss, shrub, tree, drift-wood: just slate. We ate our rations of frozen horse-meat and biscuit. The Cossack grew so weak that I had to lash him to the horse for each day's journey. At length, we stopped at a yourte for five days, to see if I could restore the Cossack; I failed in that attempt. I departed therefore with another Yakuti guide – a great glutton, stupid, obstinate and immovably lazy."

John Cochrane paused for reflection. "One might think," he said, "that all Yakuti are bone-idle and insatiable. It is an impression I seem to have in my Journal. Indeed, sir, many of them were. But, as in all society, many were not. In the event, I could not refuse the man's company, as he was the only one with any knowledge of the route I desired to take. By day he led me across the mountains in wind and snow; by night he would comfort himself with twenty pounds of horse-meat. On the fifth day, we ascended a stupendous path, almost of bare rock and so slippery that the horses frequently fell. We were reduced to cutting steps in the ice for ourselves, then hauling baggage up the slopes, and finally letting it down the other side. In the evening, our Cossack caught up with us, having recovered a little from his illness. On the following day, we had to do the same again, but this time we also had to haul up the horses and let them down the other side. For this, we made a staircase by hacking out with axes and strewing the steps with ice; my Cossack and I would haul the horse by its bridle, while the brutish guide would push the beast from behind. In this way, with all the horses we required for transport, and a fresh load of meat from those we did not require, we managed to arrive on the far side of the mountains.

"We came now to the valley formed by the mighty river Indigarka, and every stream, every river we crossed, rapidly flowed into it. My brutish guide was now so negligent and useless, that I was compelled to desire my Cossack to flog him with his own whip. He did so. This cowed the fellow for several days, allowing us to

TO FLOG HIM WITH
HIS OWN WHIP

cross open and agreeable country, which showed numerous traces of quadrupeds. We were frequently obliged to wade, chest-deep, across rivers, and when we did not wade, we swam; and when we did not swim, we walked. In this way, we reached the first habitations of the Omekon district, where I promptly discharged my guide, and pressed on – for if we delayed even a day there, we would have been trapped by the melting waters. The people here, I must add, combined in their own breasts humanity, justice and common-sense; and the young women were good-looking.

"I remained three days in the Omekon, where I abandoned my Cossack, who had relapsed into ill-health and despondency. With another guide, and a young lad, I set off south, visiting various villages and local princes as I went. Each was more determined than the last that I should not attempt the journey to Okhotsk in such a season: they said I should wait a month, until the waters would subside. I was HE WAS HAVING having none of it, and continued my journey, now on foot, NONE OF IT now on horseback. We came to another range of mountains, where we were assailed by a hurricane and heavy rains, and melting snow. On the fourth day, we had but one day's meat left; at four in the morning, the temperature stood at thirteen degrees of frost by Réaumur and at noon, seventy-three of heat of Fahrenheit."

Someone groaned. "Spare me your figures, sir," came the complaint.

"It is a great wilderness, sir," replied Cochrane calmly, "and the greatness of it is that it tests a man more than anything else in the world."

"More than war?" demanded one voice in quarrelsome manner.

"More than bankruptcy?" asked another, rubbing two coins together.

"More than slavery?" said a third sceptically.

"More than childbirth?" a fourth groaned.

"I would," repeated Cochrane equably, "state that a wilderness tests a man more than anything else in the world. Childbirth, I can say nothing of, but I doubt that it tests a man at all, and is therefore no concern of mine.

"At last," he continued, since no further objection was raised, "to lighten the load, I burned all my spare clothing and bedding.

"We reached our goal, the river Okhota, which was full of shoals and rapids, and may be declared useless. It was confined by beautiful natural quays of crystal ice, and roared from the velocity of its current. As we continued our melancholy route, we fell in with two white bears bound for the north; but fear, on both sides, kept us apart. At length, after running out of food entirely, and losing a horse to the river, we reached a fording place. The horses could not have crossed while loaded, so we unloaded them and they swam over. I then fastened a piece of wood to my waist, as buoyancy, and swam across. It was so cold that I lost all feeling in every limb. I threw off my clothes and took violent exercise to restore animation. It had been no wide crossing – barely fifteen yards – yet I barely accomplished it. Lord Byron swam the Hellespont, and John Cochrane the Okhota. Of the two feats, mine was surely the most difficult; his lordship was neither fatigued, hungry nor cold, nor compelled to his undertaking; while I had each and all of those evils to contend with."

"Lord Byron, as I recall," interrupted the second voice, "was also a—"

"Sir!" hissed Cochrane, "There may be ladies present!

"We followed the river for several days, obliged to cross and re-cross it, to stop and dry our clothes, to find berries in the forest to eat. We came at length to the junction of the Arka and Okhota rivers, which were so much swollen that we could go no further. It was imperative that we should cross the torrents, but impossible that we could. To starve on one side of the river, be drowned in it, or die upon the other side: all seemed alike to me. We therefore felled some timber, and I constructed a raft. It is a skill that all Navy men learn. All of our baggage and persons were loaded upon the raft, which was tied together with thongs made from leather bags; and we descended the river in a most astonishing manner, giddy and without accident, for some distance, until – alas! – we were wrecked upon a fallen tree. The raft turned over completely, bringing the baggage under water, and then emerged on the other side, with my two companions clinging to it; they fetched up against a small island in the middle of the stream. For my part, I was left hanging upon the branches of the tree; my body was sucked under the water, leaving only my head and arms free. I managed to gain the top of the tree, but, a branch giving way below me, was thrown upon the island myself. To remain upon the island was to invite Death; but again with the help of nautical ingenuity, I turned the raft into a semblance of a bridge – of whose design I am most proud, by the way – and we crossed to the far bank without further mishap. Except that I was again thrown into the river. It was fortunate that my companions were able to pull me out.

"From that short ducking, my clothes became like a firm casing of ice. We had immediate recourse to flint and steel, to produce a fire; which we did so well, I should add, that, in an instant, the entire forest caught aflame and was soon raging around us. We almost perished in the fire. Fortunately, we were able to contain the flames, which action had the added benefit of drying us out thoroughly. And thus we arrived, after seventy-five days of effort, in the third week of the month of June, at the town of Okhotsk, by the North Pacific Ocean."

HIS CLOTHES BECAME LIKE A FIRM CASING OF ICE

He paused, to gather strength, to gather memories, to gather an argument which had not yet been aired.

"The governor of Okhotsk," he continued, "Mr. Vladimir Ushinsky, than whom I have never found a better man, had long been expecting me, and had continued to expect me until he heard that I had left Yakutsk for the Kolyma; and then, to use his own expression, 'he gave me up for lost'. He gave me up for lost."

He paused once more, the better to approach the subject.

"Ha!" he exclaimed.

"Ha!" he uttered, a second time.

"Ha!" he voiced finally.

In the face of this trebly-repeated protestation, the darkness held its breath.

"He gave me up for lost? It is my opinion, sir, that one half of the difficulties, and nearly all the dangers and exposures, to which travellers in any climate are most commonly subjected, are the result of either their own physical incompetence or want of prudential foresight. I, sir, would never embark upon a journey for which I was not fully prepared; as a result, I have always reached my goal without mishap." John Cochrane reviewed all of his adventures in righteous indignation for several moments. And then he continued: "If a similar, and apparently difficult journey, were left open again for me to perform, I would not think once of refusing it. He gave me up for lost? He knew me not. Why, sir, if I were offered passage to Africa tomorrow, I would bid my family farewell and be ready in six hours! Why, sir, if I can traverse the Andes for the benefit of mankind and – in the event of my success – to my own advantage, I am ready now!"

With these defiant words, Cochrane found himself emerging head and shoulders above the spuming waves, his lungs bursting. He was greatly relieved, but not disconcerted.

"I did utter these sentiments at Okhotsk in the presence of Captain Ushinsky; I uttered them again in England in the face of Mr. Barrow; I utter them now, conscious that

"MY SPIRIT IS INCAPABLE OF DECEIT IN THIS AFFAIR."

THEY PICK UP A PEN AND CAST
DOWN AUTOCRACY.

Mr. Voronov glanced around the assembled company, then gave utterance to a sentiment which contained no fewer than three deceits: "I could not let my guests watch alone over an old friend."

The young widow offered the kind-hearted inn-keeper her seat. He turned it down courteously, and offered a further untruth to the dying man. "My wife, Colonel your Excellency," he addressed Major Sinclair, "My wife urged me to come along and pay my respects."

Major Sinclair nodded and smiled, his mind trotting down some sun-dappled track on a Caribbean island. Mr. Voronov understood the response to be a gracious recognition of his wife's fictitious concern.

Horatio noticed that Mr. Voronov wore his night-cap, and was shivering. He made no remark. Yadviga, even more perceptive, noticed that Mr. Voronov had brought along another bottle of spirits – it was once again desperately needed, the previous one having developed a leak. It was indeed a mystery, that a bottle with no cracks and with a sound seal could nevertheless be drained of its contents, with no human intervention. A mystery and – in this saintly city – a miracle. With the solemn ease of a celebrant, Yadviga relieved Mr. Voronov of his burden. The latter relieved himself of his night-cap and stuffed it into a pocket. Horatio, relieved that he had no further reason to pay a nocturnal visit to the inn, fed the stove.

"I fear I have broken into a conversation?" said Mr. Voronov mildly, as a way of breaking the silence which had once more descended on the small party.

Horatio debated how he should respond. He had a generous contribution to make to a discussion on the avarice of inn-keepers. But it seemed churlish to do so now. Indeed, Mr. Voronov had brought along some knuckles of ham. It was thus possible for Yadviga, by the application of expert measurement firmly established on scientific principles, to ration out the spirits against the knuckles. The result of her transactions was a determination that, should there be no further excitement, she could see herself fairly to the end of the night. She commenced without delay to prove the accuracy of her estimation by pragmatical means – she made no immediate contribution to the exchange between inn-keeper and her messenger-boy.

Ksenia heard a bell-tower ring once, only, solemnly, ponderously, without hope of response, as if the world and all its scurrying creatures had already died, somewhere far out below the vast flat expanse of the stars. The night had reached its true dead centre. In the centre of the night lay the true centre of her feelings. A girl – leaving her family at the age of fifteen, to wander across half the world with a man twice her age – abandoned for months – widowed too soon – obliged to return to Russia; a woman – and now, alone, travel-weary, with no desire to see what was beyond the horizon – thrown by one broken wheel of fortune against a man whose devotion could probably be sounded in nautical miles rather than in fathoms, whose adoration – were he ever to state it even once – was to be measured in leagues rather than versts, whose passion was to be measured in degrees of Réaumur rather than Celsius: what else was she to feel? She could feel no bitterness. She felt only a strong, deep-running need to stop and be stopped, to hold and be held, to offer all and to be given all in return. 'Love' is survival, but it needs to be asked for: she will ask Horatio.

Horatio replied, quite at hazard: "In the Caribbean Islands," he stated, "almost every island is named after a saint."

Ksenia's attention was immediately diverted. Mr. Voronov merely looked confused.

"As many islands as there are churches in Novgorod the Great," continued our West Indian hagiographer. An assertion which was soon exposed as shamefully false. Horatio counted off on his fingers the saints of the islands: "St Lucia, St Vincent, St Kitts, St Nevis—"

"Do not tell me that these are saints?" exclaimed Yadviga, outraged at the foreign names. "What of—?"

"—St Thomas, St John, St George—"

"—ah, that is better." The Orthodoxy of Russia was propitiated.

"—St Croix, St Martin, St Eustatius—"

"At last, the blessed St Eustatius!" breathed Yadviga with a pious swig at the bottle, forgetful that that saint had been canonized in Novgorod barely one hour previously.

"—St Christopher and St Barthelemy. That is sufficient."

"And there is no St Peter or St Paul?" queried Ksenia, after a pause.

"I regret," said Horatio, in Gallic manner.

"No St Theodore, neither St Boris nor St Gleb?"

"I regret," repeated the apologist for the Caribbean saints, disappointing in number.

Her silence told Horatio all that he needed to know of Ksenia's view of the gathered saints of the western ocean. He feared that there were far fewer islands there than there were churches here. Greater, by far, was Novgorod.

GREATER, BY FAR, WAS NOVGOROD

"I was born on the island of Guadeloupe," he continued.

"Not another heathen saint?" demanded Yadviga, bridling up at the mere possibility.

"None such."

"Just as well, you mark my words."

"Although it is named after Our Lady of Guadalupe of Extremadura in the country of Spain."

"Well, that is no help."

"The Blessed Virgin of Guadalupe?"

"All I can say is there is no such person in such a place."

"I thought not."

"Get on with your story."

He obliged.

"On Guadeloupe—" he began.

Mr. Voronov stopped him in his tracks. "Hold it there!" said the inn-keeper, his brow furrowed by more-than-common concern. "This Guadeloupe, is it in Ethiopia?"

"Not at all," said Horatio. "It is in the West Indies, in the Sea of the Caribbean."

"No!" said Mr. Voronov, shaking his head.

"On Guadeloupe—" continued Horatio.

"It is just," interrupted Mr. Voronov, unwilling to concede the point, "that black men come from Ethiopia."

"Black men come indeed from Ethiopia and many other places in Africa," confirmed the blackest man that Mr. Voronov had ever seen. Ksenia Ivanovna remembered her vision of the Devil, and wondered why the Devil was to be thought of as black. Could he not as well be blue, or some colour that men were not? There were, as far as she knew – and she had shared her bed with a man who claimed intimacy with all the native peoples of the world – no blue men. Brown, black, white, pink, red, yellow: not blue, except when cold. Or perhaps the Devil is translucent? He could be all around and never be seen, he could stand in front of one man and one would think the person thus covered was the sinner, not the Devil himself.

"But," continued Horatio, unaware of this colourful and colourless theological diversion, "black men also come from the West Indies."

"And from London and Paris and St Petersburg," added Ksenia, who had travelled in Europe.

Such a wide provenance of black men gave the inn-keeper pause for thought. The world was sometimes quite beyond his comprehension. "It is just," he said – but then thought better of it. "No – you are permitted to continue."

"On Guadeloupe," continued Horatio, "the French abolished slavery. As a result, my family was sold to a man on Dominica."

There was a sharp drawing in of breath through the teeth of both Yadviga and Mr. Voronov. But neither said a word. Major Sinclair exhaled softly, the word: "Dominica," sailing on his breath.

"On Dominica, we continued to live as slaves. But on Guadeloupe, slaves lived for a while as free men. Until Napoleon decided that black men should not necessarily be given all the rights of the white man. He re-introduced slavery. Liberty was not for us."

Horatio paused for a few moments. Mr. Voronov pondered liberty, and found it greatly wanting in orthodoxy. Ksenia Ivanovna pondered slavery, and found it greatly wanting in justice. Major Sinclair considered Dominica, and found it greatly wanting in profit.

"Have you heard," our second Moor of St Petersburg asked the assembled company, "the names of Toussaint-Louverture, of Magloire Pélage, of Louis Delgrès?"

None had. Yadviga wondered only whether the first-mentioned might be some un-Russian holy man.

"Men of liberty," said Horatio boldly. "Black and white."

"Both black and white?" asked Ksenia Ivanovna, intrigued. She had heard of piebald children from the West Indies.

PIEBALD CHILDREN   "No, my dear lady," corrected Horatio gently. "Monsieur Delgrès was white, the other two were not. It matters not – their true colour was that of liberty."

Oh, thought Ksenia: then the colour of the Devil is that of boredom, of hatred, of temptation, of resignation. And I, she considered further, followed no Devil through an open door, I followed a man of integrity.

"These black men, at least, were Ethiopian?" asked Mr. Voronov pointedly.

"Once they were, now they are not," answered Horatio. This was not helpful. Mr. Voronov found his head spinning. He took the trouble to say so. Yadviga offered him a small sip of spirits and the least appetising knuckle of ham to bring him back to equilibrium.

"The Revolution in France brought equal rights to the Frenchmen of the Caribbean. But on Guadeloupe, where, if you recall, I was born—?"

Ksenia Ivanovna nodded encouragingly at him: she, at least, had forgotten nothing.

"—the French masters decided that there should be no equality for the black man. They declared independence from France. They brought back their own laws. The slaves rebelled. The French masters turned to Britain for salvation. Britain took the island from the French. Napoleon sent a new governor. Guadeloupe became French again. The slaves rebelled. Napoleon grew worried. He sent an army. Slavery was introduced again."

Horatio paused for breath. The history of Guadeloupe was not an easy one. He had only covered half a dozen years so far.

"These men you mentioned," hinted Ksenia Ivanovna, anxious not to lose the thread. "Toussaint-Louverture and Monsieur Delgrès? They were from Guadeloupe?"

"Ah, not all of them: Toussaint-Louverture, he was a slave on the island of Haiti, who led a rebellion of the slaves. His example was like a beacon to all the other islands. His name was greatly praised. Louis Delgrès was a man of Guadeloupe, a mulatto – one who has a black parent and a white parent."

"One who is, therefore, both black and white?" noted Ksenia, remembering again, with some anticipation, the tales of piebald children.

"Light brown," said Horatio, disappointingly. "Monsieur Delgrès led the rebels against Napoleon's army, after the traitor Magloire Pélage declared himself for Napoleon. Alas, his fight was in vain, and on the 28th day of May, in the year 1802, he and his followers blew themselves up with gunpowder on the slopes of the Matouba Volcano."

"Ah," exclaimed Ksenia Ivanovna, "a volcano. They had a volcano on Guadeloupe?"

"Indeed they did, and on several other islands too," confirmed Horatio, choosing not to display any disappointment at her reaction to his story. Perhaps, he reflected, he had done better to omit the volcano.

"In my homeland of Kamtchatka, there are many volcanoes. They frequently explode," she elaborated. "But not much gunpowder." She paused for a moment. "Ah," she sighed, coming finally to the point of the story, "those poor men. They were, then, heroes of the slaves of the Caribbean?"

"They were," said Horatio gravely. "They did not die in vain."

"How true!" exclaimed Ksenia, "For is not slavery now abolished, and are you not a living proof of the equality of man?"

"It is the case," said Horatio sadly, "that slavery has been abolished in many parts of the world, and in those places where Britain rules. But for the French islands, despite Liberty, Equality and Fraternity, this is not yet the case. And as for Russia—". He could merely shake his head.

"Hateful," said Ksenia, lightly grazing the black man's hand with hers, not imagining for a moment that the sin and the hurt of slavery suffered by all his people could thus be stroked away – for it could not – in one man, perhaps, but not in a people – it was only that, between a woman and a man, a slight touch can sometimes alleviate the deepest pain – as it can between a woman and a woman – and, far less commonly, between a man and a man: the infrequency of this simple touch is to the detriment of the peoples of the world. What is 'Love', but a human touch in a world where humanity has been lost?

Horatio appreciated the soft touch, but could not prevent himself from brooding on the fate of the slaves of the British and French nations. He knew he had been fortunate, receiving both his freedom and the opportunity to travel. But for every slave who received freedom, ten more suffered in slavery until they died. For every freed slave who travelled, a thousand more continued their lives of poverty in the place they were born. He remembered those who had oppressed, those who had punished, and those who had struggled for liberty.

"Victor Hugues," he said after a while, "was a man of some worth, although he was white."

At the name, Mr. Voronov started up in a rage. "Victor Hugues?" he demanded. "Why, the man is a poet and a charlatan! How can you mention his name here, in Holy Russia? Sir, do you dare to offend our Nation?" He grimaced at Horatio, who was greatly startled by the onslaught.

"Victor Hugues, sir," he replied, "was no poet. He came from France to be the Governor of Guadeloupe, succeeding upon the late Baron de Clugny—"

Major Sinclair, who had lain as quiet as the dead in his cot, stirred at this, and called out, "Amélie, Amélie, I loved you so!"

Ksenia went to the bed and hushed the man, who continued to mutter the name of Amélie de Clugny for several minutes more, all the while clutching at Ksenia as only a dying man – or one who has no shame – the one might pass for the other – can.

"—and," continued Horatio, for the education of Mr. Voronov, who gave out no suggestion that he was willing to be educated, "purged the island of Guadeloupe of the slave-masters. He brought with him the guillotine—"

"Ah?" said Mr. Voronov, suddenly more sympathetic.

"—he attacked the slave-ships of the United States, and sought to bring revolution to all the other islands nearby – Dominica, St Martin, Grenada, St Vincent and St Lucia."

Yadviga spat a white knuckle on the floor, by way of castigating the foreign saints who dared raise their ugly heads in Novgorod.

"A great man, say I," said Horatio with inappropriate boldness and considerable disregard for the place of a guest in a strange city.

Mr. Voronov looked at the black man with a mixture of suspicion and puzzlement. Truly, he had not known what he was about when, earlier in the evening, he had been smitten with the new arrival. He almost regretted now having sent packing the commercial traveller from Krakow. At that moment in his re-evaluation of the measures of his life, however, Ksenia returned to her place by the stove, and Mr. Voronov immediately felt his hard heart soften. But not so much that he did not question Horatio.

"This Victor Hugues," said he, drawing on his substantial knowledge of the world of poetry – a poet of the Cynical School, who had invaded the Voronov inn one winter's night in 1827, had taught the inn-keeper one of the great lessons of life: a man who hates with insufficient knowledge of his subject can scarcely claim to hate at all; Mr. Voronov had thanked the man for this wisdom, then kicked him out into a blizzard and barred the door – "This Victor Hugues," therefore, "perhaps you do not know that, for all his posturing and piracy, he now lives in Paris in—"

"Poverty!" cried Major Sinclair, eagerly attending to every word.

"—luxury, and scribbles his lines. Rogues, revolutionaries and poets! Is not this man's tale of the church of Notre-Dame a great success among the deluded fools who admire such things? Ah," he exclaimed, more excited than he needed to be,

"if only I had my axe!"

"Well, in that case," said Yadviga smartly, "you may as well go out into the back-yard and find some more wood for the stove. The night is turning colder, you mark my words."

Mr. Voronov turned at once to do her bidding; he felt the need to chop the heads from a few men of letters.

"It is always the way with poets," said he, as he went, certain of his words:

"THEY PICK UP A PEN AND CAST DOWN AUTOCRACY."

23

FREQUENTLY, TRUTH IS A LIBEL. THE GREATER THE TRUTH, THE GREATER THE LIBEL.

"On Guadeloupe," continued Horatio, "the French abolished slavery. As a result, my family was sold to a man on Dominica.

Major Sinclair exhaled softly, the word: "Dominica," sailing on his breath.

"Dominique," he repeated to his comrade-in-arms. It was some time since he had spoken in French. In the West Indies, a man had to – you never knew when you might land on an island occupied – either now – or recently – or in the immediate future – by Boney's boys. He had spoken it in Paris – the pawnbrokers refused to speak English, and the broken-faced and lost women in the cafés were only open to negotiation with elderly men of doubtful means, if French was used. He now continued the conversation in the language of the enemy.

"It was on Dominique we first met, eh, Colonel? The Governor. In the year 1797, you turned up—"

Colonel Andrew Cochrane-Johnstone wanted to know if Sinclair had a bottle of rum. Sinclair denied it. The Colonel cursed until the stars fell out of the sky and God turned his back on Novgorod the Great. At last, his wrath tipped over into weariness. "I was appointed Governor of the island, Sinclair. Governor of Dominique. Don't forget that – I wasn't made Colonel of the 8th West Indian until the year after." He smote Sinclair on the shoulder. The dying man flinched and grinned horribly – Cochrane-Johnstone was a rogue, even if he was now hopeless in Paris. "And I was newly widowed. Oh aye, I married Georgina Hope-Johnstone; it was a marriage of considerable profit for myself." He paused and laughed bitterly. "And a profit for her as well.

"Do you know why, Sinclair? Because Georgina was closely related to Lord Melville himself. All a man had to do was marry the girl at Hopetoun, tack her name on to his, then wait for the appointment to come through; and sure enough, Lord Melville gave me Dominique.

Pity the woman had to die so suddenly, though. I was fair upset about that. There was a gaping hole in my heart, Sinclair, when I arrived on the island."

Major Sinclair expressed a strong opinion that a gaping hole could never be detected in a black heart. The Colonel ignored him.

"Had to leave my daughter behind – poor wee Elizabeth, only two years old. Still, I had that son of mine, John – aye, 'John' and 'Dundas', just like Melville. John Dundas was a bastard, though, I tell everyone that; born in the same year as I wed Georgina, but before the marriage, I made sure of her. You think who the mother was – 'Dundas' – that's all I'll say. Aye, the marriage was profitable for both of us."

To Major Sinclair's surprise, his companion drew a large bottle of dark rum from a coat pocket, and proceeded to uncork it and tip some of the warm liquid down his throat. Then he put the cork back in and the bottle disappeared once more into that tattered old coat he had worn while lying on his sickbed in Paris.

A LARGE BOTTLE
OF DARK RUM

"Poor Elizabeth," he murmured. "But she snicked herself a good husband when she was just one-and-twenty: that Lord Napier took her off my hands, and very grateful he was, too. He never even asked me."

"You were back in the West Indies by then, sir," observed Sinclair, "and in no position to say 'aye' or 'nay' to the man's proposal."

"I was that, Sinclair," said Cochrane-Johnstone. "Still, who was I to stand in the way of a man and his marriage? No one ever stopped me, after all."

"Except Napoleon Bonaparte," asserted Sinclair, showing poor judgement.

For answer, the Colonel stabbed the malingerer with his cane. Sinclair fell back in the bed, groping wildly for breath.

"A grieving widower was I," continued Cochrane-Johnstone, "but I had had all I needed from poor Georgina – her name, her relations, my commission, my fine daughter – yes, even my son. So I determined to make the best of my life in the Caribbean. Did I not do that, Sinclair?" He jabbed at the man again, provoking nothing other than pains in the man's chest and a sense of deep regret.

"You're right: I did very well for myself. Lieutenant-Colonel. Colonel. Brigadier. And you, Sinclair, never got past Major, did you?"

The dying man admitted he had failed to gain promotion. His superior officer allowed him a swallow of rum to compensate for the ruin of his life. Many men could hope for no more. Even more make do with less.

"And if that lying scoundrel, Major John Gordon, had not raised charges against me, I might have been there still. You too, Sinclair. What did I do to Gordon that he abused me so? I ask you."

"He claimed to be a man of honour—" suggested Major Sinclair.

"Pah! You lower ranks, you're all the same – honour, duty, responsibility! No wonder you never got promotion, Sinclair. HONOUR, DUTY, RESPONSIBILITY Major John Gordon can claim anything he wants – and he did so: had me recalled from Dominique, hauled up before the Court Martial in London. All lies, all libel."

"Frequently, Truth is a Libel," observed Sinclair, citing an authority on the matter. "The greater the Truth, the greater the Libel."

"That is possible, Sinclair. But it's the Court that decides what's truth and what's libel. Listen, what was I accused of?" Cochrane-Johnstone put one foot up on the side of the bed, and leaned an elbow on a knee. He tucked his cane under a shabby sleeve. He counted off the charges easily on the fingers of his right hand.

"Firstly, the embezzlement of two sums of money from my regiment: to be exact, 500 Pounds Sterling and 140 Pounds Sterling.

"Secondly, issuing orders that subsistence to the tune of 1000 Pounds Sterling should not be paid to my troops for two months in succession.

"Thirdly, arranging that negro troops in my regiment should be employed as unpaid labour on my own plantation.

"Fourthly, ordering the wrongful arrest of two civilians."

Major Sinclair nodded as each charge was read out. The President of the Court-Martial – the Earl of Harrington, no less – and a baker's dozen of Generals, Lieutenant-Generals, Major-Generals and Brigadier-Generals who sat at the bench, nodded sombrely in suit. It was a serious affair.

"And each charge I showed to be a libel," said the accused triumphantly.

"As I have just said," remarked his Major, ambivalently.

"In respect of the first charge, my Lords, I freely stated that I had issued a credit-note for the £500, to help me purchase my estate at 'Stewart Hall' for £5000; it was my stated intention that the bill would be paid in full by myself – and immediately – should it ever be presented. There was no question – ever – that the bill would likely be presented. There was no embezzlement in it."

"None whatsoever," agreed Sinclair.

"As for the £140 – that was money due to me for three years, to repay a purchase I made out of my own pocket in the year 1799, for cloth and buttons for uniforms for the Regiment."

"Cloth and buttons," noted Sinclair, "for the 8th."

"In respect of the second charge, I only noted that my position as Colonel never at any point permitted me to exercise any authority over the paymaster of the Regiment. It could not be done. I was not empowered to do so. For the record, let it be known that I took Mr. Salton with me to Dominique in 1797, as my secretary. From 1799, when I was briefly back in London, until April 1802, when he had to leave the West Indies due to ill-health, Mr. Salton was the Paymaster. If anyone was to blame for not issuing the wages, then it was Mr. Salton."

"Ill-health," noted Sinclair, "and of course Mr. Salton."

"In respect of the third charge, sirs," continued the defendant, confidently waving the emptying bottle at the bench, "two things are to be said: one, that new recruits to the Regiment were usually in poor physical state and had to be exercised; two, barracks had to be built to accommodate them. By combining these two imperatives, I saved the Government £429 16s 6d in construction and labour costs. But – note this, your Honours – let it be made quite clear that the troops were never used on my plantation, but only in draining a swamp. Further, lest there be any confusion, I ordered that forty-three negroes from my own estate be employed on the plantation. Never a black soldier was used. My butler, George Pringle, swore an affidavit on this."

"A fine man, Mr. Pringle," noted Sinclair, raising an invisible glass in his memory. "He knew his wines."

"As for the fourth and final charge, I gave the facts of the case and demonstrated clearly that the two civilians in question were detained for perfectly justifiable reasons."

"There are no other reasons," observed Sinclair. "Civil Justice and Martial Law so dictates."

"In short, my lords, you will find me innocent of all charges."

"Indeed, you were so found. Every charge a libel, every libel a—"

"The twenty-fifth of March in the year 1805, after seventeen long months cooling my heels in London, and a month in court –fully acquitted. I was free to return to my post. But, almost immediately after that, and before I could take any advantage, I lost the dearest member of my family."

Major Sinclair puzzled for a moment. "But Georgina was already dead, God rest her soul, eight years – and Elizabeth was barely nine and not yet married. Young John – no. Then who—?"

"You never had a very sharp mind, did you, Sinclair?" Cochrane-Johnstone poked him with the cane. "Family, family – of family, the dearest is the one with the money and the power: our Henry Dundas, our Lord Melville was caught out and disgraced, and resigned his office. The man was, after all, a fool: he got caught."

OF FAMILY, THE DEAREST IS THE ONE WITH THE MONEY AND THE POWER

Sinclair coughed and struggled weakly on his cot – he had arrived over-swiftly at enlightenment, which is never a good thing for a military man, unless one is on the Road to Damascus. Few of them can claim that excuse. Major Sinclair remembered family – his foolish father, his more foolish mother, a sister who had never liked him and who had run off with an adventurer from Danzig, and a brother who was sickly and had inconveniently died when only twelve years of age. The demands of army life had never run to the expense of a wife. Frequently, in these past years, he had regretted that. A wife would have been something for a man in his position, when he returned to Britain. Cheap – and perhaps undemanding – if he had chosen well.

"But," he wondered rashly, "did you not love your wife more than you cherished Lord Melville?"

"Love, sir?" said the Colonel, incredulous. "Do you dare talk to me of love? What lunacy is this? I never loved anyone in my life."

Sinclair considered briefly what 'Love' was. He decided that he had loved some but had liked none of them. What did that say to him about love?

"I took them to bed, and they liked me well enough for it. Is that not sufficient in this world?" The impoverished Parisian had clearly measured and weighed every day and night of his life, the six-and-sixty years he had spent among men and women.

Sinclair said nothing, but remembered only the vices of the women of Dominique.

"Those were good days, were they not, Sinclair?" murmured the Colonel, corking again distractedly – having uncorked it only a moment before – no drink was taken – the bottle of rum.

Sinclair said nothing, but remembered only the virtues – or were they vices? – of the women of Dominique.

Colonel Cochrane-Johnstone followed his memories down tracks on horseback, along the hills of Dominique and Guadeloupe. His estates and his negroes, his soldiers and his plantation. And then he hit upon a name and was enraged. He called out for those that could hear: "But did not that treacherous Frenchman Hugues betray the hopes of all decent white men?"

"Victor Hugues, sir," replied Horatio, "was no poet. He came from France to be the Governor of Guadeloupe, succeeding upon the late Baron de Clugny—"

Major Sinclair, who had lain as quiet as the dead in his cot, stirred at this, and called out,

"AMÉLIE, AMÉLIE, I LOVED YOU SO!"

24

SHE CONSIDERS MARRIAGE;
HE CONSIDERS ESCAPE.

The wolf kept a steady eye on the back door of the lodge. He had heard the voices within. He had scented the smoke from the chimney and sniffed the salt of the ham. He remained alert, half-crouched in the tangled briars and brambles and the beds of twigs and leaves of the abandoned garden, waiting, as a wolf can wait.

The inn-keeper stepped out of the back door of the lodge. He breathed heavily, muttering to himself of poets, pens and autocracy. He stood briefly, waiting for his eyes to adjust to the pitch blackness of the night. The wolf needed no such time. But still he lay in ambush. Finally, Mr. Voronov looked about him and began to gather branches and sticks. His professional eye discovered an old axe lying propped against the wall, rusty, blunt, the foot of the shaft worm-eaten and mouldy. But the head was not loose, a small thing to be thankful for in these days of treacherous behaviour.

"Now I shall have you," whispered the inn-keeper, smugly lifting the axe and dusting off the wood-lice and cobwebs. He laid out the branches and small logs before him, selected one, and smote into it with the axe. The axe was blunt. But Mr. Voronov was keen. The branch flew apart neatly.

"Ha!" exclaimed Mr. Voronov, "there you go, Monsieur Victor Hugues or Hugo, or whatever is your nom-de-plume. Now for all those other Frenchmen – Lamartine—"

With unseemly haste, the axe-man picked up another log, struck it a blunt blow, then another and another, until it fell apart.

"—Rousseau—"

The harvesting of a surprisingly detailed catalogue of the flowers of literary France continued.

"—Chateaubriand – Beaumarchais—"

The pile on one side grew smaller, on the other side grew larger. The wolf watched silently.

"—into the night with you, Musset—"

Another log burst apart under the mighty strokes of the armed critic.

"—off with your head, Monsieur Chenier! Pah! – here's your Marquis de Sade, and here's your Madame de Staël, and here the honourable Balzac—"

Mr. Voronov stopped to wipe the sweat from his brow. The wolf inched forward, silently, his teeth aching. Another heap of logs was lined up.

"Let me see the redness of your blood and the blackness of your soul, Monsieur Stendhal! Pah! There you go, Benjamin Constant – pah! – George Sand – pah! – Messieurs Nodier and Béranger – pah! pah! pah! The century suddenly turns ill for you, heh?"

At last, the sound of the axe ceased. The inn-keeper stood, wiped the honest sweat from his brow. The wolf inched forward some more. In a last burst of triumphant energy, Mr. Voronov hurled the heated axe into the undergrowth. It hit the wolf squarely on the forehead; the wolf tipped over into a pile of last year's leaves, without a whimper. Leaving the beast to consider his rightful place in the orthodox order of things, Mr. Voronov returned indoors, carrying with him a large pile of fuel for the stove.

Yadviga welcomed him as best she could: "Well, at last! All I can say is you took your time, Ivan Ivanovich," she scolded. "What were you doing out there – playing with the wolves? Come on, feed the stove and let me warm myself up. There's no use two of us dying this night, you mark my words."

The inn-keeper did as he was told, and was rewarded with a careful measure of vodka. Horatio and Ksenia were again asleep, leaning comfortably upon each other, he breathing exactly once to each of her two breaths, as if they had known one another for many years.

"Will you just look at them," said Yadviga in a tone mixed of one part bitter despair, two parts jealousy, and a dash of admiration – stirred and shaken well and at once fermented.

Mr. Voronov looked. He was once more assailed by a strong emotion, something that told him he must –against all natural practice and economic sense – he must offer these two people every hospitality when they returned to his inn. The stove would be fired to breaking point, a dozen eggs would be placed on the table, some ham, pickles, some bread – Voronov racked his brains, ransacked his memories – how should honoured guests be treated? Clean knives, that would do. Tea, obviously. And he himself would wear a white apron – did he have such a thing?

"Are you listening to me at all, Voronov?" demanded Yadviga, looking at him sourly.

"No, not at all, you old crone," answered the inn-keeper, with no hint of malice. "Did you have something to say that I have not heard a thousand times before?" To his very great surprise and embarrassment, Yadviga began to sob. This was not behaviour he found unusual – guests burst into tears all the time, at the treatment they received at his inn; but it was the first time he had witnessed Yadviga in such weakness. Her face turned red, tears coursed down the many wrinkles and furrows of her cheeks, skittering this way, dribbling that way, collected in her several chins. It was, he supposed, like the thaw on the vast desolate plains of Siberia. He waited for her to dry up. She did so quite soon enough.

THAW ON THE
PLAINS OF SIBERIA

"All I can say is this reminds me," said she, snuffling one last time and spitting the resulting phlegm on the floor, "of my youth."

"Old people," declared Ivan Ivanovich Voronov, "are reminded of nothing else. Much good may it do them."

"He says it does me no good: what does he know?" retorted Yadviga. "What else is youth good for, in any case, than to be remembered when you're old?"

In the face of such timeless philosophy, Voronov fell silent.

"In any case, was I not," she continued, "but sixteen when I met Alexei Alexandrovich? He says he loves me, he says. Liar. What he means is to take me into the woods and do what men do. Men. In any case, he does it and there it is. When I find there will be a baby, I consider marriage; he considers escape. As luck would have it, my brothers are at home that year, and Alexei re-considers his decision. You mark my words, we get married before the child is born."

"That was indeed fortunate," said Voronov carelessly.

"You may say so, but the child dies after three days. It is a girl."

"That was indeed unfortunate," said Voronov carelessly.

"Alexei considers escape once more, but my brothers talk some sense into him. In any case, he walks with a limp for the rest of his life. Yes, he does. So he stays. And then the children begin to come, you mark my words. Twenty of them, all told, after that first one. Six more than my mother managed. Would you believe it – thirteen boys, seven girls? Life is hard—"

"Life," interrupted Voronov with some asperity, "has always been hard. For everyone. But we must put our faith in Tsar and Church."

Yadviga crossed herself, but gave no other sign of listening to the inn-keeper. "Two of my daughters die before they are a year old; my sons are stronger, but still three die before they can work in the fields. When one child dies, Alexei gives me another."

"Ah – love!" murmured Voronov reflectively.

"All I can say is – love is the love of my children," replied Yadviga, verging again on the emotional. "In any case – do we not support each other through the bad times and make children?"

"That," indicated Mr. Voronov, "is what love is."

"Now what are you talking about?" demanded Yadviga, instantly confused.

"Love, of course," said Voronov, as if it featured in his conversations all day and every day; he attempted thereby to conceal the fact that he had never talked about it to anyone, least of all his wife – and never to his children, who had fled. He had thought about it often enough. But it was always a diaphanous dream, hauled by the horses of whimsy – poets might write about such things – and he was, on every occasion, constrained to banish such thoughts with his axe.

As Yadviga continued to look sourly upon him, he felt – unexpectedly, like a sudden flux of the bowels when feverish – a small twinge of pity for the old woman. "Your children," said he conversationally, "are they all married now?"

"And did I not say," said she, "they are all married and dead?"

"All of them?" he queried.

She began to enumerate: "Of those who reached a proper age—"

"Which would be?" asked Voronov, for the sake of science alone.

"I am talking about the age of marriage," she said acidly.

"Or escape?" he commented lightly. Lightness was not a proper mood; he felt stinging on his cheek.

"So, in any case, Alexei and Andrei are killed at Austerlitz, fighting the French.

"Anna dies in childbirth, in the year 1807.

"Vassily drowns at Friedland in the same year.

"Grushenka, of smallpox, 1810.

"Ivan, the young fool, off he goes to Bessarabia to conquer the Turk, since the French were no longer available, and dies there in 1811.

"Katerina is taken off by Cossack soldiers in 1812, and raped by a whole platoon. Well, of course, she dies of her injuries, which is not a surprise. But not before her husband has hunted down the Cossacks and fought them."

Voronov was doubtful of the legality of this proceeding against the Tsar's soldiers. "He did not kill them, surely?" he asked disapprovingly.

"Of course not – what is one peasant armed with a scythe against ten mounted Cossacks? They toss his body at Katerina's door before they leave the village. Of course, she drops dead at the sight. He has been slashed a hundred times. There is no blood left in him, you mark my words.

"Then Mikhail, Pavel and Pyotr go off to fight the French and two are killed at Borodino. Mikhail's wife tries to stop him from going, by hiding his clothes."

Treasonable, thought the inn-keeper to himself, shaking his head. Where would the might of the Imperial Russian Army be, if all the wives hid their husband's clothes? What would happen to battles and war if clothes were to be concealed? Unimaginable.

"So, in any case, he rides off, wrapped in a blanket. Of course, we never see him or Pavel again. In the meantime, Natasha is carried off and raped by the French army; she hangs herself – what else? – the day before her husband returns from Borodino with the news of the battle.

"At this, Sergei and Thomas set off with General Kutuzov to avenge themselves on the French. In despair, my youngest daughter Olga goes off to the ruins of Moscow, and all I can say is that she abandons herself to prostitution."

"Sometimes," said Voronov, shaking his head, a hard-pressed parent himself, "sometimes young people do not choose wisely."

"Well, in any case, within a six-month she is dead of drink and the clap. No sooner has she done so than we get news that Pyotr – what else? – has expired at Krasnoye. Which leaves me only with Yuri, since Sergei and Thomas have up and died of disease in Poland."

Mr. Voronov hesitated to ask. He did not need to wait. "Yuri leaves home in 1820 and is killed by the Persians in 1826." She had run out of fingers long ago. Voronov had been adding up the numbers, however, and established that all her children were now officially dead.

"And your husband?" he enquired, sympathetically.

"Was never in Persia, more's the pity. But does he not die of a bloody flux in the year 1814?" she replied, thinking rather of each and every one of her children, sacrificed – one way and another – to the greater glory of Russia and the Tsar. The ungrateful wretches: did she not need them more than the Tsar? Did a mother not love her children CHILDREN – so that they could look after her in her old age? Had her UNGRATEFUL children ever thought once about this love? She thought not. WRETCHES

Voronov knew little what to say. He had never regarded Yadviga as a person with a history. To find that she had lost so many children – fifteen, was it? – to his miserable three, was a little uncomfortable. And hers all dead, and his, as far as he knew, alive. Is it not better to lose three children to Life than fifteen to Death? Life, at least, could be fought, while Death was invincible. Something was nibbling at Voronov's mind, and he knew it not.

To fill the deep silence which had descended on the lodge, he noted that her sons and her daughters had died in strict alphabetical order.

"As they were born," she confirmed. "In any case, the priest insisted on it. Alphabetical, he says: it's easier to remember."

"Orthodoxy," said Voronov, pleased, "and learning."

Yadviga sniffled for a few moments then dried her eyes. "And, of course, after all that, I am left," she said grimly, "with three stupid sons-in-law, ten weeping daughters-in-law, and thirty-six screaming grandchildren."

"That is a comfort," suggested Voronov recklessly.

Yadviga snorted. "A comfort, he says? A comfort, says he? You mark my words, that is no comfort! They crowd round me like horseflies. Each wants something of me. I have nothing else to give. Instead, I offer my personal services to the young Prince Labanov, who owns all the land around."

The inn-keeper tried to calculate Yadviga's age and weight when she was thus offering her body to the Prince. It was an impossible thought. He said so. She slapped him hard again. When the tiny dancing lights had subsided, he approached her words from a different direction.

"So, all I can say is I had served the Prince's father as a nurse-maid when I was younger, before Alexei Alexandrovich whispered his worthless words in my ear. His son, whom I nursed – God preserve him and all his family – learning of my troubles, takes me back into his domestic service in St Petersburg as a cook; and then, when he sets off on his travels in Europe, he writes me a letter of recommendation to Governor Gerebzov of Novgorod, whom I serve faithfully until he retires to Odessa. Of course, he gives me a pension, which has supported me these past three years. That's all very well, eh? And have I not been tending older gentlemen in their extremity?"

"In short," said the inn-keeper, "you have retired from your family."

FROSTBITE AND SCURVY? THAT IS NOTHING COMPARED TO FAMILY!

"In short," replied Yadviga, "I tell you this: I have had my fill of my family. All I can say is it has given me nothing but heartache, pain, sorrow, suffering. Travellers pass through Novgorod, admiring this, gaping at that, boasting of all the other sights they have seen, the farthest ends of the earth which they have reached, monsters and mountains, rivers and devils. But they have not seen or felt half of what I have seen and felt, I, who have barely travelled a hundred miles in all my life! Hardship? Endurance? Misery? They know nothing of it, you mark my words. Frostbite and scurvy? That is nothing compared to family!"

"There is something in what you say," admitted the inn-keeper, who was protected from starvation and ignominy by these very travellers, but who had daily and nightly contact with their boastfulness, their lack of respect for Church and Emperor, their propensity – many of them – to read secretively in books. He had seen them. He had even heard them muttering to themselves. The words were certainly not Orthodox. If he could be an inn-keeper without the necessity of entertaining guests – ah! now that would be a fine thing!

While he considered what a fine place Russia could be, Ksenia stirred by the stove, found her proximity to the slumbering Horatio perfectly comfortable, and sat quietly, observing Yadviga.

"You are awake again, then," said Mr. Voronov solicitously, noticing her movement.

"I am," replied Ksenia. "Were you talking of something pleasant?"

"Well, all I can say is: I've been talking about my family," said Yadviga bitterly.

"There were many in her family," commented Voronov gloomily.

"Oh," said Ksenia in a more lively tone than he, "I have a large family too. I have ten brothers and eleven sisters."

"And does your mother still live?" exclaimed Yadviga, expecting that a woman more fecund than herself would have been unable finally to drag herself from her bed.

"When last I saw her," said Ksenia quietly, wondering now if she would ever hear if her mother died: Kamtchatka was so far away, and the post was so frequently eaten by bears.

"Alive, she says. And your brothers and sisters, all alive?" questioned Yadviga further, in full pursuit of the science of infanticulture.

"All alive, I'm sure," answered Ksenia. "And several married, and the mothers and fathers of all my nephews and nieces."

"All I can say is it's a healthy place you come from," said Yadviga, astonished and yet doubtful.

"Ah, Kamtchatka! One of the healthiest places on earth." Ksenia found an unusual tremor in her voice, a sudden rush of home-sickness. She suppressed it with one thought: "Apart from the volcanoes," she added.

Under normal circumstances, Mr. Voronov would not be inclined to believe in the existence of Kamtchatka, any more than in the existence of the Man in the Moon; but this night he felt suffused with unusual charity. Indeed, had Kamtchatka not existed, then he would have had to invent it.

Horatio had been awake for several moments. He laid his hand upon Ksenia's – knee, need not be said – and stated in the deepest of

A KNEE   voices that he, for one, would dearly love to see that place, for Kamtchatka must surely be as beautiful as its daughters. Yadviga looked at him disagreeably. The inn-keeper looked at him with a mixture of admiration and disbelief. Ksenia, daughter of Kamtchatka, and sister of many similar Kamtchatkans, looked up at him hopefully.

"If you could follow me," said she softly, "then I would show you all that you would dearly love to see."

Horatio, battered into sheer recklessness – by the night – by the place – by the heat of the stove – by the slightly sour smell of her hair – by the after-taste of pickled cucumbers – gazed upon the young widow.

"I can think of nothing better," he replied. Did he, by this, mean that he had lost the thread of Rational Understanding, or that he stood upon the threshold of Paradise?

Ksenia gazed at Horatio for several moments. All around, silence had descended like thick curtains upon a drama in a St Petersburg theatre. She knew that she had something to say, and that the words would be like a sharp knife, delivering a cut both to her who held it and to him who met it. The curtains would rend, the drama would be exposed for what it was – painted actors avoiding the harsh reality of the road.

"Before we go too far, sir," she said at last in a low voice which she hoped that only he would hear,

"I AM OBLIGED TO TELL YOU—"

25

IF ONE SLEEPS ON *A RAISED BEDSTEAD, THE ALLIGATORS WILL NOT CARRY YOU OFF.*

Major Sinclair, who had lain as quiet as the dead in his cot, stirred at these words, and called out, "Madame, I am obliged to tell you that Admiral Cochrane wished to liberate the Emperor Napoleon from St Helena."

"Admiral Cochrane?" exclaimed Ksenia, starting up in surprise, much to the alarm of Horatio. "His son Charles wished intemperately to console me."

"Indeed, no, madam," said Major Sinclair impatiently, unable to remind himself that a lady may mistake one Admiral for another and not be chastised, "not that Admiral Cochrane. I refer, of course, to Admiral Thomas Cochrane."

"Ah," said Horatio, setting aside for the moment Charles' intemperate desires and the concerns of Ksenia, "the hero of the Basque Roads."

"And of many another glorious battle in which Monsieur Frenchie was trounced," said the Major patriotically.

At the mention of battles and Frenchies, Yadviga slowly and deliberately spat on the floor.

"And this Admiral Cochrane," demanded Mr. Voronov, "why should he wish to liberate such a scoundrel as that? What was his game?" To liberate Napoleon? – such was the act of a madman or a poet – in any case: an apostate.

"The story I heard," replied Sinclair concentrating on the facts; remembering only the haziest outline of a rumour and embellishing it as he saw fit, "was that Admiral Cochrane – Thomas, madam – was on his way to liberate Chile and Peru from the grip of the Spaniards – a race for whom, since my very earliest days, I have nothing but contempt. As he sailed past St Helena, where the Emperor Napoleon had been incarcerated, he discussed with his lieutenants the practicality of freeing the prisoner, carrying him off to South

America and employing the man's treacherous skills in assembling armies against the Spanish king. I have heard tell that, in the dead of night, he made the attempt, but was thwarted by a change in the wind. But, at all events, he did not succeed, and he sailed on."

Mr. Voronov, in a fit of exasperation at the craven foolhardiness of the English, swallowed a pickled egg whole; and so felt, by a change in the wind, a greater antipathy towards this Admiral, whom he had never met, than ever before.

"Had he succeeded, of course, the young fool would have joined half of the rest of the Cochranes in front of a court-martial." Sinclair lifted his cracked lips from yellowed teeth in a grin that seamlessly changed to a grimace. "A court-martial," he repeated. "Ah, if it had not been for that Major Gordon and his pernickety morality, we would have stayed out there in Dominica, and not been dragged back to that filthy, stinking, damp city of London."

At the mere recollection of the capital city of the greatest empire in the world, Major Sinclair groaned.

His two nurses hastened to his bed-side – the younger one arriving first – the older one some time later. A foot-stool had obstructed her. Then a remembrance that the stopper was not in the bottle. Then a suspicion that the stopper was indeed in the bottle, but might perhaps be loose. A foot-stool was required after that excitement. And then she raised her spirits and arrived forthwith at the Major's bed-side.

They shooed away the gentlemen of the party, and set about his breeches with a pan and a cloth. The mere recollection of London was pissed away with a great effort. Mr. Voronov whiled away the time in an internal struggle with that last egg, and wondered hopelessly what would happen were he to return to his inn, where there was no talk of wicked Frenchmen. Horatio wished he had thought to bring a pipe with him, and reflected soberly on the white man on the island of Dominica. Not with much sympathy: he had met them all –the brutal officer, the fawning subordinate, the pale wife shaded from the sun by an umbrella and two slaves, the boats and ships that came and went with their cargoes of soldiers and sailors, all changing year on year, never changing from one to the next.

The attentions paid to Major Sinclair in his extremity did not seem to lift his spirits.

When all complaint – largely from Yadviga – had subsided, the old nurse carried the pitiful pan of liquid down the corridor to the back door. She open the door, filled the door-frame with her bulk, took careful aim, then hurled the contents out into the darkness with an energy surprising in one of her age and condition. The wolf, by then sufficiently recovered from a recent assault, had spent the past few minutes creeping forward to the door, cautiously, at every moment prepared to turn tail at the sight of an axe. Unhappily, he arrived within a convenient distance at the precise moment of Yadviga's opening of the door, and received the tepid stinking liquid full in the face. Without even a howl of anguish, he slumped down upon the ground.

In the meantime, Major Sinclair had passed on from thoughts of London to thoughts of Death: it was an easy passage. He looked at the faces clustered about him, and seemed scared at what he saw. With Yadviga's re-appearance, he let slip a groan.

"In all my days," said Yadviga loudly mis-understanding the significance of the exhalation, "are you about to piss again? Am I not an old woman? I don't have the time for it, you mark my words."

The dying man did not mark her words, only the severity of her command.

"I do not fear," said he untruthfully, remembering briefly a childhood, a nightmare and a minister in the kirk, "the angels of death."

Mr. Voronov looked around him anxiously. There was no evidence of any angels. He attributed the delusion to an excess of poetry in the corrupt British Empire.

"One – two – three – four," counted Sinclair. "The angels of death walk hand in hand and not alone. You have come for me, then?" he asked, conversationally. The four angels of death looked at each other in consternation. They stood not hand in hand. Neither did they walk.

THE FOUR ANGELS OF DEATH LOOKED AT EACH OTHER IN CONSTERNATION

"No," said Ksenia kindly, mopping the poor man's brow, ignoring the fact that it was as dry as bone can be – not the bones of ham, with the last of which Yadviga now comforted herself – rather the bone that has lain on a sun-bleached Carib shore. Fever had passed; all that remained was the short walk up the path to death's door. "No, we are not the angels of death, and we have not come for you."

"Not yet," added Horatio unhelpfully.

It was clear that Major Sinclair did not believe his young nurse for one moment, nor yet the apparition which – measured against current religious wisdom – was no angel, unless a fallen, or liberated, one – being black as the night which surrounded the edges of his eyes. However, he had no qualms in conversing with the angels of death, if all others had now abandoned him. Major Sinclair had had one great skill in life: he could talk to anyone. About anything. It had done him no good – some people wished to talk to no one, about nothing – others to no one, about anything – the remainder to anyone, about nothing – but he never knew that. Nor would he know it now. The days and nights of learning were over. Instead, he told them the full and unabridged history of the Empress Josephine: her birth and days upon Martinique; her wooing of the small Frenchman; her undoubted hatred for Amélie de Clugny, French mistresses having – as Major Sinclair thought he knew from having lived in Paris these past few years – a great jealousy of each other, their progress through life leaving reputations and rivals bobbing in their tempestuous wake. Having exhausted his knowledge of the Empress Josephine, he drew the attention of his supernatural watchers to the Emperor Napoleon, now dead – at which news, the patriotic angel Voronov and the orthodox angel Yadviga expressed great approbation – and the man's willingness to sacrifice grieving widows, marriageable girls, thousands of slaves and the odd reputation to his own ambitions.

"In a word," said Major Sinclair in a fit of indignation, "no self-respecting Briton would take tea with Monsieur and Madame Bonaparte." No one would have it otherwise.

"But perhaps," said Horatio unable to eschew the observation of a connoisseur, "he would sleep in Madame Bonaparte's bed?"

Mr. Voronov and Ksenia Ivanovna looked in horror at Horatio. Major Sinclair, on the other hand, laughed: the sound was much like a death-rattle.

"Her bed, sir, her bed." The Major looked up at the massive head-board where, in the dim shadows, it was just possible to see the carving of a swan. Never once did Josephine omit to have a swan carved on her furniture; it prevented any misunderstandings. "The Emperor Bonaparte, having no more use for wife or bed, carried it to Russia when he visited Moscow in 1812, and then aban-doned it without a backwards glance. It was brought here in 1821 by a Jewish merchant, and has served me well in recent days."

HAVING NO MORE USE FOR WIFE OR BED

All attended closely to the Empress' bed. It was difficult to imagine Monsieur and Madame Bonaparte lying there in each other's arms after a tumultuous day of imperial conviviality. Where once was sleepless Napoleon and his sultry concubine attended by an army of sycophants, now was Major Sinclair attended by an army of bugs. Had Josephine yet lived, she would not have recognised the bed. Such is love. The French are known for being inconstant. Especially with each other. Major Sinclair had witnessed that with his own eyes, and felt it with his own heart.

"Cousin Charles," continued Ksenia, pursuing her own train of thought entirely, "advised me once that, if one sleeps on the beaches on a raised bedstead, then

THE ALLIGATORS WILL NOT CARRY YOU OFF."

26

A LARGE SNAKE, WHOSE STING IS INSTANT DEATH.

It was clear that the thoughts of Ksenia were fixed not upon the pro-liferation of Admirals in the Cochrane clan – as they should have been, rather than rowing about amongst the lesser ranks of the family – or indeed upon Emperors; but upon Charles Stuart Cochrane, son of the Admiral Sir Alexander Forrester Inglis Cochrane; and, yes, beds. In the night, a bell sounded twice, marking the hour. At the sound of the bells, the dying man slipped away – not yet into the arms of Death, now stamping his feet and drawing upon a flask of brandy to keep warm in the night outside – but into a Parisian's dreams of Josephine. From which, in due course, he will emerge.

"My cousin Charles," continued Ksenia "spent more than twelve months in South America, marching through the thickest jungles and over the highest mountains. Colombia is a hot country. In the port of La Guayra, the temperature was frequently at ninety degrees—"

Horatio opened his mouth, and then closed it again hurriedly. Ksenia observed the movement.

"—Charles measured only in Fahrenheit," she continued, "and a traveller newly-arrived will suffer inflammatory fevers from the heat alone. And those, as I know to be the case from my poor dear husband, can become putrid fevers, from which a man will die."

Yadviga snored.

"Did your cousin Charles suffer much from fever?" asked Horatio, interested to divert his friend from the sad topic of her husband.

"Oh," said she carelessly, "he contracted fever as many another man did. But only later in his journey. For he took good advice and immediately ascended from La Guayra to the city of Carracas, which is the capital of Venezuela province."

"Little Venice," noted Horatio knowledgeably. "Named after the native villages on Lake Maracaybo."

"I am sure that Charles would have said so," replied Ksenia, flushing slightly. "Cousin Charles was always telling me much that I did not wish to know, and little that would be of use."

Horatio blushed in turn and resolved once more to hold his peace. He had acquired much profitless wisdom in his travels, which brought him the admiration of Prince Labanov, but of few others. In Love, an Encyclopaedia is not necessarily a mighty weapon.

"Charles told me also," continued Ksenia, pursuing her attack, "that the great earthquake of 1812 killed between nine and ten thousand souls. Why would I wish to know this? I, who lived with volcanoes and earthquakes for all my years in Kamtchatka?"

Horatio shook his head: he did not know why. Mr. Voronov shook his head: he did not know why.

"Then he told me that those who still lived after the earth had shaken and the churches had fallen and the houses were smashed – those who lived were driven to acts of morality: those who had neglected for many years to sanction their union by the sacerdotal benediction, were promptly married; those who had abandoned their children due to poverty or ill-will, were re-united; those DRIVEN TO ACTS who owed money, sought out their creditors and paid OF MORALITY them without being asked; those who had sworn bitter enmity, became friends."

"A most beneficial effect," commented Mr. Voronov, hoping that the earthquake also persuaded poets to give up their game. "Did it last long?"

"My cousin Charles did not say."

Horatio knew of another occasion, after the eruption of a volcano, when friends became bitter enemies, marriages flew apart, children were abandoned, murders were committed, lovers of life retired to dark and dank hermitages; while, of course, some senseless acts of morality were committed. Should he say so? He thought not.

"Cousin Charles sailed up rivers and through jungles. He told me that the most valuable item a man could have when sailing on the rivers was a small bedstead, so constructed as to be easily taken to pieces."

"Indeed?" said Mr. Voronov in an interested tone.

"Alligators," she reminded him shortly.

"Ah yes," said Mr. Voronov, gathering his wits. He wondered whether the same domestic arrangements could be employed to ward off fleas and cockroaches. He thought not. In his experience, bedsteads attracted, rather than repelled.

"Charles said to us: 'You talk of the dangers of wolves and bears. But in the jungles of Colombia there are alligators twenty-five feet in length, there are musquitoes from which you cannot escape even clad in gauze and leather, there are large snakes, which hang in coils from the trees, and whose sting is instant death. There are tigers and monkeys.' When he was in the town of Cartago, he observed through a good spy-glass a herd of carnivorous elephants with enormous teeth. And, of course, there were the poisonous frogs."

A HERD OF CARNIVOROUS ELEPHANTS

Yadviga mumbled angrily in her sleep at this idle talk of frogs and elephants.

"Your cousin Charles saw many things," said Horatio doubtfully.

"Cousin Charles saw through the eyes of a fool," countered Ksenia, with spirit. "He told my dear husband John these things, and John was afire to go and see them for himself, to sail up the endless rivers and hack his way through the jungle with a machetta and climb the towering mountains as Charles had. Except Charles had climbed them on a mule or while carried in a chair on the back of some poor native, whereas John wished to climb them with his own two legs."

"Quite understandable," said Horatio charitably.

"Had Charles said nothing, then John would be my husband still," concluded the widow ferociously.

"Alas," said Horatio in a low voice, hoping that his sigh would be misunderstood.

"What, madam," asked Mr. Voronov, "did this man wish to do in such a wild country?" It was clear that it would take a madman or a Briton to place a foot on its shores.

"Which man?" asked Ksenia in turn.

"This Charles," said Mr. Voronov for the sake of clarity.

"He wished," replied Ksenia scornfully, "to secure the exclusive rights to the Colombian Pearl Fishery."

"Commendable," said the inn-keeper, now satisfied. Greed and the hope of profit was something he could understand.

"On behalf of Messrs. Rundell, Bridges and Rundell of London," she continued with unaccustomed precision.

"Aah!" exclaimed Major Sinclair, not out of enlightenment, but for more pressing reasons altogether. Ksenia roused Yadviga from her comfortable sleep, and the two women applied themselves to the contents of the Major's undergarments.

"In whose enterprise," continued Ksenia, some minutes later, "he invested one thousand pounds, only to lose every last penny within four years. The loss was a great disappointment to him. He told me that the same Colombian government gave a native of Scotland, Colonel James Hamilton, exclusive rights to navigate the Orinoco with steam-vessels. Charles is a fool, and said he would have been better to strike in with Colonel Hamilton. He knew as little of steam-engines as of the machinery for extracting pearls from oysters."

"So, do these Colombians have any churches?" asked Yadviga, now awake and anxious to divert the conversation towards higher things than steam-engines and oysters.

"Indeed, they do," said Ksenia with due respect. "In the capital city of Bogota there are no fewer than three-and-thirty churches, convents and monasteries—"

Yadviga laughed in derision. Such a paltry number would scarce fit into a Russian village. Such miserly heathens, these Colombians.

"—and in Carracas, the church attached to the monastery of the Dominicans has a most remarkable picture."

"Does it though!" exclaimed Yadviga, brightening at the thought of a religious picture, while certain it would be not a patch upon the ikons and murals of the many churches of the Saints of Novgorod the Great.

Ksenia bent towards the old woman and whispered in her ear: "It portrays St Dominic as an old man with a grey beard, suckling at the breast of the Virgin Mary. He was thus cured of a violent pain in his chest."

Yadviga crossed herself, marvelling both at the unwholesome demands of old men and the selfless actions of the Mother of God.

Mr. Voronov, whose hearing was sharpened by years of eaves-dropping at the internal doors of his inn, was astonished and intrigued: were such things as this possible? So disturbed was he that he neither WERE SUCH THINGS heard Horatio's diverting questions on the state of the AS THIS POSSIBLE? roads in Colombia; nor attended to the answer – that some had been eroded to twenty or thirty feet below their original level, by the passing of floods and the passage of wheels and mules.

"Worse, indeed, than the roads of Siberia," conceded Ksenia Ivanovna.

Horatio did not fail to ask after the rivers and canals of the region and he was correctly informed that Charles Stuart Cochrane had demonstrated the possibility of draining Lake Guatavita armed only with a Syphon, an experiment carried out with two pails and a tube, to the ever-lasting astonishment of the gathered gentlemen of local quality; but had later carried out the project by having a canal dug. One day cousin Charles had advised Ksenia – who had expressed no interest at all in the matter – that the Atlantic and Pacific Oceans would be joined by a canal at Panama – it was only a matter of time; many good men had already carried out surveys.

Horatio then wished to complete his general knowledge of the area, by inquiring after the principal mineral and agricultural products of the country; the reluctant geographist replied: copper, silver, gold and platina, tobacco, indigo, sugar, coffee, cocoa, cotton.

Horatio considered these products with little interest.

"And chocolate," added Ksenia.

"And chocolate?" responded Horatio with more enthusiasm.

"And chocolate," confirmed Ksenia, "at every meal, as much as you could hope for." She sighed in her turn, and stared long and hard at her hands.

"Chocolate drink?" asked Horatio.

"And chocolate paste," nodded Ksenia.

"Chocolate sauce?" asked Horatio further.

"And chocolate figures," acknowledged Ksenia.

The lovers – of chocolate only – dreamed. A land of wonders, Colombia the Grand, Gran Colombia the happy land.

"Captain White," interrupted Major Sinclair with some vigour as he sank further into the bed of the Empress, "painted a small donkey with chocolate paste."

Yadviga pursed her lips. She had heard this story more than once in the last few weeks. Should a man about to come before the Almighty Judge not concern himself with higher matters? Did he not need a priest, rather than a donkey? And did she not need a pickled egg? She applied herself to two at once, one for each free hand.

Mr. Voronov was sufficiently deflected from his musings on the cures for the aches and pains of middle-age to enquire further. The dying man obliged.

"This donkey was then rowed out to a ship that lay at anchor off Dominica. It was not an easy task. Once on the ship, the donkey was placed in the hammock of Mr. Miers. Mr. Miers had been drinking heavily and was asleep. The donkey kicked out and woke him. Mr. Miers imagined he was in the whorehouse on Melville Street. A most amusing scene resulted."

PAINTED A SMALL DONKEY WITH CHOCOLATE PASTE

No one laughed, not even Major Sinclair. It was a memory that spoke too easily of lives that have lost their way, hopes that have been abandoned: wasted lives, and wasted chocolate.

"The ship sailed for Gravesend with the donkey still aboard," added Major Sinclair. "Some men return from the West Indies with wives, others with fond memories. Mr. Miers thought he took back both." But his words went unheeded.

"What happened to your cousin Charles?" asked Horatio at length.

Ksenia did not immediately reply. She considered the flickering flames of the stove for several moments. At last she said:

"When the news came that my dear husband had died in Valencia, Charles was most solicitous. He declared that he wished to console me."

Horatio considered these words with the greatest of care; each one was written as clearly in the dim light of that room as a star in the clearest of winter skies.

"For two years, he tried to console me. He even confessed that he loved me. I asked him at last: what is 'love'? He told me that he knew of nothing more delightful than to chat with a woman (a pretty one, he stipulated) in a cottage bonnet – I happened to be wearing one that day," she explained, "so that Charles could not get too close with his whiskers. He seized my hand and said that, although he had been in the Royal Navy, he knew nothing of ships and had a particular dislike of the sea: therefore, he said, he would never again leave the country. Charles declared that I was the most charming little lady he had ever set eyes on, and that, if I would allow him to marry me, he would be the happiest man alive."

Horatio was torn between agreement with the sentiment and outrage at the fool's persistence.

"But Charles was the dullest man I had ever met. I told him so."

Horatio regarded the young widow with increased admiration.

"He turned to the window and admitted it was true. I told him that love was a palpitation of the heart. He said he had that feeling in his heart. I told him I had not. That was the end of it. The following week, I left for St Petersburg."

"And Charles left you alone?" asked Horatio nervously.

"He did. Cousin Charles found the life of a troubadour more desirable, and soon after my departure he undertook a tour of Great Britain in the dress of an Iberian, for the benefit of the exiled champions of Portugal's Freedom. Perhaps you would like to hear about it?"

"The troubadour—" began Horatio, wishing to know more about this tour of Britain. But he got no further. At the very hint of the word 'Freedom', Mr. Voronov thumped the end of the bed with his fist. The FRENCH IMPERIAL remaining three posts of Josephine's throne shook with BED-BUGS the violence of his onslaught, the French Imperial bedbugs fled for the darkness and Major Sinclair waited for the sky to fall upon him and snuff him out. Forever.

"Everywhere there is Freedom – Freedom for the North Americans, then Freedom for the French, then Freedom for slaves, then Freedom for the South Americans, then Freedom for the Portuguese, then Freedom for the Greeks. Is there no end to this Freedom?" Mr. Voronov was distraught. "It seems to me that the ships that trade between nations carry a great plague with them, the plague of Liberty.

Ah," he continued fiercely, "but it is not for the Russians: we have no need of Freedom."

"Your time will surely come," suggested Horatio, more in hope than in certainty.

"No, we will not let that happen," said Mr. Voronov resolutely.

"The prowling Wolf of Freedom will never enter our Homes."

And with those words, he stepped out to the front of the house, to smoke a pipe, castigate Freedom, and admire

THE STARS IN THE RUSSIAN HEAVENS.

27

THE FREE ENJOYMENT OF A PASSION.

"Since it had not proved possible to reach Bering's Straits, and since now Mr. Ushinsky explained to me that boats for America were unlikely to leave Okhotsk within the year, I now had that freedom which a lesser man might have spurned – to pursue my adventures in a part of the Russian Empire which is little explored. I refer of course to Kamtchatka. It lay some distance to the south, over a raging sea.

"The circumstances which induced me to determine upon a return to Europe, previously visiting Kamtchatka, were set out in a letter to His Excellency, the Governor-General of Siberia, on the eighth day of July 1821. I will summarise this letter in two brief sentences:

"'I am not allowed to act with the expedition of Baron Wrangel, nor can I act against them, and therefore I cannot act at all. And the circumstances which have arisen in Okhotsk are such as to render useless my proceeding to America, even if a conveyance offered. There are other parts of the world in which I can better employ myself, more improve myself, and probably do better altogether. I have the honour to be etc. etc.'"

"And that," croaked the elegant lizard which sat upon the window-sill like a tiny South American god dressed all in scarlet finery, "you call a Freedom?"

John Dundas Cochrane looked blankly at the lizard.

"Because you are prevented from doing one thing, you are obliged to do another, as a poor second choice," persisted the lizard, which darted from one spot to another in a manner which much disconcerted the eye, "and yet you still call it Freedom? I," said the lizard grandly, "do not." With those words, the creature turned in a blink on its tail and vanished through the shades into sunlight.

John Dundas Cochrane shut his eyes at the glittering movement, and called the darkness Freedom.

At some time, it was difficult to tell precisely when, it was difficult to tell exactly where, he had taken a room in a small inn, named

El Precursor after the Colombian hero. This room had a roof, – or most of one, the remainder having tumbled off during the great earthquake of 1812 – a door, a vast portrait of Francisco de Miranda illuminated by a bonfire of candles, and – as an afterthought – two uncomfortable rooms. One room was already occupied by a group of travellers, passing themselves off as magicians, who were on their way to participate in the festivities marking the founding of the newly-independent country of Bolivia, and who were determined, it seemed, not to let one moment pass without celebrating the good fortune of the citizens of that country.

In this second, smaller and damper room of the inn, John Dundas Cochrane and Andrew Cochrane-Johnstone lay on their beds, staring at their lives, waiting for the end of time, or the end of the fever, or the end of the siesta, whichever one came first. In the event, the hours of siesta were swiftly overtaken by the hours of the night, and the hours of the night by the strangled crowing of a cockerel at the start of a new day. And neither gentleman noticed the passing of the hours, nor distinguished the grey moments between darkness and lightness.

"It was," mumbled John Cochrane, staring at a wall which had cracked from floor to ceiling on that grim day of the 26th March in 1812, and had horrified guests ever since – small lizards and enormous spiders darted in and out of the gap that was thus opened up – above, on the ceiling, a pair of flies made a fitful crossing of the pale grey expanse, "two months before a ship sailed from Okhotsk to Kamtchatka. On the 24th August we left aboard the Imperial transport brig Michael, with a crew of thirty-two and a handful of passengers. It took us," he sighed, a sigh which lingered long, and became a cough almost, if there had been strength enough in the chest, but satisfied itself with a long-drawn wheeze "two full days to cross the bar at entrance to the port, having struck on the first attempt. Okhotsk: a miserable port, father, perhaps only outdone in its difficulty by La Guayra here."

His father, who had been contemplating the shadows on the wall cast by a broken tree, which persisted in growing through the broken window, blinked at the mention of a boat. "Aye, the despatch boat we had when I was Governor – remember I had that hidden safely, so we could use it when I came back to Dominica? Mr. Diamond, he captained that for me and we managed to seize some prizes from the fishermen out there. What a sport, eh?" He laughed in fond memory. "Privateer work, and no one to complain."

"The voyage was thereafter uneventful," said the son, "apart from a small incident in which I was near drowned by the unsailorlike conduct of the crew. No matter. On the seventh day, we passed the Kurile Islands in safety, and after ten days we made the peak of Avatcha. I gazed up at that smoking volcano, but saw nothing there to rival the eruption we witnessed, father, on St Vincent's in 1812. But it was a further five days before we anchored in the harbour of St Peter and St Paul's, such were the contrary winds, the unpredictable currents, and the general lack of practical knowledge in the commanders of the vessel."

NEAR DROWNED BY THE UNSAILORLIKE CONDUCT OF THE CREW

"Privateer work was fine," continued the father, "but not half so good as the sport my brother Alexander provided. Made me prize-agent in Tortola when I got back – everything I could seize, sell, and more: all the loot from St Croix, St John and St Thomas. What about that cargo of slaves, eh? – one hundred fine dusky chaps: sold them all for the Havannah market, hard cash. Made me rich – in six years I bought how many houses on Dominica, son?" Hearing no answer, he reminded himself. "Four. And how many slaves did I have? Sixty. Sixty slaves. No, two-and-sixty, sir, two-and-sixty – and don't you forget it. Never mind the Holy William Wilberforce! And how many acres to my estates, eh?" Cochrane-Johnstone shook his head, trying hard to remember the best years of his life. "How many acres, sir, come on, how many acres? Ah! I'll tell you – six hundred and seventy-one acres. Not bad for a couple of years as the prize agent appointed by the Crown, whose representative was my fine brother, the Admiral Alexander Cochrane, who sailed the seas in his fine ship, and did not bother me."

"What?" asked John Cochrane, hearing a question, but not the one that had been posed. "What ships were there in St Peter and St Paul's? Sir, firstly there was the expedition of Captain Vassiliev, who had failed in his attempt to get round the north of the American continent. Had he persevered, he would almost certainly have reached Captain Parry's Melville Island."

"Melville?" asked his father. "Melville? What was he? A danger to himself and others, that's what he was. Surely you remember that our Henry Dundas, our Lord Melville was caught out and disgraced, and resigned his office. The man was, after all, a fool: he got caught. But for all that, I suppose he appointed me to Dominica. I married into his family, after all, the Hope-Johnstones – ah, Georgina, you died too fast for me." A breath was released, but it was not a sob. "Do you remember your mother?"

John Cochrane continued his own line of thought. "No, it is my firm opinion that, with proper caution and people qualified for the task, a ship might sail from Kamtchatka to survey the Mackenzie River. Perhaps I will return there. Perhaps – not. No." He shook his head. "I will never return to Kamtchatka. Never, do you hear!

"Also in the harbour was a brig under Portuguese colours, and another from the Sandwich Islands. The former brought a cargo of flour from Macao, and the latter a cargo of salt for the Emperor, for which they received, in return, some animals with a view to propagating the breeds. Bears, for example – I doubt that bears on the Sandwich Islands will be of much utility. But it was a fine vessel, the Sandwich Island brig, officered by three Englishmen."

"Sandwiches, now." The old man sat up suddenly, feeling hungry. "The beef must be red and bloody. The bread must be fresh but cold. And there must be relish." He called out aloud, perhaps hoping that a servant would come running: "Relish! Or pickles."

"Astonishing though it might seem, my arrival at Kamtchatka coincided with the largest number of vessels ever to congregate in the harbour: eight, all told. And, even more astonishing, FLOGGED, KNOUTED, apart from the three English officers mentioned, there were AND EXILED three other Englishmen there. An Irish Englishman, Mr. Dobell, the Russian consul-general to the Pacific Ocean; then a Bostonian Englishman; and finally a cockney, flogged, knouted, and exiled from Moscow for forgery, but well received in every house."

"Forgery, now that is an honourable profession," observed the father. "Though it's not one I've tried." He counted them off on the fingers of his hands, his professions. "Governor, gambler on the Stock Exchange, trader in slaves and guns, importer of sheep, grower of coffee, Member of Parliament. A man has to do all manner of things, mind, if he's to get on in the world. The world doesn't owe you a living. Honourable professions, all. I've tried them all, and here I am in the land of the free. I've a plan, oh, I've a plan." He tapped the side of his nose and winked with one watery eye at the musquitoes that whined in the surrounding darkness.

The son continued. "With so many ships and so many visitors, the society of St Peter and St Paul's spent every possible day and night in suppers, balls, routs, masquerades, dinners and breakfasts. Some were given by the Chief of Kamtchatka, Captain Rikord, and his amiable lady; others by Kamtchatkan notables; others yet by the chiefs of the expedition and by the captains of the various ships. Not to be out-done in any of this jollity, I myself hoisted the British flag over Kamtchatka, and gave a fête in honour of all my acquaintances.

"Two full months passed in this way; I was unable to leave until Vassiliev's expedition had left the bay. I was left – father?" The dusk had fallen, and from the narrow street outside came the sounds of evening. Within the inn, some kind of argument went on down the stairs, perhaps indicative of the preparation of food and drink. John Cochrane turned in the darkness towards his father. "I have not told you, father."

Cochrane-Johnstone emitted an indistinct grunt, which could have signified encouragement.

"In those two months, I was left to the free enjoyment of a passion, which was to be crowned with the reward of marriage."

A deep silence suddenly fell upon the world, as if the glorious high loneliness of the Andes had been brought on giant feathered wings to the city of Caraccas. Not a sound was permitted.

"Marriage?" at last laughed Colonel Cochrane-Johnstone, struggling for breath. "Marriage?" he repeated, in a tone of deep disbelief, once he had regained his powers of breathing. "What do you know of marriage? I've had marriages, my boy, that you couldn't believe. First there was Georgina, your mother, boy – remember her? Fine young girl, even if we got too intimate before – no, I will say nothing. And no sooner had I my appointment to Dominica than she ups and dies on me. Leaving me with you and your sister Elizabeth. Sad days, sad days. And then there was Amélie de Clugny," he said gloomily. "The things I could tell you about Amélie de Clugny, my boy – that would change your opinions on marriage forever." He enumerated to himself, with a warm glow of remembrance, the many charms of Amélie and the arguments they had had, husband and wife.

"My airy phantoms," mused young John, "my bold desires and my eccentric turn were at once dissipated by one woman. I found her amongst all the youth, beauty and fashion of the town of St Peter and St Paul's. She looked up to me, saw my qualities at first glance, as I did hers. It was as if, after so many thousand miles, and so many months of walking, I had found a sheltering port. A place where I might rest my weary head and gather strength for the morrow. Mrs. Cochrane – as she was to become, after several thrilling weeks of waiting – had that dove-like fondness of which the poet speaks."

John Cochrane halted a moment, the better to reflect. It was not a happy moment. He had left his wife in London, and now he was alone again, two thousand miles away and more; in this long night no one would take his head in her hands and look up at him, and with one word, one gesture, make him feel, even briefly, like a man who was wanted for his own sake. "But," he continued, shivering off the weakness that had crept up on him, "before I took her to the altar, I deemed it necessary to make a tour of the peninsula. I did so. On the twentieth day of November, I left my friends, one of whom, on parting, implanted on me a kiss—"

"A kiss? A kiss?" The father was outraged. "You find a woman, and all you can think of is – a kiss? When I was your age, there was far more than kissing to be done. Yes, and even when I was far more than your age. I remember – what was her name, now? Ah – Louise, was it? Sixteen and damned pretty. Of course, no sooner had I bedded her than she got herself with child and we had to take her for a cruise to get rid of the bloody thing. That cost me a pretty penny." The Colonel laughed to himself at the memory.

"—a kiss that I carried with me for six weeks as I made my way across the desolation, over the mountains, into the valleys and through the villages of Kamtchatka. From the village of Avatcha, I travelled to Nachiekin, where I had to combat a drunken postillion, several bad dogs, a saucy chieftain and an annoying shipmate from the Michael. From Nachiekin—" John Dundas Cochrane at last halted in his tracks. "From Nachiekin—" he repeated and stopped again. There was a long, dark silence, broken only by the sound of snoring from his father. The silence lasted all night, until the early hours before dawn, those hours in which the soul dies within all who lie awake, those hours from which even the brightest dawn is no relief, those hours which dissect Time and lay out its bones one by one, to dry and crack.

"I had travelled nine thousand miles and more to reach Kamtchatka. I had met enough useless Cossacks and drunken guides than a man can tolerate. Now I wandered around Kamtchatka for six weeks, and truly saw more of it than I cared. I saw the neglected village where my wife had first seen the light of day. I crossed the mountains from west to east. I was obliged to admire the wild garlic and I fell into an abyss. I met a man who had met Captain Cook's associate Captain Clerk. I saw native dances performed by females who should have known better, in which advances are made in a most unbecoming posture and the dancer's hands commit outrages upon a male partner. I visited the sulphur springs at Malka, whose waters are most unpleasant to the taste, and which is otherwise deserving of little notice. And I returned at last, to find my betrothed true and all that I could desire."

HE ADMIRED THE GARLIC AND FELL INTO THE ABYSS

John Cochrane shivered violently, his teeth chattered. He supposed that the fever was passing. Shivering was a good sign, even if, perhaps, the irregular slicing pain through his head, and the maelstrom in his bowels, was not.

"No matter," he said to himself, since no one else was attending, "no matter. On the eighth day of January, in the year 1822, Old Style, I was married. I am certainly the first Englishman that ever married a Kamtchatdale. The ceremony was attended with much more pomp and parade than if it had been celebrated in England. The winter was passed in a constant round of hospitality and comfort, and hardly anything remarkable occurred. Three earthquakes were felt, two of them very severe. The volcano of Kliutcheska Sopka emitted flames and lava. It was a peaceful time. Only a few individuals died of scurvy. The snows disappeared at the beginning of May, and by the start of July, I was ready to sail back to Siberia."

He pondered for a while, then the colic in his stomach obliged him to make haste to the bed-pan. He swung his legs over the edge of the narrow bed, tried to stand up. He failed to do so. He was in any case too late.

"St Peter and St Paul's – a place of two-and-forty dwellings, all wretched, the public buildings emblems of misery. I have never seen, even on the banks of the Frozen Sea, so contemptible a place, hardly meriting the name of a village, much less that of a city. With some relief, on the fifth day of July, I sailed away." A CONTEMPTIBLE PLACE

There was no summoning sunrise, only a dull start to the day. In the world outside, the town awoke unwillingly from its slumbers. Cochrane fell back on his bed, cold and damp with his sweat, stinking from the outflow which he had been unable to control; he slipped into a deep and greatly troubled sleep, while his father, now awake, looked on dispassionately, wondering how an incontinent simpleton like that could be

HIS ONLY SON.

28

I FORWARDED MY WIFE ON, IN THE CHARGE OF A COSSACK.

His only son had stirred from his greatly troubled sleep towards noon, when a deputation of Good Society had arrived, alerted by some nameless admirer to the presence of a famous traveller. The deputation announced itself down below, much to the annoyance of the inn-keeper, who supposed there had been some mistake, and insisted – but in vain – that the Mayor try some other inn. After some argument, both philosophical and physical, the party forced their way to the upper floor and knocked officiously on the door of the Cochranes' room. The elderly Colonel opened up.

"Commander Cochrane?" asked the Mayor respectfully, lifting his hat an exact inch.

"Colonel," snarled the guest. "Governor. The Honourable. Brigadier once. If you have any manners," he added.

"Brigadier Cochrane," the Mayor corrected himself, lifting his hat to two deferential inches, "I am Señor de la Cruz, the responsible authority in this city. I believe you are the cousin of the great Admiral himself, Thomas Cochrane, famous Liberator of Chile and Peru, loyal friend of Bernardo O'Higgins, First Admiral of the Emperor Pedro's Navy in Brazil—"

"That young fool," interrupted Cochrane-Johnstone sharply, "is my nephew. He has no more brains than his father."

Not expecting this rebuff, the Mayor halted. In the ensuing silence, there came a hoarse voice from the gloom of the midday room:

"Who is it, father?"

"Never mind," came the familiar paternal advice. "Now," he said, keeping his eyes firmly on the Mayor, "let me tell you a thing or two about Thomas, Lord Cochrane, Admiral of This and That. Did you know that he swindled the London Stock Exchange in the year 1814?"

The collector of taxes and elegant man of fashion, José Avido, who was foremost in the entourage, whistled in admiration. "He swindled the Stock Exchange? Do you have any details, señor?"

Cochrane-Johnstone had more than enough details, and was willing to share them with the gathered company; but the Mayor with creditable single-mindedness interrupted: "If you are not that Commander Cochrane, then perhaps I can be introduced to the one who is?" He peered round the door, as did all of his retinue; the combined weight of their peering forced the Colonel back from the threshold and into the room. The delegation took a united step forward; and then one united step backward, as an unmentionable stench reached their nostrils.

"Who is it, father?" repeated the same hoarse voice.

"Is that Commander John Cochrane?" asked the Mayor.

"I am he," confirmed the heavy sleeper.

"In that case," said the Mayor, suddenly more confident in his dealings, "the town-council has the great honour to present to the Incomparable Pedestrian a token of its esteem. Pablo," he ordered over his shoulder, "step forward with the items!"

A small man, one-legged and bearing a large bundle, hobbled into the room.

"We have here," said Señor de la Cruz grandly, "a full set of traditional clothing, such as, I am sure, you will wish to wear during your peregrinations through our green and pleasant land. We have, firstly, a hat." The mayor's tailor stepped forward awkwardly and laid a large straw, broad-brimmed hat upon Cochrane's bed. ITEM, GENTLEMAN'S PANTALOONS The recipient sat up as best he could, blinked the sweat from his eyes and expressed his thanks. "Item, a cloak," continued the Mayor magnificently. A long green cloak was laid out. "Item, boots." There was a murmur of surprise and awe at this munificence, as Pedro solemnly placed a pair of boots, fitted with spurs and the most enormous rowels anyone had ever attempted to attach to a spur. Amid the mounting cries of admiration, the boots were placed at Cochrane's bed-side. The Mayor called for silence, the better that he might reach the climax of the ceremony: "Item, gentleman's pantaloons." And a pair of light cotton pantaloons, striped dark and light blue, was held up for everyone's approbation.

"Sirs," said Cochrane, hoisting himself to a sitting position, the better to shake the drops of rank moisture from his tangled hair, "I am deeply honoured. It is my custom, when I travel in a foreign land, to adopt the dress of the inhabitants. I am grateful for your attentions in this matter, and will be sure to wear these articles when I leave. You can be sure that, when I come to write in London the narrative of my perilous journey across the Andean Mountains, the generosity of this benevolent town will be described in the fullest detail, as an example of the greatest kindness and hospitality of the native peoples." So saying, Cochrane fell back on his bed and shut his eyes. "It proves my point," he added weakly.

The Mayor, abundantly satisfied with the result of his civic largesse, hustled his counsellors from the room. "The honoured traveller must rest," he whispered, very loudly, "let us leave him until tonight. Commander Cochrane," he called back into the pungent darkness, "we expect to see you this evening at a Grand Reception in your honour, at the town-hall. We will commence at nine o'clock. Do not fail us. There will be many, many beautiful women there." After issuing this invitation, the Mayor slammed the door and hurried himself down the stairs. He needed a drink. The entire Town Council accompanied him, almost unable to bear the exciting prospect of a civic reception, something that had not taken place since 1819, when a lady purporting to be the Four-Breasted Seductress of Taprobana had arrived in the town – disappointingly, she had been unmasked as the painted wife of a Mexican charlatan; and, aroused by the Mayor's unprecedented and altogether incredible announcement, all the gentlemen burned with desire to see many, many beautiful women.

Cochrane-Johnstone, also, was of a mind to attend the reception. It was certain that, as the father of the celebrated traveller, he would be permitted a seat at the high table, a place from which any red-blooded male could doubtless pick and choose whatever he wanted. With this prospect firmly before him, he cheerfully set about polishing his military accoutrements, whistling a jaunty military air as he did so. His son, oblivious to those preparations in his honour, slept without rest for six hours longer.

His dreams were endless, criss-crossed by gluttons and bears, fiery volcanoes and icy torrents, horses and ship-wrecks. In vain did Mrs. Cochrane cry out to him that she was drowning in a Sea of Shadow: the sea had been poorly charted – there was nothing he could do. One by one, Mrs. Golovnin, the three daughters of Mr. Major, Mrs. Bentham – all drifted past and were swept away to their deaths, while Commander Cochrane stood on the tilting deck and did nothing.

At eight o'clock in the evening, John Cochrane felt strong enough to travel. He went out into the yard behind the inn, and, with three buckets of brackish water, he gave himself a bath. His nakedness offended no one fortunately, least of all the kitchen-maid who admired the manly apparition for a period not measured by a clock, while distractedly pulling the head off a chicken. At twenty minutes after eight, John Cochrane stood before a large mirror, a stained and shattered survivor of the earthquake, brought to him by the self-same maid; he was now dressed in the blue striped pantaloons, the large boots and spurs, the green cloak and the broad-brimmed hat of the people of Gran Colombia. Had his moustache perhaps been a few inches longer both to right and left, then it would have been hard to distinguish him from any other traveller on that great continent.

"This will do," he proclaimed, and surrendered his old clothes to the maid. He picked up his small knapsack and turned to his father, who had been watching these preparations with some disquiet.

"Father, I must be on my way. The mines and the mountains call me, and I cannot delay here."

"But they are expecting you at the town-hall. In an hour. You cannot leave!"

Cochrane the son shook his head firmly: "I have a journey to make, I cannot linger. I have received their compliment, now I must make the journey by which I will repay their confidence. Goodbye, father, I will see you again in two years."

Cochrane-Johnstone cursed violently, partly because he thought it unlikely that he would see his son ever again, partly in disbelief at the boy's stupidity, and mostly because he thought that he himself would not longer be welcome at the town-hall, for the promised festivities. On the last of these matters, he need not have worried.

John Cochrane embraced his father, strode optimistically from the room, clattered down the stairs and found himself a mule. In less than half an hour, under the rapid darkness of the night, he found himself where he had so much wanted to be – alone, on the open road of Gran Colombia, and on the distant horizon the dim outlines of the mountains.

The mule required entertainment, said its owner, otherwise it would not move.

"On the fifth day of July I sailed away," began therefore the travel-ler, striding out ahead of the mule. The sounds of merriment and expectation which filled the town had been left behind. The avid mule, anxious not to miss a word, finally caught up with the great pedestrian. Without a moment's thought, Cochrane seized the bridle and placed himself on the creature's bony back

THE AVID MULE
CAUGHT UP

"As we sailed forth from Kamtchatka, the volcano of Avatcha erupted, setting fire to immense tracts of forest to the north, and lighting up the night-sky as if it had been an Aurora Borealis. There was a great gale blowing, and there had been a severe concussion of the earth during the night. The gale drove us 150 miles to the south-east, and then we had to wait for a south-east gale to drive us back to the Kurile Islands, which we reached, though not without a great danger of ship-wreck, which would have left no one alive to tell the dismal tale."

The animal trotted along with a commendable lack of emotion. On such a cool night, there were no flies to bother it, and the calm tones of its rider were like sweet music to its large ears. Besides, the road to Los Teques led downhill on an easy gradient.

"Finally, by Providence alone, we were driven between rocks and breakers, into a bay which had never yet been charted, and which I did not have time to survey. Men, women, children, live lumber – all beheld our peril with the most awful countenances. It was only on the twentieth day out of St Peter and St Paul's that we managed to clear the Kurile Islands, and on the thirty-third day we arrived at the outer anchorage of Okhotsk. Feeling anxious to get ashore, I took a boat through the surf and reached land safely; six of the twelve in a boat which followed me, were swallowed up by the surf. On the following day, Captain Rikord, his family, and Mrs. Cochrane, reached the shore safely, and we were well received by my friend Captain Ushinsky and his amiable wife.

"It was three weeks before the party was ready to depart on the long journey to Yakutsk, some eight hundred miles to the west. The season was already late for travelling, but I could delay no longer. My present situation upon leaving Okhotsk was too different from the last, to escape my observation. Then, I wandered about alone, careless of the past, unconcerned for the future, and, like this brutish mule, alive only to the present hour."

At these insulting words, his steed kicked out with its hind legs. In his weakness, John Cochrane almost slid to the ground, but he held on with uncommon skill. The mule set off once more, remembering the indignities of the past and hatching a plan for vengeance in the future.

"Now, by contrast, our caravan amounted to two hun- PRUDENCE AND dred horses, of which I had thirteen. Provisions were laid FORESIGHT in for six weeks. And now, of course, I had a young wife to protect through an execrable journey on horseback: I felt, and felt deeply, that prudence and foresight were peculiarly necessary."

John Dundas Cochrane at that moment noticed that the traditional costume of a Colombian traveller was not well-suited to a night high in the Colombian mountains. Colombians, it might be supposed, did their travelling in daylight, with the sun beating upon their backs, not having learned the secrets of a great pedestrian. Their cloaks were thin, and pantaloons thinner still. It was for this reason, Cochrane supposed, that he shook and shivered and his teeth chattered in the cool night air. He sneezed five times in quick succession, each one a jolt of electricity in his skull. At last he dismounted and, leading his mule by a halter, began to walk briskly to warm himself up.

"She had no knowledge of horses. No matter – she bore it well."

Cochrane whistled a short tune to himself, reminded by the words 'she bore it well' of a verse or two of some Royal Naval shanty. It amused him, so long as no one was listening.

"There was little of interest in that journey. In the mountains, we met the post from Yakutsk, and then were overtaken by the post from Okhotsk. The latter had met a bear, which had destroyed most of the letters and papers – the Journal of Captain Vassiliev's Expedition, in particular, suffered much from this ursine depredation. We lost horses to the rivers, to the weather and to the difficulties of the road. In one day, six dropped dead on the road. Of my thirteen, only one reached Yakutsk alive."

The mule shook its head in disbelief and horror.

"As we approached the River Aldan, our baggage had to be transferred to oxen, and I was obliged to forward my wife on, in the charge of the Cossack, and remain behind for thirty-six hours to buy or exchange horses as could best be done. The inhabitants of that part of the world are all Yakuti. They are civil, obliging and hospitable. And if I met one who was knavish, then he would retort, with justice: 'Who taught the Yakuti to be knaves?' Ah, who indeed, my friend?"

Man and mule, thus cunningly questioning the ways of the world, approached the sleeping town of Los Teques, situated at a strategic pass high in the hills. From there, the road was said to lead downwards and onwards to Maracay.

"At last, on the first day of October, we came to Yakutsk," growled Cochrane from a tightened throat, as he moved like a ghost through the single deserted street of the town, having walked ten thousand miles in less than a week. "Yakutsk." He paused once more to collect his thoughts, then made up his mind: "Yakutsk. If my former opinion of it was bad, it was now worse. And in particular, Good Society was wanting – do you hear that, my friend?" The mule made no response, but Cochrane paid no heed. "There was no one there with whom I could spend the endless evenings. Not one. I passed two long months at Yakutsk, preparing a sledge that would take me on to Irkutsk. The cold was extraordinary – falling to 32 and 35 degrees of frost by the Réaumur scale. But I was never compelled to wear other than my usual clothing – shoes, worsted stockings, coat, waistcoat, trousers and hat. No gloves. I did not feel the cold."

He shivered – his entire body convulsed – the world turned black – he drew the cloak closer around him. Together, man and beast began the long road down the hill.

"On the fifteenth day of November, I left Yakutsk, and on the seventeenth day of December I reached Irkutsk. Fifteen hundred miles was thus covered, at a rate of around fifty miles per day. A feat not likely to be matched here in Colombia. The Russians are, I believe, the fastest travellers upon the earth. In winter, upon good trails, a man on a sledge may travel two hundred miles in a day. A Russian courier on Imperial business may travel one hundred miles per day from one end of the Empire to the other – as Holman discovered to his cost."

Cochrane remembered Lieutenant Holman, the blind traveller, who inched his way across Siberia and into the arms of the widow Bentham, only to be reeled back at great speed by an emissary of the Emperor himself, as if he had been attached to a gigantic fishing line: after which, he was ejected with all expedition and great ignominy from the Empire. Poor old Holman.

"I never suffered such a fate!" he laughed cheerfully, and brought upon himself a great fit of coughing that forced him first to his knees, where the rowels on his spurs threatened severe laceration to his buttocks ; and then to the ground. The mule stood idly by, waiting for the end. It never came.

"Having arrived in good time to breakfast with my old friend Captain Koutigin, I presented myself to Governor Tzedler, who insisted I take up residence in one of the comfortable apartments in his mansion. I was pleased to do so, as my young and ignorant wife could not fail, in the society of his lady, his sister and his daughter, to acquire so many of those little graces so necessary to the female character. There was but little society in Irkutsk; public balls had fallen off, but I received many invitations to more private ones, and to one memorable masquerade. The time of carnival was a time of much amusement, and many well-dressed characters went from house to house, I, of course, among the merriest."

The mule continued its own merry amusement of munching at the short grass. This rhythmic music calmed Cochrane sufficiently to continue his story.

"Now that I had reached Irkutsk, a great opportunity was offered to me, to make a small journey south into the mountains that border the mysterious lands of China. At Irkutsk, I was, of course, introduced to the new Governor-General, Mr. Lavinsky, whom I found – let there be no mistake – as amiable as Mr. Speransky. I expressed to Mr. Lavinsky my great desire to visit Nertchinsk and Kiakhta before continuing my journey to Europe. A gentleman named Mr. Strannack was about to make an inspection of the post-offices in Irkutsk and Yakutsk, beginning with those very places I hoped to reach. Mr. Strannack being agreeable to my company, and Mr. Lavinsky issuing permission for my expedition, we set off with great energy."

Cochrane lay deprived of strength at the side of the road. A figure stooped over him in the darkness, and spoke his name; the voice was like that of the kitchen-maid. Then two pairs of arms lifted him from his resting-place and carried him, weightless, indoors. It was a surprise, but not a shock, to find that he had returned once more to the shattered inn he had recently escaped. It was a shock, but not a surprise, to find that his clothes stank and his face was bloodied, and that his bed was as damp with sweat as if he had barely left it. Much may happen to a guest at the inn of

EL PRECURSOR.

29

THIS MAN SMELLS WORSE THAN THE MAJOR'S BED-PAN.

A wolf crept in at the back door of the building at the very instant that Mr. Voronov stepped out at the front. But this wolf was no wolf at all: rather, it was but a book-seller, or traveller, from the Polish town of Krakow. That same surprised traveller from Krakow with large ears whom the inn-keeper had ejected from his house of hospitality earlier in the evening. It was that same man, much the worse for wear, cold, bloodied, stinking of piss – much may happen to a guest at the inn of Mr. Voronov.

Curiously, it was the man lying dying in the ghostly arms of Josephine who first noticed the new arrival. Major Sinclair peered through the dark concentric rings which were gradually closing in on his vision, then struggled to lean on an elbow.

"Isengrim, Isengrim, have you come to pray for me at last?" he inquired, a catch to his breath.

Those would-be mourners who yet remained in the room looked at the death-bed and then blankly at each other.

"Isengrim?" asked Horatio.

"Isengrim – the wolf, damn you," said the Major snappishly. "Use your eyes – there he is!" He pointed with one hand – foolishly, the hand attached to the elbow on which he leaned. He fell back on the pillow, the air rushed from his lungs and he succumbed to a fit of coughing. Ksenia, having seen at a glance the poor condition of the wolf, was torn between attending to the injuries of the one, or the coughing fit of the other. In the end, Yadviga struggled over to the dying man and beat his cough from him with five dextrous blows to chest and back.

"Now," she said confidently, "you will not be doing that again in a hurry, you mark my words."

Ksenia, meanwhile, ran to the dark corridor and – with the aid, naturally, of Horatio – supported the injured man who swayed there before the door. Together, they brought him to the stove and sat him down. The man was old, perhaps sixty or seventy years of age, his hair white, his pointed face – such as could be seen behind a matted mass of grey-black whiskers and beard – crumpled by the years and the wind. On his forehead was a vast red weal, and blood was still trickling from the nasty gash at the centre of the redness. And the smell from his clothes was most objectionable. Horatio recoiled with a stifled gasp, regretting his lack of a handkerchief. Yadviga was more subtle.

"By all the Holy Saints of Novgorod!" she exclaimed, "What is that stench? This man smells worse than the Major's bed-pan, you mark my words."

Therein, of course, was the pith and essence of the matter.

The injured man warmed up and the smell intensified. Soon, steam drifted upwards and outwards to fill the room – it could have propelled a Scottish boat on the Orinoco River. But Ksenia had smelled worse in her short life. She removed the man's coat gently and gave it to Horatio to hang in the kitchen: she had no sympathy for the resident rats of that apartment, who, to a man, protested: to no avail. By the time Horatio had returned, the man had been wrapped in a blanket borrowed from Josephine's bed – in one night, the woman had done more good with her bed than in all her glorious days as Empress. Now she – Ksenia, no Empress, but a woman of far greater quality altogether – had organised some warm water and commanded Horatio and Yadviga to assist in cleaning the man's wounds.

"How did you come by these injuries?" asked Horatio in an interested manner.

"I don't know – something flew at me from out of the night," answered the man. When he spoke, he nervously scratched himself behind the ear.

"A bat?" asked Horatio.

"An owl?" asked Ksenia.

"An assassin?" asked Yadviga, more prosaically.

None of these suggestions merited a response.

The injured prowler of the night seemed quite agreeable to his new identity: Isengrim, the Wolf, late of Krakow; he tried it out, then nodded in satisfaction. Such things happen frequently to old men, and this was an old man both axe-stricken and age-stricken.

While the three mourners questioned Isengrim, late of Krakow, Major Sinclair was fully awake and striding firmly through the years 1805 to 1814 as if they were but yesterday. The ghost of Cochrane-Johnstone was back in the room, much the worse for drink, much the worse for the manner in which he had lived his life.

"You might have thought that, once Melville was lost, I was lost too. You thought that, did you not, Sinclair?"

Major Sinclair swore upon the heads of all his children – of whom he had none to speak, none that he knew of – that he had never considered the Colonel would go under at the first assault. Colonel Cochrane-Johnstone was irritated at the Major's use of the similes of war: "War," he had frequently said, "is not about fighting and dying: the point of war is to watch, to wait and to profit. Nothing more. Please do me the honour of remembering that.

THE POINT OF WAR IS TO WATCH, TO WAIT AND TO PROFIT. NOTHING MORE

"That fool Melville may have fallen in 1805, but I was elected MP for Grampound, in the county of Cornwall in 1807. Never a more respectable man than me then, Sinclair, eh?"

Sinclair agreed.

"And did I not, in that session of the Westminster Parliament, campaign most rigorously, most energetically, and most convincingly against corruption?"

Sinclair agreed.

"Corruption in Parliament and in the Army and the Navy?"

Sinclair agreed.

"Oh, I did, sir, I did indeed. I was a man of the people, and – had I stayed a little longer – I would have been purer than the fleece of a spring lamb. Luckily, I found myself a post back in the West Indies, handed the job of MP to my brother George, and left before I could be castrated like a spring lamb." The Colonel laughed uproariously and prodded his Major with the cane. "Where's that rum, Sinclair?" Sinclair obliged.

"Aye, man, do you remember those cruises we used to take?" The Colonel examined the rum-bottle. The level of spirits was dangerously low. "Is this the best you could do, Sinclair? Damn your tight fists!" He made himself more comfortable on the bed and looked around. "Fine bed, sir, fine bed. Amélie had one like this – white sheets, red blankets, sky-blue canopy suspended overhead. Red, white and blue, just like the Union flag. That was 'Love', sir: a soft bed, a sunny morning, gauze drifting in the breeze from the window; it was the finest place to be, I tell you. Where d'you get this bed, sir?" Without waiting for a reply, he continued. "The easy acquisition of money, that's what it was all about. Nothing more and nothing less."

"A robber?" demanded Yadviga.

"A wolf?" wondered Horatio.

"A bear?" proposed Ksenia, instantly startling herself. Horatio and the widow looked at each other for a moment. Both had stood in the garden to the rear of the house, innocent, alone, unprotected by light or by fire. What if...?

"You mark my words: it was a Flying Devil," stated Yadviga, in total disregard for the rational advances of the eighteenth and nineteenth centuries. Perhaps she meant to speak of a meteorite, with which Russia is liberally sprinkled – some larger than others – and which was more likely to have struck a man down on a night such as this: but not a devil, which rarely flies.

"Perhaps it was poetry?" thought the man aloud, dimly remembering some literary discussion as a prelude to his accident.

Horatio shook his head in pity: the poor man was clearly dazed. A robber was the more plausible explanation. Horatio put himself on the alert – if there was a robber abroad, there were women to be protected; he should deal with all that came.

"But you wouldn't know about my deal with the Spanish Government, though, eh, Sinclair?" asked the Colonel, in a patronising manner.

The Major resigned himself to being told the story for the hundredth time. Since the Colonel seemed not about to depart, he knew, after thirty years and more of friendship – friendship? Sinclair wondered about that more and more these days: had he ever had a friend? He doubted it. Acquaintances came and, more frequently, went. Friendship with the Colonel? – never in a thousand years – to the Colonel, he was just a financially-convenient comrade-in-arms. The nearest he himself had to friends were these angels who now fluttered around his death-bed, who would never go away again.

"No, sir," said he, "I was not there. I remained in Tortola."

"Aye, that you did, you simpleton. Tortola – there was nothing left for me there after that man Mackenrot started with his accusations. The man was no gentleman – a magistrate and no gentleman. Had to get out, too hot for me there once they started asking questions. So I did a deal with the Spanish Government. Good God! It was like stealing pennies from a blind man. One hundred thousand muskets they wanted, to fight their war against France. One hundred thousand muskets, says I: that will be – watch me here, Sinclair—" The Colonel made a mime of ticking numbers off on his fingers: "—that'll be three hundred thousand guineas, Señores. Por favor! Well, of course, they didn't have three hundred thousand guineas – I got some in Spanish dollars, and the rest was to be made up in sheep."

Colonel Cochrane-Johnstone paused for effect.

"Sheep, Sinclair. What was I supposed to do with sheep? I had all the women I wanted, I didn't need sheep." He laughed fit to burst at this ribaldry. Sinclair laughed dutifully, because he knew that was his part in this small, select drama, played out in gloomy clubs and seedy cafés over the past fifteen years. Had he not laughed, the Colonel might have forgotten his lines. Had the Colonel forgotten his lines, he might have died. Had he died, Sinclair too would have died.

"Sheep, then, could be sent to the United States of America. I had the muskets manufactured in Birmingham – finest British workmanship, seventeen shillings apiece. They didn't all function as they should, but in one hundred thousand, who is going to notice?"

"Perhaps the man whose musket didn't fire when it should have?" suggested the Major.

"Perhaps that man, sir, perhaps that man," agreed the Colonel gravely. "But his disappointment probably didn't last long in battle."

With that consoling notion, which could not have failed to bring tears of gratitude to a widow's eyes and comfort to a clutch of penniless orphans, the Colonel re-considered Sheep.

"Sent them to New York, but they were all dead by the time they arrived. A lot of mutton, sir." The Colonel kicked at his cane in an ill-tempered manner. "Then they accused me of swindle! Me, sir – can you credit it?"

The Major found it hard to believe, as he should, and harder still not to give credit.

"Sixteen thousand, three hundred and one Pounds Sterling – that's what they said I owed; and a small matter of half-a-crown on top. I needed to do something, and quickly. So I got myself elected to Grampound again in 1812 – that settled things for a while. Until that young fool Thomas, Lord Cochrane ruined me completely."

"Mammon," observed Isengrim slowly, as the women dabbed at his MAMMON   cuts and bruises, "is the god of the greatest part of the Cochrane family, and there are but few instances of their love for glory."

Horatio frowned at Isengrim, late of Krakow. The blow to the head had disrupted the man's sense of place.

Ksenia looked askance at the wounded man in pity: the blow to the head had disrupted the man's sense of time.

Yadviga rolled her eyes, finding herself confirmed in her professional opinion that injured men who had lost their senses simply needed a purge of their bowels. Did not St Theodore possess the perfect holy instrument for that? – of course he did – but it was not a pretty thing to see. She crossed herself and prayed to St Theodore that he would roll up his sleeves, extend his holy middle finger and drive the Devil from this man.

"There is but one Cochrane," said Isengrim with considerable assurance, "who acted out of motives which had little to do with money." To add weight to this opinion, he scratched his left ear energetically. It was a large ear, to be sure: any larger, and Ksenia would have been obliged – against all social propriety – to pass comment aloud.

"And that was?" asked Horatio, interested at last.

"That was the time," replied Colonel Cochrane-Johnstone, "when my nephew Thomas swindled the Stock Market and

BY HIS STUPIDITY

led Lord Chief Justice Ellenborough right to my door."

30

CONFOUND THE KEY-HOLE,
HE EXCLAIMED.

"That was Charles Stuart Cochrane," replied Isengrim. He took a sharp breath as Ksenia inadvertently flinched and jabbed his cut. "I know him well. If he has a fault, it has nothing to do with money."

"That is true," allowed the young widow, gently drying the latest flow of blood from Isengrim's grizzled face. "You have met Captain Cochrane, then?" she asked politely.

"Indeed," said Isengrim, scratching his interesting ear, "on more than one occasion. Mr. Cochrane is a man with whom one might enjoy innocent pleasures."

"H'm," observed Ksenia doubtfully, not willing to upset the injured man.

"H'm," agreed Horatio, having heard enough of cousin Charles.

Isengrim chose to ignore the combined pursed lips of his medical attendants and embarked on the tale of Juan de Vega.

"Juan de Vega?" interrupted Horatio, once more at a loss. At times, he felt that the night moved too quickly: he had not yet come across Juan de Vega.

"Perhaps he means Lopez de Vega," suggested Mr. Voronov, the literary inn-keeper who, having decided that the Russian Motherland stood safe still from the Prowling Wolf of Freedom, had felt chilled and re-entered the frontier-land of death. He was surprised to find yet another watcher here, but made no further comment, other than to propose El Fénix de España as the subject of Isengrim's story. "Born in the year 1562, Lopez de Vega was a man of the greatest passion, the pre-eminent playwright of the—"

"No," said Isengrim grimly, "I do not mean Lopez de Vega, the butcher's assistant; I mean Juan de Vega, Spanish troubadour, also known under his black wig, straw hat and Spanish unmentionables, as Charles Cochrane, once of Colombia. He did, of course," he conceded with a slight bow towards Voronov, who refused to reciprocate, "name himself after the more famous playwright."

"Did he so?" said Horatio, now clear on the name, if not the motive.

"In August of the year 1828, after suffering a disappointment in his life—"

"Did he say that?" asked Ksenia quietly.

"He did indeed, madam," replied Isengrim gravely, "although I am not privy to the facts of the case. It may perhaps have been a financial disappointment, for he had invested heavily in some South American Oyster stocks; or it may have been a matter of passion."

"I believe it was both," said Ksenia Ivanovna. Horatio patted her hand. Ksenia Ivanovna patted the wolf's long forehead. Yadviga patted the empty bottle. Major Sinclair, who was somewhere in Paris, patted the lumpy leg of the sweaty woman of easy virtue who had placed herself beside him. Mr. Voronov patted the hand that wielded the axe. He had just recognised Isengrim as the traveller from Krakow.

"Sir," said he without the slightest hint of regret, compassion, embarrassment or any other emotion which might signal sentimentality, "you had the audacity earlier this evening to enter my inn and ask for a room."

Isengrim scratched, rather than patted, both of his ears, one after the other: to have scratched them simultaneously, which was entirely practical, would have provoked concern. He regarded his late host. "Yes," he said frostily, "I made that mistake. But a book-seller may not always stay at the costliest inns, and frequently has to choose the smallest and meanest and dirtiest."

Voronov bridled up, as any inn-keeper would at such words: rarely had he been so insulted to his face, in such a cool manner.

"Book-seller?" he demanded, "You admit to being a book-seller?"

"I have that honour and that pleasure," confirmed Isengrim unashamedly. "You may, should you choose, examine my stock."

Mr. Voronov was almost lost for words. The two men stared each other down for several moments, while Ksenia and Horatio took a cautious step backwards. At last the inn-keeper gave voice to his outrage.

"Had I known, sir, that you were a book-seller, I would have thrown you out of my inn without a second thought!"

"Sir, you did throw me out," replied Isengrim, "without a second thought, for no reason that I could see."

"Ah," said the inn-keeper, feeling slightly ill-at-ease, "but my reason was a perfectly good one. Only, it was the wrong one."

"You threw me out for the wrong reason?"

"I threw you out for the wrong reason, but it was a good one."

Isengrim shook his head in disbelief. Whatever reason was adduced, the fact remained: he had been thrown out from his cosy place by the fire, and the imminent prospect of a warm meal and a bed, into the cool and inhospitable night of

AXES, BAD POETRY
AND PISS-POTS

Novgorod, and had ended up in a shadowy garden, assailed by axes, bad poetry and piss-pots.

Ksenia intervened, feeling that in some way that she could not identify she herself had been the cause of a misunderstanding between the two men. She wondered whether Mr. Voronov might make himself comfortable and whether Mr. Isengrim might continue with his story of Señor de Vega. Mr. Isengrim indicated that he would be delighted to obey.

"Beginning his journey on the 26th day of August 1828—"

"Not long after I left London for St Petersburg," confided Ksenia to Horatio. They sat close together. Although it was the coldest hour of the night – a bell had at that moment tolled three times in a nearby bellcote – it was not cold in a room now occupied by no fewer than six people, give or take some ghosts.

"—Charles Stuart Cochrane, hereinafter known to all who met him on the roads and in the towns of England, Wales, Ireland and Scotland, as Juan de Vega, Spanish troubadour, with five-and-twenty shillings in his purse, made his way to Canterbury and Kent, thence to Ramsgate – Dover – Worthing – Brighton – Southampton – Salisbury—"

Kazan – Yekaterinburg – Omsk – Irkutsk – Yakutsk – more familiar names rattled uncalled-for through the mind of Ksenia Ivanovna—

"—Bath – Bristol – Pontypool – Abergavenny – Welshpool – Bangor – Dublin – Belfast – Greenock – Glasgow – Edinburgh, stopping only to play upon his guitar, to collect money for the cause of the exiled democrats of Spain and Portugal—"

"Pah!" exclaimed Mr. Voronov, unable to hide his disgust. "These exiles, these democrats – bring them to Russia, I say, and they would have a troubadour strumming his guitar above their Siberian graves." With which musical threat, he folded his arms and glared upon Isengrim.

Horatio had encountered many Spaniards and Portuguese in his travels, but rarely those of the democratic persuasion: he now regretted that omission.

"—and to enliven his spirits in the company of ladies—"

"Alas," whispered Ksenia, holding Horatio's hand for comfort. "Charles believed himself to be a ladies' man."

"Was he not?" inquired Horatio, anxious never to let go that hand.

"Almost anyone who wore a dress was considered fair game, sir – it was not a pleasant sight to observe him in a room containing ladies." This oblique answer gave Horatio a clue as to the man's nature. Out of sympathy, nothing more, he gently patted Ksenia upon her left hand. The left cheek turned a rosy red. Ksenia turned her face to the right and raised her right hand ever so slightly. Horatio made so bold as to kiss it just once. The right cheek, now invisible, glowed. Then he held that hand in his own for several minutes, soft, yielding and quite bewildering.

Horatio wondered whether this night was all a dream, for he had never, not once in his life, felt so much that he had become quite another man altogether – one who had hope and love and had all the world to offer a woman.

Ksenia pondered the wisdom of her actions, and then immediately dismissed her doubts, for – just once – she knew that she could give herself entirely to a man without fear or doubt.

Mr. Voronov's spirits were considerably raised by this interlude. He forbore to interrupt Isengrim's narrative. Isengrim made so bold as to quote from Juan de Vega's ballad, The Spanish Exile, composed for him by a young friend and printed on sheets which sold for half-a-crown each:

"*From Spain I have come, a minstrel to wander,*
Over Britain's free shores, and all quite alone—"

Isengrim interrupted his recitation. "Although the words are English, when they were sung with a Spanish accent and a colloquial muscular movement of the features, they brought tears to the eyes of all who heard it. Especially the women. In every town of Britain, Juan captured feminine hearts."

Ksenia broke off from her distraction to repeat: "H'm."

"H'm," echoed Horatio, using the opportunity to draw breath.

The book-seller scratched his right ear and continued regardless: "He told me once that he didn't know any thing he liked better than an innocent romp with girls of sixteen. Such was his love of life and youth."

"Disgusting, I call it," said Yadviga, little convinced by this enthusiasm for life and youth.

Horatio considered the woman re-attached to his hand and reflected that, at the age of twenty or so, this widow would have been an easy prey for a man such as Juan de Vega.

"He had a wig, you say?" he asked, at something of a tangent.

"Señor de Vega was indeed shaved quite bald," confirmed Isengrim, "having fallen ill as a result of his recent disappointments. He was anxious to have his skull examined by Mr. De Ville, the famous London phrenologist."

"The Devil, he says?" asked Yadviga, her hearing quite sharp. She fingered the cross around her neck in preparation for the answer.

"No, madam," said Isengrim, "Mr. De Ville. Quite a differ- A MAN'S BACK ent person altogether. In Ramsgate, I believe, Juan de Vega SETTLEMENTS encountered a female phrenologist who agreed to visit the front parts of his head, but refused absolutely to have anything to do with his Back Settlements."

Yadviga nodded approvingly. Never should a woman have anything to do with a man's Back Settlements – those were, it was understood, the work of the Devil himself.

"Oh sons of free Britain, who are truly so loyal,
Wouldn't you fight for your country when in distress—"
continued Isengrim, only to be interrupted by Mr. Voronov, who wished to know more about Phrenology. The book-seller ignored this

request for enlightenment, considering – with scant justification – that a man who had little time for books would have little time for the advanced sciences of the day. Instead, he asked Horatio to find a sack of books which had unaccountably been left in the garden. Horatio and Ksenia left the room together: both understood quite well that they should not be separated in these hours of the night.

Together they stepped out into the fallen remains of the garden. After several minutes of fruitless searching in the darkness of the undergrowth, they fell over a large sack which had been abandoned under a bush. It took some time to disentangle themselves from the sack which had wrapped itself around their arms and legs, in much the same way that the Subtle Serpent had wrapped up Adam and Eve and snapped open their eyes.

What is 'Love'? – it is, thought Horatio in that instant, the courage to love someone even more than yourself; no, said the Subtle Serpent, that is not courage, but cowardice; I concede that, admitted Horatio: in that case, it is the need to cry halt and seek rest after so many miles.

What is 'Love'? – it is, thought Ksenia in that instant, the need to love someone even more than yourself; no, said the Subtle Serpent, that is no need, it is but a whim; I admit it, conceded Ksenia: in that case, it is the courage to cry halt and seek respite after so many versts.

At length, when the Serpent of Beguilement had gone its way upon its belly and the companions of the night had raised themselves from the dust, they returned to the house. Isengrim took the sack upon his knees and delved into it. He drew out two battered volumes. Mr. Voronov glowered upon seeing them: how many more such weapons of unorthodoxy did that man have in there? Was there no end to the Arsenal of Freedom?

He need not have become agitated. The books Isengrim now set to rights upon his lap were the two volumes of A Journal Made by Señor Juan de Vega, the Spanish Minstrel, of 1828–9 through Great Britain and Ireland (London 1830). They contained little of Freedom, beyond a copy of a letter written to The Times in October 1829, announcing the donation of a figure no smaller than fifty-eight pounds Sterling to the Committee of Spanish Gentlemen, for the Benefit of the Recent

Emigrants from Portugal, a sum which Juan de Vega had collected in his tour around the Isle of Britain.

"There are amusing things in here," announced Isengrim, languidly scanning the pages of Volume II, a man at ease with himself, fully aware of the words which passed below his fingers. He scratched his ears in over-familiar manner, one after the other: truly, they were large ears, well-furnished, both inside and out, with luxuriant hair. "Ah now – here we are: the affair of Widow E. of Bath: he plays the guitar in the street and looks up. 'Veux-tu monter? she exclaims, beckoning to him from the window; and a very curious idea enters his head at this question.' Now," he beamed at Mr. Voronov, the last man in the room he should have tried to entertain, "is that not a witty thing?"

From the bed and the lips of another man came the dying echo: "Veux-tu monter, ma chérie?" More wistful than lecherous, although the woman concerned was of meagre virtue: "Veux-tu monter?"

Nothing discomposed by this repetition, the book-seller continued to explore the pages: "Juan de Vega wrote most charmingly of his adventures in Bath, finishing with these words: 'Had it not been for one of the little children coming in with a light, in one unlucky minute, Señor Juan de Vega's virtue, like the salad, would have been devoured by a widow of forty.' 'Like the salad', sir, like the salad!" He chuckled at the comparison.

"Is there nothing more in that book," asked Horatio sternly, "than such lascivious gossip?"

"Nothing, sir, nothing!" confirmed Isengrim enthusiastically. "Widows, young ladies, school-girls, young gypsy women, the wives of cobblers and tailors: a trail behind him of outraged husbands, broken hearts and damp handkerchiefs. And at five shillings per volume, it is a bargain. Where else, might I ask, could you read a curse set upon a key-hole?"

Where, indeed? No one at present in that room could adequately answer. Mr. Voronov suspected, but could not prove, that this would turn out to be a line of poetry.

Isengrim read aloud: "'Confound the key-hole, I have hated these things ever since.' The husband of the woman whom our Juan had been kissing had spied them through the key-hole."

"And sought satisfaction? The matter ended with a duel?" asked Horatio, at last interested.

The book-seller shook his head, tapped his nose, and scratched his ear.

"And did nothing?" asked Ksenia much astonished.

Once more the book-seller tapped his nose conspiratorially, and was so much encouraged by the reaction of his audience that he repeated his offer. "Five shillings per volume, while stocks last." Alas, he had no buyers this night in Novgorod the Great.

"Had that woman been my wife," said Horatio boldly, "I would have killed the man on the spot, Democrat or no."

"Had that woman been your wife," replied Ksenia, unaccountably out of countenance at the implication, "she would certainly never have kissed the scoundrel."

The two would-be lovers avoided each other's eyes for several moments; their hands, conjoined, slid apart. Between their hearts crept momentarily a delicate wafer of ice.

The book-seller was not so naïve – he was, after all, seventy years old,

HE WATCHED
A PUNCH AND
JUDY SHOW

of a maturity in which naivety is long past and idiocy is attributable only to the narrow horizons of old age – not so naïve as to lose a sale on a question of individual taste. He had the measure of Ksenia and Horatio. Accordingly he remarked: "Juan de Vega suffered many hardships during his journey, which lasted ten months. In Edinburgh, for example, as he watched a Punch and Judy show his purse with all his money was stolen from him."

"Ah," said Horatio, more satisfied. "Was it much money?"

"Ten shillings."

Horatio had not been to Edinburgh, but was alert to the dangers of standing gaping in a crowded street. He considered Juan de Vega to have been a fool.

"It was in Edinburgh also," continued the trader in books, pursuing the scent of a sale, "that Juan de Vega ascended a great mountain, and experienced much physical discomfort."

"Oh, read me that passage!" exclaimed Ksenia, unable to contain her emotions. Much physical discomfort upon a journey was something that might redeem even the worst of men, especially since that journey had encompassed merely all the spas, seaside resorts, withdrawing-rooms and similar places of comfortable retreat in the South of England.

"Of course, of course – let me see..." Isengrim of Krakow turned to the end of the second volume, flicking the pages between practised fingers. "Yes – here we are –" He cleared his throat and read aloud, in a voice full of drama. "'I then proceeded on the celebrated hill called Arthur's Seat. Climbing this ascent I found my mechanical force did not keep up with the ardour of my wishes, and in my hurry I was obliged to stop two or three times to inhale more of that vital air which the exertion caused me to lose.'" He slowly closed the book. "Is that not, madam, a most exhausting description, and a fitting end to a long, long journey?"

Mr. Voronov marvelled at the mountains of Scotland. How high must they be, and how many brigands might they contain?

"But the whole, while lengthy, was not, of course, a journey that bears comparison with that of my first husband, who walked across every land in the civilised world." Ksenia was decided upon this matter, knowing little of the pro-Iberian journey, but much of the pseudo-Iberian journeyer.

Horatio doubted whether anything east of the Ural Mountains might be regarded as part of the civilised world, but was himself civilised enough not to say so. There is, he knew, a time for reckless behaviour, and a time for reflective behaviour. Both are right for their moments. While he recklessly congratulated himself on his identification of the moment, Ksenia was reflecting on her own words.

"And Siberia," she conceded.

Horatio approved of the reflective concession and pushed the matter no farther.

"Siberia?" asked Mr. Voronov, appalled. "Your husband walked across Siberia? Was he then—" he paused, delicately: "—of the criminal classes?"

"Decidedly not, sir!" Ksenia bridled up. "What do you take me for?"

Mr. Voronov retreated in haste, cursing his own obtuseness. After all, even if Decembrists, anti-religionists and other treacherous scum were sent to Siberia, that did not suggest that everyone in Siberia was like-minded, did it? There had to be guards and jailers and governors. And it was, he had been told, a very large country. Not all, who went there, came back; not all who came out, had gone in. It was a country where souls might be lost – could it not therefore be a country where souls might be found?

While the inn-keeper was thus distracted, re-considering the fundamentals of Religion and his own position on Souls and Siberia, Isengrim the book-seller had dived headlong into his sack of literature; he now emerged clutching a triumphant pile of books. "Siberia?" he asked, his mercantile instincts much excited. "I have here two books on travels in Siberia, which may enlighten and entertain. The SHE KNEW one is by Lieutenant James Holman and the other by Captain THEM BOTH John Cochrane. Each printed in two volumes, octavo, bound in leather and board, in London. Would you like to – perhaps?"

"Sir," said Ksenia kindly, "I know them both."

For no reason, the dying man from his bed seized the opportunity to exclaim that he once more needed to piss. No one paid him any attention. He soon relapsed into silence.

"Ah, the young lady is then an energetic reader!" exclaimed Isengrim with no small measure of condescension, having found years before that condescension spread thick commonly made a sale. Not in this case. "Perhaps you would care to read them again?"

"No," said Ksenia, "I mean that I know both gentlemen."

The book-seller from Krakow was – what was infrequent – deprived of eloquence. In consternation, he rubbed his left ear vigorously.

Ksenia continued: "And despite having spent almost a full year crossing Siberia from Yekaterinburg to meet the famous Baron Wrangel at Nizhney Kolymsk, the worthy Captain Cochrane found that Siberia held very little of interest. It was, he said, one immense wilderness: there was so little to be seen that it was hardly possible to find anything of interest to write about."

"Truly spoken," said the book-seller glumly, recognising at once that the widow knew whereof she talked. Disconsolately, he replaced Captain Cochrane's two volumes in his bag.

"Except mice," continued Ksenia, after a few moments.

Isengrim was puzzled by this. "Mice, madam?" said he. "Mice?" Of men, he knew, but not of mice.

"Is it not wonderful how each creature has its own skill?" asked Ksenia, racing after her own thoughts. "The mouse travels many miles in search of food, and knows always where she should go."

"Indeed," said Horatio enthusiastically: "The bird with its flying—"

"The deer with its running," mused Ksenia.

"The cat with its pouncing," suggested Mr. Voronov, whose thoughts ran now on murine matters.

"The dog with its ability to lick its own—" began Major Sinclair.

"The priest with his singing," interrupted Yadviga.

"The raven with his counting," contributed Isengrim, "the owl with its wisdom."

"The bear with its ease in the cold," admired Horatio.

"The cockroach with its scuttling," pushed in the dying man.

"The poet with his vexatiousness," proposed the inn-keeper.

There was a lengthy pause, as those gathered in the lodge in Novgorod the Great considered the wonders of Creation.

"Siberia, then," said Mr. Voronov, anxious to summarise the findings of the evening: "A land of many things, and none of them good."

"But not expensive," countered Ksenia in a positive tone. "Cucumbers were one hundred for a penny in some places—"

Voronov whistled in undisguised admiration – was this indeed a land of milk and honey? Why send criminals there? They could not die, if cucumbers were to be found so cheap.

"—and my husband calculated that he had travelled the three thousand five hundred miles from Moscow to Irkutsk for the total cost of thirty-two roubles—"

"One hundred and sixty-five versts per rouble," calculated Horatio for the benefit of his Russian mind. "In pounds sterling, one hundred and forty miles per shilling. And in French kilometres and francs—"

"—barely a sou," said Major Sinclair, whose ability to subsist on barely a sou had been admired for years throughout the English quarter of Paris.

"—which sum included the purchase of tobacco," said the widow in fine. "My husband," she continued, reminded of certain matters, "frequently remarked upon the custom of flogging peasants in advance. He considered it to be a Siberian habit."

"In advance?" asked Mr. Voronov, puzzled, but not disturbed.

"No matter," replied the young widow, whose thoughts on her dear departed first husband had run away with her in a different direction, much as he himself had run away with her when she was but fourteen years of age. "In Iberia—"

"Siberia," corrected Mr. Voronov.

"Indeed, not, sir: Iberia."

Mr. Voronov was left to consider the many choices: Siberia, Iberia, doubtless – in these Times of Liberty – Liberia; maybe Hiberia and Tiberia also; but the day would come when just a simple SIBERIA AND Beria would do. He blamed the poets of the time with their OTHER BERIAS continual need to rhyme.

"In Iberia, my husband marched over the rocky Pyrenees and the snowy sierras and slept in the open air; in Quebec, he marched for days to Lake Ontario on routes that broke many another man's strength; in America, he traversed the Cordilleras and ascended the Andes."

"And still you say," asked Isengrim, seeking clarification, "that he walked across every land in the civilised world?"

"Have I not mentioned Iberia?" she demanded fiercely. "Spain and Portugal, and also France?"

At the mention of France, Yadviga spat patriotically. Horatio, on the other hand, was more than willing to concede that France was indeed civilised.

"And the purpose," asked Mr. Voronov, little able to understand the urge of men and women to leave their own firesides to explore the world, "of all these journeys?"

A long silence followed this pointless question.

"The purpose, sir?" asked Ksenia, clearly stalling for time.

"Need there be a purpose?" demanded Horatio of the ill-mannered inn-keeper, unable himself to think of any. Journeys and exploration – they led but to wars and disagreeable ends: think of Mungo Park; think of Captain Franklin; think of Mr. Clapperton.

Try as she might, the widow could not think of any good purpose. Her brief marriage to John Dundas Cochrane had been a series of very painful journeys interspersed with the lengthy absences of the beloved, in the name of 'exploration'. The acquaintance of explorers did not seem to find much happiness: think of John Cochrane, think of James Holman, think of Captain Pyotr Anjou, explorer of the Novosibirsk Islands – hastily, she thought of a diversion:

"You might equally well ask, sir: what is the purpose of love?"

Voronov, who had never even thought of such a question, put it to himself: "Shto takoy lyubov?"

The Major, Parisian exile and past admirer of Amélie de Clugny heard the word and rolled it lovingly over his dry lips: "l'amour, qu'est-ce qu'il est, l'amour?"

This faint double echo was enough: the ever-perceptive young widow advised her audience that across the foot of those vast plains of Siberia there flowed the mighty river Amour, that Russia had the mightiest rivers of all the world: the Ob, the Irtish, the Yenisey, the Lena, the Yana, the Amour, the Indigirka, the Aldan, the Kolyma, the Okhota. And on an instant Mr. Voronov was filled with the hot glow of patriotic fervour and the question – or questions – of purpose, of journeys, of exploration and of love were at once resolved and then were put aside.

Ksenia had arrived back at her proposition: "But to feed every river requires a thousand miles of bog and snow. For Amour as for any other. Commander Cochrane walked twice the length and breadth of Siberia, then he decided that there was little of interest there."

"But in Kamtchatka," replied Horatio handsomely, "there was enough to make the journey profitable."

"Oh yes, indeed," she said, modestly.

"HE HAD NO REGRETS."

31

'TIS THE COLOUR THEY CALL BLACK!

Outside, the night was filled with regret.

The night was at its coldest. Anyone who chose to peer outside at the night – and none did – would have detected a slight lightening in the sky; but it was a lightening born more of expectation than critical observation.

Mr. Karamzin walked by on the road outside the house, stamping his feet and drawing upon a flask of brandy to keep warm, up and down, his brow furrowed, unable yet to enter, unable to pass on. He was reflecting on his famous work, Marfa the Mayoress, or: the Fall of Novgorod. Marfa Boretskaya was a wealthy widow of Novgorod – never the Mayoress: the citizens may have been republicans in those days, but they were never foolish enough to let a mere woman rule over them – a wealthy widow of Novgorod who had the bad luck to come up against Ivan the Great (not the Terrible), a man with autocratic designs upon the city. Being Great (and not Terrible), Ivan had the lady taken as prisoner to Moscow with a handsome escort of upright Muscovite knights. Mr. Karamzin had long had niggling doubts about the authenticity of some points in his popular work, and so had come to the declining city – having all eternity on his hands – to verify a few facts. Which were these: in 1471, at a time when the treacherous Archbishop Feofil of Novgorod—

At that very moment in his recapitulation of the facts, Mr. Karamzin was distracted by the sight of a figure weaving about on the road that led to the western gate of the city. The pedestrian had not passed Mr. Karamzin, but was nonetheless heading away from him. Anxious for company, Karamzin glided after the shadow, and came suddenly and noiselessly upon a young man in the last transports of despair.

The young man in the last transports of despair screamed when he saw Karamzin appear beside him from out of darkness.

"Who are you?" he cried, his eyes, already wide with anguish, now white with terror. "Are you natural? Are you Death?" He prepared to recoil.

"My name is Nikolai Mikhailovich Karamzin," said he, offering a hand for the young man to shake.

Surprised, the young man ignored the hand, saluted and introduced himself: "Private Ushakov. Sir!"

"You have not, then, heard of my name?" asked Mr. Karamzin, after a pause, and in a disappointed tone.

"I am in the army, sir, the civilians of Novgorod are but strangers to me," explained Ushakov apologetically. "I am, besides, sir, in the last transports of despair. Grief! Horror! Blackness! Darkness enfolds me!"

GRIEF! HORROR! BLACKNESS! DARKNESS

Mr. Karamzin sighed wearily – tonight was a night for ignorant strangers. However, he was not so impolite as to mention his disappointment, and offered some words of comfort. "The life of the happy is all hopes; that of the unfortunate, all memory." These were not his words – he could not remember whose they were; but they were spoken by him, and that was, after all, what really mattered. He was, however, a little surprised at the answer the young man gave:

"I am unfortunate, I have only memory. I cannot weep," he sobbed, tears streaming from puffed eyes, "the fountain of tears has been long dried up within me, like that of every other human blessing." These – equally – were not his words: he could remember whose they were; had but little inclination to reveal his sources.

Mr. Karamzin was intrigued, and fell in with Private Ushakov as he continued to weave his way towards the western portal of Novgorod the Great. "You have, then," he supposed, "been unfortunate in love?"

Private Ushakov turned red-rimmed eyes towards Mr. Karamzin. "Love?" he demanded. "What is 'Love'?"

Mr. Karamzin, pleased to be able to answer, found that he was not permitted to do so. For Private Ushakov continued relentlessly: "I can tell you what it is not – it is not succumbing to the tortures of rose-bud lips and a bright eye; it is not that glorious, holy, mystical union of two souls, wandering alone on this Earth until that moment comes when, in the graveyard of shadows, we meet a kindred spirit;

it is not brute lust, nor possession, nor power, nor the brief mastery of the body of another; it is not that moment when Heaven opens its gates and lets flood into a man's soul the sublime fountain of self-sacrifice and joy and—"

Mr. Karamzin felt obliged to intervene. He laid a cautionary hand upon Private Ushakov's sleeve and prepared to offer words of comfort. He was disappointed.

Sergei Ushakov tore the proffered hand from his sleeve, ripping the thin cloth of his coat as he did so. "Lay your hand upon me not!" he cried, metrically. "For I am Accursed, I am Lost, I am He who is Damned. Ah!" he cried, further, for in these circumstances, one cry is scarcely enough to make the point. "What is this?" He clutched at the torn cloth of his coat and brandished it at the star-light, blocking out even those frozen lights of hope. "Ah! 'Tis the colour they call black! Black, black! That is the colour of all my nightmares – black! – no more the red blush of a beloved cheek, no more the white of a dropped handkerchief, of a hastily-scribbled letter, no more the blue of a free sky and a babbling stream, no more the green—"

Mr. Karamzin cut in. This time he was more successful, employing, as a new tactic, a hold he had learned from another stranger an hour or two previously. Had Mr. Karamzin been engaged by any one of the twelve Imperial Offices of Censorship to gag the Romantic outpourings of that desperate youth, he could scarcely have honoured the profession more. Mr. Voronov would have expired, almost, in ecstasy. Silence descended once more over the western suburb of Novgorod.

"Tell me, young man," he said in the most soothing of voices, for he was at heart a kind man, "have you perhaps lost one that you loved?" Mr. Karamzin was nothing if not perceptive.

The cold and ghostly hand released from over his mouth, Sergei took a breath and shouted "Have I—!"

"Quietly, sir, quietly," urged Mr. Karamzin.

"Have I," whispered the troubled young man, in tones of dullest despair, "lost HER?" Tears sprang to his eyes. "SHE who lights my life like the sun and the moon, for whom the word Love was struck from the song of angels? Have I lost HER?" He paused, shaking, sucking in lungfuls of air, lest he lose his mind as well as HER. He decided, after a moment, to laugh terribly.

"Well?" said Mr. Karamzin patiently.

"We should have been married, SHE and I," continued Sergei, "we should have fled into the east, to the Urals and beyond, to Siberia, to Kamtchatka maybe, made a new life far from the eyes of men, and lived in each other's arms until we died."

"And why, pray, have you not done so?" asked Mr. Karamzin, smelling a good story here, and prepared, if necessary, to listen until the crack of dawn when, like any other ghost on the streets of Novgorod, he would have to disperse back into the tombs and churches of the city.

They were passing a low wall, which surrounded a stable attached to the Church of the Nativity of the Holy Virgin. All of a sudden, Sergei Davidovich Ushakov sat down on the wall, his hands entwined between his legs. "Why did I leave Nizhney Novgorod!" he cried, not as a question. Mr. Karamzin, having some knowledge of that place, asked himself why anyone would not leave? "I left it," replied the Private, although it had not been a question, "to seek my fortune, to escape the tyranny of my father, to find my heart's desire."

Mr. Karamzin nodded agreeably. So far, so common. Of those who joined the Imperial Army of His Holiness the Tsar of All Russia, the vast majority joined because they had to: they had no rights, only the right to be bought and sold, to be dressed in uniform and handed a gun – if they were lucky – and to go forth and die for Russia. A misfortuned few joined the army to seek their fortune. And a shiftless minority joined the army simply to get away from home. The slicing sabre of death and the biting bullet of oblivion, however, made no distinction: a soldier was a soldier, a corpse was a corpse

"And now," said the tall and fair-haired youth, "instead of obeying my father, like any man, I obey the sovereign of the world – His Majesty the Cannon." He did not know it, but Mr. Karamzin had an encyclopaedic knowledge of quotations and witticisms – 'His Majesty the Cannon' was recognised straight away. He made no comment – the weeping Private was yet young.

"I have no father, he is long dead, I buried him the night I dug my mother's grave!" The youth had read well, decided Mr. Karamzin, and with it he had acquired the voice of ANOTHER.

"I languish here," said Sergei, "amid the trees of Russia – oh, those trees!" he cried in despair, "they cast their shadow over my soul!"

"But are not these trees the Soul of Russia?" asked Mr. Karamzin, in all honesty bewildered that anyone should lament the forests of the Motherland.

"There are," cursed Sergei Ushakov, "so many trees!"

With which observation, made as a philosophical or poetical, rather than as an economical or arithmetical point, Mr. Karamzin could not disagree. But Private Ushakov, wandering alone, anguished, and almost certainly against army regulations, in the night, had strayed from the point.

ANGUISHED, AGAINST
ARMY REGULATIONS

"She—?" hinted the ghost.

"Ah, SHE, SHE, SHE," murmured Sergei, as quietly as he could in capital letters; he cast his eyes upon his companion. "I do not even know HER name."

"Ah," said Karamzin, now quite understanding the affair. There was a love which sparked into flame at the sight of one quite unknown, and there was another love that kindled at the sight of one so familiar. He himself had written much on the matter, and was even now prepared to lecture Sergei Ushakov on the advantages and disadvantages of each. His words, however, would have fallen on deaf ears.

"Nothing – nothing – nothing!" cried the young man in a ghastly voice, making up for the obscurity of his meaning with a perfect clarity of intent. "I fall – I sink – I blaze – I shriek!" Accordingly, the youth fell, sank, blazed and shrieked. "And the clock of eternity rings out its awful chime!"

At no distance at all, a cracked bell tolled, four times. As the final echo of the fourth bell faded rippled across the carpet of stars, the boy recovered some of his senses and sensibilities.

"SHE came past me today; I stood sentry-duty, on the road from St Petersburg; SHE smiled at me; SHE spoke softly; SHE laid her hand upon my arm; SHE captured my heart: I cannot," declared Ushakov quite boldly for one so young, "live another day without HER, I cannot," he struck himself upon the chest quite violently, "trudge my weary way through this life if SHE," he turned his wild eyes to the falling moon, which took fright at the horrid sight and slipped behind a cloud, "be not my companion!"

So saying, Private Ushakov sprang to his feet, and ran down the street which led to the western suburbs of Novgorod the Great, his torn great-coat flapping behind him, tears falling from his eyes like jewels scattered from the fleeing carriage of an overthrown monarchy, his feet pounding the dust as if in every footfall a world was crushed. In hot pursuit lumbered Karamzin, breathless, desperate to remember all the words of the youth in his grief, so that later he might write up vicarious agony for the discerning reading public of the Underworld. Together, almost side by side, they reached the last gate of Novgorod. The sentry was fast asleep beside the fire, expecting none at this early hour. Together they burst through the gate and out across a final meadow, towards the dark threatening wall of the forest. With barely the time to stop and cry, "let HER be anything but MINE!" and again

"BLACKNESS!"

Private Ushakov plunged between the nearest trees, and flung himself upon the back of a passing bear, which turned with startled speed and vanished, bearing Despair, into the forest of Russia.

32

HER BEAUTY WOULD MUCH EXPOSE HER.

"That may be the case," countered Isengrim the book-seller of Krakow, once more reaching into his stock. "But I have a sack full of other accounts of journeys made to all parts of the world. Each one is almost certainly of more interest than Siberia. Such adventures, of course, were the daily trade of my old friend, John Melmoth," he continued, rummaging in his sack of books for some unlikely volume.

"Melmoth?" demanded Mr. Voronov sharply. "I had a fellow of that name in my inn last winter."

"Then he lied to you," replied Isengrim distractedly. "The Wanderer died some time ago. Now, where did I put those books from Jena...?"

Mr. Voronov turned instantly pale. "The man was dead?" he asked.

In answer to Voronov's question, there came a distant and hopeless shriek from the silent streets of the town; and then the awful tolling of the bell: one; two; three; four times.

From Josephine's bed, Major Sinclair continued to babble of Paris and the torn petticoats of whores, of Reynard the Fox and Isengrim the Wolf, of monks and adultery, and of being woken by the Archpriest Awakum – this latter name an understandable misunderstanding of saintly Old Believer Avvakum Petrovich, much admired in some parts of Novgorod, little mentioned in others – defrocked, imprisoned and finally burned at the stake, perhaps for his intransigence, perhaps for publishing his Life of the Archpriest Avvakum by Himself – Literature, as Mr. Voronov often enthused, can surely be the death of a man.

Unaware that her passage through Novgorod the Great was about to load the full Burden of Despair directly upon the back of an innocent bear – she would have wept had she known it – Ksenia sought anxiously to divert the conversation into channels less favour-able to the book-seller.

"Is it not remarkable," she proposed, "that the desolate lands of Siberia should be populated by so many foreigners?"

Mr. Voronov had long suspected this to be the case; his judgement of Siberia now veered back with renewed violence to his original opinions – Criminals, the Wretched of the Earth, Assassins, those whom the Tsar had set aside – and now foreigners. Foreigners, he was sure, were the fundamental cause of unhappiness in the world. He said so. No one heeded him.

Isengrim, faster than his appearance would suggest, was down on Ksenia's words like a Wolf Upon the Fold; before anyone could say "Is that so?" with a hint or tone of interest in their voice, and before the inn-keeper could upset the young widow for a second time with his suspicions about her famous first husband, the book-seller had whipped out John Dundas Cochrane's two volumes and was eagerly thumbing through Volume I.

"We have here," said he, turning immediately to the passage wherein John Cochrane describes his journey along the coast of the Gulf of Finland, "a most extraordinary circumstance: no sooner had he entered Russia, than Captain Cochrane met with a foreigner, a black man who was known to him from his childhood." He paused and eyed Horatio speculatively.

Feeling himself obliged to pass comment on this unlikely tale, Horatio uttered the one false word: "Incredible."

"This black man," continued Isengrim, scanning with raised eyebrow the following paragraphs, "seems to have been a man of some passion and no little deception. In the inn of Narva, for example—"

Horatio turned to Ksenia hurriedly: "Madam," said he, "did you perhaps meet any interesting foreigners as you crossed the wastelands of Siberia?"

"Mr. Horatio," she replied, "we came across the prettiest of all women in the town of Tobolsk, a town in which my dear husband counted no fewer than one thousand eight hundred and seventy houses, eight thousand males and ten thousand females—"

Horatio's lust for arithmetic here got the better of him, and he was obliged to distract himself with the calculation that each house must have contained – on average – some four-and-one-quarter males and five-and-one-third females. In reality, of course, any one house would have had fewer or more, fewer males and more females, in some there would have been—

The young widow stared at her friend in exasperation, and waited. When finally he had the numbers tidily ordered, he looked up; and then looked down in shame. She continued at last: "When we came through the town, the temperature was bitterly cold and our Cossack took frost-bite. We were entertained at the house of the Governor and the Governor-General, and in the home of the explorer Mr. Gedenstrom, and discovered in the house of the latter gentleman a very young and pretty Englishwoman, named Miss Norman, who was on her way to educate the children of the Governor of Krasnoyarsk."

A VERY
YOUNG AND PRETTY
ENGLISHWOMAN,
NAMED MISS NORMAN

"She was, of course, neither so young nor so pretty as the woman from Kamtchatka?" suggested Horatio gallantly.

"Sir," replied the young and pretty woman of Kamtchatka, pouting, "you should not mock me."

Horatio was mortified, being unaccustomed to teasing. He grew hot, he grew cold, he felt the sweat appear on his brow, he cursed the day that he was born. Only when he felt her gentle touch on his arm did he realise his error, the simplest of errors, one which boys and men from fifteen to fifty and nine to ninety are obliged to make while being trifled with by females.

"Miss Norman and I spent many hours together," sighed Ksenia, realising now with some pain that this one young woman had been, perhaps, the only friend she had had in the world since leaving her home in Kamtchatka, eleven years earlier. "Miss Norman was most amiable and greatly accomplished – playing the flute, reciting the verses of several Italian poets—"

Mr. Voronov was observed to stiffen and his fingers to fumble around, searching after something well-honed. He said, happily, not a word.

"—conversing in French, Russian and Latin. She could sew tiny pretty things and she tied such delightful ribbons in my hair that my husband was obliged to drop to his knees with ardour."

There was a general silence among the male audience at this unprovoked revelation. Yadviga, being the sole female paying any attention, wondered aloud at the foolishness of all young women.

"And this charming person," said Horatio after a while, "was off to Krasnoyarsk?"

"She was", replied Ksenia Ivanovna.

"Alone?" continued Horatio.

"All alone," confirmed the young lady. "All alone, and quite excited."

"But is not Krasnoyarsk—?" asked Horatio with some hesitation, and little sure of the geography of the vast lands east of the Ural Mountains.

"—one thousand miles east of Tobolsk," she agreed. "I am not certain," she added, after a few more moments, "that Miss Norman realised just how far it was to Krasnoyarsk. Nor what a hard place it would be to live. I dared not tell her," she said sadly, "for what could she have then done? My husband later suggested that her beauty and accomplishments would much expose her in that distant town, and that she would shortly be obliged to marry or to return to her family."

"I trust it was the latter," said Horatio with a shiver, imagining for himself vast lands full of predatory gentlemen.

"But marriage, sir, is not so bad?" asked Ksenia.

"Marriage, madam," observed Mr. Voronov sadly, "is like 'Love': it is a regret for the good times."

"Nonsense," answered our widowed woman of experience, red spots of anger starting in her cheeks at this impudent assertion. "If you examine your soul closely, you will that what you have said is what you wish to believe, not what is true."

The inn-keeper, careful – for once – not to upset a guest, diverted himself for the next few minutes in this task which she had MICE RESIDED set him. In truth, an examination of his own soul was no WITHIN easy one, for it required him to establish first which of many possible souls was his. A man keeps in the wardrobe of his mind, he had decided, several souls, one perhaps for each day of the week, some worn, others threadbare; but each item hanging there, moth-eaten, is no more than a shabby cover, is only what passes for a soul. Mr. Voronov's wardrobe was dark and dingy: mice resided within.

"Marriage," stated Yadviga, sure of what she said. "All I can say is it is to be much regretted. You mark my words: it is a great disappointment."

Ksenia Ivanovna charitably conceded the point. "I instructed Miss Norman in the secrets of marriage," said she, picking up her story again "and we shed many a tear together at the very thought of some things a woman must do." She arched an eyebrow at Horatio, who pursed his lips and for several moments gazed thoughtfully into her black eyes.

"I have heard no more of Miss Norman," she added regretfully and spent some minutes reflecting on the possible fate of a very young woman, alone and thousands of miles from her home. It seemed that Miss Norman had replied to a newspaper advertisement for a woman of singular accomplishments, willing to travel and interested in the education and up-bringing of young children in a distinguished – though distant – household. Miss Norman's parents had encouraged her, since there were some pressing financial difficulties to distract them, and no obvious marriage in sight; and off she had set, clutching a letter of introduction, across Europe, across Russia, across the Urals, across Siberia – in short, across the world. Much like Ksenia, except in the opposite direction. Krasnoyarsk, for those who had not seen it, was neither a place to dread nor a place to anticipate eagerly. For those few who had seen it, it was not a place to choose to live: windy and exposed, set in a countryside that was fertile but full of flies; the buildings neat, but wooden; the inhabitants – merchants and officers and policemen. Miss Norman, all innocent, had keenly viewed the sights by day, and shed tears by night. In the brief company of Ksenia, she had found a friend, and more than a friend: one whose position was similar to her own: so far from her family, travelling with no respite into the unknown. As Ksenia had trembled for Miss Norman, so Miss Norman, doubtless, had trembled for Ksenia. The two young women had passed in the vast plains, and continued on their way, swept along by the heedless rivers of Siberia.

Miss Norman, what became of you?

"If a young person chooses to go to Siberia," said Mr. Voronov, a man on whom the subtleties of a guest's mood were perpetually lost, "then she must expect hardship. A swift marriage would have been the best course of action, and the least hardship."

"Are you not," said Yadviga, unexpectedly taking the side of the absent Miss Norman, "a blind and worthless fool? Might a woman not make her way in the world without being ambushed by lecherous wolves at every turn? You mark my words, inn-keeper: St Theodosius will cast cinders upon your testicles and place fleas in your mattress." The second part of this Christian blessing was, of course, already fulfilled. Mr. Voronov adjusted his stance in an unconscious deflection of the former.

CINDERS UPON HIS TESTICLES

Ksenia returned from her sad thoughts to the theme of the moment. "Besides," she said, "might a young lady in Russia not meet a gentleman of her own nation? Did not the Governor of Nizhney Novgorod marry an English wife? Siberia itself is liberally sprinkled with Cockney butchers and shoe-makers, colonies of Scotchmen, English missionaries, Frenchmen—"

"Pah!" spat Yadviga.

"—Spanish gentlemen, Persian princes, the inventive Mr. Major, brought up in the Birmingham trade, any number of Scotch gardeners, and a blind English traveller—"

"I have here," interrupted Isengrim without an instant's hesitation, hauling from his sack, "the volumes of Lieutenant James Holman's Travels Through Russia, Siberia, Poland, Austria, Saxony, Prussia, Hanover etc. etc., undertaken during the years 1822, 1823 and 1824, while suffering from Total Blindness, and comprising an account of the author being conducted a state prisoner from the eastern parts of Siberia." And he prepared, for general diversion, to read from them. Alas, he was not swift enough, for Ksenia was on a road of her own choosing.

"—such a traveller as got no further than Irkutsk, where he fell in with the beautiful widow of Mr. Bentham, with whom he spent some happy days, only to be arrested and rushed back to Krakow by a Feldjäger in the service of the Emperor himself. Sometimes," she sighed,

"THE WAY OF A BEAUTIFUL WIDOW IS LITTERED WITH OBSTACLES."

33

HE PREPARES TO TALK LONG AND LOUD OF LIBERTY.

The five fellow-travellers were, in the moments of reflection which followed upon this last discussion, rapidly overcome by lethargy. Perhaps it was the mention of exposed young ladies and helpless widows; perhaps it was the mention of colonies of Scotchmen; perhaps it was merely that the human body, accustomed to daylight, cries out for rest at this fourth hour past midnight, with the dawn not yet visible. A deep and unsullied silence descended upon the draughty room of the broken-down lodge in the abandoned city of Novgorod the Great. All that could be heard was the crackling of a fading fire in the stove, the shallow breathing of a man dying, and the scampering of the rats in the scullery – not, Mr. Voronov thought glumly, sounds from which much hope could be drawn.

At length, as the minutes wore on, the small group dissolved: Yadviga arranged her fingers around the bottle – now almost empty, and completely hidden – and with a perfect sigh abandoned herself to a profound consideration of the orthodox saints of Russia, a meditation from which she should not – for the sake of some peace and quiet at last – could not – even if one were short-sighted enough to make the attempt – and would not – for her slumber was judged to be well-deserved – be roused; Isengrim dragged himself and his sack of books, and entered the Empress Josephine's capacious bed, presuming, as men of questionable trades sometimes do, that a woman who would allow one old man in her bed, would surely allow a second one, and arranged himself under the blanket beside Major Sinclair, to their mutual satisfaction; Mr. Voronov, judging himself to be one too many in the company of Horatio and Ksenia, and abandoning himself once more to a warm feeling of decency, charity and sympathy, stole quietly from the room, padded down the short hall-way to the front door, and stepped out into the unvaulted night.

Outside, Mr. Karamzin was wandering perplexed along the road, stopping every five paces to turn and look over his right shoulder: he presented the appearance of expecting someone to appear round the corner he had just turned. As he divagated thus heedlessly, he bumped into Mr. Voronov who was himself looking over his shoulder, the left one, with a sense of deep longing.

"Oh!" exclaimed Mr. Karamzin, unaccountably – it seemed to the inn-keeper – agitated. He fell back two paces.

"Ha!" muttered Mr. Voronov, strangely – it seemed to the historian of Russia – distracted. He advanced two paces upon his assailant, trying to see who it was.

"Ah!" said Mr. Karamzin nervously, backing away further, supposing – with that native caution which has preserved many a man and woman, boy and girl, from the cruel intentions of their fellow-creatures – the worst.

"Ho!" announced Mr. Voronov, grabbing in desperation at his assailant's coat; alas – the ghost of Karamzin was too slippery for him, and the figure flickered into darkness like breath on a cool night. As it, indeed, was.

Nikolai Mikhailovich Karamzin, had he but known, should have stayed, for he would have learned much of interest and value from the inn-keeper on the subject of Ivan the Great; had he not come to Novgorod, after all, to complete some research for his revised History of the Russian State, research still outstanding when Death had overtaken him? – Ah, missed opportunities, Mr. Karamzin! Oh, missed opportunities, Mr. Voronov!

While these gentlemen were thus engaged outdoors in a Contredanse of Confrontation, an Allemande of Antagonism, a Kazatchok of Combat and finally a Minuet of Misunderstanding; back indoors, Horatio and Ksenia kept warm side by side, heads leaning back comfortably against the tiles of the stove, looking from under tired eyelids at the dim flickering shadows on the wall opposite. They conversed quietly. Their conversation was wordless, neither the one nor the other having the boldness to speak aloud.

"I should tell you," thought Horatio, full of good intention, "of the day I left the island of Dominica, and sought out a new life for myself.

I was a free man. I should tell you of the weeks and days before that when I considered what should be my destination – should it be South America, where, it was said, a black man could enrich himself with gold and silver from the mines? Against that, Ksenia, I weighed the rumour that the Spaniards and Portuguese of the South American countries had not as yet abolished slavery and that a man, depending on the colour of his skin, was as likely to end up in chains of iron as in chains of gold."

"Why not America?" thought Ksenia to herself, considering if she might yet find a home and a loving husband who did not harbour the unstated intention of abandoning her. "From Kamtchatka, it is but a few days' sail to America, or so they say." Her knowledge of geography was sketchy, but she had been persuaded by her late husband that America was a vast and not entirely uninviting place – perhaps a welcoming one for a young woman with dreams.

"America?" said Horatio under his breath. "America was no place for a black man, for they seemed there to have thrown off the yoke of British oppression but had not yet turned their attention to the yoke they placed on the black man's shoulders. I would step off a ship in Boston, or Virginia, and before I knew it I would have traded my freedom as a Man for the freedom of a Nation. No: America, I knew, would not be a place to go."

TRADING HIS
FREEDOM AS A MAN

"Or Europe?" wondered Ksenia, turning over in her mind the places where a young widow might find solace. "France, Germany, Spain? It is such a small place, but each town is like another country, so I am told."

"Europe, I thought," thought he, "Europe must be the place, home of Liberty, land of Opportunity. A man might find a place there to set down roots and make a name for himself. Each country is like another continent: France, with its talk of Brotherhood, Britain with its talk of Abolition, Italy and German with their talk of Revolution – surely that would be a place to go?"

"Or Africa or India, I wonder," she wondered, shivering slightly at the very thought of those hot and jungly places, full of wild beasts, wild women and wilder men – or so she had been informed by those who had travelled thither.

"But not Africa," reflected Horatio with a shudder, remembering the fate of his ancestors. "A black man could come to real harm in Africa." But then he remembered that Ksenia's first husband had considered, before embarking on his pointless footsore quest across Siberia, an expedition into the heart of Africa. Had he done so, then Ksenia could well have been an African woman, not a pretty pale girl from Kamtchatka. He slid his eyes sideways and looked fondly upon her folded hands: the thought was just as enticing.

"No, not Africa." Ksenia remembered with a dull ache that, no sooner had she and her new husband regained London in the summer of the year 1823, scarcely stepped off the ship from St Petersburg and placed their bags in the hallway of a cheerless house in London, than Commander Cochrane had applied once more to make a trip to find the source of the River Niger in blackest Africa. Alone. Why had he done this? She had asked herself the question often, both when she was in his arms and when – more frequently – she was not in his arms. "Was it something I said? Was I too young in mind as well as in body? To have travelled in his company over a period of twelve months and more, through ice and snow and heat and mud and rocks and gorges, without a murmur or a moment of complaint, although the journey would have broken many another girl, to have come ten thousand miles, and then to find that my husband's first thought was not to stop and build a home with me, and perhaps a family, but to make a long and dangerous journey with-out me. Would it have been different if he had received permission to make that journey? Would he not have died? Would I be in London now, and not travelling the roads of Russia? Could I have gone with him to Africa? Would he have taken me?" She strongly doubted it: an Explorer, it had been made clear, was a man who travelled alone, with little luggage and fewer cares: a wife did not commonly figure in the inventory. Even had I done so, and then he had died as all explorers to Africa do, would I have found a man such as Horatio in all of that black continent?" She stole a sideways glance at her companion: the thought was seductive – a woman alone, a brave black warrior, the fortunes of war and romance.

A WIFE DID NOT COMMONLY FIGURE IN THE INVENTORY

"Fortune," though Horatio. "That is what 'Love' is – good fortune, coincidence, a chance romance on a long journey. I chose Europe and then Russia, she chose Europe and then Russia. Had I chosen Africa, we would not have met in Novgorod the Great."

"But had I chosen Africa," she thought, "then I would not have met this man in Novgorod the Great."

There was a short pause as each of the two fortunate and romantic travellers examined the other without either noticing it.

"I chose Europe," continued Horatio, "as I would tell you in great detail if I thought you would be interested. Perhaps," he dreamed further, "perhaps when we have a small cottage, a fruitful orchard, a cat and one or two books of poetry, I will sit at the corner of the fire on a winter's night and tell you all of my journeys through Europe. Of course, to reach Europe, one must pass through Great Britain. It is, as you doubtless know, a damp and dismal place. None more dismal than London on a wet winter's night."

There was a groan from one of the two men in Josephine's bed. It was not clear if it was a groan of remembered pleasure, or a groan of present anguish. Horatio chose to ignore it. Ksenia was so lost in her considerations of the remembered loftiness of Commander Cochrane, that she did not hear it at all.

"In London I found the employment of a free man. The employment of a free man is to wait at doors and open them discreetly in order to admit white ladies and gentlemen – and sometimes they were neither the one nor the other – who seem never to realise that the free man exists. After a while, the white ladies and gentlemen cease to exist, and we are therefore in a perfectly harmonious relation of employment. At night, one may sleep in a cupboard, along with two or three other free men, and once in every eight weeks a free man is permitted to walk out in the parks of London and enjoy the rain."

"In London," Ksenia remembered, "I was immediately introduced to those members of the Cochrane family as wished to meet us. God knows there was an endless web of uncles and cousins – but they all seemed to have their own troubles and cares, and did not seek to burden themselves with the baggage of others. Of course, they came to look me up and down, and the younger ladies were greatly amused to find that I dressed in fashions that their mothers had worn, and one or two even offered to dress me comme il faut, and Kitty, who is the unfortunate wife of Admiral Thomas, who had had much to put up with over the years of their marriage, took me to have my portrait drawn, and was, for a week or two, very attentive. But the others, having congratulated John on his safe return, made themselves scarce and we were not much disturbed for several months. John took me out a walk every other day, when he was not working on his book and firing off angry letters to the scoundrels of the Royal Society. We strode around the dismal parks and great grey streets of London and beside the stinking river. It made me greatly regret the mountains and the seas of Kamtchatka, and John himself was always in a black humour, since he wished eternally to be away from the city and its dirt and smoke. We returned to our rooms, usually soaked through, steaming with the effort, our faces and boots covered with mud, and then he would sit and rage at the Admiralty while I made him a pot of tea with toast and tried to bring a smile to his face again. He said once, that when he returned from his next expedition, he would be such a wealthy man that he could build me a castle in Scotland and take me there. He said that Scotland was much more like Kamtchatka. But I never saw it."

"London?" sighed Horatio, "I never saw it. I saw the parks, but had to be sure not to look as if I were a citizen. I saw the rain, but was sure never to enjoy it. I rarely saw sunshine. I saw dogs and cats, and once observed a horse throw its master into the mud. I lifted the unfortunate man from the road, and calmed the horse, but was chased off by passers-by who took me for a robber or worse. A free black man in the service of Great Britain is not thereby a Great Briton."

"It was in Perm, I think," recalled Ksenia, "that I first realised that a girl from Kamtchatka is not a girl from Russia, and even less a girl from Europe. My husband kindly tried to conceal from me that the Governor of that place considered me to be a foreigner, who spoke no Russian, who was not white, who had no proper religion, a Tartar, a Mongol, a Pagan of the worst sort. But I wondered then what they would make of me in England." She blushed at this humiliating memory, hoping that Horatio had not been listening to her thoughts.

She need not have feared. Horatio was half a continent away, pacing the wet streets of London on a day when even the cast-off bonds of slavery seemed to hold some attraction. "But on that day, I would tell you – if I had the courage to tell you – I caught the eye of one who was not a Great Briton: it was the Russian Prince Labanov, who was hopeful, perhaps like Peter the Great, of finding some mighty African who would be an asset to his household. That night he appeared in a very brilliant toilet before my master and, speaking none but French,

HE APPEARED IN persuaded him that a servant such as myself could readily
A VERY BRILLIANT be exchanged for another. My master, being venal, accepted
TOILET this argument along with a bag of gold and did not bother
to bid me goodbye. So from one captivity to another and thence to another, I made my way across the world, not as you did, in one great journey, but little by little, step by step, each step taking me from my old home and never bringing me to a new one."

"From the age of fourteen," confessed the young widow, addressing no one except herself, showing her tears to no one but herself, "I have been without a home. In London, whatever my husband may have thought, we had no home such as I had dreamed of, for we lived in rooms in the gloomy house of another, made worse when he left me for months on end, made worse still when he left me forever. Perhaps I should have accepted the kind offer of Charles—"

"But when I hear the story of this woman," thought Horatio, finding courage in the contemplation of far worse cases, as a person will do who has a tendency to despondency, "I can only admire her courage, her refusal to accept her fate and the advances of such predators as cousin Charles—"

"—but then I should never have returned to Russia. Oh, but would that have been such a bad thing?"

Horatio heard his companion breathe in and out suddenly, a snatched breath; he turned his head towards her. Her eyes were fixed upon shadows, not those that played upon the crumbling plaster, but shadows in places that he knew he would never visit. Love, he thought stumbling under a sudden revelation, is the finding of a home with another, after years of solitude and wandering.

"And now," continued Ksenia, her silent thoughts spiralling towards hope or despair, "and now shall I find a home ever again? Shall I—?" She stopped, looked sideways at Horatio. The good man was lost in shadow, dreaming no doubt of his merchant's coach, his fur coat, his comfortable rooms in St Petersburg. What thoughts could he have for a young woman travelling in a diligence?

Horatio gazed into his own shadows, wondering where and when he would find rest and peace and a woman he could serve with all the power of his heart – he, ageing, a mere servant, and as black as the night. He sighed, raised himself to his feet and padded quietly out of the room, down the passage-way, and out into the street.

Observing with a deep rush of despair her friend's silent departure, Ksenia sat for a dark moment; then concealed her homelessness in the only activity which can create a home from nothing – tidying another's room of the detritus of the night. She added more wood to the stove; she gathered up the bones and the empty bottles; she hung wet cloths upon the back of the chair; she drew the blanket more tightly round the two old gentleman on the bed, dabbing the forehead of first the one and then of the other, for two entirely different purposes; then she seized an ancient and bristle-less broom and began to knock with it in corners of the room; and then she added more wood to the stove.

While Ksenia was thus engaged in the endless arrangement of homelessness, Horatio found himself, with some discomposure, in the immediate company of Mr. Voronov, a man he suspected of harbouring malevolence and mockery, despite all his actions of the past few hours. Behind his black bushy beard, did this man know Horatio's true position? And if he did, would he reveal it to the young woman left indoors? There was no way of telling, and Horatio could not force the issue.

Mr. Voronov, who, with the axe in his mind, had for the past many minutes been chopping away at the green logs of the value and worth of his life, and the void that had suddenly appeared within when he had observed the kindling of passion between two strangers; Mr. Voronov, who now felt very cold in the wood-yard of his soul, remembering that both his wife and his bed were soft and warm; this same Mr. Voronov – who was now a very different one – regarded the large black man with nothing other than respect and benevolence. He would have fought alongside him against packs of ravening wolves, just as he would have thrown himself in front of galloping horses to save the young woman. But he was not the man to say so. He was, after all, an inn-keeper: all offers of positive assistance are to be with-held. And – fortunately – he was not called upon to do either the one thing or the other. Such desperate acts are the preserve of the young and foolish: Mr. Voronov may have been foolish, but he was certainly not young.

HE WAS NOT THE MAN TO SAY SO

The two men, therefore, stood gazing into the middle distance, saying nothing to each other, as follows:

"It is in my mind, Mr. Horatio," said Mr. Voronov to himself, "to ask you how a man may reconcile himself to a wife and family from whom he has been a stranger – no, an enemy – no, an outcast – no, a traitor! – no, a stranger these past years. Are you a family-man yourself?"

"There are matters, Mr. Voronov," said Horatio gravely, without opening his mouth other than to breathe in the stars and the evil smoke from Mr. Voronov's pipe, "of which a man such as yourself will have little or no knowledge. What it is, for example, to have no home, to have no family, to be fated forever to wander the world as a stranger, much like a man condemned to immortality by the Devil."

Little did he know just how many women and men feel themselves condemned to immortality – the Devil invariably and tediously being held to blame – why not God or a well-meaning angel? – almost as many as those who feel the scythe has swung too much in the other direction.

"Of course, sir," said the inn-keeper, agreeing with no one other than himself, "perhaps you have no family to speak of. You cannot therefore know the pain that a man may feel when once he takes a step back and examines his situation, and finds himself alone amidst family. When your children are gone, they are gone and never will you get them back, except perhaps in their own children, and that breaks your heart. When your wife turns her face from you every day in anger, she breaks your heart." At this precise moment, Mr. Voronov was struck by the axe of regret. The realisation of his loss came to him like words of poetry, although – mercifully for his sanity – he failed to realise the fact. "It breaks your heart, but you never even realise that it's broken."

"Can a man," wondered Horatio obliquely, and no one, not even the ghost of Mr. Karamzin who lingered anxiously nearby, would hear him, "who has lived most of his life without a home, suddenly find one and hope to remain there? Or would it," he countered, "be an impossible struggle to remain in one spot with one woman for the rest of his natural life? I have spent all of my life as a slave or a servant, and while I would willingly serve one woman—" he paused and looked back at the lodge "—I wonder if I could again be a slave?"

No one replied immediately. But Mr. Voronov, the inn-keeper and keeper of silence, had this much to say: "I have this night considered Love, Mr. Horatio. Until this night, I have considered it to be National – for which reason I married a Russian woman – and to be Orthodox – for which reason I married a Christian; but I have until now not realised that it must also be Autocratic. A man cannot take those parts of love which suit him well and ignore those parts which suit him less well. A man in love must take the rough with the smooth. A man," said the inn-keeper with such conviction that the words at last burst forth in speech, "a man in Love must be a slave to Love."

A MAN IN LOVE MUST BE A SLAVE TO LOVE

Startled by this sudden outburst, Horatio took several steps back. He eyed the inn-keeper with some misgiving. Had the man actually replied to Horatio's unspoken questions? In a reckless moment, Horatio decided that, if the inn-keeper was prepared to discuss matters of intimacy with him, then he was equally prepared to discuss matters of intimacy with the inn-keeper.

"Sir, in these my later years, I am no longer the slave to anyone," he boasted aloud, striking a bold attitude with chest and fist. "I am, you will find, a free man." With these words, at which the inn-keeper displayed manifest signs of unease, Horatio stepped up on a pile of rubble and prepared to talk long and loud of

LIBERTY!

34

DEGENERACY, RHUBARB AND MILLIONS
OF SQUIRRELS.

"Should the Siberians wish to gain their liberty from the Russian yoke, then they have only to fire the steppes, and so starve the cavalry horses, to cut off the two miserable roads that make the Kemtchouga swamp passable, and they may defy all the powers of Europe. And if they retained mastery of Lake Baikhal, they would be a great and free nation. Had the aborigines of this vast land had the foresight to do this earlier, when the first Russians arrived, then they would not now be a dying race, like the Mexicans after the arrival of Cortes—"

"What, in the name of God, sir," interrupted Andrew Cochrane-Johnstone, awoken from a colourful dream of drink and money by the unheralded return of his son, "are you havering about? Can a father not get some peace? Is it not dark, may we not even sleep?"

"My words," said John Cochrane mildly, "were but an introduction to the greatest wonder of all Siberia, Lake Baikhal."

"Lake Baikhal?" asked his father. "Is it so big than that you need wake me? I have seen great lakes, let me tell you. Why, not far from here is Lake Tacarigua; we may take a carriage out tomorrow and see it from the top of the hill, if that's what you want. Aye," he continued, having hit upon a convenient solution, "let's do that – we'll do that tomorrow – show you Lake Tacarigua, and then we can both die happy. Will we do that, eh, son?" Cochrane-Johnstone got up in the dark and relieved himself painfully in the chamber-pot. He groaned loudly as he did so.

"Lake Baikhal," persisted his son, encouraged by the tinkling of the waters, "is some four hundred miles long, and thirty wide, and slopes to unknown depths. In winter, it is frozen from shore to shore, permitting a man to cross it by horse and sledge, as I did when I left Irkutsk in the company of the Inspectors of Post."

"Most interesting," said his father, turning his attention to the ignition of an enormous cigar, which he had won at dice in the celebratory evening in Caraccas. "Was there much to see at Irkutsk?"

Ignoring this remark – had he not already explained in great detail what there was at Irkutsk? – the intrepid traveller continued: "It is fortunate that I crossed in winter, for in the summer the seas can be mountainous, and, as the boats are badly manned and worse officered, numerous accidents occur."

The old Colonel nodded in satisfaction, but it was not certain whether this was because of the strength of the cigar, which was of the most exquisite quality, or because Cochrane had confirmed his own deepest suspicions about travelling over water.

"The lake is unfathomable and may be considered one of the grandest sights in the world. The mountains everywhere round the lake are of the most elevated and romantic appearance. They are bold, rocky, much indented and very dangerous for vessels in summer, as no anchorage is anywhere to be found. The winds are most violent and subject to instant changes, resembling hurricanes, and it is not infrequent that a ship may take twenty-five or thirty days to cross the fifty miles of its width. And yet, when it is frozen, we might cross it in only two hours and a half.

"Having crossed the Baikhal, we went firstly to the town of Verchney Udinsk, a place of little interest, and then – seventy miles in the space of seven hours, sir! – to the town of Selenginsk. Here, amid the wild mountains and the Buriats – a Mongolian people subsisting only on tea-leaves and fat – I was received by Messrs. Stallybrass, Yuill and Swan, the English missionaries."

"Missionaries?" asked Cochrane-Johnstone, for a moment interested. "Is Russia then a heathen country?"

"Not at all," replied his son earnestly. "Much of it is quite Christian, but there are areas – like those adjacent to Mongolia – where the people are neither Christian nor Muslim; and so are likely material for Christian zealots."

"I have known them," confirmed the elder, sucking hard upon his cigar.

"These Christian gentlemen, and their families, have much work to do, I believe. For not only do the Buriat people ignore their very presence, and not only have they been made to build their homes outside the town of Selenginsk, on the opposite bank of a wide and fast river, but the local people had also recently brought thirty waggon-loads of their own religious books from Thibet, at the expense of twelve thousand head of cattle."

"It would be hard," reflected the respected financier aloud, "to change their religion after so great an investment."

"My own opinion exactly," agreed Cochrane eagerly. "In any case, I cannot think that justice is done to the people of Britain, to say nothing of the poverty and ignorance of a large portion of the people of Ireland, in squandering money in every part of the world while there are so many poor and religiously ignorant in our own empire. But that is not to say that the three missionary gentleman had been idle. In barely three years they had taught themselves much of the Mongolian language, and were busy at the translation of the Bible. But they had not been the instrument of converting a single individual."

"It is sometimes that way," said his father without much regret. "And what else did you see," he asked, "on the borders of China?" It was not that he was greatly interested in his son's interminable stories, only that he feared, should Cochrane cease to talk, that he would never fall asleep again.

Cochrane brightened up at this exhibition of curiosity. So much, indeed, that he fell to coughing, and only after a drink of tepid, brackish water from a jug which he found by his bed – which made him retch from an empty stomach – did the coughing stop again. During this lengthy exhibition, his father eyed him with some impatience.

"Not far from the town of Nertchinsk," he continued at last, "we passed a monument erected to the memory of the wife of the late Governor, Mrs. Treskin of Irkutsk. It seems she had fallen from a horse while travelling to the warm baths near that place and had been literally kicked to pieces. Surprisingly, perhaps, neither of her attendants were in the least bit hurt. A tragedy, no doubt, but from what I heard, most people would have been glad to have her name buried in oblivion rather than carved on a monument."

"I have known women like that," nodded Cochrane-Johnstone once more, sucking hard upon his cigar, which was now coming to an end.

"The baths, now," he asked further, "were they of a pleasant nature, or unpleasant?" He had heard of both, although he had experienced neither. But he was a man who liked to collect facts that could prove useful.

"The baths of Verchney Udinsk," replied Cochrane, "are, like those of Kamtchatka, most sulphureous. Fine vegetables grow rapidly in their vicinity. I myself found their effects quite over-powering—"

"The vegetables?" asked the other, for clarification.

"The baths," explained Cochrane, "—but they are strongly recommended for the cure of all chronic and rheumatic diseases. Indeed the Governor of Irkutsk, Mr. Tzedler arrived there at the same time as myself, to take the cure. But I must warn you," he raised his voice, in case, in the midst of these cool Colombian mountains, at THE SIBERIAN three o'clock in the morning, there might be those who were CURE on the point of packing their bags for the Siberian Cure, "the lakes are said to be very poisonous."

"Indeed?" said his father, raising his eyebrows.

"Indeed," echoed Cochrane, contracting his. "When I left the town, I passed numerous lakes, some of which are so poisonous in nature that ducks, geese and other birds cannot live after drinking the water."

"Unfortunate," observed Andrew Cochrane-Johnstone, for he suspected that wild-fowl which died in this way might not prove suitable for the pot.

"But swans are not affected," concluded Cochrane, looking with some surprise upon the endless waters of Lake Baikhal, which seemed to darken before his eyes. "No, swans are not affected." At that instant, the waters of the lake rose up and he went under and under. His voice tailed off; his father's cigar went out; all was quiet.

"At last," muttered Cochrane-Johnstone; he turned his head to the wall, and fell asleep.

In the first hours of dawn, Cochrane rang the bell which summoned, after some delay, a hirsute servant – a janitor, perhaps, or waiter – of the inn.

"What do you want?" demanded this person, highly annoyed at having been disturbed before he had had time to drink the cup of scalding coffee the kitchen-maid had just brought him.

"It is so cold here," complained John Dundas Cochrane, "far colder than in Siberia. Do you have a fur blanket?" he inquired of the attendant.

For answer, the attendant merely laughed uproariously, then rubbed his fingers in the universal language of bribery.

"In the wild lands of Siberia," muttered Cochrane through chattering teeth, "money was almost unnecessary for those who wished board and lodging."

"Siberia, wherever that might be," replied the waiter with some indignation, "is apparently a place of fools. Do you wish to be warm, or do you wish to die like a dog?"

Cochrane fumbled in his coat pocket for some coins. He found them, but lost them immediately to gravity. The man-servant had no difficulty in plucking them up expertly as they rolled in six different directions over the grubby floor. He was impressed by their weight, and, much against habit, stood to receive further instructions.

Cochrane went on. "When I was in the town of Kiakhta, on the frontiers of Mongolia, I was advised that I was only fifteen hundred miles from Peking. I could," he turned unseeing eyes to his attendant, "I could have made my way there in two, perhaps three weeks. Perhaps I should have," he whispered.

"Do you have a fur blanket?" he asked again.

"Not at all," came the swift reply, "I have one made of wool, perhaps that would do you?"

"Not at all," answered Cochrane. "When I was in the town of Kiakhta, on the frontiers of Mongolia—"

"You have just told us that," snapped the servant. "And I have no furs."

"—there was some trade between Russia and China. The chief articles of import into Russia are teas, cottons, nankeens, silks and satins and—"

At this moment, Cochrane-Johnstone awoke. The first words he heard were:

"—and a considerable quantity of rhubarb."

A look of astonishment crossed his father's face. Rhubarb – what manner of nightmare was this?

"Three million pounds of tea were imported into Russia in the year of 1822."

At the mention of this unnatural hot drink, the servant spat violently, and turned to leave: his coffee awaited.

"The exports from Russia, are, as I have been trying to tell you, furs." Cochrane said this in a slightly peevish tone. "Furs" he continued. "Foxes of every sort, sables, river-otters and sea-otters, wild cats, beavers and millions of squirrels. The lightness, warmth and durability of the latter have made them a favourite with the Chinese. Rhubarb and millions of squirrels," he repeated in a hoarse voice, "it is so cold."

"Look," snapped the waiter, seeing that would be no peace at all until he supplied a blanket, "why don't you lie down? I'll find another blanket, if you'll only be quiet." So saying, he left the room, and was heard to shout downstairs for a blanket "from the stable, mind!" After several minutes, he returned, clutching a cup of coffee and a blanket. The latter was spread out over Cochrane. And still he shivered.

"My friend," said Cochrane, teeth chattering, "can you come and keep me warm?"

There was a little confusion at this request. The servant supposed it had been directed at the other gentleman in the room: it was scarcely a proper suggestion, but he knew that English travellers had their own customs and habits. The old man, for his part, saw that Cochrane's gaze was fixed upon the waiter, whom he knew to be a man: it was scarcely a decent suggestion, although it had its merits. The servant, when he realised the truth of the matter, said nothing, put down the mug of coffee with which he had revived his spirits and general feeling of well-being, and lay down on the mattress next to the weary traveller. It was an act of the kindest thoughtlessness.

"When I was in the town of Kiakhta, on the frontiers of Mongolia, I visited the Chinese fortress which lay at a little distance. During the fair, it contained about fifteen hundred men and boys. The female sex are prohibited. There are no windows. There is a total absence of everything that can interest even the most ignorant or careless."

"And the name of this place was – Kiakhta?" asked his father, making a note of it. Life was short, a man did not wish to waste time visiting places of no interest.

"Maimatchin," corrected Cochrane, "next to Kiakhta. To the absence of the fair sex is mainly attributable that dreadful degeneracy which is said to pervade all ranks of society among them." He drew closer to the waiter, and felt some warmth creep back into his bones.

The waiter stiffened for several anxious moments. To his great relief, Cochrane then spoke again, of a different matter.

"Furs," he said. "On my return journey to Irkutsk, I made so bold as to buy two skins of the Baikhal silver seal. I thought perhaps to make a present of them to my wife."

"Ah," sighed the servant, breathing now more easily, "your wife. A beautiful lady, I expect, eh? You had left her at home for your long journey, then?"

HIS WIFE WAS A LITTLE YOUNGER

"No, indeed," said Cochrane, "I had merely left her in Irkutsk. It had been her birthday on the twenty-fourth day of January, as it had been mine on the second day of February. I had now reached the age of thirty years, my wife was a little younger." John Dundas Cochrane reflected briefly on his marriage and his younger wife.

"She would be how old – twenty-five, perhaps?" inquired the waiter almost tenderly. He had realised that the longer he lay here, the less work he would have to do downstairs. The inn-keeper could, after all, hardly fault him for his attendance to the needs of the guests.

"Fifteen years old when I found her again in Irkutsk."

The waiter weighed this fact in silence.

"So young, and now I have left her all alone in London." There was the trace, only, of regret in the explorer's voice. "No, not entirely alone, for I have friends there. Ah, Mrs. Cochrane, when will I see you again? You are truly my dove, my chaste hope, I love thee so!" With this exclamation, he burst into tears and clutched at the waiter's greasy shirt, on which his tears dripped one by one. There were, in total, eighteen tears, one for each year of Mrs. Cochrane's life at that very moment. A wife could wish for no more than that. "Should I perhaps have stayed with you in England?" he muttered to himself. "I think not – I would have been unhappy, and my unhappiness, I know, would have made you unhappy – better," he cheered himself at this thought, "that I should make my name as the pedestrian conqueror of the Andean Mountains, and return to you in triumph, than that I should linger in the shadow of Lieutenant Holman, at home. Mrs. Cochrane, I love thee still."

With those brief, though well-meant, words, Cochrane slipped into a deep and troubled sleep; the waiter or janitor slipped out of bed, shook his head at the foolishness of foreigners, and padded downstairs,

A FREE MAN.

35

HE TOOK THE ONLY COURSE OPEN TO AN HONOURABLE MAN, AND FLED TO EUROPE.

"Free Men and Liberty?" demanded Captain Simeonov, "Who is there who cries Liberty?" He scowled at the two men outside Major Sinclair's lodge. It was still dark, and Captain Simeonov, although he would never admit it, was slightly short-sighted. Not a handicap on the parade-ground when a man could suppose, with absolute confidence, that a soldier was due a punishment – it rarely mattered which individual an officer singled out. Neither was it a handicap on the battlefield, since no one could with any precision determine who was enemy and who was friend – a gentleman could slash away with his sword and be assured of glory, regardless. He scowled forbiddingly at the likely culprits. "We know, of course, what Liberty is, do we not? It is a creeping evil. What is it? It is evil, sir! It creeps, sir! We'll have that man arrested and flogged, who talks of Liberty! Corporal Nikolaiev!" he barked at a figure who had marched up stiffly behind him, just as stiffly it should be noted, as the Captain himself, "Discover that man who talked of Liberty!"

Captain Simeonov was keen on flogging. He was of the Siberian School in this matter, where one flogged the ill-disciplined in advance.

The Corporal stepped forth, a musket in his hand. He marched up to Voronov, who, sweating slightly, edged back. Nikolaiev, for his part, also edged back. Voronov smiled uncertainly; so did Nikolaiev. The Imerach passed on. He approached Horatio. Horatio, remembering his lesson well, stepped forward and embraced the Corporal; the Corporal embraced him back, with the greatest enthusiasm. Exasperated, Simeonov called off his man: "You fool!" he cried, swiping him on the rear with the flat of his sword, "Have we taught you nothing in all these years?"

"You fool!" cried the Corporal in equal measure, "we have learned nothing at all in all these years!" He thrust at his commanding officer with his musket. The Captain was immediately en garde: he parried, and within moments, an energetic passage-of-arms was under way, sabre and musket clattering and clashing together; up and down the road they went, now yielding, now feinting, thrusting, pointing, all manner of steps, turns and stratagems; had a lady of a certain type been watching she would have fainted from sheer ecstasy; as the Captain passed Voronov, he transferred to him a large bottle of vodka from his left hand, while jabbing forward with the sword in his right; as the Corporal passed Horatio, he winked heavily; Horatio, feeling that it would only be comme il faut, winked heavily in return; until at last, getting the better of his man, the Corporal jerked the feet from under Simeonov and pinned him to the ground.

The inn-keeper, feeling that the honour of the Imperial Russian Army was at stake, hauled Nikolaiev off – not without some resistance – and released the Captain, who, feeling dusty but quite unflustered – for such minor contretemps were only to be expected if one had an Imerach in the ranks – sprang to his feet, adjusted his uniform and headed without another word towards the flickering light inside the lodge. As he reached the open door, he turned, pointed at his Corporal, and then at the spot on which he stood. Corporal Nikolaiev pointed similarly, once, twice, and then stood to attention half-way up the path. He was now on sentry-duty: none might pass. By good fortune alone, both Voronov and Horatio were closer to the door than he was, and found themselves safely inside.

Captain Simeonov saw Ksenia again and thought no more of flogging. Horatio saw Ksenia again and thought no more of Liberty. Voronov saw Ksenia again and thought of home.

"Madame!" cried Captain Simeonov, in Russian. "Madame, do we meet again? Yes, we meet again." No truer word was spoken. However, the Captain got no further with his exposition of what was manifest, for the sharp eyes of Yadviga had spotted the arrival of essential supplies.

"At last, you choose to arrive, you louse," she greeted him. "Might I hope that that is another bottle for us?" With those simple words of welcome, she relieved Voronov of his burden, and made herself busy with the lodge's poor supply of mugs. Three were to be had; she spat energetically in two of them to expel dust and wood-lice, and wiped the third with her fingers. Then, as fastidiously as were she handling an ikon in the church of St Cyril – or of St Methodius, his brother – she measured out the reviving spirit into the three mugs. One mug she passed to Simeonov, one to Voronov, and the third – the one she had wiped carefully – she retained for her own medical requirements.

While these preparations were being made, under the watchful, approving and most professional eye of the inn-keeper, Ksenia exploded a mine under the on-rushing cavalry-charge of Captain Simeonov. The Captain, taken quite by surprise, wheeled in his saddle and sounded the retreat.

"Why have we come, she asks? A good question, madam. We have come," he announced, "to pay our respects to our brother-in-arms, General St Clair—"

Looking up from her measurements, Yadviga took a moment to cross herself, for St Clair, although a new saint in the Russian constellation, was surely the patron saint of Russian Generals.

"—and having arrived, we have determined that it would be unwise to advance any further."

The other officer, he of whom the Russian patriot spoke, stirred himself on the bed, planted a kiss upon the deeply-breathing mouth of the book-seller, whispered the name of Amélie once more, then turned his attention to the new arrival.

"Captain," said he, anxious to greet a man from whom he had won a hundred roubles barely a month before, "have you come to play cards?"

"Alas not, sir," said Simeonov, "We regret. We have come to pay our respects to you, sir. You shall tell me whether you think this is due you. But we shall not step any closer, sir." He turned to Voronov, and announced in a stage-whisper that few could fail to hear: "Dying, as any child knows, is greatly infectious."

DYING – GREATLY INFECTIOUS

Voronov, to his credit, looked aghast. Ksenia and Horatio stared at the man in horror. Only the old woman seemed unaffected.

"Well," she said, "I won't say you have no sense at all, but, you mark my words: you are an imbecile. Have I not dealt with many a dying man, and look at me – am I not yet in the prime of life?"

"Not at all," thought Voronov to himself, and for his unspoken thought he received a blow to the chest from the vigorous old woman.

"Not at all," responded Captain Simeonov. "We have seen it so on every battlefield from Poland to Turkey. A child knows it to be true. Once one man dies, it is likely the man beside him will die also, and then another, until the whole line falls. The whole line falls, I say. And unless we adopt cunning tactics to avoid Death, the whole army ends up dying, line by line. I saw it at the Battle of the Iron Gorge." He nodded to Voronov. "You, sir, will know of the Iron Gorge, also known as the Gates of Iron." Voronov denied this once. "Of course you do." He nodded to Horatio. "And you, of course, will not."

Horatio denied it a second time.

Captain Simeonov brushed off these inconsequential denials. "Well, no matter that you claim to know it. It is what I expected. At the Battle of the Iron Gorge, which we fought for mastery of the Danube, it was proved beyond all doubt that dying is not a good tactic. It is also unpleasant for others to behold. Why, a man standing close to us had his limbs carried off accidentally by a cannon shot: it was not a pretty sight, and we were damned if we would let that happen to us."

Major Sinclair considered this observation, and nodded. "War," he began sententiously, with all the authority of old age, disremembering the fact that he had actually seen very little of war, except from the inside of a quarter-master's store on the far side of an ocean. His listeners expected more than just this one word; but that was not to be. The clue was in the lengthy silence that followed the single noun: "War". It was one of those short expositions, like: "Foreigners." "Time." "Children." "Men." "Women." "Death." And an old favourite: "Love." In all of these expressions – usually prefixed by a sigh – a whole lifetime, the oppressive burden of a thousand generations of experience, might be found. Thus:

"War."

Yadviga was not to be put off: "Infectious, he says. He is a simpleton," said she, with a modest amount of respect for the man's uniform. "All I can say is only the living are infectious. In any case, do the dying have any time for that sort of thing?" Delivering herself of this crowning piece of logic, of which a French Philosopher would have been proud, she drank off her mug of vodka, found it to be exactly as she had remembered, and poured herself some more. "And while we're about it, did you bring any ham?"

The pride of the Russian Imperial Army stood in the doorway to the dying man's room, and pondered these matters. At last, he reached a decision: "What will we do? We will sit here in the passage-way," he announced, "and share our comrade's last hours." So saying, he manipulated his sword in an ingenious manner and sat upon it. Horatio was frozen in horror, expecting that, at the very least, the Captain should lacerate his privates upon the blade: but no. (Such

LACERATING
HIS PRIVATES ON
THE BLADE

excitement – and more – was reserved for another night, a few years hence, after our Captain had lost a card-game in Kiev played against a lady of enterprise from Caucasia, who had wagered a place in her bed against his self-mutilation; a story there is not time for here, for it spans a full week of brutality, lust and betrayal, and requires the reader's undivided attention, a stiff drink of brandy for the ladies, and smelling-salts for the gentlemen.) The ingenious device that the Captain had tonight deployed was simply a small iron frame that permitted him to perch upon the handle of his sword, while the point sank ever deeper, as the minutes ticked past, into the rotten floorboards. He positioned himself so that he could still see into the room.

Major Sinclair was greatly enlivened by the arrival of a visitor. He had had no visitors since 1831. He sat up brightly in his bed, leaning heavily upon the bolster offered by the recumbent form of Isengrim of Krakow, and wheezed with the effort. "Captain Simeonov," he called, waving wildly with a hand that seemed not to have a great purpose in life, guessing perhaps that it, like the other limbs and appendages, would soon be rendered useless. "I salute you." The Captain on his stick returned the salute gravely.

"Did I ever tell you," he continued, "of the disgrace of Captain Thomas Cochrane?"

"You ask me about Captain Thomas Cochrane? We have heard that story many times, sir," replied the Russian, "many times."

"In that case, sir," proposed Major Sinclair agreeably, "you will have no objection if I tell it again?"

"We can think of no reason to deny you this," said the Russian, "it was always your greatest story. Your greatest story, sir, and I'll have the entrails of anyone who denies it, sir. Go to it." He pulled out a pipe, and settled his back against the wall.

"It was in the year 1814," began Major Sinclair.

Ksenia yawned uncontrollably and closed her eyes. Horatio covered her with his coat, and prepared for yet another lengthy narration.

"Ah," said Captain Simeonov, "we all know what happened in the year 1814, do we not, eh?"

There was a profound pause while all those both awake and interested considered the question. Before anyone could comment, the Captain had corrected himself: "No, you buffoon, that was 1812." Thus chastising the world in general, he permitted the dying man to continue.

"In the year 1814," began Major Sinclair. He paused; stopped; trying to remember what happened in 1814.

His Russian counterpart obliged: "One cold night in February, Colonel de Bourg arrives in Dover from France. Colonel de Bourg, sir."

"Good, good," applauded Major Sinclair, greatly pleased. He had not heard this story for some time, and it always gratified him to hear it, for it concerned his old friend and commanding officer, Colonel Andrew Cochrane-Johnstone.

"Colonel de Bourg," continued Simeonov from his perch in the passage-way, "brought great news to the shores of England—"

"Great news, indeed," enthused Major Sinclair.

"—news that Napoleon—"

"Pah!" spat Yadviga, who felt obliged to drink some more, to drown her maternal sorrows at the name of that French fiend, now in the arms of St Helena of the Oceans.

"—had been overthrown, his armies crushed, that the Allied armies had entered Paris. Is that not correct, sir?"

"It is correct!" exclaimed Major Sinclair.

"Long live the glorious Imperial Army!" shouted Mr. Voronov patriotically.

"No, sir," countered Captain Simeonov. "It is not. What were these

men, you ask? Colonel de Bourg, mark my words, he was nothing but a fraud, a man in complot with Mr. Butt, Mr. Holloway, Mr. Sandsom and one other whose name now escapes me—"

"Mr. M'Rae," chipped in Major Sinclair eagerly.

"—correct, sir: Mr. M'Rae – these five scoundrels had engineered the whole thing, intending to force a precipitate rise in the value of Omnium stocks on the Exchange of London—"

Major Sinclair did not groan, so enthralled was he by this tale of deceit.

"—of London, I say—"

No, nothing.

"—of London, where certain people who had purchased stock on time-bargains barely a month before, now found to their astonishment that they had, in the course of a day, made several thousands in profit—"

"Pounds Sterling," noted Horatio, always keen to supply valuable information of a precise nature.

"—among them, you will perhaps be surprised to learn, Messrs. Butt, Holloway, Sandsom and M'Rae, and also certain officers of the British Army and Navy then resident in London—"

"Ah!" shouted Major Sinclair with great energy. Yadviga grumbled and heaved her bulk from her chair. She propelled herself meaningfully at Major Sinclair's breeches once more, but he summoned the last reserves of his strength and fought her off.

"Leave me alone, you shameless witch!" he gasped, wrestling with her as she pursued her goal with evident distaste. His voice and his actions awakening the slumbering book-seller Isengrim from his dreams of Melmoth, Frankenstein, Manfred of Otranto and other unfortunates of recent times; finding himself assailed, as it appeared, by a dread creature of many limbs, screeching and tossing upon his bed, he leaped from the arms of Morpheus, and fled through the door, down the passage-way and into the open air, his feet barely touching the floor. There, alas, he met with Corporal Nikolaiev, who immediately set to and repelled the invasion. Several minutes elapsed and Isengrim did not return. By which time, Yadviga had, with the inevitability of a greater power, reached her goal, but was now castigating the Major for his inability to piss on her command.

When silence had settled once more, Captain Simeonov continued with Major Sinclair's story of the Great Stock Exchange Swindle of 1814: "What happened when the fraud was discovered? What happened, eh? When the fraud was discovered, and the prices fell once more, Colonel de Bourg was unmasked, and was foolish enough to seek out Captain Thomas Lord Cochrane, at his house in—"

"Have a care!" warned Horatio, alive to the possibilities.

"—in the great city, and so led the authorities to the nest of fraudsters, who were immediately placed under arrest. That was what happened when the fraud was discovered."

"The disgrace, the disgrace," groaned Major Sinclair exuberantly, recovering his good spirits.

"Indeed, sir, you shall tell me whether it was a disgrace. First among the suspects was Captain Thomas Cochrane, once the hero of the British Navy, now exposed as the worst fraud in living memory. His uncle, Colonel Cochrane-Johnstone, fearing to be tainted with the disgrace of his nephew – what did he do? I will tell you what he did. He took the only course open to an honourable man embroiled in a scandal not of his making, and fled to Europe." The implication that the land of Europe was the asylum of all disgraced men and fallen women met with broad agreement, for it was understood that all that threatened the Nation came from the west.

THE DISGRACE

"That the Colonel had made ten thousands of pounds from the sudden rise in stocks, was, of course, none of his design," observed Major Sinclair judiciously.

"None of his design: quite right, sir, none of his design and none of his asking. And who is to say otherwise? And was not the fall from grace of Thomas Cochrane a great spectacle?" asked Captain Simeonov from his perch in the corridor. "Indeed it was, for he was found guilty, condemned to an hour in the pillory, fined one thousand pounds – Sterling – and locked up in prison for a year. Was this not a shame and a scandal? Ah, the shame, the scandal! – the man was a radical and a member of the British Parliament. We know how democrats and radicals behave, do we not?" He looked around him with considerable satisfaction, a teacher at the end of an object lesson.

"Did not the people of Westminster re-elect him to Parliament unopposed, not one month after his trial?" Horatio had some knowledge of these events, for they were still the talk of servants' quarters even after several years had gone by; most particularly since the disgraced Captain had gone on to demolish the Spanish and Portuguese Empires in South America.

Captain Simeonov stood suddenly, leaving the sword quivering like an aspen bough in the floorboards. He marched up to Horatio and peered up at him. "Sir," he said in a low voice, "such is democracy: a liberty taken by fools to elect villains."

Having unburdened himself of this undeniable axiom, and demonstrating further that the words 'fools' and 'villains' could as easily be swapped, as follows: "democracy: a liberty taken by villains to elect fools" and advising, in an aside to Mr. Voronov, of two further declensions of the noun 'liberty', to wit: "liberty: democracy ridden hard by villains on behalf of fools" and further: "villainy: a foolishness taken for liberty by democrats" after which tour de force of National and Orthodox wisdom, all proving beyond doubt that Liberty, Villainy, Democracy and Foolishness were one and the very same, the inn-keeper stood dizzied and blinded by the dazzling lights of understanding; the Captain then returned with sang-froid to his perilous seat. He observed that Ksenia was stirring under her blanket. He saluted her, and, in a rare show of chivalry, concluded his history thus: "And, by being locked up, did he not abandon his young wife Kitty, barely eighteen years of age, in her greatest hour of need?"

Ksenia sighed, knowing that, in such a situation, the love of a young wife out-lasts all. On those sadly few occasions when she had met Kitty, they had agreed, simple girls that they were, that 'Love' was

LOYALTY THROUGH DISAPPOINTMENT.

They could not estimate the incidence of each of the three items.

"But Kitty's husband," she began, "was later fully pardoned and restored to his rights, and she—"

She got no further – Isengrim limped back indoors, once more bleeding and bruised. The book-seller needed more attention than Thomas, Lord Cochrane.

36

THE GOAT IS THE BEAST
WHICH MOST DELIGHTS THE LADIES
OF SCOTLAND.

Once more, the hard-pressed nurses prepared themselves to dance attendance on the sick and the injured. This was a night on which only one man need die. Kindly, Ksenia took Isengrim's arm, and led him towards the stove. Candles burned there, scarcely enough to see by, but enough for all to see that Isengrim's meeting with the Imerach had been one of reciprocated respect. The gash on his forehead had opened again and an impressive flow of blood dribbled down his left cheek. His right eye was swollen. There were bruises upon his hands and his arms, where his coat-sleeves fell away. Captain Simeonov stepped close and looked on the human devastation with a degree of satisfaction.

"What do we see here? I will tell you what we see here. We see that the Corporal has lost none of his powers," he noted, poking at the bruises and cuts with the end of a complacent pipe.

"Sir!" protested Ksenia, "Move away please – this man is injured."

"Indeed he is," acknowledged the Captain. "We can all see that, can we not? Who among us will deny it?"

"Well, then," finished the young widow, and she slid her body between the Captain and the book-seller. The Captain appreciated this move and felt greatly tempted to lay hands upon the young woman as she presented to him that aspect of woman-kind which he dearly loved. Noting, however, with a practised eye, that Horatio loomed large over him, he whistled a brusque martial air, and threw himself once more upon his sword.

Seeing that Isengrim was exhausted, and yielding to an unaccustomed sense of charity – perhaps she had fallen in love, at the age of seven-and-sixty: it happens: love is not solely the dominion of the young and foolish – any one may enter in – any one may leave – Yadviga made haste to clear some space upon Josephine's bed.

"Here," she said to Major Sinclair, "can you not move over sharpish and let this poor gentleman lie for a moment?"

The dying old soldier was used to following orders: he did as he was told without a murmur of protest. He would march down the steep hill of death without complaint. Fellow-soldiers, he reasoned, had died in far worse conditions. As a consideration of the circumstances, Yadviga rolled up the Major in one blanket; in so doing, she rolled him to the far side of the bed, where – unfortunately ending up face down, arms pinioned to his side – he contemplated at close quarters the cold rotting wood underneath the window. The two women now eased Isengrim on to the warm spot vacated so kindly by Major Sinclair, provided him with the only pillow, covered him gently with the other blanket. He lay, breathing heavily, appreciating the musky scent of the Empress. Ksenia applied warm water and rags to his injuries. Yadviga wondered, as any conscientious physician should, whether a man so badly injured needed water or something stronger; with a dedication remarkable and unusual for one of her profession, she experimented upon her own body; after due consideration and measure, she decided on water, and left the younger woman to it.

"We were just discussing," said the last-named, knowing from experience that a man ill in his bed likes nothing better than to be talked to, "the colourful career of my cousin Thomas, Lord Cochrane."

"Your cousin, madam?" exclaimed the book-seller. "You seem to have many cousins?"

"My cousin, sir," stated the young widow with no little pride. "I know that he spent some time as Admiral-in-Chief of the Chilean and Brazilian navies, and indeed, was something of a hero in Greece."

"Stop right there," urged the book-seller, referring not, it was clear, to her tender washing of his wounds, something she would never have stopped in any case; but to her further narration of any matters to do with the glorious and naval deeds of the greatest sea-hero since—

"Stop right there," urged the book-seller. She obliged.

In the silence which followed, Isengrim scratched his ears masterfully, then made it known that, in his heavy sack of books, he had one which shed light upon the career of Thomas, Lord Cochrane.

Would the dark gentleman, he asked, indicating Horatio as a likely assistant – had the man not once been a slave, after all? – be so kind as to find that book and bring it over?

Under no normal circumstances would Horatio have undertaken this menial task. Was he not a man of liberty, free to disobey anyone and everyone, except perhaps the Prince Labanov. And, naturally, the widow Mrs. Cochrane, for what is 'Love' but blind obedience? It was she whom he now obeyed, as she raised her tired, tired eyes to him and, with one slight parting of her two lips, repeated the injunction. He placed the huge bag of books upon the table, and untied the knotted string that held it shut. He placed his right hand within and pulled out a book. By the light of the candle, he examined the title.

"Travels in Scotland," he announced, "by an Unusual Route, by the Reverend James Hall of Walthamstow."

"No, not that one," said Isengrim.

Horatio hauled out another small volume: "Travels in Iceland, by Sir George Steuart Mackenzie."

"Not that one," said Isengrim.

"Travels in Beloochistan and Sinde," asked Horatio, "by Sir Henry Pottinger?"

"Sir, you are not trying."

"Mr. J.E. Coffin's Journal of a Residence in Chile during the Period of Revolution 1817–18–19?"

Ksenia put her hands over her ears. She wished to hear nothing of coffins, Revolution or death.

"Here," continued Horatio, on hearing the repeated judgement of the book-seller, "is the Journal of a Residence in the Burmhan empire, and more particularly at the Court of Amarapoorah, by a gentleman named Hiram Cox."

"That," said Isengrim, "is a most interesting book, and one which would repay the modest outlay." He found no takers.

"Another one on Scotland, sir," announced the book-seller's new assistant. "Travels in Scotland, descriptive of the state of manners, literature and science, by Louis Albert Necker."

"Newly translated from the French," encouraged Isengrim.

"Into which language, you blackguard?" asked Simeonov, not unreasonably.

"English," was the reply.

"And what do we know about Scotchmen? Do they not speak English?" asked Simeonov perceptively.

"They do, sir," replied Isengrim, all unsuspecting, "they do."

"Then why," demanded the Russian Captain, with enough triumph in his voice to quell the thought that this was a non-sequitur, "do they need a Frenchman to tell them of their own country? I ask you that – you have no reply."

"No more," replied Horatio, who had just picked out another two-volume edition, "than the Russians need Dr. Morton's Travels in Russia."

Voronov the inn-keeper was suddenly intrigued. "Why do all these foreigners need to know about our country. Are they spies, Captain?" He turned to the military intelligence.

"Spies, sir, spies? Spies buzz about us like flies upon a dung-heap. Oh, we know spies! They must be flogged in advance." SPIES – FLIES UPON A DUNG-HEAP

"I think rather," intervened Isengrim, seeing that the discussion was likely to follow a direction of little profit, "that these writers publish their books so that more travellers – sir, more travellers—" he took care to emphasise the word for Mr. Voronov's ears, "—more travellers, sir, will take themselves and their servants to this beautiful land, visit your splendours, spend money in your inns—"

"Ah!" said Voronov, suddenly getting the point.

Horatio continued to plunder the sack of books: "Captain Holman's Narrative of a Journey through France, Italy, Savoy etc.—"

"We know of him," said Ksenia quietly. "Tell me, sir," she addressed Isengrim, "do you have no books in your sack that speak of love?"

Isengrim looked at her aghast: "Love? What is that?" he demanded.

Love, of course, is blind – like Captain Holman; who managed, like many another traveller in those far-off days, to find – despite his impairment – delight in the unseen breath of a pretty mouth, or the curve of a woman felt only by all-seeing fingertips – but that is neither here, nor was it there.

Horatio moved on quickly: "Sir William Gell's Narrative of a Journey in the Morea."

"Where the Devil," demanded Major Sinclair, in muffled tones, "is the Morea?"

There was a silence. None ventured an answer, except, at length, the book-seller: "A good reason, I think, for you to purchase the book." The suggestion, unsubtly tendered, brought him no profit, for the dying man had no freedom to reach for his purse.

Horatio, wearying of these endless journeys, travels and narratives, flicked through the books ever more quickly: "Travels in Asia – Travels in Ireland – Journal of a Residence in Ashantee – Travels in Brazil – across the Cordillera of the Andes – into Khorasan – I know not, my friend – Mexico – the Sandwich Islands – from Constantinople to England – from Calcutta to Europe by way of Egypt – from England to India and home again—"

"Could they not as well stay at home, those Englishmen?" demanded Simeonov, outraged at all these travels. "To travel, simply to return home – what futility!"

"—a Residence in Bagdad – a Journey across the Balcan – Travels in Assyria, Media and Persia – Travels in Chaldaea—"

Horatio stopped suddenly, holding a book in his hands. He looked at Ksenia; she looked at him, puzzled. "What have you there, sir?" she asked.

Horatio coughed. "It is, madam, A Journal Made by Señor Juan de Vega."

"Ah," said Ksenia quietly, with a small smile upon her lips, so small that she knew not what to do with it, so there it remained. "Cousin Charles."

"Did you know," began Isengrim conversationally, "that Charles Cochrane has lately taken out a patent for the weaving of Cashmere wool in Great Britain?" He had learned, in his years as book-seller, to keep up with the lives of his authors – such tittle-tattle, he found, frequently sold a book when all other interest had faded.

This particular piece of news struggled like a swimmer in a tempest, and slowly sank without trace. Isengrim threw a life-line after it: "Mr.

Cochrane is likely to make his fortune, which is more than his uncle ever did. The goat, I am advised, is the beast which most delights the ladies of Scotland."

Captain Simeonov raised his left eyebrow; Major Sinclair choked – it may have been the dust and the position of his mouth.

Horatio had plucked out the next book. "One perhaps," he showed it to the young widow, "for you, my dear friend – Mr. Dobell's Travels in Kamtchatka and Siberia, with a narrative of a residence in China."

"Lately published," beamed Isengrim, "and fresh from London."

"May I look at it, sir?" implored Ksenia Ivanovna. The old man could not refuse. She sat down with it in her lap, and opened the pages, following the words carefully with her index-finger in the light of the flickering candle.

Horatio was reaching the foot of the pile. He paused and asked Isengrim whether he had found the book required.

"No, sir," was the flat answer. It seemed that the book-seller saw merit in all of his books being paraded before an interested audience, and was in no hurry to hit upon just one. Languidly, he scratched at his ears.

Horatio sighed. He paused at the next title: "This man did not travel far," he observed. "Narrative of a Journey to Brussels and Coblentz."

"Written perhaps," wondered Voronov, anxious to turn the tide on the on-rushing hordes of English travellers, "by a Russian?"

"Alas not," came the awful reply. "The author is King Louis the Eighteenth of France."

"Did he," asked Mr. Voronov, "stay in an inn on his travels?" His question was heavy with interest.

"Certainly not," mocked Isengrim. "The man was no simple traveller, that he would put up in the Inn of the Merry Hunter, or the Inn of the Tin Drum."

The inn-keeper gave sharp attention to this new piece of knowledge. "The inn-keepers of that part of the world give names to their inns, then?" he asked, hovering between orthodox incredulity and inventive enterprise.

"Of course they do," said Isengrim. "How else would travellers distinguish between so many inns on the road?"

Astonishment – and, in equal measure, Revelation – was written in clear Russian letters upon Mr. Voronov's face. He thought of his own inn. He paused but for a moment.

"The Inn," he said majestically, "of the Great Tsar."

"The Inn," stated the Captain prosaically, "of the Thirsty Soldier."

"The Inn," proposed Yadviga pointedly, "of the Pickled Cucumber."

"The Inn," suggested Horatio chivalrously, "of the Comely Cook."

"The Inn," put forward Isengrim slyly, "of Storm and Stress."

There was a silence while Voronov struggled with this boundless choice.

Horatio continued with his researches: "Next we have Travels in Norway, Sweden, Finland, Russia and Turkey by Captain Jones, R.N.—"

"Pah!" said Simeonov.

"—and then 'Travels in Phrenologasto' by Don Jose Balscopo—"

PHRENOLOGASTO "Now that," interrupted Isengrim with great appreciation, "is a rare delight. Published in Calcutta in 1825. It repays study, and the man who travels there need not leave his home."

"A wonder," said Voronov, shaking his head to clear it of a snow-storm of new ideas. It seemed that books – when not written by poets – might contain great bundles of usefulness. It was marvellous just how little he knew about travellers and travelling, about inns and kings. He resolved to improve his knowledge at the earliest opportunity: he would have been astonished at how soon that opportunity would come.

"All this travelling," stated Captain Simeonov, "is a sheer waste of a man's talents. We have no doubt, have we?"

"Oh, we have, sir," said Ksenia hastily. "It is the very best employment for men of strong physique and firm resolve."

"The very best employment for men of strong physique and firm resolve, madam," countered the Captain, "is war."

Horatio and Ksenia disagreed. Voronov sided with the Captain, if only because Death in Glory seemed a most Russian sentiment. There was, of course, no ground for compromise, as all parties soon recognised.

Horatio peered into the bottom of the sack. "It is empty, sir," he stated, not without a timbre of satisfaction in his voice.

Isengrim denied this. "There is one more book," he said confidently, with the air of a showman about to reveal his greatest trick. He was, of course, correct: a slim volume lay at the foot of the sack.

Horatio opened it to read the title – it was a very long one: "Secret Memoirs of the Honourable Andrew Cochrane-Johnstone, of the Honourable Vice-Admiral Sir Alex. Forrester Cochrane K.B., and of Sir Thomas John Cochrane, a captain in the Royal Navy – by Mr. A. Mackenrot."

"Indeed, indeed," agreed the book-seller benignly. "I think you will find—"

"But what is this, sir?" asked Horatio, peering at a hand-written note on the title page. "Someone has written – what does it say? – 'Mr. Mackenrot was prosecuted for publishing this pamphlet, but having also been prosecuted capitally for Forgery and acquitted on INSANITY proof of his Insanity, the Prosecution for this Libel was dropped.'"

"Never mind that," said Isengrim hastily, "give me the book. It is the only copy I still have." He snatched the book away from Horatio. "Do you know, sir, that the author of this volume was sued by that scoundrel Admiral Cochrane, for defamation of character. Character? – the rogue had none to speak of! Well, I – that is, the author – the author issued a subpoena – you know what that is, sir? – for witnesses to attest in court to the veracity of these Memoirs. Who do you think those witnesses were, who were called?"

Horatio had no idea; Voronov had no interest; Simeonov had no tobacco left in his pipe; Sinclair had no voice – he was slowly being suffocated against the wall.

"Firstly," said the book-seller triumphantly, "the Emperor Napoleon—"

"Aaah!" screamed Yadviga, who was so overcome by emotion that she was obliged to sip some more spirits.

"We know who he is, do we not?" stated Simeonov superfluously.

"Secondly, his brother Jérome Bonaparte, King of Westphalia—"

"Is that a place?" said Simeonov. "We must make a study of Europe."

"—and thirdly, the Admiral Willaumez of the Imperial French Navy."

"And did they appear in court in the defence of the author?" wondered Horatio, unable to disguise a dawning interest.

"Alas not," answered Isengrim gravely, "for Napoleon was unhappily defeated at Waterloo, just as the papers were about to be served on him, and – in the capacity of bailiff – I found it impossible to serve the papers on him during his captivity in Britain, for they kept moving him on. That was done to thwart me, sir, to thwart me, and prevent the truth about the Cochranes ever reaching the ears of the public!"

"Sir," admonished Horatio, "please lower your voice." He indicated Ksenia, once a Cochrane herself, who, by good fortune, was six or seven thousand miles away and heard nothing of this Libel.

The book-seller continued in a whisper: "And then they moved him to St Helena, which was further than I cared to travel."

"Had you done so, however, you could have written a book about it," suggested Voronov, missing the point.

Major Sinclair had succeeded in clearing a passage for air, and was able to cry for help. Yadviga, with great complaint, unrolled him swiftly and he lay, dizzily, on the bed. "Did you know," he said, when he had caught his breath and the world seemed no longer to spin like the last endless vortex of Death "that Thomas Cochrane released Napoleon from St Helena?"

"Did he, by Jove?" exclaimed Isengrim, agitated, "Did he? Did he?" WHY WAS HE He continued muttering and considering the ways in which NOT TOLD? his life could have turned out so differently. "Then why," he said at last, looking fiercely at Sinclair, as if the man had himself been concealing the French Emperor, on whose wife's bed he lay so smugly, "why was I not told?" To which rational question there was no rational answer.

Dropping like five stones into the gulf of silence, the hours struck in the distant bell-tower.

Yadviga sat up, alerted to the passage of time. "You!" said she without ceremony, pointing at Isengrim, "are you feeling better?"

The book-seller incautiously admitted it.

"Well, in that case it is your turn to fetch more wood for the fire. I'm freezing here, and poor Major Sinclair is dying of cold, you mark my words. Just look – the stove has almost gone out while you've been setting out your stall. Make shift!"

Too surprised to think of a reply, Isengrim scratched his left ear, wrapped his blanket tightly around his shoulders, limped past Simeonov, down the passage-way, out into the back garden – scene of a late accident – and began to forage for wood in the dim grey light of dawn.

THE DAY BEGAN TO RUSTLE.

37

IT WAS WITH SOME FACILITY
THAT HE DEFRAUDED THE FRENCH
GOVERNMENT.

"Sir!" reported Corporal Nikolaiev, from his post out at the front of the house, "I heard a rustling."

"Very good, Corporal," replied Captain Simeonov, distracted by the lack of tobacco and the great mysteries of Napoleon, "We know what you must do."

The Corporal entered the house in the manner of a deadly assassin, saluted stealthily to the Captain, then crept down the passage-way and into the kitchen. The mourners-to-be lost sight of him. Out of sight, out of mind.

Horatio replaced all the books in the sack. Ksenia, enraptured by the words which brought back to her in painful, golden memory all the sights of her childhood, every transformed image of her home, laid down her book with a sigh.

"Sir," she said, turning to Horatio, "if you could but come with me to see Kamtchatka!"

Horatio, emboldened by his recent employment as publisher's agent, sat down beside her. He found himself indifferent as to the end of this implied expedition, but enthusiastic as to the means. Had he not heard it truly said that it matters not where a man travels, as long as the company is good? One might readily travel the Road to Hell, for the company is frequently amusing.

The publisher of Mr. Dobell's volume on Kamtchatka had thoughtfully, and at no little expense, included some engravings of clear vistas (such as had never before been seen so clearly, even in Kamtchatka) and precipitous mountains (such as had never before teetered so precipitously) on the peninsula. With some explanatory confusion, Ksenia showed these few pictures to Horatio, who was receptive. At no time in all his years of wandering in Europe and Russia had he felt such a burning desire to visit Kamtchatka, a land that surely was close to Paradise. Decency and Liberty would, of course, have to be abandoned – these counted as nothing in the balance.

Ksenia, for her part, knew that if she, by some unheard-of miracle, could once take this man to Kamtchatka with her, she could there endure all that a woman endures, and more – yes, even mud-slides and earthquakes and eruptions – through all the remaining years of her life – for there she would be happy: she knew it, it required no argument. There was great danger here and scandal: she knew it, she need not be told.

"I cannot tell why were you not told, sir," complained Major Sinclair in battered tones, having fallen somewhat behind the rapid unfolding of events, the quick cut and thrust of conversation, the torrent of ideas and philosophy, such as were unfolding this night in Novgorod the Great. Not to mention the swift disappearance of vodka and pickled cucumbers, so fast that the human eye could scarcely follow. "If you were not told, it is none of my fault. I am sure I would have told you had I known what there was to tell. Colonel Cochrane-Johnstone," he continued, "frequently told me that there was nothing to tell. And that if I did tell, it would not be the action of a gentleman."

"We know what honour is, do we not?" announced Captain Simeonov sententiously from his madman's perch in the corridor. "Oh, yes."

"'Honour', said the Colonel," said Major Sinclair, "'is like the grave – both have one lasting virtue: they protect a man from his creditors.'" The Major stared vacantly for a moment, as if seeing in front of him the figure of the Honourable. "When last I saw him, it looked as if the grave would be his only refuge from all his debts, as honour had singularly deserted him."

"He once had some, then?" asked Horatio, unable to contain himself.

"Debts?" replied the Major obtusely. "Yes, he had some debts – debts, indeed, that would have crushed many another man. The Colonel," he stated proudly, "had the largest debts of all the Scotchmen in Paris, even greater, he used to tell me, than his two foolish brothers. Did he care a fig?" The Major laughed in hollow manner. "I think not. He had a new plan every day for making his fortune again. Poor chap," he murmured sympathetically. "After the scandalous case of his nephew Thomas, he was obliged to flee first to Calais—"

"Calais, refuge of all charlatans," remarked a voice from the gloom.

"—so it is said – and then to Lisbon, and finally back to the West Indies, where he landed only to find that all his assets had been sold, every last scrap, by those carrion who gather around a man when he is knocked flat by injustice. And even then, even then, he found his debts were not cleared."

"We believe that all creditors should be locked up," said Captain Simeonov, appalled by the lack of honour among such gentlemen as were owed money. "And the key, by order, thrown away." As if to emphasise the point, he stood up and extracted his sword from the

CREDITORS – LOCK THEM UP

floorboards, slashed hither and thither, to the detriment of several spiders who had spent long hours creating intricate webs and now found them cut to ribbons. His anger propitiated, he resumed his seat; the spiders set about their business of repair, muttering darkly.

"In the year 1819, he set off for Demarara, to plant coffee," continued Major Sinclair, "and from that endeavour, he made some profit."

The mention of hot refreshments induced Yadviga to turn her attention to the samovar, long since neglected in this night of dissipation. With the assistance of the young widow – for it is the role of women, in all romances, to furnish the basic necessities of life, while the men undertake the burdensome tasks of Reflection and Philosophy. To his credit, Horatio offered to help, but was soon shooed away. While tea was brewing, the dying man mentioned that, due to some unpleasantness in South America—

"Creditors?" demanded Simeonov.

"Once more," confirmed Sinclair.

"Pah!" spat Simeonov.

"Scum!" concurred Sinclair.

"—Colonel Cochrane-Johnstone was obliged to retreat firstly to the island of Dominica—"

"Aha!" exclaimed Yadviga, at this hour of the morning entirely unclear why she did so.

"—and then, finally, we made our way to Paris, to which city the Colonel's elder brothers had already retired. There, sir," the Major shook his head, "there we were obliged to live on our wits."

"An outrage!" exclaimed Simeonov, who had heard of men living on their wits – it was not an idea with which he felt greatly comfortable. Far better, he judged, to be a soldier and to live by the sword and to die by the—

"Pox!"

interrupted Yadviga savagely, "where did I put that bottle? This is an outrage, you mark my words." She scowled at Voronov, who was pleased to demonstrate, for once, his innocence. Ksenia swiftly located the missing item and restored it to the head tea-maker.

"An outrage, indeed," agreed Sinclair. "I considered myself fortunate to fetch up in that city with a man who knew how to make money from nothing."

"As I would be, sir," intervened Mr. Voronov, who had spent the past twenty-five years of his life wondering what was the difference between money and nothing – for he saw little of the former to make a comparison with the latter.

Sinclair babbled on: "Scarcely had he arrived on French soil than he had set up the National Pullet Investment Fund, of which, no doubt, you will have heard?"

There were blank looks. The word 'National' rang alarums in the heads of the Russians, while Horatio was attracted to the Pullet.

"Le Fonds National des Poulets," elucidated the Major. "Founding capital, five millions of French francs."

Simeonov whistled: "A fine sum from a man in debt."

"On the promise of a fixed return of fifteen on their investment, some land-owners in the Fontainebleau forest agreed to make the Colonel master of ten thousand chickens."

Voronov shook his head doubtfully. He kept chickens himself, and knew how even a dozen could cause turmoil and tears. Ten thousand? – not to be imagined: feathers, dust and droppings everywhere. To say nothing of the cackling.

"The Colonel remained master for three days only, and then he handed them back, explaining that an intervention by the National Board of Security—"

Simeonov clicked his heels smartly and saluted.

"—had made it impossible for the scheme to continue: small returns only could be expected, he told them, and he knew they were not men for small returns. They agreed, were refunded their entire investment, and set off for home with their chickens."

"A complete failure then," observed Horatio, unsurprised by the abortive scheme.

Major Sinclair laughed fit to die. When he had defied all expectation in this respect, he replied: "Not at all, sir, not at all. He made enough money to set us up in a splendid apartment at number 96, rue du Faubourg St Honoré."

"Not possible, sir," stated the Russian army officer imperiously.

Major Sinclair gathered his strength for the surprising punch-line, then coughed it up:

"Eggs."

It took some moments for the import of this one word to sink in. When at last it did, every head was shaken in wonder.

"Thirty thousand eggs at two sous per egg. No sooner had we settled in to our new lodgings," continued the Major relentlessly, "than he turned to me: 'Sinclair,' he said, 'one French egg is not enough.'"

Horatio nodded in weary appreciation of a witticism he had first heard at the age of ten. Voronov, having no familiarity with the French language, nodded in agreement only at the insufficiency. Simeonov, in a National Frenzy, considered one French egg to be more than enough, and said so.

Major Sinclair ignored them all and continued: "It was with some facility that the Colonel defrauded the French Government. For he had a grander scheme in mind. This time he aimed higher than hens."

"Geese?" asked Voronov eagerly. He had a soft spot for a goose's egg: his first day of married life had begun with a goose's egg, and it was perhaps the happiest meal of all his days. He longed – he now realised, with a great longing that stuck in his throat – for another goose's egg. And for those emotions and comforts and hopes which went with it – all now, lost.

"Ducks?" demanded Yadviga, who had foggy memories of a morning spent in a barn with a Cossack soldier, some years before – no, in truth: it was many years before – in which a duck's egg had played no inconsiderable part. The egg she remembered, the Cossack and his ways – she did not.

"Swans?" proposed Ksenia dreamily, for no other reason than that she had found the swans of London, when left uneaten, to be extraordinarily beautiful.

"Carnivorous elephants," said Major Sinclair.

While the dreamers indoors considered the significance and magnitude of elephants – and, since Major Sinclair gave no sign of elaborating on the matter, they could not tell whether the projected enterprise, by which the French Government was to find itself so easily defrauded, was founded upon the beasts themselves; or, taking into account the moral turpitude of the Colonel and the experiments in Agricultural Improvement of his brother Archibald, the ninth Earl of Dundonald, their excrementa – a drama was unfolding outdoors in the back garden.

Corporal Nikolaiev, upon reaching the kitchen, stopped still. He listened for the rustling sound which had alerted his fine-honed instincts – he was a man who had stood sentry-duty for days and weeks and months on end. The rats, observing his furtive movements, were wise enough to freeze in the midst of their pattering, to make not a sound, as if turned to solid wood by the eye of Baba Yaga. In this artificial silence, the soldier could clearly hear what he wished to hear: a rustle, a snuffle, the sound of a creature breathing out in the opaque twilight of the garden. He crept forward and eased open the door, which stood already ajar.

Something was moving in the mists. Something with four legs under the bushes, under the trees, brushing aside brambles and fallen branches: tracking, foraging, hunting. Then, in one moment, one shaft of morning sunlight, reflected by some miracle – had Yadviga been here, at this moment, she would surely have been smitten down with religious awe, died, and gone to Heaven, there to sit and look down upon all Unbelievers, and eat celestial cucumbers – the rising sun, somewhere far to the east, almost under the horizon, shot a single beam to a high window in the tower of the Church of Spilled Blood – a most religious edifice which has not been mentioned until now, for it stands a little to the west of Novgorod the Great, and was noted only for the quality of its glazing – a single beam reflected back down to the ground, into the garden, to illuminate in a golden haze one small patch of the undergrowth: in one moment that would have done credit to the lighting-master of a fashionable theatre in St Petersburg, the holy ray of light picked out from the rising vapours of the earth the grey shape of a wolf, as it stopped and scented the air.

Well, said the Corporal to himself, an Imerach knows how to deal with a wolf.

Scarcely taking the time to draw breath, he leaped out from the doorway and in one – two – three – strides he was across the open flower-beds, now overgrown with weed, and had grasped the wolf by A SOLDIER FREE the throat. As he expected, the ferocious beast put up a AND BOLD struggle that would have done honour to the greatest grey wolf of all Siberia. Locked in each other's grip, man and beast tussled, snarled, bit, kicked, turned, wheeled, bared their teeth. They stared into each other's eyes and saw there only themselves. It was a horrible sight and they set to once more, a fight to the death. After a few moments, a blanket, which had unaccountably been caught in the struggle, finally trapped the wolf's hind legs. With one swift and practised movement, the soldier wrapped the rest of the blanket around the wolf, thereby muzzling it, stood up, slung the hapless beast over his shoulder, whistled a merry line or two of 'A Soldier Free and Bold', and set off back to the house.

In the passage-way, he stood to attention in front of Captain Simeonov.

"What have we here, Corporal?" demanded the Captain fiercely. "Do I know what we have here? I think not!"

"We have here a wolf, sir!" reported the soldier.

At this news, the Captain felt obliged to stand up; he took a long step backwards, then he poked the trapped beast circumspectly with his sword. The beast howled, and then the burden sagged. The cry was almost human. "Still alive, eh?"

"Sir!" acknowledged the Corporal. "Yes, sir! Still alive, eh, Captain, sir!"

"Well, take it back to barracks, Corporal. Should you let it out of your sight? No, I order you not to let it out of your sight. We'll have some sport with it, eh? But if it gives you any trouble, cut its legs off."

"Barracks – sport – trouble – cut its legs off, sir!" said the soldier smartly. He shifted the burden from his right to his left shoulder and stepped out on to the street. A trail of dripping blood from the captured creature marked his road back to the kremlin. With an unvanquishable sense of pride in his men, Simeonov watched him march away.

"The fiercest, most bloodthirsty elephants you ever saw," stated Major Sinclair, returned to consciousness by the sudden military drama; but his words fell upon deaf ears.

"ELEPHANTS IMPORTED FROM COLOMBIA."

38

OMELETTES.

"Legs," advised Captain Simeonov steadily, "what are they? Are they not the things a wolf values most in life? Of course they are." He eyed the shocked circle of people in the little room, who had clustered together without a moment's hesitation on learning that the Corporal's burden was a wolf. He wondered idly whether one of them might argue on the subject of vulpine values. Civilians, there was no argument, are argumentative – more so than an Imerach: it was the principal distinction between an army-man and a civilian – no argument. Come to think of it, taking the legs off a civilian was guaranteed to put a stop to any nonsense. He measured them up with his sword-blade. No, he reassured himself, none of these needed such a punishment. Not yet. He relaxed once more upon his martial seat – one false move would have unmanned him – and he straightened his moustache.

"From Colombia, sir?" enquired Horatio, wishing rapidly to change the subject. "Are there really elephants in Gran Colombia?"

Major Sinclair looked blankly at him.

"Carnivorous elephants?" prompted Horatio.

The Major shook his head angrily – some people never listened. "Eggs, you useless black fool, I told you already. With eggs you can make—" With which unending words of diplomacy he fell back once more into the brown arms of Josephine, much as an insomniac Napoleon might have done on any given night of the Empire.

So the mourners never did find out how Colonel Andrew Cochrane-Johnstone managed to defraud the Government of France. Which is much to be regretted, for knowledge of such matters is always utilitarian. On the credit side, however, the mention of elephants and of eggs did much to counter-balance the matter of wolves and to calm the nerves of those assembled, and they drifted back to their seats and positions.

Major Sinclair's last words had a profound effect upon Horatio. At this end of a long and arduous night, he was already exhausted; his every limb ached, his head thumped unreasonably, his mouth was dry. And he was, he knew, still a slave, still a servant, still a black man amongst seventy million white men and women, every one of whom was likely to view him as a foreigner and a potential enemy. Seventy million, apart from – he was sure and certain – one.

It is curious: Horatio found the word "black" insulted him most, although it could not be gain-said; Voronov found the word "fool" embarrassing, and did not even hear the adjective; Ksenia found the word "useless" to be offensive, for she knew that Horatio was the most useful man in the world; Yadviga was more concerned about "eggs", for she had just consumed the last of the pickled variety, and it had given her violent wind; Simeonov found nothing untoward in any of this – army men, he was pleased to note, speak their minds the world over, and so it should be: no argument.

Horatio stepped up: "I was, sir," he said, looking boldly at Captain Simeonov, "about to talk of Liberty."

"You digress, sir," warned the Captain in reply.

"I may digress, I think?" demanded Horatio, stepping up some more.

Simeonov looked at the much larger man and decided that a digression was, until further orders were received, tolerable. He examined his fingernails and hummed a song of Old Kiev.

"I, who was once a slave, may talk of Liberty, and the present times," he began. "We live in the Age of Liberty and Revolution – America, France, Colombia, Chile, Brazil, Spain and Portugal; and in this new Age, the renunciation of Slavery by decent men."

"And women," noted Ksenia, anxious not to be forgotten.

"By women especially," confirmed Horatio with generosity and – assuredly – truth. "But here in Russia," he continued grimly, "not a word of Liberty may be spoken, even in a whisper, even if it is the Liberty to choose another autocrat—"

"What, sir," demanded Simeonov in a terrible voice, in lieu of rattling his sabre – it is not easy to rattle a sabre if one is perched upon it – "do you mean by that?"

"I mean, sir, the followers of Pavel Pestel," replied Horatio with much forwardness, "those who wished for the Tsar Constantine, rather than the Tsar Nicholas."

"The Decembrists?" squeaked Mr. Voronov, unable to master his voice at the audacious reference.

"Certainly," agreed Horatio, still keeping his eyes fixed upon the Imperial Army man.

The latter nodded slowly as if – as indeed he was – fixing the face of the black revolutionary in his mind, his face and his name, so that he might be placed, at least in the imagination, against a wall and summarily shot. "Why do we love our Tsar? Orthodoxy, Autocracy and Nationality: the three Pillars of Wisdom," he stated. "That is why we love Tsar Nicholas. For no other reason. Why – Liberty and Revolution, they lead to—"

"Omelettes," said Major Sinclair in French, as he slipped over the edge into—

"—Death and Destruction," concluded Simeonov. "Liberty leads to imprisonment, Revolution to exile."

"Only so, I think," countered Horatio boldly, "if those who would have it otherwise stand in the way." He recalled with anger the five Decembrists who were executed for their pains, and some hundreds of others sent into Siberia.

Captain Simeonov declared that he fully intended to stand in the way.

"Narodnost," added Mr. Voronov. "Nationality is the answer to all our woes. Nationality in the face of foreign liberties." He comforted himself that Nationality was the answer to all the pressing problems of the day, including – perhaps – slavery and poetry.

Nationality, and – he had recently been advised – flogging in advance.

Horatio talked passionately of Liberty. But one look of admiration from Ksenia would have flung shackles around his feet and manacles upon his wrists, and all his wild ideals into exile.

"Ah," said Ksenia, reflecting on another matter altogether, "the love of Liberty is a tragical thing. Do you know," she asked the world in general, "that my grandfather died for Liberty?"

"For Liberty?" asked Voronov, appalled. "Do you not mean rather that he died as a result of Liberty?"

"My grandfather," continued Ksenia, feeling quite at liberty to ignore the remark, "was Joann Petrovich Loginov, son of the famous Pyotr Mikhailovich, founder of the seminary at Petropavlovsk. In the year 1771, my grandfather associated himself with the celebrated exile Count Benyovsky of Hungary, and sailed from Kamtchatka in search of the Island of Miracles. To Oonalaska first, and then to Canton."

"Ah – Canton and the fabled port of Macao," observed Horatio knowledgeably. It was a continual source of astonishment, to himself as to those who conversed with him, what useless knowledge he had stored up in his head, instantly available at the slightest opportunity. Prince Labanov was frequently obliged to call upon Horatio to provide a forgotten fact.

"That may well be, sir," said Ksenia kindly, acknowledging the reference. "My grandfather and his young companions—"

"These rebels, then?" corrected Simeonov censoriously, looking as grim as he might be permitted.

"—indeed, sir: one of them was my great-uncle – set off in their ship, and sailed away in the hope of finding freedom, for to them Kamtchatka was but a prison. They came after many mishaps to the distant islands of Japan, where they were made very welcome, until – alas – they were mistaken for pirates by the native peoples and three men were slain under a hail of arrows. My grandfather was one of them. He died on the spot and was buried on the beach of Formosa." MISTAKEN FOR PIRATES

"Natives," muttered Captain Simeonov, more interested in this matter than in any of the other nonsense. "Never trust their welcome." Assuredly the ship of Count Benyovsky would have been well provisioned with muskets and cannon, for the laudable and necessary purpose of revenge. Rebels, traitors and exiles he could forgive, as long as they exercised discipline over a Native.

"And your great-uncle?" asked Horatio, shaking his head at this sorry tale.

"When they reached Canton, many of the party died of fever; Count Benyovsky sailed for Africa to become King of Madagascar, and most of the Kamtchatkans returned home," she replied. "My great-uncle brought the tragic news to my grandmother and my first father, who was very young. He too," she advised the company, with more than a breath of sadness in her voice, "died young. Scarcely had I learned my numbers than he perished in an accident."

"You had several fathers, then?" asked Horatio, anxious to establish all the family connections of this mysterious woman.

"My second father was Joann Vereshagin, sexton of Paratunka," replied Ksenia, "who very charitably married my mother when my first father was lost; and my third father was the kind Captain Rikord, Governor of Kamtchatka, who took me into his home when I was ten years old. And he still is my father."

"Ah, the Governor!" exclaimed Yadviga with lively interest. "You can't do better than a Governor, you mark my words! So, you're a Governor's daughter, eh? Let me kiss you on the cheek, my dear!"

Which she did, without further ado. It was always wise, she had found, to make such little investments here and there; it cost nothing and could reap several roubles.

"Where," asked the inn-keeper of a sudden, the leaky ship of thought having led him inexorably from blighted voyages to benighted travellers to the matter of Journals and Narratives, "is the book-seller?"

Ksenia's hands leaped to her mouth. That the book-seller was missing in the garden while a wolf had been captured in the garden could mean only one thing. Horatio's thoughts slid along a similar icy roadway.

Yadviga was more concerned that the book-seller had not returned with wood. With the clarity of mind of a strategist, which Simeonov could only sit and admire, she therefore combined the inconsequential need to search for the missing man with the more pressing need to collect more fuel for the stove. Horatio and Voronov were despatched to the rear of the house. The army man proposed that he stand guard over the women and the sick man – "just in case." He spread a very thin blanket of comfort upon them by declaring that a wolf cannot hide it, should a man be in his stomach: therefore, he argued, the book-seller was not eaten.

A WOLF CANNOT HIDE IT, SHOULD A MAN BE IN HIS STOMACH

Unconvinced by the iron logic of this case, the two seekers after fuel stepped cautiously into the garden. The light spilled by the rising sun upon the limpid skies above made it possible to see far more now than Corporal Nikolaiev had ever seen. It was clear that Isengrim was not moving around.

"Either he is asleep," proposed Horatio: Sleep, the Twin of Death.

"Or has fled," muttered Voronov: the Flight of Dead Souls in the Arms of Angels.

"Or is dead," wondered Horatio aloud: a Thousand Doors opening upon another Realm.

"Or has found another book," pondered the inn-keeper under his breath: a Life Beyond Life.

But a thorough and thoroughly nervous search in every corner of the garden, which took some time, revealed neither sleeper, nor fugitive, nor corpse, nor book. Nor, although it had never been expressed aloud as a possibility, a wolf. It was, therefore, with some relief that the two men set to and gathered enough wood to fire a funeral pyre, before stepping back into the house: there they were greeted by those who still watched within – with relief, exasperation, and coolness: all in equal measure.

"The book-seller is nowhere to be seen," reported Horatio gravely.

"And that being the case," added Voronov eagerly, casting his bundle of wood at Yadviga's feet, "I will look after his books. The gentleman may yet return and will wish them kept safe."

So saying, Vladimir Ivanovich, who until that night had treated all books as any orthodox and national man should treat poetry – with a focussed mind and a sharpened blade – now gathered up all the Journals and the Narratives and the Travels, and replaced them lovingly and one by one in the sail-cloth sack.

An inn-keeper had found an enthusiasm for travellers: the world was turned upsides-down. It was a dawn of another day in

NOVGOROD THE GREAT.

39

THE SWAGGERING JACKS IN OFFICE.

Had it been the dawn, surely there should have been some sound of humanity or of nature? John Cochrane pondered this curious fact as he lay, as at the foot of an abyss, upon his sick-bed. He had been awakened by some sound, it was sure, but since his awakening there had been nothing – not a bird, or a dog, or the rustle of a leaf; neither the sound of men labouring nor of women keeping starvation and disease at bay. Even the sunlight seemed of a curious quality – grey, pearly perhaps, as if seen through a snow-storm. But the heat was oppressive. He tried to sit up. It was a great difficulty. When at last he had succeeded, he was unable to stand, so the effort had been almost pointless.

"You have reached the end of your travels," said a voice he did not recognise. It came from a corner of the room still wrapped in profound gloom.

"Father," asked John uncertainly, "is that you?"

"Indeed it is," said the voice, still sounding unlike any voice that John knew, past or present or future.

"I cannot see you," said the son doubtfully.

"That is true," came the reply, "but I can see you. You have reached the end of the road."

"In Siberia," replied John Dundas Cochrane, caring little for the pessimistic answer given, and setting one foot before the other to dispel any notion of suffering from a weakness, "the roads were frequently so bad that I believe I never saw the like in my life. My sledge was broken from the falls and concussions it suffered, the road was so full of ruts that I expected to be laid up. Sometimes, I would be going along at ten miles per hour, on a level, when suddenly the vehicle would pitched into a hole of two feet deep and six or eight feet wide, which nearly killed the horses with the shock. I may say," he concluded boldly, "that my travelling expenses from Moscow to Irkutsk amounted only to twenty-five shillings, which included my purchases of tobacco. I left Irkutsk on the eleventh day of February, and had high hopes of reaching Moscow again without greater expenditure than before."

"And did you?" asked his new companion more out of politeness than interest.

Cochrane did not continue that discussion. He strode forwards along the long road that stretched from Maracay to Valencia, keeping his eyes fixed upon the distant mountains, and blind to all other sights and questions.

"The Cossack who conducted me to Tobolsk was nothing but a drunkard. He sold all of our copper cooking utensils in order to buy drink. With the result that we had nothing to cook with. It did him no good: he fell asleep beside the road and was severely frost-bitten as a result. But that was the least of my troubles. The farther west I travelled, the more frequently did I encounter the contemptible usages of Europe among the manners of the native peoples. It was not a pleasant sight: Siberia is advancing backwards in the score of humanity and civility. In Omsk, for example, I was almost prevented from bidding adieu to the Governor-General by one of those swaggering Jacks in office, who insisted that I bid adieu to him instead, and that he would relay my fare-thee-well to the Governor-General himself. Of course, I persevered and was finally admitted to the presence of the Governor-General. Shortly after that, I encountered another of these young gentleman on a narrow road; my Cossack asked the officer for his rank; on being informed that he was merely a Lieutenant, my Cossack laughed and said that I was a Commander, and therefore of greater rank. The young man, being still unwilling to give way, forced his way past." Cochrane nodded in happy remembrance. "His sledge ended up in the ditch."

There was a pleasant silence for an uncertain length of time, as Cochrane buried himself in his memories of the long road from Irkutsk to Tomsk and Omsk. To his right, had he indeed been marching towards Valencia, a thick forest loomed over them from the steeply-rising hills. The sun travelled from east to west with the most unexpected swiftness, behind a layer of featureless cloud – already it was in decline. Missing his step as he examined the unfamiliar sky, Cochrane suddenly veered off the dusty road and fell headlong into a bush at the edge of the forest.

Just at that moment, a brave company of Gran Colombia's militia came marching along. Cochrane's sudden movement was spotted by the leader of the company, and suspicions were immediately aroused.

"Arrest that man!" he commanded, standing well back, and urging two of his soldiers forward. "Slay him if he is armed."

Two soldiers stepped forward eagerly and hauled Cochrane from the bush. His face was scratched by the thorns, and his eyes were wide open.

"The postage," he complained, "must be paid in advance."

"What postage?" demanded Lieutenant Gomez, standing over the European who had clearly been trying to escape. "What postage?" he asked The Companion, who was edging away from the scene.

"The postage in the Russian Empire," replied Cochrane with some asperity. "How surprised would you be to learn that, in that country, the postage for letters must be paid for by the sender, a circumstance WHEN TO PAY which appears to me to keep back education more than POSTAGE IN RUSSIA anything else? There is a great difference, I presume," he continued, grasping the collar of one of his captors and so terrifying him with his insistent tone that the soldier dropped his musket, "in paying to send a letter, with the contents of which a person is acquainted, and paying for the receipt of a dozen letters with unknown news from a parent or friend. Is that not," he demanded, "the case?" The soldier, disarmed entirely, nodded his head insistently. This earned the strongest censure from Lieutenant Gomez.

"Why were you trying to run away?" Lieutenant Gomez wished to know.

John Cochrane had no answer to this. It seemed to him that all that his cousin Charles had told him about the poisonous frogs of South America, while incredible, scarcely reflected the truth: these frogs were gigantic, the size of a man, and armed to the teeth. One of them had just man-handled him from the road. What was it Charles had told him? – do not touch the skin, the skin is what kills a man stone-dead at the slightest contact. He tucked his hands into his armpits and gazed down at his feet.

"I think," volunteered The Companion, something against his better judgement, and with the utmost hesitation: a strange man in a strange land, even a liberated land, had best never volunteer anything, "that my friend here has a fever."

At this, the entire company stepped back several paces, leaving Cochrane sitting on the road, his head hanging down loosely over his chest.

"A fever, you say?" asked the lieutenant cautiously. "Do you think it is putrid?"

"I rather fear so," confirmed The Companion with some enthusiasm. "He showed signs of it when he landed at La Guayra—"

"Ah, La Guayra," interrupted Lieutenant Gomez, laughing bitterly, "you need say no more. Many is the traveller who has landed at La Guayra in the finest of health, and died before he even reached Carracas. This man," he jerked his thumb at the great pedestrian, "is stronger than most, I think, to have come this far."

"But not much farther," suggested one of the soldiers gloomily. With military precision, the entire company fixed eyes upon Cochrane and shook its head.

"His name?" asked the lieutenant suddenly.

"Commander John Dundas Cochrane," reported The Companion, "late of the British Navy."

There was a collective gasp. "Cochrane?" said Gomez excitedly, "of the British Navy? The Admiral—"

"Not that Cochrane." The Companion was not anxious to raise the entire countryside in expectation of welcoming the great hero of Valdivia and the liberator of Bahia, only to disappoint.

"There is another, then?" asked one soldier, astonished.

"There are several," confirmed The Companion, who, in the course of his duties, had listened to many stories of that family. "This one is a cousin."

"Should we not, however—?" asked the lieutenant, unsure of the niceties of dealing with the fevered cousin of a revolutionary hero.

"We should not," said The Companion, grasping the opportunity. "It is best, I think, to leave him in peace; the fever will perhaps pass."

Respectfully, the company saluted Cochrane as he sat on the ground, wheeled smartly into line and marched onwards in the direction of Maracay. When the sound of footsteps had died away, Cochrane announced: "the conduct of post-masters is one of the greatest nuisances in the Russian Empire." The Companion let the remark pass.

"It was a singular circumstance," continued Cochrane, "that not only must postage be paid in advance, but almost anything a man might require – a bed, a horse, a sledge – all must be paid for in advance, and no one may travel even half-a-mile if they have not yet paid for it. Inhospitality, incivility and general distrust everywhere prevailed in Russia; while in Siberia, an honest man may be treated with civility and trust by anyone he comes across."

With these words, he struggled to his feet. The Companion lifted Cochrane's powerless arm around his shoulder, and together they walked at a funereal pace into the north-west. The sun was setting fast. A cool rush of air lifted like a vast shroud from the endless lake to their left and settled upon them.

"The roads are no better. The winter road across the Ural Mountains was to end at the city of Kazan," continued Cochrane, pausing briefly to cast his eyes once more upon the distant peaks. "But the roads had been so bad, and the sledge so knocked about, that I fell ill. So ill was I that I considered the palpitations of my heart as a prelude to dissolution. Had I not been taken in by virtuous and humane people at Kazan, I am sure I would have died."

THE PALPITATIONS OF HIS HEART

At length, after barely three miles of walking, Cochrane could walk no farther. At a distance of perhaps one hundred yards, a dark shape stood beside the road, some simple dwelling. The Companion hoisted the compact form of Commander Cochrane upon his back, a task which came naturally to him, having spent eternity hauling corpses; he set off down the road and came abreast of a dilapidated hut, once made of wood alone, now an architectural wonder of thick

spider-webs, creepers and night-flowers. Inside, something rustled
and scuttled in a panic, and then all was silent. The Companion,
adjusting his eyes to the darkness, saw that there was nothing in the
hut except a bare earth floor. But it was dry. He laid Cochrane gently
down on the floor, placed his knapsack under his neck and head as
a pillow, and squatted down beside him. Cochrane's breathing was
fast and shallow, and his skin burned to the touch. But he was awake
and desirous of talk.

"Are you married, my friend?" he asked.

The Companion stated that he was not. The Companion had
neither home, nor wife, nor children.

"A wife and a home, sir, that is a simple ambition, is it not? But is
it for men like us?"

The Companion remarked unequivocally that he was not a man
like us; Cochrane ignored the sentiment.

"A wife, a home and children – three artless pleasures. But pleasures
only when compared to the life we lead for the best part of the year,
the trials, the agonies, the discomforts of a voyage or an expedition;
all of which would be almost for nothing if we did not have a wife
and a home to come back to. Am I correct?"

The Companion denied this, but in a low tone. There was no point
in exciting the invalid any more than necessary.

"When we travelled back from Kamtchatka, my wife fell seriously
ill. This was in greater part due to the state of the roads – have I
mentioned the state of the roads to you? Many was the
time our wagon or sledge fell into ruts four and five feet
deep. In the end, I was obliged to walk alongside, in order
to avoid further injury. But what to do with my better half was a
difficult and serious question. By dint only of labour and patience
did we reach our destinations. But it was the day that we reached
Kazan, myself more broken than hale, that Mrs. Cochrane was taken
so alarmingly ill that she could not be moved from the spot in which
she sat, drinking tea with the Governor's niece. For twenty-three days,
she was confined to her room, and for more than that time I too
suffered a species of torturing pain in the heart and left side, a pain

which still afflicts me now and then. Now, for example, as then." With these words, John Cochrane sat up rather alarmingly, clutching his left side and gasping for breath. The Companion held him erect and gave him to drink from one of several bottles of a liquid that could bring oblivion. Then, as the patient's breathing calmed again, he let him gently back down on to the earth. Outside, the insects and frogs of the night called out in rich harmony.

"When we came to Moscow, you know," continued Cochrane, brightening at the memory, "I spent several days in examining a document which detailed the buildings and conveniences of the city. In Moscow there were, in the year 1818, just six years after being rendered to ashes by Napoleon: ninety-eight wooden bridges; five hundred and thirty-nine alleys, lanes and narrow thoroughfares; three thousand seven hundred and ninety-three wells for drinking-water; two hundred and fifty-three fish-ponds; nineteen slaughterhouses; one edifice for the instruction of military orphans; nine military barracks—"

He paused to gather his breath, for it, unlike the buildings of Moscow, was very scarce; then plunged onwards.

"—fifty-seven beer-houses; one hundred and thirty-two gin-shops; fourteen burial grounds—"

The Companion expressed the opinion that this was insufficient.

"—one mad-house; thirty-three public baths – thirty-three too many, sir; one hundred and forty bun-houses; one hundred and seven hot-houses; three hundred and sixty firemen's watch-towers—"

"Far too many," observed The Companion.

"—twenty-five apothecary's shops; four thousand three hundred and forty-one street-lamps; and twenty-five public squares."

There was a silence for several minutes. The Companion, staring out through a gap in the roof of the little hut, noticed that there were nineteen visible stars in that one patch of sky. Truly, coincidence was a very fine thing: he would now remember how many slaughterhouses there were in Moscow.

"Two hundred and eighty churches; fourteen convents for friars and seven for nuns; and thirty private chapels." Cochrane sipped some more liquid, and subsided.

"And here," said The Companion, "there is but one hut, ten thousand trees, and countless stars."

"Yes," agreed Cochrane, seeming to take comfort from the fact. "In my night-journeys across Siberia, I tried counting the stars, but I moved too fast and they moved too slowly. It is my belief that no man is permitted to count the stars."

"Unless," countered The Companion, "he has eternity in which to do so."

"Even if," argued John Cochrane, "he has eternity in which to do so."

"Nonetheless, shall we begin?" asked The Companion, thinking that he could divert his companion from his excitement. Quiet and rest are most desirable during a fever. There could be nothing more calculated to abate excitement than an enumeration of the stars in the sky. So thought The Companion.

"If you are blind, James," said Cochrane to some unknown acquaintance, "you cannot see one star in the sky, let alone dozens, or hundreds, or thousands. You cannot navigate by the stars, you cannot contemplate their motions, you cannot comprehend eternity. What object can you have, in going to Siberia? You are welcome to my Cossack and my conveyance, and you can make your way out of Moscow towards Siberia. But what good will it do you? There is so little of interest in Siberia, so little to be seen that it is hardly possible to form an interesting work on that topic. Siberia is, in fact, one immense wilderness, that five or six hundred miles are passed by the traveller without seeing an individual, much less any works of man at all worthy of description. The matter of interest is to be compressed in a small space. And a blind man wishes to pass through it? Indeed, you may go there as anywhere else, for you will see just as much.

"A wise traveller lives with the people of the land through which he travels. He will find that he will be treated as a guest, and not as an enemy. A man alone may safely trust himself in the hands of savages. But can a man who is blind travel in this way? I think not.

"I put my opinions to Lieutenant James Holman; he did not heed my warning. Indeed, he took my words to be a criticism, an intention so far from my thoughts that I found him ridiculous. He was, he said, sensible of my mental obscurity. The man was blind in spirit as well as in the eyes. What could he possibly tell of me? A man, surely, must endeavour to tell the truth, regardless of the consequence?"

The Companion sighed. The stars were meant to sedate. John Dundas Cochrane, it seemed, was not a man who wished to be sedated. There was more annoyance, more anger with fools, more disparagement, more frustration in his short frame than in many another taller man.

HIS WHOLE DEMEANOUR WAS A FEVER.

40

WITH THESE SENTIMENTS,
HE CONCLUDED HIS NARRATION.

The stars, finally, sedated mankind. Both traveller and unwitting servant fell into a profound sleep, which remained undisturbed as the constellations performed their cartwheels overhead, and untroubled by a mist that crept up from Lake Tacarigua and hid their shelter from the view of all, save a large number of excitable bats which navigated easily around it as if it had been lit with a thousand bonfires. With the rising of the sun, on the twelfth day of August in the year 1825, the thin clouds of the night began to disperse, revealing a blue sky. But the mist remained draped over the lake, leaving within sight only the ripples at the very edge of the water.

John Dundas Cochrane awoke, feeling himself free of all care and relieved of all aches. He sat up and peered eagerly out of the doorway of the hut. There, high and framed in the gap, were the mighty peaks of the Andes.

"The Andean Mountains," he said resolutely to no one in particular. "What a journey I will have, up there, on the heights, living among the native peoples, eating with them, sleeping in their simple huts or under the stars, day by day consuming the miles until I reach the very tip of the continent of South America. And what a Journal I will write: The Narrative of a Pedestrian Journey Along the Andean Mountains of the South American Continent, from the Coast of Gran Colombia to Cape Hoorn, in Three Volumes. That should make them sit up and notice, at last. With Accompanying Maps and Plates. That would do the trick: accompanying maps and plates. It will make my fortune and establish me as the foremost explorer of the British Isles, I can have no doubt."

Cochrane rubbed his hands at these elevating thoughts, and tried to stand up. He failed. He tried again, tottered two or three steps and sat down again heavily upon a rotten log. He was alone.

Cochrane experienced a naked thrust of terror and cast off the blanket from around his shoulders. "When once the Andes are conquered, I am left only with Africa. On my return to Britain, in two years, and after publication of my journals, I will set off immediately for the Niger River. Or the Congo River, perhaps, should it remain unexplored. I will go alone. My only regret is that I was not permitted to do so before now."

He felt utterly empty and drew the blanket round him again as comfort. He trembled at some distant memory.

"If I should not move today from this pleasant spot, let me tell you just this." He addressed his remarks to the distant waters of the lake. "I am a proud husband, not ashamed of my wife. I have, on several occasions, defended her character against those who, wishing to slander me, slandered her. In the town of Perm, for example, once we had found a stable in which to rest, the police offering us nothing more comfortable, I had to obtain from the Governor a fresh passport. I endured his absurd and ill-timed questions regarding my wife. He suspected my wife of being a Tartar, a Mongol or some sort of Pagan.

'Of what country is she?' he demanded to know.

'Of Kamtchatka,' I replied easily.

'Is she a Kamchatdale?'

'As much as you are a Russian.'

'Who and what is her father?'

'He serves.'

'What is his rank?'

'A priest.'

'But does he speak the Russian language?'

'He does.'

'Is he a white man?'

'In appearance, but I cannot answer for any few shades by which he may be removed from a Tartar, or other tribe.'

'And your wife, where was she brought up?'

'In Kamtchatka.'

'What has been her education?'

'To respect everybody,' I replied pointedly.

'Well,' says he, 'I give you joy, but I confess I would rather you go to Kamtchatka for a wife than I.'

"I informed his Excellency that I thought it better to have a wife as mine, who would go where I chose, and would consider it her greatest delight to do so, than such as his, who would not accompany him although in her own country. We parted on the worst of terms."

John Dundas Cochrane smiled in grim satisfaction that he had bested the Governor of Perm.

"But what I had to endure on my return to my own country was as insolent and impolite as anything I had to endure in the unsophisticated parts of the Russian Empire. Mr. Barrow, of the Royal Society, in making remarks upon my published Journal, lost all sense of common civility. He termed my wife – in print, do you hear? – a 'Kamtchatka girl'! As far as her age could warrant this HE LOST ALL SENSE impudence, he may have been correct; but I should have OF COMMON CIVILITY expected his very refined notions of propriety might have induced him to have called her a young lady. Naturally, I was mistaken in that."

Cochrane brooded for a while on this matter.

"Mr. Barrow," he continued at length, "seems to have had a lurking desire to condemn me for more than referred to in my narrative. This need not concern you," he added rapidly, "as the causes were discussed in private between myself and that individual. It was suggested in some parts that my marriage to a fourteen-years-old girl was perhaps – no, no matter." Cochrane waved the subject away; and then forthwith returned to it.

"I have no need to apologise for the airy flights of my heart, nor for the transports which induced me to marry so young a girl. A man who travels across the world may find a kindred soul wherever he might wander, may he not? Mrs. Cochrane reciprocated my feelings. And she reached the age of fifteen within days of our marriage. A girl – a woman of that age can speak for herself, I believe? Nor is it the business of the Royal Society how a man makes his family. What is it to them – they have not stirred from their comfortable chambers, they have not suffered, they have not thrilled at the sight of a pretty face and the sound of a charming voice. No matter." Once more he brushed the bothersome flies of romance away from his face.

"This need not concern us. My only regret is that people have chosen to criticise my Journal for the worst of reasons. I, John Dundas Cochrane, walked – and sailed and rode – from Dieppe to the furthest point of Siberia; I suffered extremes of cold and almost lost my life in the most deserted wildernesses; and came home again, bearing a tale that no one before me had ever told, and that none, least of all that man Holman, is likely to do again."

A vast flock of water-birds emerged from nothingness and wheeled over the shore, shrieking, before vanishing skywards.

"Mr. Barrow and the Royal Society, of course, had no wish to deal with me with any respect or decency. I was not of their model of explorer. I was not one of a vast party of dandies and half-pay black sheep, who sail off into the waters of the Arctic to freeze to death or, at the orders of a man who sits dreaming in London, march in numerous and noisy company into the interior of the dark African continent, to die of thirst or on the spear of some native warrior. No, sir, I am not Ross or Parry or Franklin or Clapperton, or some other creature of the Royal Society. No, sir, I am that wise traveller who goes into his journey, dependent only upon the reception which the ignorant and brutal will give him. A man alone may safely trust himself in the hands of savages. A man alone may discover more about the dark patches of our maps than any number of Mr. Barrow's parties.

"And he has done so, has he not? From Nizhney Kolymsk, having the leisure to do so, I sent a long letter to the Royal Society, taking issue with the geographical description of that part of the world set out in a highly erroneous document by Captain James Burney of the Royal Navy. Burney had scarcely been anywhere near the shores he described, but this did not prevent him from amalgamating hear-say with half-digested fact, conflating legend and travellers' tales, ignoring the difference in years between previous narratives; I, on the contrary, who had made that journey to north-east Siberia, who was still there, and who had talked at great length with Baron Wrangel who had thoroughly explored the shores of the Frozen Sea – in short, I corrected Burney according to known observations and accurate measurements and wrote to the Royal Society detailing my objections to Burney's farrago."

BURNEY'S
FARRAGO

Cochrane fought for breath. His throat was greatly constricted. He attributed it to his outrage.

"Sir," he whispered hoarsely, "Sir, what did they do with my letter?"

No one replied. Cochrane lay alone in an immeasurable and emptied landscape.

"They ignored it," said Cochrane wheezing angrily. "They did not even acknowledge receipt, until, on my return to London, I wrote asking how it had been received. It was not discussed, neither was it published. A slovenly way of dealing with the business of the Society, and one which astonishes me to this day. They would not tell me even when it had reached London."

"Had you," came a distant voice, which seemed to come from a boat out beyond the edge of the mist, "paid the postage in advance?"

Cochrane caught the remark, but in his anger, did not seek out the speaker. The dark shape of a boat slowly emerged from the obscurity, parting the mists, making its way towards the near shore.

"And yet, had they read my letter and had they discussed the observations, then perhaps I could have made a valuable contribution to the exploration of the North–West Passage, emerging, as it does, into the Icy Sea of Siberia. And my remarks upon travelling by land in Siberia would doubtless assist in the exploration of the frozen territories of northern America. But – ah!" he exclaimed, as if he had just thought of this point, when, of course, it had been festering in his mind these past two years: "There's the marrow of it:

I WAS MEDDLING IN THE NORTH-WEST DISCOVERIES,
and Mr. Barrow does not like a man to do that. I have no regrets that I am not a Fellow of the Royal Society. I have no regrets that I travelled as I did. I have no regrets that I went out alone. I have no regrets." With these sentiments, he concluded his narration.

41

THE BREAKFAST OF CHERNOBOG,
MASTER OF THE INFERNAL DARKNESS.

It was the dead hour, the hour of great regrets and unconsummated sentiments, the lowest hour of just another night in Paris, City of Pleasure. On that ninth and twenty-first night of August in the year 1833, far to the west of Novgorod the Great there still slumbered women and their men, children and their cares: Paris nestled in the troubled arms of Sleep. Between Paris and Novgorod there lie more miles than is healthy to contemplate – one thousand and seven hundred, perhaps: that would be two thousands and five hundreds of versts if one were a French adventurer, probably longer if he had his ex-mistress's bed to transport; or two thousands and seven hundreds of kilomètres if one were a Russian count dreaming of French sophistication.

Between Paris and Novgorod, however, a moment only elapsed.

Major Sinclair looked up and found his old friend, Colonel Cochrane-Johnstone, wandering in the dark, along the stinking banks of the Volkhov. They looked, in the darkness, much like the stinking banks of the River Seine. In the night, one slow-flowing river may readily be mistaken for another. The Colonel, old beyond his years, peered at him. "Damn you, Sinclair," he said, "you here too?"

The Major confirmed eagerly that he was, but the Colonel had already lost interest. "It is my greatest regret," he began; but with these words, the old man closed his eyes, breathed his last breath, and slipped forever into the black chasm of the final dawn.

Accompanied by his faithful subordinate, Colonel Cochrane-Johnstone arrived at the centre of the Earth, and halted at the gates of the underworld. The attendant there was pleased to see them. He laid down the axe with which he had been chopping logs of the yew-tree, and informed them that there would be a slight delay – "their worships being at their breakfast, sirs. Make yourselves comfortable while you wait."

The two army officers, too wearied to complain any more, sat upon a stone bench outside the janitor's hut, with a view to the Gates of Hell.

"Where have you been?" demanded the Colonel, moodily poking his cane in the dusty ground at their feet.

"I, sir?" asked the Major, slightly surprised by the tone of the question.

"You, sir," confirmed the Colonel in a sarcastic tone. "Or is there another man here I should speak to? You, sir," he addressed the janitor, "do I wish to know where you have been?"

The janitor demurred and picked up a dusty volume to renew his acquaintance with the amusing Narration of a Journey by Dante Alighieri. As he read, an uncountable number of grey faces half-appeared from the misty distance beyond the Gates, listening and listening.

"Well?" pressed the Colonel, turning back to Sinclair.

"I have been," replied Sinclair, "in—"

"No matter," interrupted the Colonel fiercely. "You were not in Paris. You missed nothing. Do you know," he continued, with a slight whine in his voice now, "that in these past few months, I have heard nothing but the tales of the Cochranes?"

"I, too, sir," answered Sinclair over-eagerly. "I have been—"

"Did they not know that I was one too?" demanded Cochrane-Johnstone. "Damn them – I was on the point of dropping Johnstone from my name – little good did it ever do me in life! What do you think, man: should I have done that earlier?"

Major Sinclair, never a man of many deep thoughts, had no opinion to advance on this crucial matter.

"Don't bother, Sinclair," said the Colonel wearily, "don't bother. All I've heard is the praise of brother Alexander and what a great hero he was – conqueror of America, wasn't he, all on his own? He's been dead over a year, and still they prattle to me about him, thinking they do me an honour. And when they've mined that seam to the dross, then they start on that mendacious and rapacious little scoundrel Thomas: Commander-in-Chief of the Chilean Navy, THE BOSOM FRIEND they drool, was he not the bosom friend of Bernardo OF BERNARDO O'HIGGINS

O'Higgins, Liberator of Peru, did he not rise to be the First Admiral of Brazil, oh, they cry, was he not Admiral in charge of everything Greek! Did I not admire him, they wanted to know? Was I not proud to be the uncle of Lord Cochrane, now the tenth Earl of Dundonald? No, said, I, he can't keep his wife in harness, the man is a cuckold and a grasping fool. But they didn't want to hear that."

A scarab beetle crept out from under the bench on which they took their ease. The Colonel stabbed at it with his cane. The cane splintered, the beetle tottered onwards, oblivious to the ways of men.

"And in any case, I hate ships, boats and the sea," muttered the Colonel. "Water is meant to be admired, not sailed upon."

Major Sinclair could only concur. "In Novgorod, too, they could find nothing to talk about," he added, "but Cochranes." He was uncertain as to how the news would be received.

"Where?" demanded Cochrane-Johnstone impatiently.

"Novgorod," said Sinclair. "The Great," he elaborated, for the avoidance of uncertainty.

"Never heard of it," said his friend contemptuously. "Never want to."

The janitor at the portals of the underworld coughed discreetly in an effort to attract attention. "Your honour," he said, "I can tell you much about Novgorod and its history, of Ivan the Terrible—"

"I said, sir," hissed Cochrane-Johnstone, "I never want to!"

Everyone fell silent; but Sinclair was roused a minute later by a blow to the side of the head. His commanding officer thus alerted him to his desire to hear more about Novgorod and what was said there about the Cochranes.

"Mostly about your son, sir," admitted the Major.

"What, that unprincipled mooncalf John?" The Colonel was astonished.

Sinclair admitted it – the Colonel, after all, had no other son that anyone could recognise.

"What's he been up to now?" the Colonel wished to know, forgetting that the boy had been dead these past eight years.

The Major tried to explain as succinctly as possible, but got no further than a mention of Siberia.

"Oh – that pedestrian nonsense," he said, in three words dismissing the finest three years of his son's short life. "Why did the simpleton want to go walking around the world?"

Major Sinclair had, of course, no answer. He only offered the further information that Charles Cochrane had also been mentioned frequently – at which thought, the Colonel laughed so much that he lost control of his bladder – and that Sinclair had made it his personal business to mention certain key passages in the brilliant life and career of one Andrew Cochrane-Johnstone.

"Didn't do you any good, eh?" inquired the man of that name, almost with a trace of sympathy.

Major Sinclair tried valiantly to bluff, but ended up conceding defeat.

"My son?" said the Colonel after a few moments of thought. He was not a man given much to introspection, either in this life or the last. Thus, the question, "Where did I go wrong with him?" – the question that every father asks in relation to his son – came to his mind rather unexpectedly. It was, of course, the wrong question.

"Do you know," continued the unrepentant father, voicing none of these doubts, looking neither right nor left, and certainly not backwards, "that I accompanied him on a wild-goose chase to South America, and he went off and left me high and dry in some God-forsaken stink-hole, not a penny to my name. Went off, took the fever – or was it the pox? no: not the pox – he hadn't the wit for that – and died. My only son – didn't even leave me his purse."

Major Sinclair and the janitor both waited in respectful silence, while the Colonel dabbed at what might have been – and indeed certainly was not – a tear.

"Children," said the Colonel, adopting that well-known tone of succinct wisdom, but without the accompanying sigh.

The janitor nodded his head wistfully. "My own children," he proposed to observe—

"Elizabeth, having snared Lord Napier, no longer knows me," persisted Cochrane-Johnstone angrily. "Me, her own father, her only parent! Indeed, I am told that my daughter has gone so far as to apologise to Lord Cochrane for my behaviour in the Stock Exchange matter. For my behaviour? mine? – unbelievable!" The Colonel was so outraged at this further instance of familial treachery that he ceased, for the instant, to talk.

The janitor took the opportunity to ask: what is the 'Love' of a child to a parent or of a parent to its child? Major Sinclair, having no children and having almost forgotten that he had had parents, could not comprehend the question. Cochrane-Johnstone considered the question unpalatable, and scowled.

In the ensuing silence, the janitor, Velos, Slavic god of death, remembered at last to embark upon his introductory talk. "The Underworld has seen many stirring times," he began, settling down upon a well-worn wooden stool which stood beside the gate. He placed a pipe between his teeth and patted his dog Simargl on the head. Simargl lay down and kept his eyes on the visitors, ready to growl if either dared to shift a limb. "Let me tell you of the arrival of Ivan the Terrible in the year 1584—"

Alas, at that very moment he was interrupted by the entrance of Belobog and Chernobog, their fast broken. They now had some business with the supplicants. Velos sighed, then fell silent. Caught in the eternal battle between Chaos and Order, in the conflict of Dark and Light, in the perpetual confusion of Love and Hate, in the cosmic struggle of Good and Evil, a man would do well to absorb himself in a study of his fingernails. Velos was a man who did well.

A STUDY OF HIS
FINGERNAILS

Belobog, god of Day, god of Heaven, the bringer of Good Luck and master of Heavenly Light, made the two old army men welcome. Dressed only in white, and with a long flowing beard, he had the appearance of a wise old man. "And where have you travelled from?" he wished to know.

The Colonel, thinking it was none of this old padre's business where he was from, refused to answer. The Major ventured tentatively that he had lately come from Novgorod. Belobog was most interested: "Ah, Mother Russia?" he nodded cheerfully. "And must one still pay the postage in advance?"

Chernobog, the god of Night, the god of Hell, the bringer of Evil Luck and master of the Infernal Darkness, cast his malevolent eyes upon the Colonel and the Major. "Never mind this old simpleton," he said roughly. "Tell me of Siberia – did you travel there?"

The Major admitted that he had not had that pleasure.

"Pleasure, man? Pleasure?" Chernobog laughed. "I did not lay down the plains and bogs and mountains and rivers of Siberia so that people could take pleasure from them!"

"Ah, Siberia: rather the Land of the Unfortunate, than that of the Criminal," observed Belobog charitably.

"The Russians are the dirtiest people in the world," said the Colonel, having met one or two in his long career.

"You too have come from there, then?" asked Belobog.

"No, sir," replied the Colonel proudly. "I have come direct from Paris. And," he added sourly, "the French are the noisiest people in the world. It is a relief to escape from their babbling. Now then, sirs," he continued impatiently, "can't we make some haste here? Am I to understand that one of you is St Peter?" He looked sharply from one to the other.

The two gods raised their eyebrows.

"Perhaps we should begin with the questions which we ask everyone who passes this way," suggested Belobog. With some difficulty, he extracted from his white robes a large leather-bound book, stained, dog-eared, the spine peeling off and drooping sadly, pages crumbling and falling out. He shuffled through the pages, which had been filled with writing, and came at last, near the end, to a clear space. He produced a pen and an ink-horn, and cleared his throat.

"Our first question: what is 'Love'?"

Both the Colonel and the Major groaned, for entirely different reasons – the former since he had no idea and could not have answered under pain of perpetual damnation – which, if he was to believe at all in these two gods and the portals of the underworld, was precisely his position. The Major, for his part, racked his brains – there had been something about all that recently; if only he had paid some attention, perhaps—

"It is," went on Belobog placidly, answering his own question, since none was otherwise forthcoming, "the avoidance of Death."

There was no sense to this – how can one avoid death? The Colonel said so. The god of happiness and peace, the judge who rewards goodness, replied that a person who had loved and who had been loved would leave behind in life part of their soul, and so avoid death.

Chernobog snorted: "Bloody nonsense, man, and you know it. Love is the avoidance of Life."

"I think not, my old friend," said Belobog mildly.

"I know you think not," replied Chernobog, re-engaging in an argument which the two divine old gentlemen had been conducting for ten thousand or more years past. "Love is an excuse, a gloss, a dress put on to disguise the most basic of animal needs. Love is Romance. It gets in the way of Life." Chernobog turned with an unerring sense to the Colonel. "Is that not the case, Colonel?"

For the first time in his life – notwithstanding the fact that he had gone a shade beyond that now – Colonel Cochrane-Johnstone made a deep observation. "I am an army man," he said slowly, "but I have seen the seas: it seems that the furrows ploughed by ships in the seas are soon lost."

THE FURROWS
PLOUGHED BY SHIPS
IN THE SEAS ARE
SOON LOST

"As it is with life," remarked Belobog condescendingly.

"As it is with love," remarked Chernobog meanly.

"As it is," added Major Sinclair, misunderstanding everything that was being said, "with the roads of Russia."

With a sigh, Belobog made a mark or two in his ancient ledger.

There was a long pause. Simargl fell asleep. A fly landed on his muzzle and rubbed its legs languidly. The pipe of Velos had long gone cold.

"And now," demanded the Colonel at last, impatient for his breakfast, "can we move on? What is the next question?"

Belobog smiled indulgently: "That was the only question."

"There were once other questions," explained Chernobog, "but we grew tired of them. They were never answered. We might have asked, for example, how you managed to defraud the Government of France. But we shall not – it no longer has any significance." He rubbed his hands in easy expectation. "And now you can move on." Velos sprang up and began to push open the gates of the underworld. The massed ranks of grey shades beyond fell back uneasily. The dark shape of a boat slowly emerged from the mist, making its way towards the Gates.

Chernobog, the god of Hell and master of the Infernal Darkness, drew his brows together, for they were much separated, and spoke thus, speaking only words of punishment: "You shall make a voyage into Eternity, and as you sail, you shall talk only of John Dundas Cochrane, the Great Pedestrian Traveller, and of his cousin Thomas, Lord Cochrane, the Great Admiral, and of their famous uncle, the Admiral Alexander Cochrane, late of London."

The colour – mostly grey – drained from Andrew Cochrane-Johnstone's face. At that moment, he realised he had left Life behind. Forever.

Major Sinclair groaned once and twice in sympathy, and called for a bed-pan.

IT NEVER ARRIVED.

42

AN AXE MAY STRIKE MORE SWIFTLY THAN A BOOK.

It was a dawn of another day in Velikiy Novgorod. The Major seemed quiet; he did not groan even once. Mr. Voronov, examining his nails intently, and trimming them with his teeth, gazing bleakly at the lightening square of the dusty window, thought of his departed family. Reading of so many travels to so many distant places makes a man yearn for home. A home that never was. The mere fact that he had not yet read a single one of these books scarcely altered the effect. Mr. Voronov was no different from any other father – his two sons had long ago left home, no longer able to bear the joy of living under the parental roof, and his daughter lived with him in a state of perpetual war. The inn-keeper, spitting his nail-trimmings out – sideways, into the passage-way, so as not to offend the pretty young person – thought that, were he to be a wanderer returning home from the Urals or the far coasts of Africa, the polar wastes or the thousand rivers of Iberia, he would like nothing better than to find his wife and his children waiting at the threshold to his happy home. The words sprang unbidden to his lips: "where did I go wrong with them?" he murmured, and a tear or two pricked his eye. That moment of introspection came from the books. The man might have served himself better with an axe: an axe may strike more swiftly than a book, but to less injurious effect.

While the inn-keeper turned suddenly into a man of great sentiment, and Captain Simeonov idly recalled some good luck he'd had at cards just a few hours previously – the two of them, therefore, considering the hands they had dealt themselves – while they were thus distracted, Ksenia fretted.

At last she turned to Horatio – for to whom else should she turn, having not a friend in all the world? – excepting everyone she had met that day – and some were false friends, and others were not: it is the lot of a person abroad to mistake one for the other, until sometimes it is too late. Not in this case: Horatio bent his ear towards his new friend.

"I am worried about Mr. Isengrim," she said.

"I too," said Horatio, not untruthfully. But the whole truth, not expressed, was that he was a tidy man, and hated to mislay things. Or people.

"I think we should try to find him," she continued, "now that the sun is risen. All the wolves will have left the town."

"Do you think so?" asked Horatio, more in response to the second than to the first opinion.

"I do," replied Ksenia, confirming the first opinion and leaving aside the second.

"Let us then," said Horatio with a sudden onslaught of decisiveness that he did not feel, but which was thrust upon him by a great and unstoppable force, "let us then step out and see if we cannot find the book-seller."

Ksenia gazed at him for a long moment in unveiled admiration. Horatio noticed, and gazed manfully over her head, as like an explorer watching the horizon as anyone was liable to see in Novgorod that day. Mr. Voronov, had he observed this, had he been paying attention, would have wept more copious tears of home-coming.

Pausing only to wrap her cloak warmly – and to inform only the inn-keeper and the military captain of their intentions, Yadviga having fallen into a short slumber – Ksenia led Horatio out to the street.

"Shall we go left?" asked Ksenia.

Horatio paused to consider.

"Or shall we go right?" she wondered.

Horatio was not certain. "We cannot go straight ahead," he observed, indicating a high fence which surrounded some dilapidated residence of old Novgorod. "We should go left."

"Perhaps we should," thought the widow. Horatio made to move off to the left. "We shall go right," she decided. Horatio quickly veered to the right. "To the left is the kremlin, and I do not imagine the poor man will have gone there."

Neither the reason for not turning left, nor the reason for not walking straight ahead would have stood up to scrutiny. But a decision made by the heart, thought Horatio, has more value than one taken by the head.

Their steps took them in the direction followed by Private Ushakov less than two hours previously, a despairing youth now enjoying the slightly questionable company of a hungry bear. The street, in the cool morning light, was beginning to fill with citizens, several of whom dodged back into hidden doorways at the sight of a black man and a pretty woman; others took the precaution of engaging in deep discussion on the state of Russia with neighbours whose existence they had barely acknowledged before that moment.

Taking little account of this amiable behaviour, the happy couple wandered down the street, she with her arm in his, eagerly looking right and left to see if perhaps a book-seller lay in the bushes, or was A BOOK-SELLER LAY curled up neatly in a kennel. There was, of course, no sign IN THE BUSHES of him. But it was a quiet and beautiful hour, a morning full of promise, that brief instant when all is not yet lost. The absence of Mr. Isengrim no longer seemed uppermost in the young widow's mind. Ksenia talked, instead, of the night and the day. Horatio attended carefully.

"We have passed a long night, sir," she began, as a bell tolled once.

"A pleasant one," replied Horatio hurriedly, as the bell tolled again.

"A pleasant one despite the unpleasant duty that lay upon us," she agreed, as the bell tolled once more.

"An unpleasant one," observed Horatio gravely, as the bell tolled for the fourth time.

"And yet the old gentleman is still with us," she sighed, as the bell tolled again.

"I fear," answered Horatio, "that it may not be for long." His fear was entirely unfounded.

"The number of our years," she said after a while, "is sometimes not great." The bell tolled for the sixth and last time.

Horatio patted his companion on the hand which lay against his coat.

"But is it not a miracle that, while we yet live, we may find friends and lovers?" she said finally.

Horatio was startled into silence. In one sentence, the young woman had said all that needed to be said of Love, of Friendship and of Human Existence. At length, after one hundred and seventeen steps on the road, he turned to her with tears in his eyes and said—

"Look," Ksenia interrupted before he had even had a chance to say the first of several words, "this church is open. Shall we go in for a moment?"

The church in question was the one from which the hours rang throughout the night, reducing the life-span of its close neighbours by several years. However, in their disturbed nights, these neighbours could at least find additional hours in which to improve their minds, so – ultimately – no time was lost. It was the Church of the Holy Seven Youths. Inside, the church was already thronged as the devout of Novgorod came to make requests of their deities – no longer those such as Chernobog and Belobog, who now live in well-deserved retirement, apart from the odd visit from those who have lost their way. The ikons in the church, such as could be seen through the dim light and smoke of the candles and censers, depicted various martyrs, heroes – and the occasional heroine – of the faith: St Theoctistus, Archbishop of Novgorod; Blessed John 'the Hairy'; the Martyr Ia of Persia (with, in the background, some of the 9,000 others who bravely expired with her); the Martyr Paphnutius and his companions in Egypt; the Blessed Hesychius 'the Silent' of Mt. Athos; St Barsanuphius, the Bishop of Tver just down the road; St Eudocimus the Unknown, who remains largely incognito to this very day; the Blessed James of Borovichi, wonder-worker of Novgorod; St Cosmas, eunuch and – perhaps consequently – hermit of Palestine; the malingering St Poemen, known as 'the Much-ailing'; another wonder-worker, this time St Gregory of the Kiev Caves; and St Jonah; penultimately the most fortunate Martyrs Felicissimus and Agapitus; and then St George Limniotes. All of whose ikons Horatio barely glimpsed as Ksenia led him speedily down the path of sweet-smelling martyrdom.

At the far end of the corridor of gloom, a priest was intoning the words of the prescribed six psalms, while, in the background, a small chorus of men was winding itself up like clockwork for the Great

Litany. Ksenia threw herself without a backward glance into religious contemplation. Could Horatio, for all his radical ideas, blame her? Alone, having passed a night in the close company of Death, Sorrow and a Wolf, with several hundred miles of hard road ahead of her – who would not seek the protection of the higher powers?

Horatio was more circumspect in his actions, having given up Religion in favour of Liberty. However, he was a Rationalist, and felt free to rationalise his presence here. He was here to protect a young widow, in whose company he had felt the stirrings of the gentle breeze of dreams and the rumblings of his own deep malcontent. Standing in as religious a manner as he could manage, head bowed, he observed the ceremonies and surreptitiously took in his surroundings. He fell into deep contemplation of the miracle of the Seven Sleepers of Ephesus – whose names, he was able to learn, were: Maximilian, Jamblichus, Martin, John, Dionysius, Antonius, and Constantine. For SLEEP AND THE one hundred and fifty years the youthful sleepers slept, ADOLESCENT while outside their families and great-nieces and great-nephews were obliged to offer pagan sacrifice – such is the nature of the human adolescent that little has changed in two millennia; sleeping the sleep of the just until, in the reign of the good Emperor Theodosius the Second, they were led stumbling and coughing into the bright morning air, there to comprehend the meaning of miracles and promptly to expire. To Horatio, a sleep of such a length seemed little compensated even by such a holy death and having a church named after them in Novgorod the Great. But he was an Unbeliever, and his thoughts counted for nothing. A common man, thought Horatio further – ever the arithmetician despite his enthusiasm having embroiled him in troubles before – might live for twenty-five years before he persuades a woman to bear their children. In one hundred and fifty years, then, a man could sleep and then awake to feast his surprised – and doubtless disappointed – eyes upon the sixth generation of his descendants, who would stare back at him with nothing more than astonishment – certainly not pity or respect or love, and least of all: recognition. They would be strangers to each other, having strange names. Would they even believe his story? He thought it unlikely – in one hundred and fifty years, even small children would be Rationalists and Reasoners. These would be his great-great-great-great-grandchildren – was that correct? He counted them out on his fingers—

Ksenia pulled him out of the church, and he emerged, coughing and blinded by the heady light of morning, as one emerging into Ephesus.

"You were saying your prayers?" asked the young widow, gazing up at him with shining eyes in a flushed face.

"I?" stuttered Horatio, still adjusting to the streets of Novgorod.

"Counting out the saints on your fingers," hinted Ksenia.

Horatio mumbled something which sounded suspect to those who suspect and credible to those who will believe.

"I was thinking also," he said boldly, as they continued their stroll in the morning air, "of the names of children."

"Ah?" exclaimed Ksenia in a manner that sounded over-interested.

"What would I name my children," he explained, setting off down a road that could yet see him carried off, like young Private Ushakov, by the Bear of Despair. He fell silent.

Ksenia waited for a moment, her thoughts wildly rushing around her head. "And?" she demanded impatiently at last, shaking his arm.

Horatio coughed in embarrassment. "Voltaire comes to mind," he began, "or Rousseau, and perhaps Victor—"

The young widow gave none of those names great encouragement. Hurriedly, Horatio changed tack. "There was a man in Brazil," he stated inconsequentially, "Senhor de Carvalho, the founder of 'The Confederation of the Equator', who named his daughters Philadelphia, Carolina and Pennsylvania, in honour of the United States of America."

THE CONFEDERATION OF THE EQUATOR

"Oh!" murmured Ksenia with some disapproval. There seemed little of humanity, of family, in such a course of action.

"Perhaps," he added hastily, "my daughters could be named Iberia, Siberia and Kamtchatka." But it was too late; Ksenia had withdrawn her arm from his, the easier to show her disapproval.

They walked on in silence, Ksenia with eyes cast down, Horatio with eyes directed straight ahead, both in misery, neither with a thought for the missing book-seller on whose trail they had ventured out. Had he fallen in their path, they would not have noticed: such is the power – not of love, but of self-recrimination. They came to the town-gate, where they paused to gaze upon the forest which stood beyond. Behind the trees, a bear considered the dark complexities of life and the infrequent moments of light-hearted spoil.

Hearing a growl from the depths of the trees, the two companions hurriedly turned back. Simultaneously, they thought to talk of less contentious matters.

"Aleksander Radishchev—" said he.

"Captain von Kotzebue—" said she.

Horatio inclined himself slightly, relieved to find that interruption was possible. She, still inclined to punish the man, proceeded.

"—Captain von Kotzebue was very kind to me when he discovered that I was born in Kamtchatka. He is a man, you know, who has circumnavigated the world three times."

Horatio was astounded.

"Could he not stop?"

Ksenia laughed. Indeed, it is worth pointing out that she giggled. Horatio did not understand what it was that he had said to cause this, but he smiled crazily.

She continued: "The Captain wrote a book which Mr. Isengrim appeared not to have in his sack: A Voyage of Discovery into the South Sea and Bering's Straits for the Purpose of Exploring a North–East Passage, Undertaken in the Years 1815–1818. It was a very long journey."

"With a very long title," said Horatio to himself.

"On his return from his last journey, which took him round Cape Horn and then to Kamtchatka, he visited my step-father in St Petersburg. Ah – and he was accompanied on that occasion by Captain Anjou—" She stopped suddenly, and averted her eyes.

"Captain Anjou?" enquired Horatio politely, failing to notice something.

Ksenia shook her head energetically and threw herself into the road, in front of an early-morning carriage, causing the horses to rear up and the driver to curse in the traditional Russian manner. Horatio dashed out and saved her from an untimely injury. They walked on, rapidly, breathlessly – for different reasons.

"And you?" asked Ksenia at last, as they found themselves in a street they had not been before. All seemed unfamiliar.

"And I?" asked Horatio in his turn, his mind leaping back and forth like a dog upon the trail of a rabbit. Had he missed something?

"Aleksander Radishchev—" said she.

"Ah," he said, relieved. "I was thinking only that Aleksander Radishchev also wrote a book of travels. His Journey from St. Petersburg to Moscow took him into exile in Siberia for seven years."

"The poor man!" exclaimed Ksenia, wondering if she had seen that unhappy journalist among the ironed convicts whom she passed in traversing the land some ten years before. Puteshestvie iz Peterburga v Moskvu.

"But it is not yet a crime to travel from St Petersburg to Moscow?" she asked in tremulous voice, remembering that she now did precisely that.

"Not yet," Horatio reassured her. "It is just that Mr. Radishchev described some of the wretchedness of serfdom and brutality of autocracy which he saw as he travelled. The Empress Catherine learned much from it."

Had Mr. Voronov been there, he might have thought twice about the sack of books which he now guarded so eagerly. Who knows what revolutionary ideas might lie within? Fortunately, he was dozing by the stove and learned noth- THE DANGEROUS POSSIBILITIES OF TRAVEL ing of the dangerous possibilities of travel. Fortunately, also, such books as Mr. Radischev's were rare – a man who writes the truth about his travels may find himself on a journey he little cares for. Far better, one might suppose, to flog such travellers in advance, that they think twice about writing libel and calumny.

"Is it not strange," mused Horatio, as they found themselves once more, quite to their astonishment, before the dilapidated lodge, "that we have both been thinking of travellers and journeys?"

"And of the names of children," added Ksenia, rather to Horatio's embarrassment. She continued to look at him. What is 'Love', but a lingering glance, an attraction of dark eyes and red lips, a deep pool in which to drown. And the offer of that glance, those eyes, that pool – the very offer is a woman's love. Horatio, quite unused to these signs and signals of abandonment, remained confused and uncertain. He hesitated. He hesitated too long.

She could suppress her words no longer: "You talked of your children," said she. "Do you have any?"

"No, alas," said he sadly, "neither children, nor any wife." He took a sudden decision, infected as he was by a morning full of promise. "I was about to ask—"

"There is one thing I must tell you," Ksenia interrupted, "before you say anything more. I have no children, but I am—"

But at that very moment, from the interior of the lodge of Major Sinclair, a long wail burst upon them. It emerged from

THE MIGHTY BOSOM OF YADVIGA.

43

NO SOONER WAS THE BOTTLE EMPTY THAN SHE FELL TO MOURNING.

The long wail that burst from Yadviga's bosom came close to causing the emasculation of Captain Simeonov: he had been considering the several attractions of a number of low women who frequented the kremlin of Novgorod, and did so – from propriety – with his eyes closed. At the sudden, and deafening, wail, he span off his seat and managed only by good fortune to avoid the thrust of his own blade, as the sword fell away, then rebounded menacingly from the floor-boards.

Mr. Voronov, hunched up in corner of the room, dreaming with the sack of books, was jolted into consciousness; he made for the door, terrified. There, he encountered the on-rushing phalanx of Simeonov, Horatio and Ksenia; for a moment, there was a confused mêlée of bodies, of which no Russian Imperial Army officer could possibly feel proud; then, together, all four stumbled back into the room.

Yadviga sat upon the dying man's bed. He was dying no more. He was, for the first time that anyone had noticed, dead. The old woman clutched the last remaining bottle of spirits. At the arrival of her fellow-mourners, she made shift to determine whether anything was left in the bottle. There was but a short mouthful, she soon discovered. Sometimes, as she well knew, making a fuss over so very little was not worth the effort; she therefore made very little fuss. No sooner was the bottle empty than she fell to mourning.

"Would you believe it," she exclaimed, "he is here one moment, and gone the next."

With every outward sign of sadness, Horatio covered up the dead man's head with the grubbiest of sheets, while Ksenia tended to the unhappy old woman who had at last been left bereft, after so many fruitless hours of waiting.

"Did he have any money?" asked Captain Simeonov, hovering at the door in an interested manner. "You know what I mean: money, eh? I believe I have some notes in my quarters, showing that he owed me a few roubles."

"If he had money, sir," said Yadviga forcefully, "do you not think it is due to me as his last companion and servant? In any case, he had no money. I tended him out of charity."

Ksenia glared at the military man. "How can you think of money at a time like this?" she demanded. "Have you no shame at all, sir?"

Simeonov muttered that shame had no bearing on any of this, that a man of honour—

"You," ordered Yadviga, pointing a finger at the Captain. "Instead of counting a dead man's money, should you not go and make yourself useful? Perhaps you should fetch some vodka, eh? –do we not need to raise a glass to poor Major Sinclair? Believe me, we do, you mark my words."

The Captain shrugged his shoulders, buttoned up his tunic, picked up his sword and sauntered out into the street. By the simple act of threatening the first passer-by with a death so painful that the civilian awoke in a cold sweat every night for ten years thereafter, he swiftly returned with not one, but two bottles of pure spirit, one of which he passed carelessly to Yadviga, the other being shared with Mr. Voronov.

Considerably comforted in her distress at this sight, Yadviga poured out a good measure for herself, and two shorter measures for Horatio and Ksenia, on a principle of sharing which would have done credit to the very best inn-keepers of Europe. Having made these careful preparations, she raised her glass to "Lieutenant-Colonel Georgiy Sinclair!" – downed the contents in one, then, in the best traditions of Russian hospitality, dashed the glass from her hand. It bounced on the rotten floorboards and rolled under the bed.

Her fellow-mourners followed suit, with greater or less success in the matter of smashing their glasses, while Yadviga made herself comfortable at the foot of the death-bed – the Major's spindly legs had to be pushed to one side. He did not feel a thing.

"In any case, no one can now deny," said she, indicating with one hand the dead man's head, now covered by a sweaty sheet, "that Colonel Sinclair comes to Novgorod the Great two years ago. Fresh from St Petersburg, he says – he says he has spent an hour with the Tsar himself." At the very mention of the Orthodox Autocrat, she crossed herself devoutly. Captain Simeonov emulated her with a desultory motion of the hand, while Voronov stood to attention. "Does he not tell me with his own mouth that he has travelled from France and across all of Prussia and half of Russia – and for why? And for why?"

She paused to glare at everyone around, daring them to know the answer.

Captain Simeonov dared: "To escape Liberty?"

Horatio dared: "To escape Justice?"

Voronov dared: "To spend his last days among Russian warriors?" It was a decent thought, for once, and not utterly erroneous, although the reason which no one dared to state – 'gambling and fraud' – was probably more honest.

"It is, he says," said Yadviga majestically, rising above the mean suggestions of jealous men, "with the express purpose of visiting all the churches of Novgorod the Great. Is that not remarkable? Well, I won't say it's not."

This intention came as a surprise to most. But Ksenia, charity alone in her heart, sighed: "Ah, to visit all the churches? If only I had time."

Simeonov remained stubbornly convinced of the correctness of his own answer, and Horatio of his.

"Alas!" said Yadviga in sombre tone, "he has so little time, you see. In any case, he gets struck down with the disease of – what was it? – lassitude? – that's it – lassitude, he says, when he has THE DISEASE OF LASSITUDE visited barely two of our famous and holy churches. It comes from his early days in hot countries. So, does he not take money to the shrine of Blessed James of Borovichi, wonder-worker? Does he not visit the Weeping Ikon of the Most Holy Theotokos? Do they hear our prayers?"

"No, madam," suggested Horatio, ever the Rationalist. "Not at all."

Yadviga scowled at him. "All I can say is, perhaps our saints cannot understand the words of a foreign gentleman, our brave General Sinclair. Who knows? In any case, our priests tell us that we are merely mortal, do they not?"

"But he still found the energy," said Simeonov, "to sit down to a game of cards and take all the pay of my battalion. Do you know what that man had? He had luck. The man needed no saints and ikons, madam, just some devilish luck."

"In any case, weakened though he is," conceded Yadviga – and her word was not to be doubted, for she had seen many a weakened and weak man in her time, "he finds some small comfort among fellow-soldiers, which is a fine thing to behold."

She allowed herself a tear or two, shed not for Major George Sinclair, but for all those soldiers – boys and men – who had died, and who were yet to die, leaving the mothers of Russia at home to eke a living from a wasted land.

Ksenia embraced her and wept in sympathy – not for Major George Sinclair, but for her first husband and the young men of the world, those who had died and who were yet to die, leaving the women of Russia at home to rear children in an empty land. And for the children who were not yet born, and the men who have been deceived and must not be told. So many deaths, so many deceits, so many tears.

The three men stood back, apart, embarrassed, thinking not for a moment of Major George Sinclair, but of their own concerns. Of the three, only Voronov mourned: for the loss of two of his own children, roaming the world with strangers and – more importantly – without a single traveller's guide-book to the morals and sights of strange places. He had, he now realised with a pain much as if he had dropped an axe on his foot, been a poor husband and a poorer father. Now, only now, did a tear breach the rampart of his eye. It trickled over his cheek and was soon lost in his beard. Another followed, then another; the inn-keeper began to shake and to sob.

Alarmed, Horatio found himself placing a strong arm around his host. Had the Major in fact been a worthy person? Was he alone in not regretting his death? Then came the darker thought: who would shed a tear for Horatio, if he himself died at this very moment? Who – after the night had adjusted its rumpled clothing and splashed its face with icy water and placed its felt-boots once more upon the roads of Russia – would mourn? Not – he answered his own question – one.

Or perhaps just one. His face clouded over. So much was uncertain between life and death.

Seeing the undisguised regret upon the faces of the two other men, Captain Simeonov was for a long moment assailed by a doubt: had he allowed himself to be seduced by these maudlin civilians? If he stayed here any longer, would he make a fool of himself? It was a danger, and he was a man greatly accustomed to avoiding danger. Resolute and bold, therefore, he stepped forward, gave a final smart salute to the shrouded corpse of the Scotch officer – who undoubtedly owed him several roubles, the scoundrel – bowed gravely to the women, then turned on his heel and strode out into the street.

At the foot of the walls of the citadel, the Captain stumbled across Corporal Nikolaiev, whom he had ordered to return to barracks.

"Corporal," barked the Captain, "are you lying on the ground? The ground is no place for a soldier. Why are you lying on the ground? The ground is hard. Is the ground not hard?"

The Corporal, uncertain which question to answer first, stood up, slightly dazed. This prompt action, at least, enabled him to reply "no" to the first question, and, after some encouragement, "yes" to the third question. The second question, as is commonly the case, was more perplexing.

THE SECOND QUESTION WAS MORE PERPLEXING

Corporal Nikolaiev pondered it in a slow, but perfectly methodical, manner. To begin with, he stepped over to the blanket which contained the captured wolf. Raising his foot, he gave it a smart kick. There was a long-drawn, muffled groan – such as a wolf might make if captured, kicked and rolled in a blanket. Or, for that matter, any other creature out foraging in the night. Next, he turned to each point of the compass in turn, his sentry's eye looking out for any irregular movement, or a trail of footprints. Thirdly, he examined the waters of the moat – such as could be seen, since for the most part the stagnant pool was covered with green slime. Lastly, he stepped back and stared straight upwards, scanning the over-towering walls of the citadel of Novgorod the Great for any soldier or large bird of prey.

"Sleeping, sir!" he reported, at the conclusion of all of this.

The Captain advanced upon him, and smote him on the chest.

"Sleeping, sir? Do we sleep when carrying out orders? No, we do not. We obey the orders of the superior officer, even if it means marching into the jaws of death. And we know, do we not, that it frequently does? Yes, it does. Yes, sir, we know."

The Corporal frowned. "A man may sleep," he insisted, contrary to the orders posted very clearly on the barrack-room walls and at intervals read out – with some embellishment – to the assembled hordes of the Russian Imperial Army.

"A man," insisted his Captain, "may not sleep. He may not rest. He may not sit. He must not lie down. Not," he emphasised with a slap across the Corporal's left cheek, "without," with a slap across the right cheek, "permission," and a further slap across the left cheek. And then, for good measure, and in case, as sometimes happens, there was any doubt about the instruction, a second slap across the right cheek.

It may have been that last slap, the one issued as a sharp reminder – the Captain never knew. At all events, the Imerach stirred and without asking permission, as would have been the case had he been paying attention, he repaid the Captain in the coin he had received. In no time at all, the two men were once more grappling in hand-to-hand combat, a sight that might, under other circumstances, have burst a Russian heart with pride in the ever-vigilant warriors of the fatherland. Back and forth they went, like the double-headed eagle of the Empire, now tripping, now dodging, running and advancing, throwing and punching. By sheer mischance, they both came up against the wolf encased in the blanket and the force of the collision rolled the whole package to the edge of a steep slope; it quivered briefly on the edge, then plunged down into the moat where, leaving a mound of bubbles, it vanished with but a single sound under the surface.

Several minutes later, the Imerach managed to gain the upper hand, knocked the Captain unconscious, then immediately did the same to himself. The dance of death was ended. The dust slowly settled. As did the bubbles.

In the house of the dead, at length, mourning could not decently be extended. It was time for the celebration to end. Various bells announced the hour across the gentle breezes that woke Novgorod the Great to another summer's day. Some bells rang seven times, and were correct; others rang twelve or four times, in a more or less cryptic fashion. Others simply tolled, knell after knell after knell, doubtless for the dead, perhaps for the quick, but for reasons known only to initiates. At the sound of all the bells, Ksenia bade farewell to Yadviga. There was much sobbing. The old woman was suddenly struck with the strong belief that Ksenia was the one true daughter she had never had. Ksenia, for her part, abandoned all reason and declared that Yadviga might have been a mother to her – "I have only had two," she stated, almost with regret.

Horatio and Voronov stood by, waiting for these false declarations of relationship to die away; as, indeed, they did, in face of the more practical matters of breakfast and obsequies.

BREAKFAST AND
OBSEQUIES

In that order.

Exhibiting all the boldness of their nocturnal familiarity (when all other answers are exhausted, what is 'Love', but familiarity?), Horatio and Ksenia stepped out together, without a word being spoken, to the street. Constrained to wait for Mr. Voronov to struggle down the path with his unaccustomed sack of books, their thoughts wandered.

"My first husband," whispered Ksenia, "was obliged on one occasion to breakfast upon the remains of a wolf and a horse which had fought each other to death in the Siberian night."

Horatio, having no ready reply to this extraordinary revelation, simply reached for her hand and patted it consolingly.

Voronov swung the bag of books energetically over his right shoulder and strode out with a look of hope upon his face. Their road at first took them towards the kremlin, but then, as Horatio had done late in the night, they turned aside and skirted the outer walls, thus by good fortune avoiding a small scene of tragedy, which would have dampened their common cheerfulness. They came to the bridge over the River Volkhov which continued to pour the waters of Russia in slow and majestic waves to the sea. Once the bridge was crossed, Mr. Voronov's eager steps began to slow. At last he drew to a stop, some fifty yards from his own home. He turned to his companions.

"I wonder—" he said, with caution in his voice.

"Sir?" asked Ksenia after a few moments, since the inn-keeper said no more.

"—if I might—" he continued, with hesitation.

"Sir?" inquired Horatio when the inn-keeper seemed lost for resolution.

"—trouble you to wait for a few moments outside while I explain matters to my wife who doubtless has some questions to ask of me not least where I have been all night and indeed where I have been for the past twenty-five years. What I intend to do with all these books I don't yet know myself so if you will excuse me I shall try to set my life to rights and my wife—" Without waiting for the full-stop which in any orthodox sentence would be used to invite an answer or licence from his companions, the inn-keeper bolted from the spot, swinging his sack of books in front of him both to protect himself from what lay before and to propel himself forwards with no chance of stopping. He launched himself through the door, falling immediately upon his wife, who had seen him coming from afar.

For a few minutes, for the sake of decency and out of respect for the intimacy of a husband and wife, Horatio and Ksenia left them. Content with a few more minutes of solitude, they stood and gazed at the river that flowed from Lake Ilmen and past the walls of the kremlin. They should be warned, however, of this: that this Imperial city of Novgorod has seen many unhappy times; a breakfast at that inn of marital bliss was perhaps to be

THE UNHAPPIEST OF ALL.

44

VLADIMIR IVANOVICH, SHE CRIED, YOU HAVE LOST YOUR MIND.

Mr. Voronov launched himself through the door of his inn, falling immediately upon his wife, who had seen him coming from afar.

Not one word was spoken. Not one sound was made, except for a sharp inhalation of breath as the inn-keeper shot past his wife and crashed into the table used by infrequent guests. None were resident on the preceding night – all being otherwise occupied – so none were clustered around the table, anxious to break their fast. Which was fortunate, as the sack of books, in its flight across the room just a few feet from the floor, would surely and swiftly have decapitated them all. Such is the power of the printed word. The sack clattered against the far wall, and tumbled noisily but harmlessly to the ground.

When the inn-keeper had caught his breath, he picked himself up from the greasy floor, adjusted his cap, and turned to face his wife. She stood with arms folded, beside a door not yet closed, neither inviting an explanation nor refusing it, neither asking him to stay nor asking him to leave. Not yet.

"My dear—" he began, inauspiciously.

"You have returned then?" she interrupted, an icy edge to her words of welcome.

Mr. Voronov sighed and tried another approach. After years of such jousting, he had exhausted them all, but never gave up trying. Which, in the judgement of some, might be described, and circumscribed, as 'Love'. "I was," he said humbly, "mistakenly locked out."

"By me," she confirmed, leaving little room for further manoeuvre. "It was not a mistake."

"I thought not," acknowledged the lady's husband. "You were, of course, quite right to do so."

This concession made only the slightest dent in her armour. She felt it, but did not flinch.

"Can we sit down?" asked Mr. Voronov further.

"Why?" demanded Mrs. Voronova.

"I have something to say," confessed Mr. Voronov.

"It can be said standing up," stated Mrs. Voronova, reducing to dust – in a manner which her husband had always secretly admired – every attempt at closeness.

"It can be said standing up," conceded Mr. Voronov. "But perhaps the door can be closed?"

"The words will not blow away if there is a draught," announced Mrs. Voronova. And here, she was wrong: some words, such as those that a man might say after a night of revelation, could turn like a feather if touched by the gentlest breeze from an angel's wing, or the passing of a fly – which two events could well prove to be the same, should the unhappy couple have chosen, at that moment, to consult a mystic.

The inn-keeper pondered. This was not going well. It was his own fault – the price to pay for many years of neglect, the penalty for being a man without feeling. He breathed deeply.

"I miss my children," he said.

Mrs. Voronova's astonishment at these words was so great that, in a distraction, she closed the door.

"I wish they were all still living with us, in our home," he added.

Mrs. Voronova felt dizzy; she walked shakily towards him. He stepped back cautiously. His fears were misplaced – she grabbed at a chair and lowered herself into it.

"Further," he announced, "I now know that I have neglected you sorely for many years, and I regret every lost moment."

His wife stood up abruptly, struck by the awful truth.

"Vladimir Ivanovich," she cried, "you have lost your mind!"

"No, my love," said Mr. Voronov in tones which justifiably gave his wife further cause for concern, being as they were: meek, low and sweet, "I believe I have found it."

"Explain yourself," she asked patiently, "before I take this knife to you." So saying, she whipped out from her petticoats a large kitchen knife, which had seen useful service over many years, not least in dealing with tripe. She found it an admirable counsellor in debates with her husband.

"Can I sit?" asked the inn-keeper, seeking, despite his best intentions, to pursue his advantage.

"You cannot," replied his wife without a pause. "You have either lost your mind, or you have lost our savings at a game of cards. Nothing else can explain it. If you have done the one, you are no longer my husband and can no longer sit with me. If you have done the other, you are no longer the keeper of this inn and can no longer sit with me. In short," she concluded, having run over all the probabilities, and several possibilities, to her own satisfaction, "you can only stand." She seated herself once more, to emphasise the point.

Mr. Voronov conceded defeat on this question, and continued to stand.

"My children," he began hesitantly, "our sons Ivan and Nikolai—" He faltered.

"My" interrupted his wife, "sons," emphasising greatly the possessive pronoun: "What of them?"

"Are they not my sons too?" asked Mr. Voronov, suddenly bewildered.

His wife looked at him with disdain. "Who else would they be the sons of, I wonder?" She held his eyes, and he knew that she spoke the truth.

"They are your children," he continued bravely, "which we created together – you mostly – and I fear that perhaps I drove them off. A father should never do that. What are children for, but to protect and to nourish, whatever may become of them, whatever roads they take, however foolishly they behave? If they stray, they need forgiveness; if they return, they need a welcome. They made but one mistake and I drove them away: what was I thinking?"

His wife looked at him oddly. Was the man babbling or did he really believe what he said? It was a difficult matter to determine.

"No child should ever be driven away by its parents," she agreed "regardless—"

At that precise moment, the only daughter of this inn, Yekaterina by name – she of the swaying hips and knowing smile, upon which several travellers had gazed with avidity but not dared to comment aloud – entered yawning and rubbing the sleep from her eyes.

"Begone, you wanton hussy!" shouted both father and mother with parental concern for her peace of mind.

The girl pouted, ran into the kitchen and out into the yard, where she could be heard screaming obscenities at the chickens who scratched a living there.

"—of what they have done," concluded her mother.

"My very thoughts exactly," agreed Vladimir Ivanovich Voronov with mounting enthusiasm. "What if we never see either of them again – perhaps they will be called to war and be killed, and we will never see their broken bodies, nor the slashes made by the swords, never have our dear Ivan, our dear Nikolai home to bury in the graveyard under the old yew tree—"

At this vision, their grieving mother gasped and turned pale. As did the inn-keeper, but more quietly. His words were now far outstripping his courage.

"What have they done," he concluded nervously, "but run off with the maids?"

"Thieving little bitches," muttered his wife with threefold inaccuracy.

"What young man would not do the same, if he was kept in the same house as them day after day, night after night?"

Mrs. Voronova saw the justice of this observation and dried her eyes. "It is only natural," she admitted.

Her husband continued on this romantic vein of thought: "Until that night when, all being quiet, he slips on his boots and coat and—"

"A young man will always follow his—" judged the wife.

"—breeches," finished her husband, continuing to paint a simple picture of elopement, "and set off into the world without nothing but a knife in his—"

"—heart," she concluded.

"—pocket and a girl on his arm." Voronov sighed unnecessarily. Might he not have done the same, had his own father not kept him – and the maids – under lock and key, for the good of the business? And where were they now, his sons? He had, in shutting them from his thoughts, shut them from his life.

"Where are they now, our sons?" he asked.

"Little Ivan," she said, "who ran off with that maid with a broken tooth—"

She had, remembered Mr. Voronov, master of the inn and connoisseur – he imagined – of maids, also a head of hair that both concealed and promised much—

"—is now in Kazan. He works in a small inn there. They have a child, a son."

"I have a grandson?" exclaimed Voronov, full of astonishment. "Why did no one tell me?" The emotions of the night overwhelmed him suddenly and he gazed wide-eyed at his wife, the grandmother, the mother of his children; tears ran endlessly down his throat, as if he were the mighty Volkhov when the thaw had set in.

"And darling Nikolai," she continued, "went first to Chudovo—"

"Aha, Chudovo," said her husband, in an instant recalling two superb details. "That is where that girl Dunya came from, the one with the—"

"Poor Dunya," interrupted Marfa Petrovich Voronova, "died in childbirth, as did the child, leaving our Nikolai all alone in the world; he left for St Petersburg; he now works in a gilded theatre."

Mr. Voronov was astounded beyond measure. Grief and pleasure overcame him in equal amounts: grief for the loss of another grandchild, for the death of Dunya, for the tragic revelation about Nikolai's chosen profession; and pleasure for the unexpected news that he still had a family. 'Love', he had suddenly and alarmingly discovered, was Family. Were it not for that, his second son's headlong descent into the gutter would be beyond bearing.

Without one word more, he threw himself into the arms of his wife. The chair on which she sat gave a loud crack, before tipping itself, and its occupants, on to the floor. There they lay, racked by each other's sobs. Out in the yard, Yekaterina continued berating the chickens. Neither mother nor father heard her. Inured to the noise of humans, neither did the poultry.

"We must," proposed the inn-keeper into the left ear of his wife, an ear now largely unaccustomed to such intimacy, "go and visit our sons and our grandson."

Mrs. Voronova pondered this carefully for a few moments, weighing each word as if it were a suspect cabbage at the market. Then she, in turn, whispered into his right ear: "Vladimir Ivanovich, have you lost your mind?"

"No, my love," he murmured, "I believe I have found it again." He kissed her not with passion but with a deep tenderness. "We have some money saved, we can close our inn for a week or two, and we can find our family again. Perhaps we can persuade them to return to Novgorod and take up their lives here with us?" Startled at the audacity of his own words, and unaware of their cruel and ridiculous naivety, he raised his head and looked deep into the eyes of his wife, those same brown eyes into which he had fallen when a young man, the eyes full of passion and compassion, sensitivity and common-sense, and – most importantly – all the cunning and rapacity required in an inn-keeper's wife.

She, as if hit by a bolt of lightning, yielded. Here was a man, she thought unexpectedly, who still wants to know me, who has been on a long journey, but has now returned, who has been reported dead but is found alive. Either that, she concluded, or I have lost my mind.

And perhaps, said Voronov to himself, as the happy pair lay in each other's arms and refreshed their memories; perhaps, when we return, I will write a book of our travels and name my house

'THE INN OF WAR AND PEACE.'

45

IT WAS, UNFORTUNATELY, A VERY EMPTY BOAST.

The decision to enter the inn at that precise moment was not necessarily the best one. For, as Horatio pushed back the door and ushered his friend before him, his glance fell upon the inn-keeper and his wife, who were both on the floor, entwined in the closest possible discussion of the meaning of the words 'War' and 'Peace'.

"Oh," said Ksenia, unable to avert her gaze. At length, she addressed Horatio, unaccountably reminded of an omission: "Sir, I have not yet told you of the peculiarly becoming nakedness of my first husband."

"Ah," replied Horatio, looking thoughtfully at the ceiling, and attentively avoiding the blissful domestic scene before him, "but I believe I have heard that story."

Ksenia sighed and moved her gaze to that very same spot. "Perhaps I told it – I do not remember." A large bluebottle was on the ceiling taking its ease, oblivious to the matters beneath it – or above, since it walked upside-down. She considered a bluebottle, in whose life there was neither up nor down, neither truth nor falsehood, nor travel nor husbands. On such a sunny morning, the fly was briefly enviable.

Suddenly aware of a cool draught, the inn-keeper's wife turned her head and saw the two honoured guests standing in the doorway. For no obvious reason they were admiring a patch of ceiling; she must suppose it was some cockroach. Seizing the brief moment of their inattentiveness, she hoisted herself and her enraptured husband from the floor, dragged man, loose clothing, knife and broken chair into the kitchen, then pulled the door fast shut behind them.

When he heard the slamming of the door, Horatio looked obliquely at the scene. It had been vacated. One single item of intimate cloth-ing remained, upon which he advanced with two long strides before kicking the garment skilfully into a dark corner. Ksenia pretended not to have noticed it.

"We may now," announced Horatio, "breakfast."

It was, unfortunately, a very empty boast.

Five minutes went by, spent in companionable silence on the one side of the kitchen door, and in noises reminiscent of great culinary activity on the far side. After five minutes, the commotion reached a peak and then immediately died away. There was a heavy silence. Another five minutes passed.

At length, Ksenia grew worried. "Do you think they have murdered each other?" she inquired.

Horatio considered the possibility. A judgement depended on whether he had interpreted the previous scene correctly. He weighed the possibilities, and decided that—

"No, I think not. But perhaps I should—" He advanced upon the door and tapped lightly.

There was no answer.

He tapped more loudly.

"One moment," came the breathless voice of the landlady.

At length, Mrs. Voronova poked her head round the door. Her face was flushed, her hair in great dishevelment. For no apparent reason, she clutched a goose's egg in her trembling hand.

"You will want your breakfast?" she asked. On receiving a positive response, she slammed the door once more shut. Preparations were soon to be heard in full swing. Yekaterina was summoned sharply from the yard. Fires were lit. Water was pumped. The inn-keeper was dispatched with his axe. After a lengthy interval, the young Miss Voronova flounced into the public room, skimmed some plates across the table and launched cutlery after them, leered evilly at Horatio, glanced disdainfully at Ksenia, then marched out again.

The inn-keeper himself was next to arrive, dripping with sweat from – the travellers supposed – his wielding of the axe, and bearing a steaming samovar, some butter, and a basket of cucumbers. "There is no bread," he apologised. "It was forgotten about. Like many things." He lingered beside the table, contemplating the cucumbers. "Like many things," he repeated, and cast a distracted smile upon the young widow, as if waiting for her to ask. She was afraid to oblige. At length, with not another word spoken, he placed the samovar and butter upon the table and returned to the kitchen with the cucumbers.

Ksenia, in an attempt to gloss over these uncommon preparations, drew hot liquid from the samovar. Tea-leaves had also been forgotten about. Like many things. There came, in time, a bowl of eggs, some cooked, others not cooked, all from hens. Horatio could not bring himself to eat two of them.

Finally, Mr. Voronov returned, bearing a large pot, which he left without a word on the table. He returned to the kitchen with the ease of a sleepwalker. Through the open door, Horatio observed inn-keeper and wife subside into a long embrace, while their only daughter stood to one side, upon her face a look composed equally of utter disbelief and unalloyed disgust.

Ksenia lifted the lid from the pot, peered inside. She stifled a scream. Gently, but nevertheless with urgency, she replaced the lid.

"Is there Death in the Pot?" joked Horatio, remembering the subject of the adulteration of food discussed at the Royal Society in London when last he was there with Prince Labanov. He IS THERE DEATH IN THE POT? spoke nevertheless a little anxiously, as he was aware that a long day of travelling would lie ahead of him: he was now beginning to feel hungry.

Ksenia shook her head. "Not Death," she informed him. "Mice."

Horatio did not care to ask whether the mice were cooked or yet living. It did not seem to matter.

Ksenia thought that this breakfast could never be made any worse. She did not know she was wrong.

Horatio, perceiving that the young woman was shaking slightly, wrapped his coat around her and made efforts to coax some life from a badly-neglected stove. While he was engaged in this task, to all appearances as if he had been doing it for hours, Ksenia breathed in the slightly acrid smell of the man's clothing and succumbed to one last lingering moment of madness. And then she said: "There is one thing I must tell you."

Horatio looked up, pretending to be terrified. "There was a wolf in the pot, or a mare?" he asked.

"No," laughed Ksenia. She pulled his coat closer around her, despite the fact that the room was now warming rapidly. "No, it is something else."

"I have told you," said Horatio, inordinately pleased with his ability to raise a smile after so many grim hours of the night, "I cannot eat more than two eggs."

Inexplicably, Ksenia did not laugh, despite the witticism being an old friend. On the contrary, she looked serious. Horatio held her eyes for several moments and then he looked away to the flames that now leaped up within the stove: he saw a finality he did not understand. Ksenia paused for a moment further and then she said: "I have told you that I am a widow. However, I have not told you all: you should know that I am—"

The front door of the inn was pushed open. Ksenia, who had her back to the door, saw a look of blank despair fall upon Horatio's face and drain it both of joy and sorrow. She stopped in her confession, and turned. A man stood at the open door, dressed for a long journey.

"Horatio Alexandrovich," he said, nodding to that gentleman.

"Boris Ilyich," replied Horatio, rising slowly from his knees and avoiding Ksenia's eye.

"It is time," said the son of Ilya, a shade ominously, as if he were the long-expected Mercury of Death – he was, after all, dressed all in black. "Prince Labanov awaits."

THE LONG-EXPECTED MERCURY OF DEATH

Horatio nodded. The man withdrew a single step, leaving the door open.

"Prince Labanov?" asked the young widow nervously. "He is here in Novgorod?"

"No," replied the black man quietly. "He is in St Petersburg." There was a pause; and then the five words which destroyed one long dream: "I am in his service."

"Then—" began Ksenia, but could say nothing further. Except for that one moment of girlish excitement, when Captain Cochrane took her away from Kamtchatka, she had always been the one who was left behind. When the Captain wished to explore the wilder regions of Tartary, he had left her behind; when horses were lost on the journey from Yakutsk, she had been, in her husband's words, 'forwarded in charge of a Cossack', like some parcel; on their return to London, he had hastened off to Colombia, she had been left behind; after her return to St Petersburg, she had been left behind. And now—

"I have to go," confirmed Horatio wearily. "I am sorry."

He knew, having studied the matter carefully over the years, that the word 'Sorry', like 'Love', has no meaning on its own. It languishes like a beggar on a St Petersburg boulevard, without a kopeck to its name. It hopes for much, but cannot pay its way. The vocabulary of apology and forgiveness is as extensive as that of love, for much the same reasons.

"Sorry?" asked Ksenia, in as low a voice as Horatio had heard in his entire new life. She said nothing more.

"I am sorry," repeated Horatio helplessly.

"What are you sorry for?" asked Ksenia, looking steadily at her hands.

"I am sorry," began Horatio. He stopped. He began again: "I am sorry for having deceived you. No," he ended, "that is not right." He felt that he was being led down into a maze of mirrors, at the end of which he would have no idea whether he had advanced or retreated, or – indeed – what it was he was 'sorry' for in the first place. He was sorry, perhaps, for having to apologise.

"What then," asked Ksenia quietly, "is right? When a man says that he is sorry, all I know is that he is confused."

Horatio nodded miserably, not knowing whether the woman was right or wrong. It mattered little now. "I am sorry," he whispered once more, without hope and without meaning.

"I, too, am sorry," said Ksenia, as much to herself as to Horatio, and said no more. The end of one thing is not always the beginning of another.

Horatio and Ksenia looked for the last time – perhaps that day – perhaps forever – upon each other.

There was an indiscreet cough from the doorway, followed by the more-than-discreet snorting of an impatient horse. It was Boris Ilyich who coughed; the horse, through good manners, remained outside. Horatio walked heavily to the kitchen-door, interrupted Mr. Voronov in his dreamy contemplation of family life, and paid his fee for the night's board and lodging. The inn-keeper, so distracted by the comforting surroundings of his new world, did not think to argue the amount with his guest, to whom he had provided little board, no lodging to speak of, and the most memorable breakfast in Novgorod.

Horatio turned then to Ksenia. For a long, long pause, the man and the woman gazed at each other, as if from a great distance, assessing and measuring, falling and falling away. Eyes were locked, but seeing beyond. The rest of the world, even the many distractions of the inn of Mr. Voronov on this morning of revelation, vanished. All sound stopped, two hearts ceased to beat. It was one of those moments, rare in a life, to which every succeeding regret must be tethered.

And then the door opened wide, and closed on silence once more.

THE BREAKFAST, SUCH AS IT WAS, WAS OVER.

46

HE FINISHED – AS ALL MEN DO – WITH A GREAT DEAL OF NOISE.

When at last all was quiet, the ill-matched foreigners having left, Yadviga gave a deep sigh, expressive of all the sorrows of Mother Russia, past, present and future, then lowered herself to her knees beside the last bed and resting-place of Major Sinclair. It was a scene that would have inspired compassion in all but the most hard-hearted of souls – an old woman settling to pray for the departed soul of a good master.

It would indeed have been such a scene, had she not continued her descent further than is commonly the practice for prayer, stuck her head under the bed, exhaled heavily, groaning with aches and pains that she had all but forgotten about; and finally pulled out two small boxes, which had been concealed below the Imperial Mattress.

On one were carved, in the British script, the words 'Cards + Dice', and on the other were carved the words 'Padre + Deus'. To avoid any confusion – and to the untutored or careless eye, confusion was a certainty – the former had a small corner of a face-card – a joker or a king – pinned to it with a rusty nail; while the latter had tacked to it a small image of a person with a halo – possibly a Saint. Yadviga looked upon the two ikons, and crossed herself. Since the face-card could have been a picture of the Tsar himself, and the ikon might have been a knave, the old woman crossed herself once more and then applied the surest test of all: carefully she shook one and then the other. Both clinked with the comforting sound of coin. The one with the playing-card attached was decidedly heavier. The old woman grunted with no small satisfaction and heaved herself unsteadily to her feet. Remembering that the priest had often urged her to render unto the Tsar that which is the Tsar's, and unto God that which is His, she tipped the contents of the 'Cards' box into her own pocket. Casting one last bleary-eyed and aggrieved look around the room, and leaving two candles burning for the deceased, she set forth into the day with the box marked 'Padre' carried ostentatiously before her in both hands.

A funeral had to be arranged. The British military gentleman had given his nurse and servant clear instructions in the past week regarding the obsequies to be mounted in his honour. A likely spot in a pauper's graveyard had already been identified. Such objections as had been raised by the priest of the chapel of St Onuphrius the Silent, regarding the schismatic nature of Major Sinclair's stated beliefs, had been finally resolved to everyone's satisfaction with a votive candle or two. Mr. Volchovsky, the Major's frequent companion of the round table, at dice, who spent his spare time in digging graves and building coffins – a profession to which his father had told him every ambitious young person should aspire, for, like the wind, the tides and the stars, there will never be any shortage of death – Mr. Volchovsky had been engaged for that certain hour which Major Sinclair saw before him. A small squadron of mourners could also be rounded up at short notice, with the promise of a few coins.

NO SHORTAGE
OF DEATH

All arrangements being in place, no trouble at all should therefore have risen up to face down Yadviga.

But is it not always the way with arrangements, that some fool will step in the way and throw them all asunder? Or, in this instance, some fool will step in the moat, and call Mr. Volchovsky away, just when he was most needed?

On arriving at the gravedigger's house and being informed of this unforeseen circumstance, Yadviga justifiably raged against the lack of consideration shown by others.

"Well, I can't say that that is very helpful. Could they not find another time to die?" she demanded.

Mrs. Volchovskaya, habituated to such transports of grief, refrained from observing that it is the way with Death, that it comes frequently unexpected and uninvited. Instead she said: "My dear Yadviga Petrovna, I am sure my husband will be home soon. In the meanwhile, will you not have a little something to fortify you against the day?"

Yadviga accepted this medical attention, measured out in hot tea with a dash of vodka. A young apprentice was then summoned, encouraged with a clout round the head and a baneful threat, and dispatched to seek out his master and inform him of the emergency. Having taken all possible measures to please the customer, Mrs. Volchovskaya inquired:

"And how did the gentleman die?"

"All I can say, Irina Ivanovna," replied Yadviga, shaking her head, "is that he finished – as all men do – with a great deal of noise."

Mrs. Volchovskaya nodded agreeably, satisfied in the confirmation that what men lacked during their life – the ability to string a sentence together – they made up for on their death-beds. Her belief was that Mr. Volchovsky would be obliged to chatter on for a week, just to make up on lost ground, before being permitted to fall silent forever.

"And it will be a grand funeral?" she asked further, in rhetorical manner, with no suggestion of partiality.

Yadviga held out her cup for a further restorative before answering. "The gentleman concerned, Irina Ivanovna," she said at length, "had a great deal of money, you mark my words. Otherwise," she added, looking sharply at her companion, "I would never have agreed to serve him."

"Quite right, my dear Yadviga Petrovna," murmured Mrs. Volchovskaya.

"In any case, he specifically asks that as little as possible is to be spent on his funeral, and all that remains – a great fortune, he says—" here she patted her own pocket where some heavy coins made a pious jangling sound "—is to be given to the priests for the benefit of his eternal soul."

Mrs. Volchovskaya, knowing that the departed gentleman had been a close associate of her husband's at the gambling table, had reservations about this pious picture. But she crossed herself regardless: a fine, professional gesture – who can tell what might pass through the mind and conscience of a person upon their death-bed?

"He had no," she probed a little, knowing something of the ways of old gentlemen and those they left behind, "ah – no intimate friend?"

The very thought appalled Yadviga. "The gentleman," she replied, "was of a respectable age."

Precisely, thought Mrs. Volchovskaya.

"No," confirmed Yadviga, "I was his only true companion at the end." She sniffed a little.

Mrs. Volchovskaya sniffed too – perhaps in sympathy. "What is 'Love', after all?" she added philosophically. "It cannot reach beyond death."

This was an interesting observation from one whose daily bread was earned by death, and who should therefore have been aware – perhaps more so even than Velos, janitor of the Underworld – that Love can reach beyond Death. And vice versa.

Yadviga, after a third professional cup had sufficiently revived her, now set out to find the priest, and herd together a respectable number of mourners and standers-by. The priest was pleased to be offered as an advance a small sum of money from the spiritual – that is, less corporeal, or heavy – box of coins; and made his way to the house of Mr. Volchovsky, where he received all the hospitality due to a man of God, all the while evading any questions as to the financial arrangements made by the late Major Sinclair. All he would say on the matter was that "The blessed St Onuphrius is glorified, but remains, as always, silent." With which theological evasion, Mrs. Volchovskaya had to remain content

Now nearing the limits of her energies, Yadviga descended upon a sprawling wooden hovel that lay close to – and just outside – the western gate of the city, next to the encroaching forest. Its design owed little to the human mind; it was in places round and in places rectangular; its roof was now flat, now like a mountain-range; in one corner the walls were embedded in the surrounding mud, in two others, the house appeared to stand on a wooden leg; in a fifth corner, the walls had mouldered away completely and the bushes of the forest had forced an eager entrance. More smoke billowed from its one window than its chimney, since the latter was blocked by a dead crow that no one had bothered to remove last winter. To the untutored eye, there was no door to the residence, but Yadviga, succumbing to an old habit, muttered the magic words "Turn your back to the forest and your front to me", and easily found the door in the mouldy wooden walls. Without knocking, she threw open the door, releasing enough smoke to cloud a respectable battle on the frontiers of Turkey, and marched in.

It was, after all, her home.

In the murk and gloom inside, some figures were moving around slowly, mumbling.

"Pyotr, Pavel," snapped the old woman, "are you there?"

"Yes, mother," came two weary replies. Sons one had thought to find lying on the field of battle, one at Borodino, one before Moscow, their bones picked clean, were apparently alive – but only just – in Novgorod: is not the Mercy of God great? Untold thousands of men had died in defence of their country; hundreds of others had deserted the ranks in self-defence; nevertheless two of Yadviga's sons had not only stood firm, but had also escaped with their lives. Yadviga was not grateful at all – the pair had been a burden upon her ever since, except when engaged in the robbery and divestment of passing pedestrians upon the highway.

THE ROBBERY AND DIVESTMENT OF PASSING PEDESTRIANS

Pavel was engaged in cleaning the mud of the streets of Novgorod from a battered barrel-organ, one so decrepit that it seemed unlikely that it could play a single note, let alone delight children and old people at fairs. When the handle was turned, indeed, it took a few moments for any sounds at all to be heard against the background of flaking rust. And then, at last, the first few bars of the second movement of the German Beethoven's Third Symphony might be heard. Not one of Yadviga's family knew the name of the tune, and few outside of the family would have recognised it. One cultured gentleman, arrived from St Petersburg on a holy day, did determine the nature and name of the tune, but thought it best not to advise the hulking war veterans, who manned the machine, of its dedication.

At the arrival of his mother, Pavel ceased his labours and gazed slack-mouthed at her, ready to obey as a good son should.

"And where's that no-good daughter of mine?" bawled the distraught mother. "Olga – are you not awake yet?"

A heap of clothes stirred upon a low bed. "What do you think, you old hag?" demanded the daughter, miraculously cured of the clap – or so it is said – as soon as she had arrived home from Moscow – a result, it was understood, of an intercession by the Virgin Martyr Theodora, who took pity upon the Russian victims of Napoleon's cruelty: a religious marvel that was a useful lever for negotiations in dark corners with credulous and desperate men.

Impervious to the ingratitude of her sole surviving children, whom she had never stopped loving, Yadviga announced that the attendance of all three was required at the state-funeral of the great British soldier, Major George Sinclair. She rattled a few of the smaller coins to gain her family's attention – a ruse which succeeded admirably. A good half-dozen adults clustered around her, forcing themselves on her attention. Not all were sons and daughters: if they had been, one might have had to doubt Yadviga's own tragic autobiography; as it is, one has to consider either her arithmetic, or her alphabet, to have been at fault.

Within minutes, Yadviga and the selected three companions in grief were on their way to the house of Mr. Volchovsky, all sombrely – if patchily – dressed; Olga, thanks to her untended coiffure, gave every appearance of having suffered in the most desperate distress for several days and nights past. Pyotr and Pavel trundled the barrel-organ along, in expectation of adding a dignified and profitable tenor to the whole affair.

All things considered, Major Sinclair would have been proud to have attended his own funeral.

Mr. Volchovsky had hurried back to his home from the scene of the unfortunate accident at the moat, with the body of the drowned stranger in a handcart, covered by a dripping blanket. Captain Simeonov, reported the gravedigger, had been intemperately annoyed with the circumstance, but had been persuaded to cough up two roubles to cover expenses.

"A most charitable man," he announced. No one, least of all Olga, who had had recent financial dealings with the Captain, was deceived by this charitably false assertion.

At the ninth hour, sharp, the procession set off, the priest in the lead at a swift pace, Mr. Volchovsky and the apprentice in hot pursuit

– the latter bearing the cheapest possible coffin upon his back as if he were some ill-sketched tortoise – the four mourners shuffling and stumbling as best they could, shading their eyes against the bright sunlight of that August morning, the wheels of the barrel-organ cracking and protesting all the way.

As the party rounded the last corner and entered the street on which stood the Major's lodge, they became aware of citizens in disarray ahead of them. Not only of citizens in disarray, but also of a disciplined column of rats which bore down upon them and CITIZENS IN rushed past, clearly fleeing some event of grand consequence. DISARRAY

"Ah!" cried the priest, preparing for a miracle. He crossed himself.

"Ah!" cried Mr. Volchovsky, preparing for a procedural hitch. He smote the apprentice sharply upon his coffin.

"Ah!" cried the young man, prepared for nothing, but fearing the worst.

"Ah!" cried Yadviga, preparing to negotiate a discount on the funeral expenses. She leaned breathlessly upon the greasy shoulder of Pyotr, who in turn lurched up against his brother Pavel. They awoke briefly from their dreams.

It was indeed a miracle worthy of the attention of Saints Peter and Paul.

An hour previously, in her haste to settle matters, Yadviga had left the stove burning, the door open, piles of wood nearby, and two candles sputtering over the bed. By some freak chance, which could not have been foreseen, flames had spread from one thing to another, and a fire had taken hold of the old building. At the very moment when the party were setting off on their procession, the flames had set their tongues upon the Empress Josephine's bed, and now the old hero was ablaze upon the most expensive funeral pyre seen in Novgorod the Great since the times of Ivan the Terrible, who, in the year fifteen hundred and seventy—

But there was no time for comparison. Following the example of the neighbours, the members of the party broke into a run and stood before the burning house: at a safe distance. Every piece of wood, though damp, was burning merrily and a huge pall of smoke rose into the sky, carrying with it flaming motes and sooty diamonds. Framed by the window, the deceased blazed darkly.

"A pious cadaver, wrapped in inextinguishable flame," commented the priest, whose sole vice, apart from money, was poetry; for this very reason, he had never advanced far in the hierarchy, and would certainly never be given charge of a church which was other than silent. It had been made clear to him that Orthodoxy precluded Poetry, in the same way that Virtue precluded Vice, Autocracy precluded Democracy, and so forth. Vice and Democracy were strangers to him, but Poetry—

"This is as fine an inferno," said Mr. Volchovsky, rubbing his hands with unqualified appreciation, "as when the Palace burned at Tsarskoe Selo in 1820."

A FINE INFERNO

At that moment, the roof of the lodge collapsed, spraying a huge fountain of ash and flame into the air. All who could, stepped back sharply. Those who could not, turned to dust.

"Grand, grand!" enthused Mr. Volchovsky further.

Yadviga cooled his fervour a little by noting that his professional services were no longer required. "And," she added darkly, "neither are those of the mourners, you mark my words." Her few remaining children in this world turned away disheartened, but mingled long enough with the crowd to gain a few roubles in the exercise of their several and undoubted skills.

Mr. Volchovsky sought to argue with the executor of Major Sinclair's estate.

"We have a contract," he stated.

"We have not, I think you will find," replied Yadviga, on sure ground.

"This coffin cannot be used for another," he argued. "The wood cost me five roubles."

"All I can say is, that coffin can be used for anyone at all, save respectable people" she countered, "and is made from odd scraps of wood which you found in your yard. Mr. Voronov and his axe could make you another in five minutes."

"My time—" he continued, desperately, to itemise.

"—would be better spent at home with your wife than at the gambling-table," thrust back Yadviga, guardian of the morals of Russia.

Defeated, Mr. Volchovsky sent his exhausted apprentice back home with the coffin, thereby acknowledging that a new and willing customer could readily be found; indeed, he already had one in mind, consumed by water rather than by fire; and he stayed only to observe the fire in its last throes and marvel at the power of flame.

The priest, Gregorius by name, was an honourable man: he stood dutifully and spoke the words of the service for Those Who Have Fallen Asleep, even if it had been inauspiciously in a bed of flames. But it was rather difficult to hear his words above the roar of the fire – they might as well have been an invocation of Svarog, the god of fire. No matter: the gods – who had already been paid – blew off the ashes and clutched to their bosoms

THE CHARRED REMAINS.

47

THE TOMB BELCHED FORTH
SMOKE AND FIRE.

The breakfast being over, Horatio stepped outside. From a great fire somewhere on the other side of the river, small flakes of ash drifted down, much as snow does at the first sign of winter. Horatio, despite the warmth of the morning, let his mind follow the suggestion made by the ash, and shivered.

In the street outside the inn, the two coaches awaited, horses eager and willing, coachmen less eager, less willing. Horatio retained sufficient social elevation to avoid any outright criticism of his tardiness, but he could tell from the idle play of their whips that his dalliance in a comfortable inn, with a pretty stranger, while they had spent the night in a cold and damp stable, with the horses, was not appreciated. That small clue of the whips and, he must suppose, the stream of spittle which was launched to a spot three inches in front of Horatio's boots by the coachman Alexei Konstantinovich – with a precision of which his father would have been proud, had he been alive, and not, as was the case, buried in a small graveyard in the town of Vassil, after being fished out of the River Soura, a little dejected and a little disjected as a result of a contre-temps with a hard-headed peasant and his three wild-eyed sons, whose appreciation of the hereditary skills of expectoration was, to say the least, lamentable. Thus, Alexei Konstantinovich in the leading coach, and Boris Ilyich in the second coach, waited, then waited no more.

It is a surprising, but gratifying, fact that the sometime maid of Voronov's inn – a maid and a maiden still, despite her recent employment and current unemployment – sat in great comfort within the coach of Alexei Konstantinovich. On resigning her post on the previous evening, she had come across the fine handsome coachman and, knowing nothing of his father and little of his inherited skills, had sought protection and assistance. Both were gladly given. In a day or two, the girl would be in St Petersburg, and Alexei would have some explaining to do.

Horatio, all innocent, climbed blindly aboard Alexei's coach.

The girl smiled at him, and brushed down her petticoat, all innocent: "Good morning, sir," she began, "I am—"

Horatio blushed, touched his hat politely, and hastily climbed out again. He hoisted himself forthwith into the coach of Boris, which had remained empty. He was in no way desirous of the simple pleasures of maids.

"—Anna," she finished, in a disappointed tone.

Scarcely had Horatio closed the door, than they were off. Horatio settled himself upon the seat, looked back at the inn, saw no one, and considered his master.

Prince Labanov was a middle-ranking member of the Russian nobility, an avid student of Scottish history, a collector of curiosities of the human-race, and – last but scarcely least – the proud owner of several coaches in both St Petersburg and Moscow. Moscow, capital of Old Russia; and St Petersburg, capital of New Russia: perhaps, one day, the positions would again be reversed. A canny prince maintained an establishment in both cities, and, just to be sure, any other large city of Europe. One never knew when one might need to flee the country of one's birth.

Horatio had been sent to Moscow by Prince Labanov to fetch the coaches, which were to be used on the Prince's imminent trip to Paris. It is a generally-understood principle of transportation that a coach which may be used in a Russian summer is not a coach which may be used to cross a European autumn. No traveller would wish to set out upon a winter's journey ill-prepared: some catastrophe might overtake him – or, less frequently, her – on the highways of Europe and leave him – or, more frequently, her – stranded and without hope, in yonder wild forest, or on that windswept plateau, easy prey to independently-minded peasants and other unflogged creatures of the abyss.

Prince Alexander Labanov: his great passion, apart from his wife and family, whom he loved dearly when at home, was the study of Mary, the unsuccessful Queen of Scots. It would not be long – measured against the yardstick of academic research – before the Prince could proudly publish, in Paris, in 1839, Mary's Lettres Inédites, 1558–1587, a work of most singular interest. For the purposes of research, the Prince frequently abandoned home and beloved family, to track down such documents as these; and then he edited them. Wherever and whenever he travelled thus far and wide, his man-servant Horatio went too, a source of great interest to those he met, a black man who, having survived slavery, could be trusted to serve white men. In recognition of which, Horatio Alexandrovich had been granted the patronymic by his master.

A WORK OF MOST
SINGULAR INTEREST

Horatio sat in his coach and chewed at his gloves. His head span with thoughts, cries, punishment, curses, which could not be dispelled by even the most violent shaking. What had he done? What had he not done? He had deceived the one woman who might make him happy, the one woman whom he might make happy. Had he set his sights too high? He had learned, through the years, to have small ambitions and aspire to simple solace, to yield to passing fancies and harvest passing pleasures and never look back. What could he expect, if he changed the habits of his life? He was, after all, but a servant – he who was now crossing the river Volkhov in the carriage of his master and about to career northwards at break-neck speed—

The horses stopped suddenly. The two coachmen cursed, cracked their whips and swore in a manner which made Horatio grieve for the lost essential goodness of mankind. He leaned over and squinted out of the window. Some sort of urban demonstration was in progress, and the participants were spread out over the street with no regard for princes, headless queens or urgency. The horses could make no progress through this idly swirling crowd, and so drew to a halt. Horatio, glad of a distraction from his own inner turmoil, lowered the window and stuck his head out. He wondered foolishly for a moment if it might be a Democratic Assembly.

The sudden appearance of a Moorish head in their midst greatly excited the more spiritual of those gathered together here, and a cry of admiration and awe went up.

"What is happening?" asked the Moorish head of a couple of citizens who stood nearby.

"You do not know?" queried one citizen, greatly astonished.

Horatio confirmed his ignorance.

"What, you do not know?" queried the other citizen, greatly troubled.

Horatio confirmed his ignorance a second time.

"Why," replied the first man, now less taken with the black apparition: an Angel, or Coptic Spirit, who did not know what was going on in Novgorod was scarcely a Being to be venerated, "a miracle has taken place. That's what."

"A miracle?" inquired Horatio, interested but sceptical.

"A miracle," confirmed the second citizen. "It seems that a young man was taken by a bear last night, but the bear—"

"—observing the piety of the young man," continued the first citizen, "and yielding to his cries of despair, did not eat him—"

"—but brought him," interrupted a young woman enthusiastically, "within the city walls and deposited him under the Eternally-Smoking Ikon of the Most Venerated Varlaam, and—"

"—and it burst into flames," finished the second citizen in triumph.

"The bear burst into flames?" asked Horatio, prepared to concede that a wild creature incandescent in the face of Religion would truly be one of Nature's wonders.

"The ikon burst into flames," corrected the second citizen, extinguishing him with a look. "Sir, if you do not have the decency to look like a Russian, then at least have the decency to think like one." With which irrefutable words, he turned away.

Horatio, in his studies of the religious edifices of Novgorod the Great, had not yet encountered this smoking Varlaam: he waited for the smoke to clear.

"There he is!" shouted the crowd, and there was a surge backwards and forwards, threatening the coach with ship-wreck.

Horatio peered up and down the road, looking for a singed bear that had at last seen the Light and the Way; but could see only a white-faced young man being led by a battalion of processing priests. The young man passed within a yard of the coach, and could be heard muttering repeatedly: "Blackness, blackness, blackness." He stopped at the coach and stared at the black face above him. "Blackness," he said once more, now in a tone more hollow than before.

"You, Moor," cried a concerned citizen to Horatio – not one of those with whom he had lately conversed – "make room for this pious youth!" At these words, a phalanx of merchants and their wives hoisted the bleak young man, lately escaped from a bear, into the coach. A pair of butchers, their aprons stained menacingly with the blood of daily animal sacrifice, leaped up beside Boris Ilyich and ordered him to turn the horses. There was a brief argument. But before argument could lead to violence, as is so often and unhappily the way of butchers and coachmen, the horses of their own volition turned their noses in the direction chosen by the passing priests, and set off meekly.

They were, by nature, devout horses. They did not belong to Prince Labanov, for those, unlike the servants, had been permitted to rest in their stable after the long haul made on the previous day. These horses belonged to a family friend, a wealthy widow of deep religious conviction whose entire ménage had been trained, by sheer habit as much as anything else, to direct their steps towards any scene of Orthodox excitement. On coming across a spiritual procession such as this, it was now their natural inclination to follow it. Only the strong hands of Boris Ilyich and Alexei Konstantinovich had restrained them in the past few minutes. But now they were free to follow their true beliefs.

A SCENE OF
ORTHODOX
EXCITEMENT

"V Khutyn! V Khutyn!" shouted the crowd obscurely.

Horatio sat back in his seat. The young man sat tensely opposite him.

"It was a bear," muttered the young man, his lips shredded, his face gaunt.

Horatio nodded encouragingly.

"It was about to tear me limb from limb," said the young man, slightly encouraged. "It proposed to eat me – oh horror!" There was a pause while he composed himself for the Wonder, eyes glazed. "And then, at the very instant that it spread its jaws around my head – oh Wonder! – through the trees we caught a sight of HER – SHE whom

I never thought to see again, SHE like a gilded angel sent down to rescue me. SHE," he added, looking askance at Horatio now, "was in the company of a dusky stranger."

"Remarkable," said Horatio, wondering how all this was possible.

"And then the bear," continued the pale youth, "growled once and abandoned its plan. Was this not, sir," he enquired of Horatio, breathing, like the bear, in short thick pants, "a Miracle?"

"Assuredly," said Mr. Karamzin, who had also, although unnoticed by Horatio, clambered aboard. He took in the scene with an expert eye. "May I introduce Mr. Sergei Ushakov of Nizhney Novgorod, late Private in the Imperial Army?" Horatio and Sergei Ushakov bowed nervously towards each other. Karamzin beamed. "Now, sirs: we are off, I believe, to Khutyn, A monastery. A most splendid place. Scene, if you will," he continued, finding himself in very familiar territory, "of a most uncanny event."

"Indeed?" asked Horatio politely, glad for the moment to be distracted from the agitated young man opposite, who – it needs be said – gazed upon Mr. Karamzin as one re-living a nightmare.

"The Khutyn Monastery of the Saviour's Transfiguration and of St Varlaam," continued Mr. Karamzin, much as if he had found employment in the Afterlife as a guide for travellers, an employment with which all visitors to Novgorod, having counted out good money for abbreviated tales from history, were more than familiar, ABBREVIATED TALES "was founded in honour of the blessed saint, who proph- FROM HISTORY esied that the city of Novgorod the Great would be inundated by the rising of the waters of Lake Ilmen—"

"Oh – come Floods!" prayed Private Ushakov, tears coursing down his face.

"—punished by the firing of arrows of flame upon the women and children of the town by a host of angels—"

"Oh – come heavenly Fire!" begged Private Ushakov with a burning heat.

"—and destroyed by the hovering of a fiery cloud over the city—"

"Oh – come Brimstone!" implored Private Ushakov with passion, stretching his arms to the heavens.

"—all of which greatly alarmed the people of Novgorod, and, it is said, turned them instantly back to the ways of piety and charity."

"Well, that was indeed a blessing," said Horatio, who had sat through this threefold threat of retribution with mounting despondency.

"The Monastery of St Varlaam," continued Mr. Karamzin knowledgeably, "was visited by Ivan the Third (the Great, not the Terrible, as you will appreciate – the grandfather, not the grandson) who, expressing in 1471 a pious interest in the relics of St Varlaam, ordered the holy tomb to be opened. But to his astonishment and the wonder of all who beheld it, the tomb belched forth smoke and fire—"

"Oh – Horror!" shrieked Private Ushakov, his nerves stretched beyond reason.

"—and no man dared approach it," concluded Mr. Karamzin in a satisfied manner. "And it was in that same year, you will recall, that Ivan the Third laid siege to Novgorod the Great and carried off to Moscow the Mayoress, Marfa—"

He was interrupted at this moment by the flinging open of the coach-door. The slow pace of the procession, as it moved towards the Khutyn Monastery, several miles out of town, had allowed even the sick and the lame to keep pace with the coach and horses. Thus, an old soldier – known to Horatio from the previous evening as the maimed veteran of the Battle of the Iron Gorge – leaped aboard, as agile as a new recruit.

"Sirs," he saluted and made himself comfortable next to Sergei. "Have you a drink about you?"

Horatio denied it.

"Not even a flask against the cold wind?" asked the old soldier.

Horatio denied it twice.

"Civilians," muttered the soldier, disgusted. He turned to Ushakov. "So, young fellow, you have had an adventure?"

In reply, the Private smote his brow. A large red weal came up. He smote it – once more. He sought – Suffering!

"I remember," continued the old soldier, not at all disconcerted, "the campaign against the Turk, when, after a night in the gorges of

Nakhichevan, every man – every man, I tell you – was reduced to a babbling wretch. This is how it was—"

It was not a tale likely to bathe the Imperial Russian Army in the eternal light of glory. Indeed, as the narrator rambled on, and as the wheels outside turned along the rutted road which led, yard by yard, to Khutyn, Ushakov's face turned relentlessly more ashen – he began once more to gnaw his lips – he beat his head slowly against the side of the coach, so that his hands might have a rest from that holy task – he prayed to the bears and wolves of Russia. As for Karamzin, he stared in speechless admiration at the old soldier and took out a leather-bound notebook.

The rhythmic battering of the young man's head attracted the attention of the accompanying priests outside, who, excited by what must be supposed to be a further Miracle, crowded upon the steps of the coach and peered in. Several of them were so animated by what they saw that they opened the door and made entrance. In no time at all, the body of the coach, designed and built for two or three noble persons, was groaning, containing ONE HIGHLY-STRUNG VICTIM OF LOVE as it did one large servant, one ghost, one one-legged veteran, four priests with very long beards and a tendency to throw up their hands, and one highly-strung victim of love.

In the coach in front, matters were no better, and Anna the maid found herself the unwilling object of desire for a pious band of enthusiasts; however, she acquitted herself well in the circumstance. She had served an apprenticeship in an inn. While impropriety was offered, none occurred.

The gilded towers of the Khutyn Monastery glinted suddenly in the sunlight. The priests murmured appreciatively. Horatio, seeing no good would come of this, made his excuses and disembarked.

He stood amidst fields and small clumps of trees. A number of fires were browsing in the stubble of harvested corn, and the resultant smoke drifted around, now obscuring, now revealing the surrounding landscape – the flat lands, the low hills, the endless forest, the abandoned towers of the city. The last stragglers of the enthusiastic crowd passed him by, hobbling towards the day's further entertainment.

"Is this Liberty?" he wondered aloud. "What am I doing, falling in love?"

An old woman, wheeled in a handcart by an idiot daughter, glanced at the black man, and shook her head. "Love and Liberty? Madness," was her cool judgement on the matter, as her carriage sped on over the ruts of the road.

Horatio dropped his head. Was 'Love', he pondered, reverting to the old question, the inescapable; or was it, on the contrary, the escapable? Was 'Love' liberty; was 'Liberty' love? Is 'Love' the escape from 'Liberty'; is 'Liberty' an enslavement by 'Love'; or indeed contrariwise? He sighed at length at such fruitless speculation. His unusual ambition, to find happiness after so many years, with a single woman who returned his fondness, was doubtless foolish. That night had been that rarest of all nights when, no more a slave, no more a servant, he could be a man of wit and wisdom, a man entirely at liberty to admire and to animate a woman of the greatest merit: a woman of independent thought. In the cool light of morning, he now saw his naivety. What man of his position could hope to attain such happiness? Happiness was not his lot. Ksenia was that woman who might, ten – fifteen – twenty years ago, have run off with him, despite his misrepresentations. But now she had been deceived by his own fantastical notions – a merchant, a man of wealth, stability and loyalty, a man who could be trusted. He had betrayed her trust. Trust, once gone, rarely returns with a smile upon its face.

Horatio breathed deeply and turned to face the city of Novgorod the Great. "Should I go back," he asked, "and apologise?"

"Never apologise," muttered a veteran forming the rearguard, who was missing one of everything – eye, ear, arm, finger, leg, foot, doubt-less other items. "Never apologise, it is a weakness. Look what it did to me!" Without pausing to offer an explanation, the veteran hobbled onwards to Khutyn, one eye shining in expectation of a miracle.

Ignoring this sound advice, Horatio stood and considered. All hope had been lost; but he had learned the curious fact that, when Hope is utterly lost, there is always one shred remaining. He was a man of great philosophical flexibility. He looked over his shoulder towards

Khutyn. Somewhere in the middle of that swirling cloud of dust, at the front of a large crowd, his two carriages neared their holy destination and the incendiary attentions of St Varlaam. It would be some time before Alexei and Boris could turn around and find their way back to the high road. There was, therefore, time for that shred of Hope.

Determined to think no more, Horatio set off at a quick pace, back towards the town. He left behind the fires and the dust and the cries of religious excitement. His eyes were fixed on the one thick spiral of smoke which ascended from somewhere in the town, dividing the blue sky north from south.

As he came within sight of the bridge over the River Volkhov, he heard a great rumbling; he stopped, shaded his eyes and observed the passage of the diligence, now repaired, now speeding on its way to Moscow, unimpeded today by those careless pedestrians and pious citizens who customarily threw themselves under the wheels of this leviathan of the road. The diligence completed the crossing of the river without major incident, turned, and came to a halt before the door of Mr. Voronov's inn. Horatio quickened his pace.

The diligence did not stay for long: from his distant viewpoint, Horatio observed a brief passage of figures entering and leaving the inn. He stopped; the heavy hand of lethargy brushed away the final shred of Hope. The coach set off again, into the south, leaving behind a broken fast, a broken dream, and

NOVGOROD THE GREAT.

48

HER HUSBAND IS ENGAGED IN
THE MEASUREMENT OF THE BLACK SEA.

The breakfast in Novgorod the Great, such as it was, was over. As was the night of groundless hopes and futile secrets. All – breakfast, secrets, hopes – had vanished in an instant, the illusion slain by a single and predictable lunge of the truth. Ksenia sat in silence at the table in the room of the inn. What, she asked herself oppressed by sadness, is 'Love'? She now knew the answer: 'Love' is hope against hope.

Marfa Petrovich Voronova, wife of a man who had recently discovered the rest of the world and its inhabitants, entered from the kitchen. Her husband was visible through the partially-opened door, sitting at the vast kitchen table, where bowls, eggs, milk, jugs, cuts of meat, pots, pans, beetroot, mice, spoons, plates and other tools of the inn-keeper's trade jostled for space with an abandoned axe, some female undergarments, and a sack whose literary contents spilled out upon the deeply-scored surface.

Mr. Voronov, finally at peace with the world, avidly scanned the titles of all Mr. Isengrim's books: he could at present do no more, since he had only learned his alphabet by rote when a boy, and had found little use for it in the intervening thirty-five years. And these printed letters suggested that he had forgotten more than he had learned. He would, he now promised himself, go to the priests and ask them to teach him to read. And then, and then – the world would be opened up to him like an endless cellar-full of barrels, an eternal wood-yard of logs, a limitless row of cucumbers. For now, he had to be content to admire the words, one by one; listen to the rustle of the paper; tap the hard covers; gaze fondly at the few lithographed images that some reckless publisher had thought to waste his money on. He did not yet know, alas, that the books were all – bar two – in the English language, and that the words, bar none, were printed in the Roman alphabet. He will be disappointed when he finds this out, when he finds that the world is indeed far broader and far less Orthodox than he had ever imagined. Perhaps an English traveller will come past one night and read to him – in which case, he would keep the traveller here, night after night, a prisoner of Russian Autocracy, for a thousand and one nights, until Mr. Voronov had gained an understanding of travel; and the traveller could again be on his way – to Siberia.

"You are exhausted, my dear," said Mrs. Voronova, observing Ksenia's red-rimmed eyes, white face and crushed demeanour.

The young widow attempted a smile and failed. Having failed, she let her tears flow. The inn-keeper's wife, awash with emotion herself, sat down heavily beside her, and the two women hugged each other as friends while the tides of disappointment ebbed and flowed over them.

At length, the sobs subsided. "You have been awake all night, and have travelled so far," the older woman pointed out gently.

"And I am alone again," said Ksenia at last.

"Again?" asked Mrs. Voronova. "But were you not alone when you arrived?"

Ksenia admitted that this had been the true state of affairs. "But—" she added, and then was unable to complete her thought.

"But you thought you had found a friend?" said Marfa.

Ksenia nodded, desperately.

"You thought you had found more?" asked Marfa further, dabbing at the tears of the younger woman with her soiled apron.

Ksenia nodded, desperately.

They embraced once more, now as wounded veterans in the war of love. There was a long silence, during which Marfa compared her situation with that of the young woman. Just one hour before, she had been as alone and as friendless as this one. And then she had discovered a husband, and something more: how long that might last, was a matter on which she had her own views, and they were not entirely optimistic. But a woman – as a man – must take such moments of peace and comfort as are offered; or else rage against the world every day and every night.

In time, Ksenia sighed and sat up straighter. "Not entirely alone," she said. She patted her stomach, where no bump could – as yet – be seen.

Marfa embraced her a third time, more tenderly still, now as a mother to a mother. "How far do you have to travel?" she asked solicitously.

"To Odessa," came the reply.

"Is that near Moscow?" asked Marfa innocently, never having been beyond the southern end of Lake Ilmen in all her life.

"Slightly further," admitted Ksenia, wondering for one final infatuated moment, whether she should take the road eastwards from Moscow, and travel, not to Odessa, but to Kamtchatka, where her mother and her family would perhaps welcome her back; her and her child. The child could perhaps be born in Bolcheretsk, erstwhile capital of Kamtchatka. Or, if things got tight in the bleaker regions

THE DEMON GODDESS ON HER BROOMSTICK

of eastern Russia, then there was plenty of scope for: Mati Syra Zemliya, Moist Mother Earth; Kupula, goddess of water; Mokosh, who gives and takes life; and, if a woman was really desperate, Ved'ma, the demon goddess on her broomstick. The very thought of a broom swept away this inane dream.

"My husband," explained Ksenia quietly, "awaits my arrival."

"Your husband?" asked Marfa, in confusion. "But are you not—?" She left the question incomplete. She blamed Mr. Voronov – the man could never get his facts right, and he was, this morning, in utter confusion. The fool had said that this was a young widow, seeking to make a husband of the handsome black guest.

Ksenia looked away, at the flickering flames in the stove. She took three deep breaths, then two more, and finally one more.

"My husband is Captain Pyotr Anjou, a man of great merit and inexhaustible virtue. Having explored the Frozen Sea and many other places of little interest and fewer people, he has been much in demand by the Tsar to establish the boundaries of the Russian Empire. He is, at present, engaged in the measurement of the Black Sea."

Marfa's eyes opened wide with astonishment. A man who can measure a sea must be a man of great prowess. And a black sea, at that. Impossible to imagine. She wondered if she should summon her husband, who seemed to have found a new interest in far-flung places.

"He has sent for me," continued Ksenia, "to spend the winter with him in Odessa, a town, I am told, that is very pretty, and has most beneficial airs. Pyotr Fedorovich wishes to be present at the birth of his first child."

Marfa shook her head. She had little time for husbands who meddled in women's affairs.

"You are but recently married then?" she asked interestedly.

"Six years," came the reply.

Marfa could make nothing of this. Six years – what, in the name of St Niphont and the Elder Mardarius, had the man been doing?

"He has been much away from home, then?" she pursued the matter.

"He has been up and down the Baltic Sea several times, back and forth to Asia – the Caspian Sea, the Azov Sea; he has been on the Black Sea for three months."

"But did he not – was he not – did he not have the time even to—?" Marfa could not bring herself to pose the question.

"He was not at home for long," came the simple reply. "and when he was, he was frequently in the company of his friends – Baron Wrangel, Captain Matiushkin, Captain von Kotzebue, Mikhael Lazarev of the Antarctic. They talked about ice and snow and ship-wrecks and the fabled land of Sannikov and of many other things that explorers like to talk about. He was happy, even if I – even if we – did you know," she continued quickly, fearing another unanswerable interruption from Mrs. Voronova, "that my husband has an island named after him, one of the Islands of Novosibirsk? I understand that there is not much of interest in those islands, but it is something for his son to admire, is it not? And almost, would you believe, did Captain Anjou meet with my first husband – they were in the north of Siberia at the same time – but my first husband went one way, with Baron Wrangel, while Pyotr Fedorovich went the other. We met, Captain Anjou and I, at the house of my parents in St Petersburg, after I had returned there from London six years ago. My father, Captain Rikord – also a man given much to exploration – recommended Pyotr to me. He was a handsome man, I was a widow. Captain Rikord expects that he will reach high office. And I believe Pyotr loves me—"

There was a note of great uncertainty in her voice as she came to a sudden halt in her outburst and lowered her eyes.

Marfa regarded her young guest with some trepidation. Had this woman been her daughter, she would have known what to say. At length, she threw caution aside, along with any pretence of being an inn-keeper's wife.

"Last night," she began firmly, "when you were with our other guest—"

She got no further in what might have been a scolding, or might have been a speech of encouragement.

"Last night," Ksenia interrupted, "last night was all the pleasure I have had for many years. Since I can remember. In all my life. Last night was when I was truly myself, a woman, on my own, with all the liberty I could hope for. I was not being taken off to a distant land, full of strangers, I was not being left behind to contemplate loneliness in the company of those who either ignored me or sought to direct my every movement. I was no longer a girl to be married off to the first comer, no longer a curiosity, no longer a widow to be pitied, no longer a wife to be ignored – I was just a woman. It was foolish, I know," she continued, lowering her eyes, "and it was a grave deceit; but it was my one, only, night of love. There may not be another." She stopped abruptly and looked up, her eyes fixed in determined fashion upon Marfa Petrovich.

A GRAVE DECEIT
AND A NIGHT
OF LOVE

Who said nothing at all, but instead took Ksenia's hands firmly but gently within her own, squeezed them, and kissed the young woman once upon the forehead and once upon each flushed cheek.

"I hope and trust," she said quietly and with only a little conviction, "that there will be another." She expressed this hope as much for her own benefit as for Ksenia's.

Into the ensuing silence, a clock-tower sounded the ninth hour; both women stirred. "Alas," said Marfa, "I have all my work to do. My husband does not look likely to do it. Rest here a while and then you can be on your way."

"No," said Ksenia, rising from her seat, "I must go and look out for the diligence. If I do not meet it, I am a lost woman."

Accordingly, she embraced Marfa one last time, and went to stand by the door to the inn, looking out into the morning. Across the river, a thick plume of smoke arose: she wondered what it might be. And somewhere, far in the distance, there was the noise of many people – a procession, doubtless, in this teeming city of saints. She forced herself not to look out for Horatio, it being certain that he was now well on the road into the north, caught up in the troubles of his own world, with never a backward glance. She told herself to think no more of him, to become, in heart and soul and body and spirit, to become again Mrs. Anjou, wife and mother.

But, despite her best intentions, it was with a somersault of the heart that she heard the sound of coach-wheels approaching. It was Horatio! He had returned! One hand to her mouth, she looked up the road.

It was but the diligence from St Petersburg to Moscow. It approached heavily, remorselessly. The coachman, a person of keen eyesight, caught sight of his missing passenger from afar, and waved in great relief and enthusiasm. A new wheel had been fitted to the vehicle late in the evening, by which time his passengers had made themselves quite comfortable in an inn close to the scene of the misfortune. Having set off as early as the sore heads of his passengers allowed, to make up for lost time, the coachman had felt obliged – against the express wishes and repeated commandments of his other passengers and the refractory guard – to call in at every inn and hovel beside the road, looking for the misplaced lady. It was, therefore, with an overwhelming sense of gladness, something he rarely experienced in his dull life, that he spotted Ksenia at the door of the inn.

The passengers within smelled strongly of fish and onions, and all were in black humour; but they were rapidly persuaded, by some well-directed kicks and elbowing on the part of the invigorated driver, to make comfortable room for Ksenia. Barely a minute passed before the diligence, with a song in its heart and a whistle upon its lips, set off again for Moscow, leaving behind the shattered breakfasts and the shattered dreams of

NOVGOROD THE GREAT.

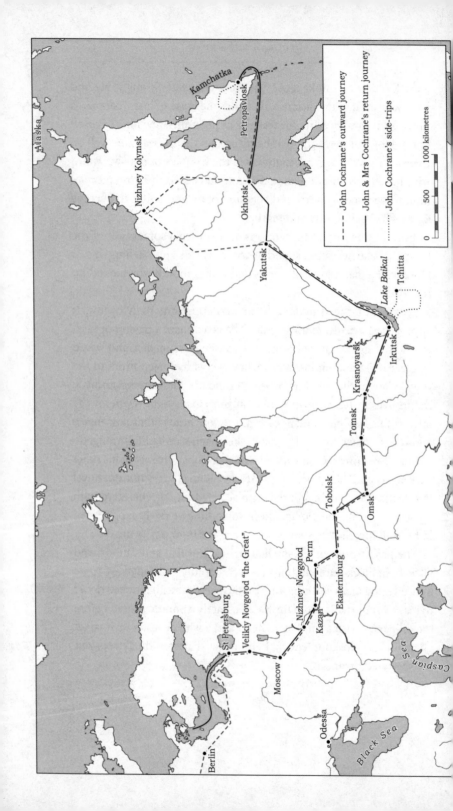

HISTORICAL AND BIOGRAPHICAL NOTES

The central characters of this story really existed: potted biographies are given below. Surprisingly little has been written of John Cochrane, who took it upon himself to rectify that omission before he died. Of the rest of the Cochrane family, much has been written, and books may be found almost anywhere. Of Ksenia, very little, and of Horatio, nothing at all, has been written.

Any dates below marked '(O.S.)' are in the old-style Russian (Julian) calendar, which in the 19th century was twelve days behind the western Gregorian calendar, and continued to lag behind until 1917.

ANDREW COCHRANE-JOHNSTONE (1767–1833)

Born 24/05/1767 at 'Bellevile' – a house near Holyrood Palace in Edinburgh – he was the twelfth son of the 8th Earl of Dundonald.

In 1791 he became MP for Stirling Burghs, for a year. On 26/11/1793, he married Lady Georgina Hope-Johnstone, the daughter of James Hope-Johnstone, 3rd Earl of Hopetoun, and of Lady Elizabeth Carnegie; the family was related to Henry Dundas, Lord Melville. Andrew Cochrane appended her surname to his. Marriage registered in 'Abercorn, West Lothian' (next to Hopetoun) and 'Ormiston, East Lothian'.

Georgina died 17/09/1797 – the same year that ACJ went to Dominica. A daughter, Eliza, had been born 26/12/1794, who subsequently married the 9th Lord Napier (William), 28/03/1816.

In 1797, he was appointed Governor of Dominica, became Colonel of the 8th West India Regiment in 1798, and Brigadier of the Leeward Islands in 1799. During this period of governmental responsibility, he was blamed for a mutiny among black soldiers in 1802; the Dominican Assembly petitioned for his recall, which occurred in 1803. He was also accused by Major John Gordon of using black soldiers as unpaid labour, of wrongfully arresting citizens, of corruption. Returned to

Britain in September 1803, to face court-martial proceedings; he was acquitted in March 1805, but then was passed over for promotion, and he resigned his commission.

On 21/02/1803, he married Amélie de Clugny, daughter of the late French governor of Guadeloupe. Napoleon himself annulled this marriage, violently disapproving of it, on 30/05/1805.

In 1807, he was elected MP for Grampound (in Cornwall) for a year, and again from 1812 – replacing his brother George – until July 1814 when he was expelled from the House, for his part in the great 'Stock Exchange Swindle' (which effectively ended the career of the popular naval hero Thomas Cochrane, and by which Andrew profited to the tune of £4931).

In his first period as MP, he conducted a crusade against corruption in Parliament and the Army. By 1808, he had returned to the West Indies – supported the revolutionary Francisco Miranda's plan to liberate Spanish America and open it up to British trade. From his brother Alexander, he obtained the appointment as 'prize agent' at Tortola (Virgin Islands). Soon accused of bribery, of not surrendering confiscated public property, and of using captor's money to buy estates and property on the Danish islands of St Croix, St John and St Thomas etc.

Fled back to England in 1809. Visited Seville and Vera Cruz, buying Spanish dollars for the British Treasury. Was accused – perhaps mistakenly – of defaulting on a deal to sell 100,000 suspect British muskets to the Spanish government, in exchange for sheep destined for North America. (The sheep all died on arrival at New York in 1810.)

After 1812, he was pursued by creditors – he owed £16,301. His Dominican property – four houses, 671 acres, 62 slaves – was seized and sold in 1814.

After his arrest in July 1814, he fled firstly to Calais, then to Lisbon, then returned to the West Indies (January 1815) where he discovered that his assets had been sold for less than he owed. In 1819, went to Demarara (Guyana) to plant coffee. In 1823 he was known to be back on Dominica. In 1829, he was in Paris, where he made a fraudulent claim on the French government. He died 21/08/1833 – in Paris, at 96, rue du Faubourg St Honoré. His possessions were inventoried – so presumably he died in poverty and/or in debt.

JOHN DUNDAS COCHRANE (1793–1825)

Born 14/02/1793, John Dundas Cochrane was the illegitimate son of Andrew Cochrane. It is not known who his mother was, but we might suppose it to be Georgina Hope-Johnstone, since she married his father barely nine months after John's birth: this is, however, mere speculation by the present author. At the age of ten, John, like many of his cousins and his uncles before him, joined the Royal Navy, probably on a ship captained by one of the Cochrane clan. Any biography of his more famous cousin, Thomas, the 'Sea Wolf', describes similar circumstances. After the end of the Napoleonic wars, John found himself, again like many another naval officer, on half-pay and with nothing to do. This rich reserve of bored, active men was tapped by men such as John Barrow, who sent them out in exploratory droves to roast in Africa and freeze in the Arctic, in search of adventure, trade-routes and Empire. John Cochrane himself preferred his adventures in solitude, and undertook his epic pedestrian journey across Europe, Russia and Siberia, between 1820 and 1823. On 8/01/1822 (O.S.), he married Ksenia Ivanovna Loginova, in Kamtchatka, and with her returned overland to St Petersburg, arriving in London in June 1823. The first edition of his Pedestrian Journey through Russia and Siberian Tartary was published by John Murray in 1823; the 2nd and 3rd editions were printed Charles Knight in 1824 and 1825; and a 4th edition by Archibald Constable in 1829. The book was translated into Dutch and German, and possibly also into French.

In June 1824, he travelled alone to South America, probably at the suggestion of his cousin Charles. Returning to London in 1825, he prepared the 3rd edition of his book in which he found ample space to argue bitterly with Sir John Barrow, and then set off again to Gran Colombia (Venezuela), possibly to oversee a copper-mine, probably with the aim of walking the length of South America; no sooner arrived than he promptly died of a fever, in the town of Valencia on 12/08/1825.

KSENIA IVANOVNA LOGINOVA (1807–1870)

Ksenia was born on 24/01/1807 (O.S.) in the village of Bolcheretsk on Kamtchatka. There is some contradictory and possibly misleading documentation about her step-father, father and grandfather – but this is not the place for any detailed discussion. From the age of about ten, Ksenia was brought up in Petropavlovsk in the household of the Governor of Kamtchatka, Pyotr Ivanovich Rikord (1776–1855), and his young wife Ludmila Ivanovna Korostovez (1794–1883). It would appear that her mother was widowed and re-married, to a priest or sexton named Vereshagin – this step-father died shortly after her departure for Europe with John Cochrane.

Not quite fifteen years of age, she married John Cochrane on 8/01/1822 (O.S.). There is some suggestion that she was married illegally, or against her will – but the fact that the newly-weds were accompanied on their journey westwards from Kamtchatka, at least as far as Irkutsk, by Mrs. Rikord, argues strongly against this.

A widow at 18 years of age after the death of John Cochrane in 1825, Ksenia remained in Great Britain – probably London (John's sister Eliza, and his cousin Thomas' wife would have been in town) – until 1827. Captain Rikord having been appointed Governor of Kronstadt, he and his wife had in the meantime set up home in St Petersburg and in 1827, Ksenia joined her adoptive parents there. Here she met the famous Arctic explorer, Pyotr Anjou (b.1796), after whom some of the islands on Novosibirsk are named, and married him at the St Petersburg 'Churches of the Sea' on 24/10/1828 (O.S.). Anjou was a man much in demand for his skills in exploration and hydrography, and was frequently called upon to make journeys to various watery parts of the Russian Empire (the Aral Sea, the Black Sea, the Baltic); he eventually succeeded Rikord as Governor of the port of Kronstadt.

Ksenia had six children: Ludmila (1834–1897), Pyotr (b.ca.1836) – who became a naval man like his father, and was on the Russian–Japan Expedition of 1852 – Fedor (1842–1858), Ivan (b.1844), Aleksandra (d.1888), and Elisaveta.

The family had large houses in St Petersburg and Oranienbaum (the summer retreat of the Imperial family). Pyotr Anjou died in 1869 and Ksenia herself died in 1870

'HORATIO'

This man lived and breathed, but, as yet, we know nothing more of him beyond his brief appearance in John Cochrane's narrative of the year 1820, and from this same narrative the fact that he was once (ca. 1807) a servant (or slave?) of Andrew Cochrane-Johnstone and his brother the Admiral Alexander Cochrane in the West Indies; and that at some later time he became a trusted servant of Prince Alexander Labanov in Russia. We have not been able to determine his name, nor his age, nor how he came to be employed in Russia, nor his subsequent fate.

CHARLES STUART COCHRANE (1796–1840)

The son of Alexander Cochrane spent his youth and early career in the Royal Navy (but later confessed he had 'a particular dislike to the sea'). Between March 1823 and June 1824, he was in Gran Colombia during the final months of Simon Bolivar's struggle for independence from Spain, and wrote a two-volume book about his travels – Journal of a Residence and Travels in Colombia. He acted as the agent for the firm of Rundell, Bridge & Rundell, and successfully won for them the monopoly rights to the mechanical exploitation of the pearl fisheries in Gran Colombia. Between August 1828 and June 1829, he disguised himself as a Spanish exile, and made a tour of Britain. His two-volume Journal Made by Señor Juan de Vega, the Spanish Minstrel describes this journey in – frequently tedious – detail. In 1830 Charles learned in France a process for spinning cashmere, which he then patented in Britain; the patent was subsequently sold to the Glasgow firm of Houldsworth & Sons.

The remaining characters of this story are – by and large – invented, here and there based opportunistically upon real people both living and dead.

The episode of the August night in Novgorod is entirely fictional and should not be supposed to reflect the real behaviour or morality of any of the 'real' characters.

A SHORT BIBLIOGRAPHY

JOHN DUNDAS COCHRANE

[Narrative of] A Pedestrian Journey through Russian and Siberian Tartary to the Frontiers of China, the Frozen Sea and Kamtchatka. First published by John Murray 1823; 2nd and 3rd editions reprinted Charles Knight 1824 and 1825; 4th edition Archibald Constable 1829. Translations published in Weimar 1825, Jena 1825, Vienna 1826, and Delft 1826.

ANDREW COCHRANE-JOHNSTONE

Defence of the Honourable Andrew Cochrane-Johnstone (Edinburgh, 1806)

CHARLES STUART COCHRANE

Journal of a Residence and Travels in Colombia, during the years 1823 and 1824, by Captain Charles Stuart Cochrane of the Royal Navy, vols I and II (London, 1825)
A Journal Made by Señor Juan de Vega, the Spanish Minstrel, of 1828–9 through Great Britain and Ireland, 2 vols (London, 1830)

A. MACKENROT

Secret Memoirs of the Honourable Andrew Cochrane-Johnstone, of the Honourable Vice-Admiral Sir Alex. Forrester Cochrane K.B., and of Sir Thomas John Cochrane, A captain in the Royal Navy, (London, C. Chapple, 1814)

THOMAS (LORD) COCHRANE

The Case of Thomas Lord Cochrane K.B. (Edinburgh, 1814)
The Calumnious Aspersions contained in the Report of the sub-committee of the Stock Exchange, exposed and refuted, in so far as regards Lord Cochrane, KB and MP, the Hon. Cochrane-Johnstone, MP, and R.G.Butt, Esq.... (London, W. Lewis 1814)
The Autobiography of A Seaman, by Thomas, 10th Earl of Dundonald (London, 1861)

See also:

Brian Vale, The Audacious Admiral Cochrane (London, Conway Maritime, 2004)

JAMES HOLMAN

Travels through Russia, Siberia, Poland, Austria, Saxony, Prussia, Hanover etc. etc., undertaken during the years 1822, 1823 and 1824, while suffering from Total Blindness, and comprising an account of the author being conducted a state prisoner from the eastern parts of Siberia (London, Whittaker, 1825)

See also:

Jason Roberts, A Sense of the World (London, Simon & Schuster, 2006)

ACKNOWLEDGEMENTS

The following people have provided great assistance during the research for this book (but the non-appearance of any name in this list does not signify that person's failure to help):

Irina Viter, of the Kamchatka Regional Library in Petropavlovsk and

Mr. Vladimir Malygin, Consul General of the Russian Federation in Edinburgh from 2004 to 2009.

John Massey Stewart for his astonishing knowledge of nineteenth century Russia and

Maria Vladimirovna Bardina in St Petersburg for her researches into the lives of the main characters.

Prof. Klaus Ebmeier of Oxford, for his kind identification of Imerachism (echopraxia).

I would most of all thank ...

... my sister, Isobel Hazelwood, who with great enthusiasm (my words, not hers) provided translations of Russian archive material,

... of course my editor Sam Kelly, who reduced me to manly tears on several occasions, and who heartlessly pushed me back into the ruins to start again,

... finally my wife Annette, who watched this whole story emerge, unravel, knot itself up and unravel again, and humoured me at several moments of my delight and triumph when Ksenia Ivanovna Loginova finally popped out of the shadows.

www.andydrummond.net